SPIDER
WEB

**Center Point
Large Print**

Also by Earlene Fowler and available from Center Point Large Print:

The Saddlemaker's Wife
Love Mercy
State Fair

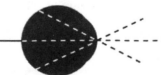

**This Large Print Book carries the
Seal of Approval of N.A.V.H.**

SPIDER WEB

Earlene Fowler

CENTER POINT LARGE PRINT
THORNDIKE, MAINE

This Center Point Large Print edition is
published in the year 2011 by arrangement with
Berkley Books, a member of Penguin Group (USA) Inc.

Copyright © 2011 by Earlene Fowler.

The text of this Large Print edition is unabridged.
In other aspects, this book may vary
from the original edition.
Printed in the United States of America.
Set in 16-point Times New Roman type.

ISBN: 978-1-61173-094-4

Library of Congress Cataloging-in-Publication Data

Fowler, Earlene.
Spider web / Earlene Fowler.
p. cm.
ISBN 978-1-61173-094-4 (library binding : alk. paper)
1. Harper, Benni (Fictitious character)—Fiction.
2. Women museum curators—Fiction. 3. Quiltmakers—Fiction.
4. Folk festivals—Fiction. 5. Police—Crimes against—Fiction.
6. Large type books. I. Title.
PS3556.O828S65 2011b
813'.54—dc22
2011003304

To Lela Satterfield and Laura Ross Wingfield,
Beloved Sisters and
Prayer Warriors of the highest order

and

To the brave and selfless men and women
of our military
Thank you for your loyalty,
your devotion and your sacrifice

Acknowledgments

Be merciful, just as your Father is merciful.

Luke 6:36

Thank you Father, Son and Holy Spirit. Please, help me to always err on the side of mercy.

With a humble heart, I also thank:

Steve Crawford—Deputy Coroner, San Luis Obispo County—for patiently helping me find the perfect gunshot wound.

Ellen Geiger—friend, agent, advocate—I appreciate your hard work, your dedication and your unmatched sense of humor about life and this crazy publishing business.

Karen Gray—Deputy District Attorney, San Luis Obispo County and part-time Red Cross nurse (you rock!)—for always being there to answer my questions and make introductions and for being my dear friend.

Pam Munns—California Highway Patrol (retired) and dynamite quilter—girl, what can I say? You have helped me with your knowledge, your suggestions and by introducing me to other people who have helped me. I treasure your friendship.

John O'Connell—Captain, LAPD (retired) and Marine Corps combat veteran—for openly sharing your knowledge and feelings about your time in Vietnam. Thank you for your help and your service to our country. Semper fi!

Kate Seaver—my beloved editor—you are enthusiastic, dedicated and smart. I appreciate your insights and suggestions. Thanks for never being cranky (even when I am). The publishing world is a kinder, better place for your being in it.

A special thanks to my friends, without whose support and love I fear I would perish in a cloud of despair—Charlotte "Bunny" Brown, Tina Davis, Janice Dischner, Jo Ellen Heil, Christine Hill, Jo-Ann Mapson, JoBeth McDaniel, Carolyn Miller, Sally Parker, Kathy Vieira.

My husband, Allen, whom I love. Your resilience amazes me and your courage inspires me.

A Note from the Author

Spider Web takes place in March 1998. It has been a little over five years in Benni Harper's life (*Fool's Puzzle* took place in November 1992), but almost eighteen years in my life. I am doing my best to remember how things were back in the nineties, but even consulting books and the Internet, it's difficult! So many changes have happened so fast in the last fifteen years. So, please, don't be too hard on me if I miss a thing or two.

There are readers who have expressed dismay with the fact that I showed readers what happened in Benni and Gabe's life a decade in the future in the book *Love Mercy*. I did that for the simple reason that there is nothing certain in this world.

I wanted to let my readers know (as with the prologue of *Mariner's Compass*) that Benni and Gabe end up okay. That seems to be the biggest worry people express to me. There was a method to my madness. I hope the Benni Harper books go on forever, but I cannot promise they will because it is not totally in my control.

I found this quote while doing research for this book and was amazed at how much it applied to all good novels.

Fiction is like a spider's web, attached ever so lightly perhaps, but still attached to life at all four corners. Often the attachment is scarcely perceptible.

Virginia Woolf

Spider Web

The Spider Web quilt design, like many old patterns, probably originated with a quilter's love for her flower or vegetable garden. Very similar to the Kaleidoscope pattern, it is often made up of a variety of symmetrical multicolored fabric pieces, triangular in shape, put together to resemble a spider's web. Some variations of the pattern are made with only two colors of fabric. It is a great way to use up extra fabric, something that was important during the 1930s Depression when this pattern was popular. Like its real-life counterpart, the Spider Web pattern has innumerable variations. Unlike many patterns where there are many names for one pattern, with the Spider Web quilt pattern, there are dozens of patterns for one name. The pattern can be traced back to the early nineteenth century. The pattern has been found in the Kansas City Star patterns of 1929 as well as the quilts of the Hmong, an ancient tribe of mountain people who migrated from China in the mid-nineteenth century. Some of the patterns called Spider Web do have other names such as Farmer's Wife, Merry-Go-Round, Mystic Maze, Amazing Windmill, Autumn Leaves and Job's Tears.

Chapter 1

Music flowed out of the old ranch house's open front door like a wash of honey water—"Are You Lonesome Tonight?"

Elvis Presley's unmistakable voice rose and surrounded me as I watched from a small rise a hundred yards away. The damp, drooping branches of a pepper-scented valley oak camouflaged me and my horse from whomever was inspecting my former home. Trixie, a new mare my father bought last week, shifted beneath me.

The song's melody was as familiar to me as the creak of saddle leather. It was a favorite tune of my gramma Dove, who often serenaded her fancy chickens. Dinner and a show, she would say, tossing handfuls of powdery feed. She claimed they favored Top 40 tunes, Tennessee Ernie Ford and on stormy days, the heartbreak songs of Patsy Cline.

"Back in the twenties, Vaughn De Leath sang it," she always told me. "Long before Elvis was a gleam in his daddy's eyes. Henry Burr sang it too. And Al Jolson." I loved knowing that little bit of trivia, though I'd never had a reason to use it.

Air fluttered from Trixie's nostrils and she tossed her head. She was not a horse, I was learning, who liked to wait. She preferred to keep moving.

On the ground behind us, something rustled in the brush. Trixie tensed, mouthed her bit, teeth chinking against metal, then calmed herself. I stroked her warm neck and softly crooned, *Good girl.* Daddy would be pleased. Fortitude was important in a horse who worked cattle. Scout, my chocolate Lab–shepherd mix, sat a few feet away, his shiny eyes glued to my face, a foot soldier poised for instructions.

"It's okay," I whispered.

One brown ear was in radar position, the other floppy but alert. Still, his eyes watched me. He sensed my anxiety but trusted my words.

Another fragment of song echoed up the hill. It sounded farther away, though Trixie and I hadn't moved, keeping still as possible on the spongy new grass. Was the person inside carrying a radio, a tape player? Had they moved deeper into the empty house?

I closed my eyes, recalling the house's interior landscape. The living room walls were knotty pine, lacquered to the color of vanilla wafers. The red and white kitchen had a porcelain farmhouse sink, chipped in the top left corner, and a milk glass chandelier with six pebbled globes that had been a pain to keep clean hung over the

14

small dining area. A scarred butcher block squatted slightly off center in the room. The strutting wallpaper roosters always seemed to be laughing, like Jack and I when we'd first moved into the house. Two bedrooms. The larger one faced east and had a padded window seat. That was the room where Jack and I had first made love.

John Harper Jr. *Jack.* My first love, husband of my youth. A hundred years ago, it seemed. Another lifetime. The Harper ranch had gone into foreclosure not long after Jack was killed in an auto accident. Over six years ago now. His family—once mine—scurried back to their home state of Texas. I exchanged western-themed Christmas cards with Sandra, my former sister-in-law, wife of Jack's only sibling, Wade. She was the one who told me a few years back that a group of Southern California investors bought the ranch with the intention of growing wine grapes, but the grapes were never planted. She thought that maybe they'd sold it, though she wasn't sure. I possessed the ability and contacts to find out. But I never did.

Early in my grief, I would ride the three or so miles from my family's ranch weekly to check on our house, traveling the same cattle paths that Jack and I rode when we were teenagers, sneaking out at night to meet under the stars and kiss. Gradually the house checks became monthly. Then once every three or four months. Now I only occasionally made the long trek to this hill. I could take the Jeep, which would be faster, but I preferred to ride one of our ranch horses, who always needed exercise. It was what Jack would do. I would pause on the rise and observe the land he and I had worked together, loved together, the home where we'd once planned our lives.

His death was no longer a painful throb but more a soft pinch to my heart. Though you never believe it in those first horrific moments of loss, life does keep moving forward. My life today was full. Gabe Ortiz, my second love, proved to me that even in the darkest times, there was hope. Five years we'd been married. I glanced at the diamond ring he gave me last August. Even on this cloudy March day it sparkled on my blunt-nailed finger. My plain gold wedding band bought in a Las Vegas jewelry store had been enough for me, but he wanted to give me more. We were on top of a Ferris wheel at the county fair when he slipped the diamond on my finger. A Ferris wheel was an apt metaphor for our marriage—the second for both of us. Jack and I had been a merry-go-round—steady, predictable, but beautiful with its detailed carving and rich, solid colors, but Gabe and I were definitely a Ferris wheel with brilliant neon lights and unpredictable seats.

". . . shall I come back again . . ." Elvis's silky voice floated up and lost itself in the high branches of the oak tree. Trixie was quiet, trusting me to be in control, to let her know when it was time to move on.

Elvis Presley. I'd been listening to his albums all my life. My mother played his music while she lay in bed dying and I scrambled over her rumpled bed quilts with my plastic Breyer horses pretending to be Annie Oakley or Roy Rogers. Dove played Elvis's albums for years, keeping my mother's memory alive for me. Right before Mama died, at my dad's request, Dove had come from Arkansas to help raise me, her oldest son's only child.

Thinking of my mother caused a moment of sadness to envelop me, like misty fog floating over the hills. She was twenty-six years old when she passed. I was six. It could overwhelm me if I let myself dwell on it. We both seemed so impossibly young for something so tragic. I was now thirty-nine—forty this month—acutely aware I was entering the second half of my life. I'd already lived almost fourteen years longer than she had, a fact that felt odd and troubling.

Here is a truth: Losing your mother when you are young changes you; the ground beneath your feet is never quite firm enough. You never completely trust happiness again.

But I had learned to embrace what happiness

was sent my way, to push the distrust into an attic corner of my brain. Despair rarely held me captive because I was surrounded by older women who tackled life as if it was the final quarter of a Super Bowl game. There was my steady yet dramatic gramma Dove, not contradictory adjectives when applied to her; my ever-surprising great-aunt Garnet, whom I grew closer to daily since she'd moved here from Arkansas with my uncle WW; the women in my quilt group at the Oak Terrace Retirement Home who, with wicked good humor, voted unanimously to name themselves the Coffin Star Quilt Guild; even Constance Sinclair, my cranky but dependably generous boss at the Josiah Sinclair Folk Art Museum where I was curator.

The timorous sound of older women's voices warmed me like a flannel quilt, softening the frantic edges of my life. These women I loved and respected had seen much in their years on earth, had experienced sorrows that would fell an ancient redwood. But they endured. They prospered. Shoot, they *laughed.* They amazed and delighted me. And sometimes they drove me head-twisting crazy.

My current project was recording their stories as part of an oral history project I'd undertaken with the celebrated photographer Isaac Lyons. The working title was "San Celina at Home."

18

He'd approached me with the idea a few months ago proposing a collaboration—he'd take the photos; I'd write their stories. It was an incredible opportunity that countless writers and historians would have killed to have been offered. Isaac was renowned for his insightful portraits, had photographed presidents and popes, movie stars and politicians. He'd studied with Ansel Adams and Edward Weston, argued form and composition with Dorothea Lange. His work hung in the Smithsonian.

It was a position I did not deserve. My education was not impressive, nor was I even that talented. However, I did have an inside track. He was married to and loopy-in-love with my gramma Dove. And because he loved her and she loved me . . . well, I got the job.

"Ask them what home means to them," he'd instructed me when we first discussed it sitting on the front porch of the Ramsey Ranch, owned jointly by my dad and my gramma. "Ask them where they feel the most at home, anything you can come up with that encourages them to talk about home. I'll take some of the photos while you're interviewing them or later if they seem nervous. The best photos happen when people forget themselves."

Because Isaac was weary of traveling, and because San Celina was now his home, he decided to concentrate on the people in San

Celina County, on the coast halfway between Los Angeles and San Francisco. Our county actually provided him a wonderful cross section of people—Cal Poly, a state university that still held strong rural roots, a rich Hispanic population, a smattering of Chinese and Japanese, African Americans and Swiss Italians, Portuguese and Basques, artists and musicians, retirees and homeless, ridiculously wealthy and no-nonsense working class, the always struggling small business owners. We'd started the project a few months ago, and it was apparent already that we'd end up with more photos and interviews than we could fit in one book. Culling them would be a painful job.

When the music from the ranch house abruptly stopped, jarring me from my thoughts, other sounds reasserted themselves; the distinct tip-tip of a downy woodpecker, the sucking noise of Trixie's hooves on the soggy March soil, the chatter of crickets. A sharp, cold wind circled around us, swooping over the hills from the Pacific Ocean. I shivered inside my denim jacket. Like Scout, I lifted my head and sniffed the briny air. Rain was coming.

I studied the gray sedan parked in the driveway. It had been there when I crested the rise. How long? The vehicle's make was nondescript, at least to me. If it wasn't a truck, they all looked the same. Was the person who owned the car buying the land? Did they plan on living there? Alone or with a family? This person was walking through the original ranch house. Had he or she already inspected the newer one where Wade, Sandra and their children had lived with Jack's widowed mother? It was more attractive and definitely bigger, but I always felt it had less history, less soul.

The thought of another family living in what had been my and Jack's first home made me anxious, a little angry. For some reason that bothered me more than when it was rumored that both houses might be razed and wine grapes planted. I could watch them be destroyed, but I didn't want anyone else to live in what had been my first home as a married woman. Unreasonable, but it was how I felt. I selfishly didn't want someone else's memories supplanting my own.

A rumble came from Scout's throat. I glanced down at his square, tense body. In that second, the front door of the ranch house opened and someone stepped out. Tall, thin, wearing blue jeans, a dark knit watch cap, sunglasses and a heavy jacket. From my distance, it wasn't apparent if the person was male or female. If I'd only remembered to bring binoculars. The person carried a radio or tape player, the source of the music. I watched the vehicle move away, braking occasionally on the rough gravel driveway. One red taillight was burned out. I

21

watched the gray car until it turned the corner and headed for the highway. An uneasy feeling pressed down on my chest; the air seemed to grow heavy, like the drop in barometric pressure before a storm.

I was tempted to ride down to see if this person left any physical evidence, but I wanted to beat the rain home. I turned Trixie around, clicking softly. It was probably nothing.

"Let's go," I called to Scout. "We've got chores to do."

Chapter 2

"Somebody's poking around the Harper place," I said, walking into Dove's red and yellow kitchen. Daddy was pouring himself a cup of coffee.

Outside, the rain that had threatened the whole ride back started an Irish river dance on the roof. Trixie, Scout and I made it back with seconds to spare.

"Hide me, pumpkin." My father's craggy, sun-browned face was desperate; his pale blue Australian shepherd eyes flashed white. "Someplace where the girls can't find me for the next hundred thirteen days."

Lord forgive me, I laughed.

"It isn't funny," Daddy said sharply. A sheen of perspiration glowed on his upper lip. "They're threatening to sign me up for some kind of nutty computer dating service." He shuddered beneath his blue plaid cowboy shirt. "It's this whole Memory Festival business. Got them all in a lather. They keep saying that I'm living in the past. They claim I need to make new memories. Benni girl, I *like* the memories I got. I don't want new ones. And I certainly don't want to date nobody off no dang computer."

I opened the refrigerator. "Meat loaf! It's almost noon. Want me to make you a sandwich? Is Isaac around?"

"Sure. Put on some of that wasabi mustard. It's pretty darn good." He sat at the breakfast bar, his work-scarred hands wrapped around a chunky tan coffee mug. "I think Isaac went to town. Said something about a new camera."

"He's been waiting for that for weeks. It's the latest thing. I think they call it digital. Doesn't even use film. Apparently you can see the photo on a little picture screen before you take it, then delete the photo if you don't like it. Crazy, huh? There aren't even any negatives. All the pictures go on a computer."

Daddy frowned at the word. "Computers are going to ruin this world. I don't want to go to dinner or anywhere else with no computer woman."

Though tempted, I knew better than to argue with him. Actually, I'd read an article in the *San Celina Tribune* a few weeks ago about computer dating and it insisted that, if you're careful, it could be helpful in connecting people with common interests. Much more reliable than bar-hopping, not that Daddy would consider either option. My dad had been alone a long time, though he'd never given any indication he was lonely. But, no doubt my gramma and her baby sister knew things about my father's life that I didn't. After all, they lived with him.

"Where *are* the sisters?" I sliced thick hunks of Aunt Garnet's spicy meat loaf and arranged them on slices of wheat bread. Plain yellow mustard for me. Scout bumped my shin with his nose, angling for a taste.

"Just a smidgen," I said, tossing him a piece of meat loaf that was onion-free. "You need to maintain that svelte figure."

I placed the sandwich with a scoop of potato salad and two pickle spears on a plate and slipped it in front of my dad. "It might do you good to enjoy yourself a little. You work really hard."

"I enjoy myself just fine," he said, picking up his sandwich. "I enjoy myself by working."

"Okay, then." Having done my due diligence in regards to his social life, I sat down across from him with my own sandwich. "So, I just rode out to the Harper ranch and saw somebody walking through my and Jack's old house. By the way, I think Trixie's going to be a good cow horse. She has a tendency to be a little impatient, though."

He shook his head, bit into his sandwich. "Shame how that place has just sat there empty all these years. Haven't heard anything about it since that fiasco with those big-city investors. Bill down at the Farm Supply said when their fancy winery fell through, they lost a bundle."

25

He chuckled, their misfortune like a touchdown for his team.

"I wonder if someone is thinking about buying it."

"I'll ask around, see what's what. What're you doing with the rest of your day?"

"That's why I'm looking for Isaac. I forgot to ask him yesterday about whether he had appointments set up for us this week. I'm trying to get everything coordinated for the Memory Festival this Saturday. Only six more days."

"Don't this county have enough festivals?"

To Daddy, the only gatherings worthy of attendance were the World Ag Expo in Tulare, the Mid-State Fair, the Snaffle Bit Futurity in Reno, the Parkfield Ranch Rodeo and, if a person felt like really whooping it up, the National Finals Rodeo in Las Vegas. He just didn't get why people needed to congregate to celebrate things like flowers or wine or quilts or memories.

I set down my half-eaten sandwich. "At first I thought it was kind of pushing it to concoct a fair around something as ambiguous as memories. But it's turning out to be really interesting."

Daddy grunted, pushing the potato salad around on his plate. "You remember things or you don't. Seems pretty cut-and-dried to me."

I sipped my Coke before answering. "You

wouldn't believe how many booths we've got. Did I tell you the city agreed to close off three blocks of downtown, just like with the Thursday night farmers' market? Took me some wheeling, dealing and whining to get that accomplished. But it enables us to have more booths than if we were just using the mission courtyard."

I pulled a list out of my leather backpack. "There'll be a story booth for kids and adults. An oral history booth where people can record family stories. The VFW has its own booth to record military memories. There are a couple of scrapbooking booths and a photo booth sponsored by Zack's Photo Shak where people can get a photo of themselves with something or someone they want to remember. Cal Poly's history department has booths for each decade starting with 1900, for people to record what they remember about that time. I'm not sure where the information is going, but it sounds fascinating. The historical society has a booth promoting San Celina history. The Farm Supply and a couple of local nurseries are giving seminars and selling plants for memory gardens. There are going to be booths for memory stones, flag cases, condolence lamps, pet headstones and urns, cremation jewelry . . ."

"What in tarnation is cremation jewelry?"

I laughed and took a bite of my pickle. "Apparently there are companies that can make your loved one's remains into a diamond that you can make into a lovely dinner ring or necklace or even . . ."

Daddy held up his hand, his expression pained. "I get the picture, and it ain't a pretty one. Leave me out of this."

After we finished our lunch, I rinsed off our dishes and put them in the dishwasher. "The Alzheimer's Association booth is selling the most amazing artwork created by people with memory impairment or dementia."

Daddy drained his coffee cup. "We need to talk about scheduling roundup."

I sighed. Normally I enjoyed roundup even with all the work of getting the vaccines ready, finding out whom among our neighbors could help, how many temporary hands we should hire, planning the menu—breakfast, lunch, snacks and the after-roundup barbecue. It was always a very long day that often flowed into two. These days it seemed like every activity in my life was listed under *let's get it done yesterday,* just another chore to scratch off my to-do list. I couldn't remember the last time Gabe and I went out for a leisurely dinner and stargazing in Morro Bay or an afternoon poking around antique stores.

"How many cattle this year?" I asked, leaning back against the sink.

Daddy picked up his dark brown felt Stetson

and settled it on his almost pure white hair. When had that happened? It seemed like the last time I looked he was more pepper than salt. "Not as many as last year—two fifty or so. We should be able to do it in a day if people don't goof around."

"I'll talk to Dove, see what's on her schedule. Maybe we can do it week from Friday?"

He came over and kissed me on top of my head. "I'll put it in my datebook."

I gave him a quick hug. "Be sure to leave some room for those other dates that Dove and Aunt Garnet have lined up for you."

He muttered like an old crow all the way out the door and probably halfway to the barn.

I wiped off the counter and left Dove a note that she was almost out of milk and yellow mustard. I added that Aunt Garnet's meat loaf was good enough to win first prize at the Mid-State Fair.

In my truck, I pulled out my cell phone and dialed my husband's cell. It rang four times, then went to voice mail.

"Gabe Ortiz. Leave a message." His police chief voice dared the person to ignore his command.

"Hey, Sergeant Friday," I said, using the nickname I'd given him when we first met, an attempt to take him down a peg, but that ended up being my version of honey or darling. "Not

29

desperate, but urgent. Need to know what you want to do for dinner. Over and out."

It was still hard to believe Gabe and I had just celebrated our fifth anniversary. This whole memory fair had started me thinking about my scattered photographs and memorabilia. I had become interested enough in scrapbooking to start going through them, dividing and organizing pictures by year. What a task it was turning out to be. What I was learning was I almost always took too many photos of the same thing and not enough of things that mattered, that is, things that were now gone. Of course, how was I to know back then that they'd disappear? I wished I had more photos of Jack and me when we were teenagers, more photos of Gabe and me when we were dating or of my favorite jeans in high school, the ones I spent hours embroidering. I wished there were photos of Jack's work boots, of his hands, of the first calf I helped deliver, the first meal I ever cooked for Jack and for Gabe. How I longed for a close-up of my mother's hands, her earlobes, her feet. I sometimes stared at my own bare feet and wondered if my toes looked like hers.

But what could a person do, mount a camera on her head and record her whole life? Sometimes you just had to make do with the memories in your mind. I suspected those memories, photographed through the cheesecloth of time, might ultimately be more kind.

The steady rain had softened to a mist during my ten-mile drive back to San Celina. The emerald hills spotted with blue lupine and the occasional early patch of California poppies were a photographer's dreamscape. It was one of those extraordinary Central Coast spring days in a year where we'd been receiving enough rain to turn our normally dun-colored landscape the brilliant green of a Disney cartoon. The beauty of this land—my home—never ceased to amaze me. I might be Arkansas born, but I'd been raised here. Rich, dark California soil flowed through my veins.

After dropping Scout off at home, the California Craftsman bungalow that Gabe and I were slowly remodeling, I headed across town to the Josiah Sinclair Folk Art Museum. Though my job often drove me batty, what with dealing with fussy society patrons, temperamental artists, the kooky and unpredictable public and an ever penny-pinching bureaucracy, I still loved it. Between overseeing the running of the museum and its exhibits and the artists' co-op affiliated with the museum, the job was never boring, and it even allowed me to utilize my dubiously valuable history degree from Cal Poly.

I pulled my purple Ford Ranger pickup into the museum's half-full parking lot. The old Sinclair Hacienda (donated by our first and most dependable patron, Constance Sinclair) looked sparkling today. The white adobe walls looked freshly painted though likely it was the rain that contributed to their clean surfaces. The double front door had been recently stained and the black hardware painted. The red tiled Spanish roof had a small amount of green algae, but D-Daddy would take care of it before it became a problem. Delbar "D-Daddy" Boudreaux was my dynamite assistant whom I'd just promoted to property manager (along with a well-deserved raise) despite the fact that he and I were the museum's only paid employees. He cared for these buildings with the same love he'd no doubt lavished on the commercial fishing boat he'd owned in Louisiana before retiring in San Celina.

I pulled open the heavy front door and entered the museum's lobby gift shop. The products for sale in the glass cases—cards, hand-painted scrapbooks, colorful signature wall quilts, memory lockets—reflected both the Memory Festival coming this Saturday and our corresponding exhibits.

The main exhibit downstairs was called I Remember When—Quilts as Personal History. It displayed a variety of story quilts that celebrated everything from a sixty-six-year marriage to a winning Little League tournament to celebrating ten years of sobriety to a Cambodian family's first year in the United States. There were twenty-five quilts accepted for the exhibit, the most we could comfortably show, and I worked hard at choosing quilts that represented a cross section of human experience.

In our smaller upstairs gallery, we presented a more controversial exhibit called Moving On: Celebrating Those Who Have Left. It also had a memory theme, but to qualify, the subject of the art piece had to have passed on from this earth. D-Daddy started calling it my "dead folks exhibit," though I pointed out we had two collages that celebrated the death of a police dog and a pet pig. This exhibit, with its center-piece Graveyard quilt, had earned us the most publicity.

"You thought up this crazy exhibit just to rattle people's cages," my cousin Emory said a few weeks ago when he helped me hang the pieces on a slow Monday afternoon. Elvia, his wife and my best friend, and their ten-month-old daughter, Sophie, were at a Mommy and Me Books & Lemonade event she was hosting at her book-store downtown, Blind Harry's. "Not to mention getting lots of free publicity."

"Not really," I insisted, "though you know we'll gladly accept any kind of free publicity." I ran a lint roller over the Graveyard quilt. It had been designed and made by the quilt guild the artists' co-op sponsored at the Oak Terrace

Retirement Home. "The ladies of the Coffin Star Quilt Guild have been working on this quilt for a long time, and I really wanted to display it at the museum. This Memory Festival was the perfect venue. Then someone in the artist's co-op asked if they could display a collage they'd made about their father's death in the Korean War, and before I knew it, we had a themed exhibit."

Emory brushed back a lock of shiny honey-blond hair that had fallen across his forehead. Even working sixty hours a week running his smoked chicken business (his father, Uncle Boone, had moved out to California last summer and promptly became addicted to golf, thus semiretiring), becoming a husband and father and active as a community volunteer hadn't diminished his rakish, college-boy look. Even wearing old corduroy jeans and a faded red Arkansas Razorbacks sweatshirt he could have posed for an Abercrombie & Fitch ad.

He stepped back to gaze at the double bed–size quilt. It was made with brown, black, rust and tan calico squares interspersed with squares of the eight-pointed Lemoyne Star pattern. The middle of the quilt was a large muslin square depicting rows of coffin-shaped pieces of fabric embroidered with tiny words. "What's the story behind this thing?"

I stood next to him. "It's loosely based on a

famous old graveyard quilt by Elizabeth Roseberry Mitchell. They copied the general pattern of her graveyard quilt, but after realizing it might creep out their kids, instead of putting family names on the coffins like Elizabeth did, they agreed to 'lay to rest' things from their lives. It's kind of a cool idea, really."

Emory stepped closer to the quilt, reading out loud the words embroidered on the tiny coffins. "Jealousy, anger, bitterness, envy, greed, sadness, fear, regret, prejudice, Bob." He turned to me, a bemused grin on his face. "Bob?"

I'd laughed, remembering when Thelma Rook embroidered the name. "He was the first boy who broke her heart. Hey, it made her feel better, and a hundred years from now, it'll make someone wonder."

"Especially if his name is Bob," Emory had said.

Back in my office, there were five messages on my answering machine. I was very stingy about giving out my cell phone number, still preferring to have some time during the day when I wasn't at somebody's beck and call, but by chairing the Memory Festival committee, I'd added to my already full plate of people wanting me to do something for them. But, I reasoned while taking out paper to record the messages, it would only last until this Saturday. Next year I'd generously pass the Memory Festival chairperson position on to some other deserving soul.

The first two messages were requests for booth applications. A bit late in the game, but I'd check with the person in charge of booth rentals to see if there were any cancellations or spaces left. Maybe somebody would agree to share a booth to save a little money. The third was from Elvia asking if Gabe and I would like to come to dinner tonight. Emory had bought a new, gizmo-rich gas barbecue he was dying to try. The fourth was Constance Sinclair wondering if I'd finished the last two applications for grants that she'd sent me (no, I hadn't, but they were on my list) and the last message was from my father.

"I'm calling from the barn phone," he said, his voice a dramatic whisper. "They're inside the house with a lady they done picked up at the supermarket. Near the frozen foods. She's Lyle Shelton's sister-in-law from Boise. She makes baskets." He paused a moment, then said, "They're coming for me. I can hear them. Save me, pumpkin." Click. The message had been left an hour ago, so I didn't call back. He'd likely been captured by the Boise basket weaver and was now beyond my help.

I passed the booth requests on to the person in charge of them, ignored Constance's message and sent up a quick prayer for Daddy that Lyle's sister-in-law wouldn't scare him too much and that he might actually enjoy talking to her. After

36

giving the rest of my in-box a promise to reconvene tomorrow, I decided to cruise through the co-op building to see if the artists needed anything. It was part of my normal Monday afternoon routine. That way if a machine needed repair or supplies needed ordering, I had all week to take care of it.

I was on my way down the stone pathway between the museum and the stable behind the hacienda that now housed the artists' co-op when I met Amanda Landry, one of San Celina's deputy district attorneys and our museum's pro bono legal guru. She was also a co-op member and a wonderful quilt artist.

"Hey, girl," she called out to me in her molasses-tinged Alabama accent. "Just the woman I was lookin' for." She had someone with her, a woman I didn't recognize. "Sweetie, I desperately need a favor."

"Whatever it is you want me to do, the answer is no. At least until next Monday. I'm swamped."

She turned to the tall silver-haired woman behind her who wore a nubby Irish fisherman's sweater and jeans. "Ignore her. She always gets pissy-pants on Mondays. I'm tellin' you, this little gal owes me. I have saved her butt just too many times to count."

"As my proper aunt Garnet would say, bull grits," I said, laughing. "But if you bake me a maple walnut pie, I will reconsider." Amanda's maple walnut pies would make a fortune if she were ever so inclined to market them.

"Done. My new friend here needs some time on one of your pottery wheels. Do you think she could buy some time?"

I glanced up at the woman and smiled. "Sure, why not?"

She smiled back and tugged at one sleeve of her sweater. Silvery blonde curls hugged a perfectly shaped head. She appeared slightly older than Amanda, maybe early fifties, and matched Amanda shoulder-to-shoulder, which meant she had to be close to six feet tall. Her rosy cheekbones were natural and her eyes were almost a teal blue.

"I'm Linda Snider," she said, holding out a hand. Her handshake was firm but not overwhelming. Two thin gold bracelets sounded a delicate jingle. "I go by Lin."

"Benni Ortiz. You're a potter?"

She nodded. "Not a very good one. I'm new at it, but I'll be here in San Celina a month or so. I want to keep my hand in."

"Are you visiting family?"

"She's looking for a home," Amanda said. "Just traveling around the country trying to decide where she wants to retire. Doesn't that sound like fun?"

I looked back at Lin Snider. "Really? Where are you from?"

Her smile became wistful. "Nowhere and everywhere. Army brat. Lived in fifteen cities in eighteen years. I was born in San Antonio. So I guess, officially, I'm a Texan."

"Lots of them around here," I said. "They seem to be more vocal around football season. You know those Dallas Cowboys fans."

"Actually, I'm not a big football fan," Lin said.

"That's why I liked her right off," Amanda said, throwing her arm around the woman. "Barbaric sport."

An unbelievably large raindrop hit me on the nose. "Looks like the rain is starting up again. Let's go to my office and check the schedule. I'll make tea."

Once inside my office, with the tea bags steeping, Amanda and I discussed the upcoming festival while I hunted for the pottery wheel's signup sheet.

Like a human metronome, Amanda waved a long forefinger at me. "Sweetie pie, I told you months ago that you were crazy as a bourbon-drunk turkey to head this Memory Festival committee. When are you going to learn that magic word 'no'?"

"You're right, you're right. One of my high school friends talked me into it. Her father has Alzheimer's and it's just tearing her up. This festival made her feel like she was doing something productive. We were going to cochair, but then she got mononucleosis."

"The kissing disease?" Amanda gave a roof-raising laugh. "Who gets that over the age of fifteen?"

"I don't think they call it that anymore." I smiled at Lin. "She's dating herself."

"Actually, I was thinking the same thing," Lin said, smiling back.

"Back to business," Amanda said. "I told you that Benni could fix you up with a potter's wheel. Now you can play in clay to your heart's content."

"Thank you, Amanda," Lin said. "Meeting you is the best thing that's happened to me since I came to San Celina. And thank you, Benni. Whenever you can fit me in, I'd appreciate it."

I found the scheduling notebook at the bottom of my desk drawer. "It looks like there's time free on Wednesday and Thursday afternoons this week. Both are two-hour sessions. Twenty dollars an hour."

"I'll take them," she said. "Where do I sign?"

After she filled out an application and paid me eighty dollars in cash, I put the money in the petty cash box, locked it and stuck her application inside the notebook to file away later.

"Great, that's done. Now let's go see the museum," Amanda said. "I want to show Lin the dead folks exhibit."

"I wish everyone would stop calling it that." I looked over at Lin. "The exhibit's actual title is Moving On: Celebrating Those Who Have Left."

Her face registered just a moment's emotion—dismay, sadness? Not surprising. Everyone had lost *someone*. That was the reason I thought the exhibit would be popular.

"I'll come say my good-byes once we're finished seeing the exhibits," Amanda told me.

About a half hour later, Amanda was back in my office. She flopped down in one of my visitor chairs. "Lin's looking through the gift shop. Thanks for letting her use the wheel. She seems nice, doesn't she?"

"No problem. The more it's used, the more money we make. How did you say you know her?"

"It was just one of those serendipitous things," she said, pulling a compact out of her purse and checking her lipstick. "I was in the health food store looking for something that would help me with my insomnia, and she just started talking about how she also has problems with not being able to sleep. We're both of 'that age,' if you know what I mean, except you don't, but you will. Anyway, we started comparing night sweat dilemmas and before you know it we were drinking green tea at the bar." She made a face. "I don't care what they say, that stuff tastes like someone dug up their lawn and threw it in a pot of ditch water. Cooked grass is all it is. And I don't mean the kind we smoked in the sixties. Give me good ole Lipton's any day."

"You said she's looking for a place to retire?"

Amanda scraped off a bit of shiny lipstick in the corner of her generous mouth. "Said she was traveling around the U.S. looking for a place to put down roots. She came into some money and thinks she might want to relocate to a smaller town. Lived in Seattle or thereabouts. I know what she means. It's nice being in a place where everybody knows your name." She winked and gave a mischievous grin.

"Right," I said, leaning back in my office chair. "Sometimes you wish everyone would forget your name. Like, for example, when you stupidly agree to chair a festival committee."

"There're rumors about starting the first annual Bush Monkey Flower Festival. The committee is looking for someone experienced to take charge . . ."

"Out!" I said, standing up and pointing to the door.

"I'm gone, Miz Ortiz. See you on Saturday. I did foolishly agree to man, or rather woman, the 1960s booth for two hours. I think I have some old love beads that I can wear. It is truly the only thing that fits me from that time." She came around the desk and gave me a rib-cracking hug.

"Thanks for being nice to my new friend. Shoot, maybe she'll end up deciding to live in San Celina. This town's got a way of reeling people in."

After Amanda left, I started to put away the pottery wheel notebook when Lin Snider's application fell out. I dug through my desk and found my three-hole punch. Then I pulled down the notebook that held the applications of everyone who used the co-op, feeling very smug that I was filing it right away. Out of habit, I glanced over her information.

Her address was for a hotel in Morro Bay—the Spotted Pelican Inn. It was one of dozens of hotels in the tiny seaside town twenty minutes from San Celina. This particular hotel was popular with birders who descended upon our avian-blessed county at various times to add to their life lists or participate in official bird counts. The hotel's lobby was connected to a wonderful French bakery called simply Pierre's. The head baker had won Best of County awards for her unusual croissants—mango-chocolate, strawberry-mint and pistachio–cream cheese. It was one of Gabe's favorite places to linger on a foggy winter afternoon, drinking their rich, dark coffee and reading the *New York Times*.

I scanned the application. Except for her name and the hotel's address, there was no other information. I needed to ask this Lin for her actual mailing address the next time I saw her, not that I expected that she would do anything illegal. Gabe's voice in my head reminded me to get all her information in case something was stolen or damaged in the museum or co-op buildings. Being married to a cop had definitely changed the way I looked at people, something I wasn't entirely happy about. But sometimes the most innocent-looking people could be people who are up to no good, and I could imagine Gabe scolding me because I hadn't checked her driver's license or some other form of identification before allowing her access to our buildings. I wrote a reminder to myself on a Post-it and stuck it on my telephone.

"Done my due diligence, Chief," I said out loud.

"Who're you talking to?" my aunt Garnet said, striding into my office.

Dove appeared two seconds later. "Hey, honey bun!"

I'd been so lost in my thoughts I hadn't heard their not-at-all-subtle voices coming up the long hallway.

"Nobody." I stood up, abruptly closing the notebook. "What're you two doing here? Last I heard you were pushing some Boise basket broad off on Daddy."

"Just finished our cane fu lesson," Dove said, holding up her lavender and white Hawaiian

44

print cane. "I'm starving, and your daddy needs a woman."

"We practiced taking out knees today," Aunt Garnet said. "Easier than one would think."

They were dressed in identical elastic-waist jeans and flowered tops. Dove's flowers were lavender to match her Hawaiian-themed cane. Aunt Garnet's were navy blue. Her cane was a glossy cherrywood. She preferred a more traditional look in canes, she informed me when she bought it directly from their instructor.

When Aunt Garnet and Uncle WW moved out to San Celina last summer from Arkansas, I was a little worried about her and Dove living in such close proximity. Make that a lot worried. They'd always gotten along like vinegar and baking soda—dramatic eruption guaranteed.

Aunt Garnet and Dove were about as opposite as two women could be. We're not talking apples and oranges, we're talking apples and carburetors. But with Uncle WW in the middle stages of Parkinson's disease, Aunt Garnet and Dove surprised everyone when they took to heart the Bible verse in Isaiah about beating their "swords into ploughshares and spears into pruning hooks." They warred no longer and had settled peacefully into a life of church activities, ranch work, Uncle WW's various doctor appointments and now, apparently, finding Daddy a soul mate. They even enjoyed hobbies together like their weekly scrapbooking class and their cane fu class down at the senior center.

Cane fu, I'd learned, was a type of senior martial arts where a person learned to defend themselves against muggers or, as Aunt Garnet called them, mashers. I'd seen some of their moves and, believe me, you didn't want to mess with folks trained in cane fu.

"At the refreshment table after our lesson, some of us were discussing the moral conundrum of whether we should put steel pipes inside our canes to give them more power," Aunt Garnet said, her wrinkled face thoughtful.

"Loading the deck, so to speak," Dove added. "My position is all's fair in war and cane fu. If someone tries to mug me, a steel pipe upside the head is exactly what he deserves." She brandished her cane which, I assumed by the ease with which she swung it, was empty . . . so far.

"What about turning the other cheek?" I asked, knowing full well that my comment would set her off.

"I smack that too!" Dove said.

"Amen, Sister," Garnet agreed.

"Well, I feel *much* better about you two being out and about after dark now. I hear that the pit bull rescue is looking for people to work with their more vicious dogs. I think that should be your next project."

46

The calculating expression that appeared on *both* their faces caused me to start two-stepping backward. "Just kidding, girls. Maybe you should stick with cane fu until you get really proficient at it. Change of topic: Why the sudden interest in Daddy's love life?"

Aunt Garnet sat down heavily in one of my black and chrome visitor's chairs. "My legs are getting a little wobbly. Has Ben been talking to you?"

Dove joined her sister, collapsing with a loud sigh. "I hear you, li'l sis. That's quite a workout. I just love our darling little instructor though. Susie Watanabe. She's got a black belt in karate and kung fu. She studied cooking at that fancy school in France—Cord and Blue. And she speaks fluent Chinese!"

"Isn't Watanabe a Japanese surname?" I asked.

Dove looked at me blankly. "Yes, so?"

I waved my hand—never mind. "Daddy's love life?"

"Pshaw," Dove said, resting both hands on the crook of her cane. "We just want him to take a few women out to dinner. He's overreacting."

"Or meet them for coffee," Aunt Garnet said. "The poor boy's so lonely. He just doesn't know how much."

"For Pete's sakes, we're not asking him to marry them," Dove said. "But we do need to get him settled . . ."

"Before we leave these earthly chains." Aunt Garnet tilted her head upward like she was receiving a message directly from the Lord.

I bit the inside of my cheek to keep from laughing. "Is there something you two haven't told me? Some inside scoop on when you're scheduled to take the A train to Jesus?"

Dove pointed her cane at me. "One never knows. We could be hit by a bus."

"Or mugged for pocket change," Aunt Garnet said, her face serious.

"Or kidnapped by pirates," I added, not holding back my smile.

"Laugh all you want, missy," Dove said, pointing her cane at me. "But no one knows the time or place of their last breath. We just want your daddy properly situated in the love department before we go."

" 'Properly situated in the love department,' " I repeated. "I think I'm going to have that printed on a T-shirt: 'Are You Properly Situated in the Love Department?' "

"Don't sass me," Dove said.

"Us," Aunt Garnet added.

So now I had two of them. Great. I almost preferred when they squabbled with each other. With those two joining forces, Daddy . . . and the rest of us . . . didn't stand a chance.

Daddy, dearest, you're on your own here. Good luck.

"Have you both received your assignments for the Memory Festival?" I asked. Since someone else had been in charge of booth sign-ups, I had no idea who was where, doing what.

"Uncle WW and I are at the 1940s booth for two hours," Aunt Garnet said. "He's wearing his army uniform. It still fits!" She gave me a tremulous smile. "That's about as long as he can handle, I'm afraid."

"Wow, I'm impressed. I haven't been able to fit in my wedding dress since I was twenty-two." I looked over at my gramma. "What about you, Dove?"

"Historical society booth," she said. "Isaac will be speaking at the bookstore. And we're both signed up to be interviewers in the story booth."

The historical society, having heard about the project that Isaac and I were working on, decided to expand on the idea and start collecting oral histories of San Celina. It was something the historical society had done a little bit of a few years back trying to record local residents' stories about World War II. I'd helped with that, going around and speaking with many of our Japanese residents who'd been interned during the war. This time people could just say what they wanted, though their memories did need to include San Celina.

"What're you doing?" Dove asked.

"I'm wearing about twenty hats on Saturday.

Just pray that no huge problems occur and for sunny weather."

"I'll make a special request to the Lord," said Aunt Garnet.

"*Gracias, tía grande.*"

"Duh nah dah," she replied slowly, enunciating each syllable. Then she giggled. Aunt Garnet's rudimentary Spanish tinged with her Arkansas drawl always made me smile. Her enthusiasm for her new life as a Californian, not pining for the past, for accepting this new season of her and Uncle WW's lives, made me realize how courageous she was. I was proud of the women in my family. If I had half their courage, I'd be set for this second part of my life.

We were in the lobby, discussing the display of books that Elvia had helped me pick out that taught how to record family histories, when Laura, one of our docents, dashed through the back door, her face flushed with panic.

"Benni, you have to come see what's happening on TV."

"What?"

"Over by the courthouse. A sniper shot at a police car!"

Chapter 3

My first instinct was to call Gabe, but I resisted. He didn't need any distractions.

We followed Laura into the woodworker's room. The room smelled toasty and sharp from sawdust and linseed oil, and the equipment, normally whining and buzzing so loud the men shouted their conversations, was silent.

Six men gathered around a small color television propped on a card table. The woodworkers liked watching sports or one of the cable home improvement stations while they made their tables, chairs, duck decoys and fancy shelving.

The men moved aside, making a spot for me.

"What's going on?" I asked, peering into the small screen filled with cop cars and people. My heart raced, like I'd just run a fifty-yard dash.

Ray, a longtime member of the co-op, pulled at his shaggy, brick-colored mustache and said, "Some punk shot at a police car parked on a side street next to the courthouse. It's a spot reserved for officers bringing prisoners to their arraignments and trials. The driver's-side window was shattered. Thank God, the officer had stepped out of the vehicle a minute before." He crossed himself.

"Lord, have mercy," Dove murmured behind me, resting a hand on my shoulder.

Filling the screen was one of San Celina's local news anchors, Tiffany Connors. She stood across the street from the scene, shifting from one high-heeled foot to the other. Big Top Pizza's large plate-glass window, painted with bright red, yellow and blue balloons, loomed behind her, an improbable backdrop. With her smooth blonde pageboy, twitchy upturned nose and enthusiastic voice, she gave every story the same high school "Let's put on a play!" tone.

"Why in the world is *she* reporting on this?" one guy asked.

"Guess," another replied.

Tiffany was a local joke because she insisted on writing her own news copy, which, because of her lack of journalistic education or experience always stated the obvious. No one dared criticize her simplistic style to her face or in print because her father, Deck Connors, was the new owner of the *San Celina Tribune* and KSCC, our home-town television station.

"At approximately twelve thirty-five p.m. a sniper fired at a San Celina police vehicle." She flipped her head around to gaze up at the second-floor apartments over Big Top Pizza, San Celina Fitness and a new coffeehouse called

Bitter Grounds. Students primarily rented the cheap, noisy apartments, built in the thirties. "The alleged shooter broke into an apartment . . ." She turned stiffly and pointed to the second floor above the pizzeria. ". . . and used it for his dastardly deed, then disappeared, like a thief in the night. San Celina detectives are investigating. More information at our four p.m. broadcast. This is Tiffany Connors reporting for KSCC." Before the camera was turned off, she'd already pulled a compact out of the pocket of her fitted black leather jacket and was checking for smudges underneath her spiky eyelashes.

"Dastardly deed?" One of the woodworkers snickered. "Where did she go to broadcasting school, *Mister Rogers' Neighborhood*?"

"I resent her sexist use of the male pronoun," Ray said. "It could have been a woman. San Celina's SWAT team's best sharpshooter is a woman, I hear."

"Maybe they should be checking to see if that officer has kept up with his child support payments," one man commented.

"Gabriel is probably fit to be tied," Dove said. "You know he feels very protective about his officers."

"I'm going to the station," I said. "Maybe Maggie can fill me in."

"Please call us as soon as you find out anything," Aunt Garnet said, leaning on her cane. "We're going on back to the ranch."

I drove the half mile to the police station where I was surprised to find the lobby completely empty. Then again, it was the middle of the day. All the officers were either out patrolling or down at the shooting scene, along with any reporters. Jacob, the officer behind the front window, recognized me and buzzed open the side door, letting me into the offices.

"Hey, Mrs. Ortiz," he said, his freckled face and spiky red hair reminding me of a grown-up Opie from the old *Andy of Mayberry* television series. "Chief's still down at the shooting scene. Crazy, huh? Who would, like, shoot at a police car in the middle of the day? And right next to the courthouse. That's crazy, huh?"

"Unfortunately, there are lots of crazy people out there. Is Maggie here?"

"Hasn't left all day. Hey, how'd you hear about it so fast?"

"I was at the folk art museum, and it came on the television. We caught the tail end of Tiffany's report. Any information about a suspect?"

He shook his head no.

Maggie, Gabe's assistant, was making a cup of tea at the credenza behind her desk. Both lines on her phone were lit, but she was obviously allowing them to go to voice mail.

"Hey, Maggie. I came over as soon as I heard."

"Bad stuff," she said, shaking her head while she dunked a tea bag. "Want some tea?" She wore a maroon business suit with thin black piping. Maggie and I had known each other since she was a girl. She and her sister, Katsy, owned a small cattle ranch outside Santa Margarita, near the Frio Inn. She'd worked for Gabe for a couple of years now, keeping his work life running smooth as a dish of flan.

"No, thanks. Any word about which officer had a really lucky day?"

"Or unlucky if you think about the nightmares he'll likely have for the next, oh, ten years. It was Ryan Jacoby. He was taking a prisoner in for arraignment. It was actually supposed to be Miguel's assignment, but he took the day off."

Miguel was one of Elvia's younger brothers. Long before he was a police officer who worked for my husband, I had helped Elvia babysit him. I'd given that tough, barrel-chested cop more piggyback rides than I could remember. "Any leads on who did this dastardly deed?"

She cocked her head, her dark brown eyes confused.

"A direct quote from Tiffany Connors, girl reporter."

"Heaven help us," Maggie said, giving a dainty snort. "Was Bart Simpson on another assignment today?"

"Have any inside scoop?"

"Nothing of significance. The detectives found the room where the shot was fired, but it's just some college kid's apartment—four college boys, to be exact—and they were all in class, perfect alibis. Still, they'll be investigated—as the detectives like to say—down to the gnat's ass. Pardon my French."

"Was the place broken into?"

She sat down behind her desk, took a sip of her tea. "According to the detectives, there's no evidence of it. Then again, it's four college guys living there. My guess is there are probably a dozen keys to that apartment floating around this county and beyond. Or they might not even lock it. But you can count on anyone who has passed through those apartment doors during the last year will be found and interviewed."

I sat down on one of her padded visitor's chairs. "I'll make a wild guess that there's little physical evidence of the shooter's presence."

"From what Detective Arnaud told me a few minutes ago the place is a pigsty—big surprise there, huh? And that finding clues was going to be like searching for an old copper penny in a swamp."

"Interesting turn of phrase. I don't recognize that detective's name. Who's he?"

She gave a half smile. "*She's* a new detective. Gabe hired her about three months ago. She's a very experienced investigator."

I held up my hands. "As Sam would say, my bad." Sam was Gabe's son, a student at Cal Poly and part-time ranch hand for my dad. "What's she like?"

"Yvette's about your age, maybe a little older. Early forties? She and her husband moved here from Louisiana, though she's originally from Santa Maria. I hear he's a pretty famous photographer who has won some big awards." She shrugged. "Not my area of expertise. They actually moved out to care for her sick mama. They're living with her over in Arroyo Grande. It's nice having more women hanging around this good ole boy's club. She and I have talked a few times in the lunchroom. I like her. She keeps me posted on things."

"And you keep *me* posted, so I like her too. Do you think Gabe will be here soon, or should I just talk to him tonight?"

"Actually, he called right before you walked in. He's on his way back to the office. There's not much more to do at the scene, and he has a meeting with the new prison warden at three p.m."

"Thanks, I'll wait in his office."

I sat down in his high-backed leather chair and amused myself by doodling laughing dog faces on his official San Celina Police Department, Chief Gabriel Ortiz message pad. He walked through the door fifteen minutes later.

"Give us five minutes, please, then get the mayor on the phone," he called to Maggie, closing his office door.

"Hey, Friday," I said, standing up and going to him. "Sorry about the shooting."

He hugged me hard, resting his cheek on the top of my head. "How did you hear?"

"I was at the folk art museum, and it was on the television in the woodshop. Is it true you have no idea who did this?"

He kissed the top of my head and walked behind his desk. "Yes, and there's not much to go on. I have my best investigators on it."

He sat down, glancing at his memo pad. My doodles made him smile briefly.

"Do you think it could happen again?"

His full bottom lip disappeared under his thick black and silver mustache.

"For now, we're treating it as a random act."

"Okay, what's on for dinner?"

"I forgot to tell you I'm having dinner with the sheriff tonight. She and I are taking out the new prison warden, filling him in on the way this county runs, and just getting to know him."

"Do you like him?"

"Seems like a decent guy. Comes from Utah. You're not going to believe this. His wife raises Pembroke Welsh corgis."

"That is an amazing coincidence." Sally Schuler, San Celina's sheriff, bred Pembrokes.

"We were possibly invited to Emory and Elvia's for a barbecue. Emory has a new gas grill. I'll tell them we'll take a rain check, and I'll go to Liddie's. It's chicken and dumpling night."

"I'm jealous," Gabe said.

"Every third bite will be for you."

There was a soft tap-tap on the door. I stood on tiptoe and kissed the bottom of his chin. "My meter's run out. See you tonight. Stay safe. If someone starts shooting at you, run like a rabbit." That scene in the Pink Panther movie always made him laugh.

He ruffled my hair, though he didn't crack a smile. "You always make me feel better."

After talking a few more minutes to Maggie, hearing the latest gossip about the June wedding plans for her sister Katsy and her fiancé Levi, I headed for my car. It was almost three o'clock. Too early for dinner, so I decided to drop my truck off at the house and walk downtown to Blind Harry's Bookstore to discuss the sniper shooting with Elvia.

Blind Harry's, the largest independent bookstore between Los Angeles and San Francisco, was Elvia's biggest dream come true next to marrying Emory and having Sophia Louisa (or Sophie Lou as Emory and I called her, to Elvia's consternation). She'd taken a small, semi-successful bookstore that she'd worked at since she was sixteen and turned it into one of San Celina's crowning business jewels, a true destination bookstore. She'd been slowly buying the owner out when she married my cousin, and he bought the rest of it for her as a wedding present. And, because my cousin was the nicest, most liberated man on earth, Blind Harry's was solely and completely in her name.

The bookstore was one of the most enthusiastic sponsors of the Memory Festival, and it showed in their amusing front window display. Elephants—stuffed, china, bejeweled and books about them—dominated the scene. A clever touch, I thought. Inside the store, there were at least a dozen displays of books that celebrated anything to do with memory or oral history. There was even a section that promoted mnemonics, the study of tricks on how to remember things.

Blind Harry's was busy as always. The bookstore was popular with the town's retired folks and tourists, and the downstairs coffeehouse was one of the favorite meeting places for college students and the town's young professionals.

I waved at the cashier, a young woman named Tara, whom my stepson Sam had recently started dating exclusively, though I'd been informed by him that it wasn't actually called "dating"—that was apparently an "old-school" term. They were "hanging out" with each other on an exclusive basis, which sure sounded like dating to me.

I headed upstairs to Elvia's French country-style office and found her bundling little Sophie into a white fuzzy snowsuit-like outfit. Two floppy bunny ears sprouted from the hood.

"Sophie Louisa Aragon Littleton, you are just downright cute enough to eat," I said, bending close to her and making exaggerated smacking noises with my lips. I loved how a grown person was allowed to behave like a reject from clown school as long as it was in the interest of entertaining babies.

"I'm going to confiscate your cousin's credit cards," Elvia said, zipping up Sophie's bunny suit. "He wants photos of her in this costume for our Easter cards, which I've informed him *he* gets to address. Want to come with us? We're going to that new photography studio next to Zack's Photo Shak."

"I've walked by that place but have never gone inside. Looks cute. What's it called . . . back something?"

"Backdrops. The Cal Poly girls like it because they have lots of clever backgrounds like the Hollywood sign or Mammoth ski slopes." She handed Sophie to me while she pulled on a gray wool jacket. "Is it still cold and rainy out? I haven't left this office in hours."

"Pretty chilly. There are dark clouds, but no rain in the last few hours. So far, it's looking good for the festival. Fingers crossed that

Saturday stays dry, because we foolishly have no alternative plan." I bounced Sophie up and down in my arms, making kazoo music with my lips. She giggled, smiling a wide, toothless grin.

"Watch it, I just fed her," Elvia warned.

"I've helped deliver calves since I was eight years old. Baby barf doesn't scare me."

"I wasn't thinking about you. She just ate some peas. I don't want her bunny suit messed up, at least until her pictures are taken." She held out her arms.

"Gotcha," I said, handing Sophie back to her mama. "Where's her stroller?"

"Downstairs in the storeroom."

By the time Elvia had rounded up Sophie's black and white polka-dotted designer diaper bag and her own purse, I had the stroller ready. Downtown was busy for a Monday afternoon. I wondered if there was something going on this week at Cal Poly. First week of March? Nothing going on that I could recall. Mardi Gras was last week, and the town had been relatively quiet since Ash Wednesday. It appeared that most Cal Poly students, as well as San Celina itself, were still recuperating from an always raucous Fat Tuesday celebration.

At Backdrops we had six spring- or Easter-themed backgrounds to choose from. I liked the giant Easter basket filled with jelly beans and chocolate bunnies, but Elvia preferred the windmill and pink tulips background. While she consulted with Emory on her cell phone, I wandered around the studio's lobby looking at the framed photograph samples. The photographer on duty was a man who appeared to be in his late forties with wavy, shoulder-length silver hair and a gold hoop earring in one ear. His even-featured face was conventionally handsome and unmemorable, like the perpetually grinning star of a cable cop show set in an unexpected, funky town like Oxford, Mississippi, or Eugene, Oregon. Right at this moment he looked extremely bored. I wondered how he ended up in this studio taking photos of college girls on fake surfboards and babies in bunny suits.

"You and Benni think just alike," I heard Elvia say. "I honestly think the bunny costume takes care of the cute department. An Easter basket background is going too far. No, it *isn't* up for discussion." Elvia made a face at me and then pointed at the door. Apparently it was going to be discussed. I gave her the okay sign that I would watch my goddaughter.

While Elvia took the discussion outside, Sophie slept peacefully in her stroller, unconcerned with such a monumental decision.

"She doesn't seem to care one way or the other," the long-haired photographer commented. He sat behind a fancy carved wooden desk, playing with a decorative pen and pencil set. "But then, they never do."

I looked at him curiously, not certain if his words were meant to be sarcastic. "It's my friend's first baby."

He arched his dark eyebrows at me. His sober gray eyes were ringed with dark lashes. "Mystery to me. I don't have kids."

I bent down and fiddled with Sophie's jumpsuit. "Me, either. But lots of my friends do."

"You're the police chief's wife."

His blunt statement took me by surprise. Though I was accustomed to being recognized by locals, this man was a stranger. I'd been married to a cop long enough to be instantly suspicious. I glanced at the door and, with no subtlety, moved between him and Sophie.

He stood up, showing pale, uncalloused palms, his face apologetic. "Didn't mean to startle you. I should know better than to pop off like that. I know who you are because my wife pointed you out a few weeks back at the farmers' market. She works for your husband. Yvette Arnaud. She's a detective."

Relief flooded through me. "Right, okay." I laughed nervously, feeling myself relax. "You're the photographer husband. Yes, Maggie . . . uh, my husband's assistant, told me about her. And you. Your wife is working the sniper case."

He nodded. "She worked a similar case in New Iberia and cracked it. Was quite the celebrity for a while. She called me about it a few hours after the incident this afternoon, said she'd probably be late tonight." He gave a wry half smile. "Deja-voo-doo, as my friend, Jay, would say. I was at our place—well, her mom's place—in Arroyo Grande. Heard anything more about it?"

I shook my head. "But it's still early in the investigation. You know how that goes."

He nodded, pushing his hair back behind his ears. "Been married to a cop for twelve years now. I know how it rolls. It'll be TV dinners until this guy is caught."

The door opened and Elvia blew in, a cool breeze entering with her. "The tulips," she declared, her black eyes shining in victory.

I glanced at Detective Arnaud's husband. "Good taste wins . . . this time."

He laughed and motioned at us to follow him to the back. "My name's Van Baxter, by the way."

"Nice to meet you, Van. This is Elvia Aragon Littleton. She owns Blind Harry's Bookstore."

They nodded at each other. "He's married to one of Gabe's detectives," I informed Elvia. "She's working the sniper case."

"I hope they capture whoever did it quickly," Elvia said with a shudder. "It makes me a little nervous to walk down the street with Sophia."

"I'm sure it won't take long," Van said, pulling out an order form. "My wife's a very good detective."

In less than a half hour, he had the pictures taken and Sophie back in her stroller. I don't know what kind of photography Van did back in Louisiana, but he certainly had a flair for getting babies to smile on cue.

"The proofs should be ready in a few days," he told Elvia, taking her deposit. "The cards take about a week. We have to send them to San Jose to the home office. This franchise hasn't proved itself profitable enough to have our own developing equipment. And I can't convince Deck the importance of going digital."

"Deck Connors owns this place?" Elvia's nose twitched like it smelled a dirty diaper.

"Lock, stock and fake backdrops."

"How long have you been here?" I asked.

"Just two months. So far business has been brisk, but I'm told it really takes a year to make a profit."

"I hope you do well," Elvia said. "We need to keep the downtown vital for consumers."

"See you around town, Van," I said. "Hope to meet your wife soon."

The front door flew open and five teenage girls rushed in. Their giggles and baby powder-scented perfume instantly filled the small room.

"We have an appointment with Mr. . . . uh . . . Van?" the shortest one said.

He cocked a dark eyebrow at them. "I'll be with you ladies in a minute." He turned back to us. "Maybe you'll meet her later this week or this weekend. I've rented a booth at the Thursday night farmers' market and the Memory Festival to sell some of my prints and cards. Yvette's supposed to be there helping me." His grin was lopsided and attractive. "That's if she still has the day off. With this sniper business, you never know."

"I'll look for you both," I said.

On the walk back to the bookstore, I remarked to Elvia, "So, Deck Connors owns Backdrops too? He's only lived in San Celina for two years, and I swear he already owns half the town."

"He's not a bit shy about letting people know that, either," Elvia said. "He dominates every downtown association meeting. Just because he owns three businesses down here, he seems to think that gives him triple the vote."

Her mouth turned down in irritation. "Arrogant man."

"Hmmm . . ." was all I could contribute. There were people like him in every town. "Are you headed back to the bookstore?"

"I'm done for the night. We're going home to see Papa try to work magic with his new grill. Are you and Gabe coming over for steaks?"

"Wish we could, but he had a business dinner tonight with the sheriff and the new warden. How about tomorrow?"

She nodded, tucking Sophie's blanket closer around her. "That's probably better. Emory was just reading the instructions a few hours ago when I called. I think it might be better for him to test the grill before we have guests."

Elvia and Emory's blue and gray Victorian was two long blocks from Blind Harry's. Gabe and I lived only a block past them. When we reached her house, I came inside for a moment.

"*Hola*, Benni," Señora Aragon said, taking Sophie from Elvia the minute we walked through the door. "Emory still with grill," she told her daughter, rolling her eyes. "Grill not happy with him."

I laughed. "Guess you'll be ordering pizza tonight."

Señora Aragon was already peeling the bunny suit off Sophie, cooing to her daughter's first child. "No pizza. I make tacos."

"Tempted?" Elvia said.

"Always, but I'm really in the mood for chicken and dumplings."

"Be careful," she said, walking me to the front door. "Watch out for snipers." She gave a little shiver. "That's something I never thought I'd have to say about our town."

"It's only a few blocks. I'll be fine. Personally,

68

I think it was just some stupid college kid fooling around with a borrowed gun."

"That's supposed to make me feel better?"

Emory walked into the room holding a metal rod in his hand. "Hey, sweetcakes," he said to me. "I know you were expecting barbecue tonight, but—"

I held up my hand. *"No problemo,* Señor Littleton. I heard you were having difficulty putting it together—"

"I'm doing fine," he said indignantly. "It's just taking a tad longer than I anticipated."

Elvia crossed her arms over her chest. "I told him to pay someone to assemble it, but he insisted that he could manage on his own."

"How unlike my normally lazy cousin," I said.

"It's not that hard," Emory said. "It's just the wheels and the—"

"Tell it to the marines." I kissed his cheek. "You won't starve. Señora Aragon is making you tacos tonight."

Emory's face lit up. "She is?"

"Really, be careful," Elvia said, opening the screen door and coming out on the wide front porch.

"Got your flak jacket on?" Emory called.

"Go back to your instruction book, barbecue boy," I called back.

"I mean it," Elvia said, encircling herself with her arms.

"I'll be fine, *mamacita.*" I blew her a kiss, then skipped down the steps. It was dark already, though it was just a little past five o'clock. I went by the house, fed Scout and turned on the heat so it would be warm when Gabe and I both got home. The temperature had dropped fifteen degrees once the sun went down, and it was probably forty degrees now. Bone-chilling for us wimpy Californians.

During the three-block walk to Liddie's, I unsuccessfully tried not to think about the sniper. I'd haunted the streets of San Celina practically my whole life. I knew every inch of this town, but walking along the uneven pavement, I could not help glancing up at the oaks, pines and myrtles lining the streets. Then I felt silly. A sniper couldn't sit in these trees without being noticed . . . could he? Besides, why would he . . . or she . . . shoot at me? Still, I walked faster and was a little out of breath when I swung open the glass door of Liddie's Café.

About half of the red vinyl booths and Formica-topped tables were occupied, mostly by local senior citizens and in-the-know tourists who found out that Liddie's served the best home-style food in town. At nine p.m. was when the real action started at Liddie's, which claimed to be open "twenty-five hours a day." That was when students, who stayed long but spent little, took hostage most of the café's booths and tables. But the owner of Liddie's was an old Cal Poly student himself, so he tolerated them. Jack, Elvia and I had certainly spent our fair share of time lingering at Liddie's.

I was in luck and my favorite booth in the back corner was free. I could enjoy my dinner while observing Lopez Street and all its nightly drama. The rain had almost stopped, and the streets were as black and shiny as fresh tar.

From behind the long counter, Nadine waved at me and held up one finger, communicating that she'd be with me in a minute. Nadine Brooks Johnson had been serving folks breakfast, lunch or supper, depending on her schedule, for the last fifty years. No one knew exactly how old she was, but the popular guess was she was closing in on eighty years old.

"Where's the chief?" she said a few minutes later, pulling a pad out of her ruffled apron pocket. Though the café's owner required the other waitresses to wear black slacks, white blouses and red and white checked aprons, Nadine refused to change from the same uniform she'd worn when his late father owned the café: a pink polyester waitress uniform, starched white apron and old-fashioned white nurse's shoes. She looked like Hollywood's idea of a vintage fifties waitress. I had no idea where she still bought the uniforms and never had enough nerve to ask her.

"He's having dinner with the sheriff and the new prison warden." I pulled off my denim jacket.

She cocked one skinny hip. "Hear the guy's from Utah. Raises corgis. He and the sheriff oughta hit it off like gangbusters." She took a pencil out of her silvery pink beehive hairstyle. Her standing Friday morning appointment at Playgirl-A-Go-Go Coiffures was legendary. Before Gertie, the owner, died, she taught the other two stylists who worked there how to concoct Nadine's teased hairdo.

"See, you know as much as I do." I didn't even bother to look at the menu. "I'm here for the special. And I'll just have water tonight."

"No Coke?" She looked up at the sky. "What's this crazy old world coming to? Benni Harper Ortiz is not drinking a Coca-Cola."

"I still think Coke is God's choice of beverage," I retorted, "but I've had too much caffeine today. I need my sleep. Especially this week."

"That Memory Festival took off like a rocket, didn't it? You'd think this town would be sick to death of festivals, but everyone I've talked to is really looking forward to this one."

I rested my chin in my hand. "It really struck a collective nerve. Maybe it's because it's so inclusive. Everyone has memories."

Nadine's face softened, her moist brown eyes crinkled behind her pink cat's-eye glasses.

"Isaac asked me to pose for a picture for that book of his. Says I need to talk to you about what home means to me."

"I'll be at the story booth this Saturday. We can do it then, if you want. Or I can interview you another time."

She nodded. "All this memory talk makes me think of my mother. Did I ever tell you she owned a truck stop café on Route 66? Outside Oklahoma City. Knew every trucker's name that came through. Their families too. She made the best butterscotch pie. Back then they used real lard in piecrust. Made it so flaky you'd want to cry with every bite."

I smiled. She'd told me the story only about a thousand times. "We need to get that recorded this Saturday so I can type it up for the book."

"I'll be there. Makin' the young'uns work on Saturday."

"Good for you."

"Your chicken and dumplings will be right up, kiddo." She gently bopped the top of my head with her order pad—Nadine's version of an affectionate hug.

I stared out the dark window, my mind on autopilot, so I didn't notice when someone walked up to my booth until I heard a soft "Excuse me?" If the person had been the sniper, I'd've been dead.

My head popped up. For a minute, I didn't

73

recognize the smiling woman. Then I remembered —Amanda's new friend, Lin something.

Her smile faded a little. "I'm sorry, am I disturbing you?"

"Not at all. I was just woolgathering. It's, uh, Lin, right?"

She nodded and brushed a lock of silvery hair from her eyes. "Lin Snider. Where did that saying come from anyway? Woolgathering, I mean."

"Good question, but I don't know. I'm a cattle rancher, not a sheep farmer."

"Really? Amanda didn't mention that. You're not just a museum curator but an authentic cowgirl?"

I held back my impatient sigh at the clichéd word. "We don't actually call ourselves cowgirls. We prefer ranchers." The words came out crankier than I intended.

"Duly noted," she said with a quick nod.

There was an awkward moment of silence. Was she expecting me to ask her to join me? Though I sympathized with her search for a place to call home, I was tired, a little cranky and not particularly in the mood to make conversation with a stranger. I just wanted to eat my chicken and dumplings and go home to wait for my husband.

"I won't keep you from your supper," she said, touching a tentative hand to her neck. "I suspect this is a little forward, but I was wondering if we could get together sometime. At your convenience, of course. Amanda told me that no one knows this county better than you, and I'm assuming she told you I'm looking for a place to retire . . ."

I nodded my head, definitely feeling like the biggest heel in the world. Had my impatient feelings been that apparent on my face? Where was my Southern hospitality? Dove and Aunt Garnet would skin me alive if they saw me act like this to anyone, but especially someone who was new to the community.

"Not very Martha and Mary-like," I could hear my aunt Garnet say.

"Yes, she did," I said, trying to keep my voice light. "San Celina *is* a great place to live."

She bit her bottom lip, obviously embarrassed. "Maybe you could give me a quick tour of the county. I've explored on my own already . . . but it's always better to have someone who knows the area show you around. Maybe you could give me some idea about where the nicer places to live might be."

I was tempted to tell her that I was a museum curator, not a real estate agent, but that was, again, being more snarky than this woman deserved.

"Oh, nicer doesn't sound right," she said. "I'm really not a snob. I just would like to weigh all my options." She inhaled deeply, her expression a little embarrassed. "I'd be happy to pay for your time, of course."

Now I felt like a complete jerk. How would I feel if I had to travel around the country looking for a place to call home? My better angel finally kicked in. "I'd be happy to show you around, and I wouldn't dream of taking money for it. This week is packed because of the Memory Festival. How about one day next week?"

"That would be wonderful," she said, obviously relieved. We both turned to look at Nadine bringing my plate of chicken and dumplings. "I'll leave you to enjoy your supper. Looks delicious."

"First nugget of San Celina insider information," I said when Nadine slid the platter in front of me. "This place has the best food in town."

Nadine pulled a bottle of Tabasco sauce from her apron pocket. "Your water's on its way." She glanced over at Lin. "Hey there, Miz Lin Snider. There's lemon chess pie on the menu tomorrow. Come for lunch 'cause there's a good chance it'll be gone by supper." Nadine gave me the eye. "Lin loves her lemon chess pie."

Lin laughed, touching Nadine's forearm. "You know me already. My grandmother Lois made the best lemon pie. It's always been my favorite."

"Then see you tomorrow," Nadine said. "I'll

put that on your tab, Benni. Tell that good-lookin' husband of yours that I'm getting a little miffed. He hasn't been here for lunch in four days." She pulled a white paper bag from her apron pocket. "Here's a couple of snickerdoodles for him."

"Hey, what about me?" I called to her retreating back.

"You need to cut back on your sugar," she said over her shoulder. "You're starting to get some thighs on you. Ain't that attractive."

I turned back to Lin and smiled, holding up a palm. "There's a small town for you. Everyone's your mother."

"I think it's kind of nice. Reminds me of a time in my life—" She stopped and gave her head a little shake. "One more question, and I'll get out of your hair. Where's a good place to get a car repaired?"

"Depends on the car."

"I have a Ford Taurus. It's only a small problem. I backed into a tree stump, actually. I need a taillight and the cover for it."

"Ouch," I said, sprinkling Tabasco sauce on my chicken and dumplings.

"Depending on how much time you have, the best bet is to go to the Ford dealer over by the Madonna Inn. It's right off Interstate 101. There are other shops where you could go, but they'd most likely have to order the part. If your car is new enough, the dealer may have any part you need right there. It's more expensive, but quicker."

"Thanks. Maybe I'll see you Wednesday at the museum when I'm using the wheel."

"Good chance I'll be there."

"Enjoy your supper." With that, she turned and walked out of Liddie's.

It took about thirty seconds before it clicked. I threw down my napkin and hurried for the door in time to see her pull out of Liddie's parking lot. Only one taillight glowed when she put on the brakes on her Ford Taurus sedan. Her dark *gray* Ford Taurus sedan.

Chapter 4

I went back to my meal, feeling a little foolish. A gray sedan with a burned-out taillight. It was odd that the gray sedan I spotted leaving the Harper Ranch this morning had the same problem, but there were hundreds of cars similar to Lin Snider's. Probably a few of them had broken taillights. Why was I looking for something suspicious in a perfectly believable coincidence?

My reputation as the police chief's wife who seemed to constantly stumble into crime scenes was already carved in granite. My name was probably right at the top of the ballot for town eccentric. Much to Gabe's relief, I had managed to maintain a crime-free profile for the last six months, and I was determined to keep it that way. Even if it *had* been Lin Snider out at the ranch, she said she'd been driving around the county. She found the old Harper Ranch accidentally, discovered an open door and decided to investigate. That's all.

I was finishing my meal, idly contemplating my busy day tomorrow, the Mexican hot chocolate I'd make for Gabe tonight, my interviews for Isaac's book, when another person interrupted my reverie.

"Hey, ranch girl," said my friend and verbal sparring partner, Detective Ford "Hud" Hudson of the San Celina Sheriff's Department. Our relationship consisted of a juvenile combination of harmless flirtation and smart-ass insults. But, in spite of our constant bickering, in the last few years a real friendship had developed between us. Actually, he was an upright guy and I'd trust him with my life . . . and had a few times. Even my husband was beginning to like Hud a little. Or at least tolerate his presence in my life without too much grumbling.

"Hey, Clouseau," I said, my nickname for him simply because he was as far from the loopy fictional detective as someone could be. "What's cookin'?"

"Just dodging sniper bullets and searching for justice for poor lost souls," he said, sliding into the bench seat across from me.

Hud wore a faded plaid flannel shirt, an olive green and blue Tulane University Green Wave baseball cap and dark blue Wranglers. His warm brown eyes and smooth-cheeked, country boy face looked every inch like a mother's dream of the dependable L.L. Bean–clad boy next door who would tame and marry her wild daughter. In reality, he'd probably be the one buying her illegal moonshine and taking her skinny-dipping at midnight. My lost souls remark to him referred to his job at the sheriff's department—investigating cold cases.

"Yeah, that sniper thing stinks," I said, looking down at my watch. "Shoot, I missed the six o'clock news. Did our lovely Miss Tiffany have any breaking news about the incident?"

"Not much more than this afternoon. The four young men who live in the apartment were all cleared. Apparently they have handed out keys to their bachelor pad with gracious and unrestrained hospitality. Not to mention that they often leave it unlocked. So anyone and her brother could have simply walked in and out of the place. But I'm assuming you know this already." He removed his hat and set it on the table. His short brown-blond hair stood up in funny little peaks.

"Part I knew, part I assumed. I spoke to Gabe at three o'clock, and they were stymied. They've apparently got a brand-new crackerjack detective working on it. She's from Louisiana."

"Yvette Arnaud. Yeah, we've met. She's sharp, but no surprise there. She's Cajun." He grinned at me. He was half Cajun on his mother's side. "Moved here from New Iberia."

"Dave Roubicheaux's stomping grounds." A love for James Lee Burke's books was one of the things Gabe, Hud and I had in common.

"Except she's real as can be. Husband's a photographer. Quite famous and in demand at one time, I hear."

"Believe it or not, her husband and I have met. Flvia took Sophie to Backdrops to have Easter photos taken. He works there." I pushed my plate aside and sipped my ice water. "His name is Van Baxter."

"What's your problem?" he asked, pointing at my water glass.

"What?"

"Water? Since when do you drink *water?* I thought you bathed in Coke, gargled with Pepsi and rinsed your hair in RC Cola."

"I drink water."

He twisted his lips into a smirk.

"All the time." I made a face. "Often."

He rolled his brown eyes skyward.

"Okay, some. I'm trying to limit myself to one Coke a day. I read somewhere that cola is bad for women's kidneys."

He threw back his head and laughed. "It's killing you, isn't it?"

I nodded miserably. "Yes, but, I'm turning forty this month. Gotta start living a little healthier."

"Forty? That's *old*. Ancient. Someone call AARP, quick. Get the defibrillator ready."

I slapped the top of his hand. "Shut up. You're older than me. How do *you* like being forty?"

He leaned back in the booth, locking his fingers around his neck. "Forty is much more attractive on a man than a woman."

"On that sexist note, I'm outta here." I feigned standing up.

"Don't go." He leaned forward, flattening his hands on the table. "You know that you'll always be my unattainable dream woman."

"That's better," I said, sitting back down. "So, are you working on any interesting cold cases?"

"Nah, same ole rusty dusty bones."

I stuck three five-dollar bills under my plate and slid out of the booth. "See you tomorrow. I have to brave the dangerous, sniper-filled streets of San Celina and walk home."

"You're walking?" A line of worry creased the space between his eyes.

"I walked *here*. It's only a few blocks."

He stood beside me, helping me slip on my jacket. "I'll walk with you. My car's parked downtown next to Blind Harry's. Had to pick up a book on California missions I ordered for Maisie."

"Hud, there's really no need. Go ahead and have your dinner."

"Already ate. I was at the end of the counter. You didn't even see me when you came in." He pointed a finger pistol and shot me. "If I'd've been a sniper . . ."

I punched his arm lightly. "Oh, shut up." I couldn't believe I didn't see him either. So much for my astute powers of observation.

"Who was that lady you were talking to? The

tall one with the silver hair. Haven't seen her around before."

I busied myself with buttoning my jacket, tucking Gabe's bag of cookies from Nadine in my pocket. For a moment, I was tempted to tell him about the car I saw at the Harper Ranch and Lin's broken taillight. But I held back, not wanting to endure his teasing about my manufacturing a mystery where there was none. "She's renting time on the potter's wheel at the co-op. Just met her today. New friend of Amanda's."

He stuck by my side the five blocks back to my house. I had to admit it made me feel a little better, though he pointed out halfway to my house that I was probably in *more* danger walking with him.

"That is," he said, when we arrived at my house, "if what everyone is speculating is true and the sniper has a thing about using law enforcement personnel for target practice. We don't actually know that for sure yet."

"Except you're not in uniform," I pointed out. Scout was standing at the front window waiting for me in the soft yellow living room light. His tail wagged hesitantly, not quite certain it was me. "How would anyone know you're a cop?"

"By my confident demeanor and movie-star good looks?"

I laughed, the sound obviously traveling through the closed window to Scout's ears. His tail went into full windshield wiper mode. "I hope someday we can find you a woman who can admire you as much as you admire yourself. It would be the perfect match. Thanks for the police protection. You're a pal."

He brought his hands up to his chest, feigning a shot to the heart. "Tell the chief hey for me and to pretty please catch the turkey shooter before he decides to go after the *important* law enforcement personnel in this town. You know, the ones with the badges shaped like stars."

"No comment." I was up the steps and unlocking my door when he called out one last remark.

"Ranch girl, you do know that you can tell me anything. You have any worries about . . . anyone, you come to me."

I turned around slowly. He stood at the bottom step, his face sober. He had obviously observed my dash through the café to check out Lin Snider's car, but chose not to mention it.

"I have no idea what you're talking about," I said, but brought my hand up in an assenting salute.

Once inside, I went over to the front picture window and waved. He waved back and started up the street.

Ten minutes later, when I was upstairs changing into my new favorite flannel cupcake-covered pj's—an early birthday present from Elvia—the front door opened. Scout bounded out of the bedroom with a happy bark, running down the stairs.

"Hey, Chief Ortiz," I called. "Want some hot chocolate?"

"Sounds great," he said, appearing in the doorway a few seconds later. "It's getting cold. A storm is coming."

I gazed up at the ceiling. "Please, Lord, six hours of sun on Saturday, that's all I'm asking. Eight hours if you're feeling generous." The Memory Festival ran from ten a.m. to four p.m. Eight hours of sunshine would cover setup and takedown.

He walked over and hugged me. His suit jacket was cold and slightly damp. "Am I glad to be home."

"How was your dinner with Sally and the warden?"

He let me go and pulled off his jacket. "Good. Stan, the new warden, and Sally have a mutual admiration society going on."

"Corgi love?"

He laughed, pulled his tie loose and unbuttoned his white dress shirt. "Something like that. I do know quite a bit more about the breed than I did three hours ago. It's helpful they have something in common since they have to work together. I was invited more as a courtesy." In seconds he had his work clothes off, standing there in pale blue boxer shorts looking very sexy . . . and very cold.

I handed him a sweatshirt and some sweatpants. "I'll go down and start the cocoa. Also, I have a message and some snickerdoodles from Nadine. She misses you."

Gabe's dark eyebrows raised in anticipation. "Snickerdoodles?"

"I hope you're planning on sharing. There are only two."

He winked at me, giving me a look I knew well. "Maybe. If you're real nice to me."

I laughed, watching him pull on navy sweatpants. For a moment, my eyes lingered on the baseball-size, spider-shaped scar on his thigh, a souvenir from a Bouncing Betty explosive in Vietnam. He'd been lucky. Many soldiers had lost limbs or their lives to Bouncing Bettys.

"You couldn't possibly be sexually attracted to me right now," I said, twirling around in my baggy pajamas. The man-style pajamas covered with pink and mint green cupcakes were very comfortable and as cute as, well, a cupcake. But on a sensuality scale of one to ten, they were a minus three.

He crossed the room and grabbed me in a bear hug. "The thing is, I happen to know very well what's under those cupcakes."

The salty male scent of his bare chest soft

with black hair never ceased to intoxicate me. "You sweet-talker. Give me one of your cookies, and maybe later tonight I'll show you my cupcakes."

"Sounds like I'm coming out on the better end of the deal."

I kissed his chest. "You, sir, are a very wise man."

We spent the rest of the chilly evening on the front room sofa watching mindless television sitcoms, surrounded by cookie crumbs, quilts and warm dog. The sniper situation only came up once.

"No other leads?" I asked when a clip advertising the late evening news came before a State Farm Insurance commercial.

"Not a thing." He sat at the other end of the sofa, his feet in my lap. I massaged them through his thick wool socks. "Let's just hope it was a random act." He pulled at one end of his thick black mustache, sprinkled now with bits of silver. He rarely touched his mustache except when he was worried or agitated.

I squeezed his foot. "We can hope."

We went to bed before the eleven p.m. news, knowing that if there'd been any progress on the case, he would have been notified. We both had busy days tomorrow and though we kissed for a few minutes, I pulled away first. "I'd really love to go further," I said, yawning. "But, if we continue, I'm afraid you'd have to do all the work."

He yawned in sympathy. "I was kind of hoping you'd be on top tonight."

I slipped my hand under the covers and stroked his chest. "Rain check?"

He grabbed the back of my neck and kissed me long and deep. "I find having a sensitive and understanding wife incredibly sexy."

We kissed again, then turned out the light. A light rain started, and the trickle of the water running through our gutters, the musical tap-tapping on the roof made it easy for me to drop off to sleep. I awoke in what felt like only moments later to the rain thrumming louder on the roof and the sound of Scout whining. Seconds later, Gabe started thrashing in his sleep, muttering phrases familiar to me now after five years. I waited, holding my breath. Sometimes it was just a word or two and then he moved out of the dream and went back into a deeper sleep. The dreams seemed to have become less frequent the last few years. When I tried to talk to him about them, he was dismissive.

"It's just old crap from 'Nam," he'd say. "Nothing to talk about."

He groaned, and an arm flew out from under the comforter, hand clenched in a fist. "No," he murmured. Then louder. "No!"

Then he exploded. *"Nada, nada!* To the left!

Take him!" His voice sounded young, terrified. His fist pounded the mattress.

I bolted up, my heart swelling in my chest. When I touched his arm, he jerked like he'd been burned with a cigarette. I instinctively jumped back.

"There, in the bush! He's hit. God, no, no . . . go, go, *go*! *Madre de Dios!*"

"Gabe," I yelled, trying to grab his arms again. They moved like snakes on speed.

"He's hit," he screamed, his whole body flailing.

Scout lunged forward with a growl, the hair on his back stiff as wheat stalks.

"Scout, back! Back!" I yelled.

Gabe screamed, "Shoot, you mother—" A sob choked his garbled words.

I tried again to grab his thrashing arms, calling out his name, attempting to break through his nightmare. "Gabe! Friday!"

Next to the bed Scout barked a continuous staccato.

A wail came from his gut that sounded like every man that had ever been hurt on a battlefield. "He's gone, he's gone . . . shit, *no mas, no mas . . .*"

I tried to maneuver through his flailing arms, to touch his face, try to wake him. He thrust his fist out, striking my breastbone with a loud *thump*. Pain shot through me, bouncing up against my spine. It felt like I'd been hit with a steel hammer. I gasped, fell halfway out of bed.

Scout jumped on the bed, baring his teeth at Gabe.

"Scout!" I screamed. "No! Off!"

Scout hesitated, looked at me over his shoulder, his body trembling, torn between my words and his instinct to protect.

"Off," I said, forcing a calm voice. "It's okay. Come here."

He jumped back down and came to my side, his warm ribs against my bare leg, a growl still rumbling in his throat.

On the bed, Gabe moaned, murmuring a name: "Carlos, Carlos."

"Gabe," I pleaded from the foot of the bed. "It's me, Benni." I moved around the bed to his side, reaching out to touch his damp forearm. He pushed my hand away, his eyes open wide in the semidarkness, not awake, not asleep, caught in a horrible in-between world, reliving a moment long buried in his mind.

I inhaled deeply and yelled as loud as I could, "Gabe!"

Gabe bolted up, his expression wild.

I lowered my voice and just started talking, praying that my voice would seep through the reel of memories that had taken his mind captive. "Gabe . . . Friday . . . please. It's okay. You're here. Everything's okay." I crawled up on the bed, touched his thigh, felt him tense beneath my hand. My chest throbbed, the spot right above my heart, the place where he'd struck me.

That stupid, stupid war. Thirty years later and still he dreamed of it. Still it haunted him.

"Gabe, Gabe, Gabe . . ." I whispered, the monotone I used to calm a frightened animal, a horse who scented a coyote or a hysterical cow who had lost sight of her new calf. "It's me, Benni. It's me."

He stared at my face, his eyes glazed and uncomprehending. I reached up and touched his cheek. He jerked, fists clenched. I fought the urge to move backward, brought my hand to his lips, their fullness dry and chapped under my fingertips.

"Gabe, you're okay. You're home. You're home." I moved my hand down his neck to his chest, placing it over his racing heart. The organ pulsed like a drumbeat under my palm, feeling like it would beat right out of his chest, dripping and bloody, dropping into my open hand.

I talked and talked, nonsense words, words of comfort, snatches of songs and his name over and over, a Niagara of words. Gradually, his body began to relax, like life coming back into something that had been dead. A memory from my childhood flashed like an electric shock—a Sunday school story told by the pastor's wife, a woman with hair the color of merlot wine.

Mary and Martha were crying because their beloved brother, Lazarus, had died. They called out to Jesus when they finally saw him walking the dusty road toward their house—Lord, Lord, come and see. Mary fell at his feet—if only you had been here, she wailed, my brother would not have died. Jesus, overcome by grief for his friend, wept. Then a miracle from his mouth—*"Lazarus, come forth."*

He was dead, but now he lives.

And the sisters rejoiced.

Gabe turned his head to look at me. His eyes opened wider, back in the present now, aware of where he was, what had happened again.

"Oh, God." His voice was agonized, his face crumpled with shame.

"Shhh . . ." I touched his unshaved cheeks with my hands; my thumbs caressed his lips. "Shhh . . . it's fine. You're okay."

"*Querida, lo siento, lo siento . . .*" he started, then choked, his words a wet garble in his throat. "I'm so sorry . . ."

"No, no, it's okay." I gently pushed him back down on the pillows. "Hush, it's okay." At the foot of the bed, Scout growled.

I crawled to the end of the bed. "Go to bed, Scout. Everything's fine."

I touched the top of my faithful dog's broad head, stroking between his frightened eyes, reassuring him. He hesitated, not comprehending what had happened. I scratched underneath his chin, assured him again that everything was fine. He believed me and went back to his bed.

Gabe lay on his back, staring at the ceiling, a look of despair on his face so profound a sob filled my chest. We'd gone through this before, though not for a long time now. And never this violent. I'd read dozens of books and magazine articles. Post-traumatic stress. It could be set off by anything—fireworks, a car backfiring, the sound of a crying child, a remembered smell, a sniper's bullet.

"I'm sorry . . ." he started, unable to look at me.

"Shhh . . ." I stroked his hair, his face, kissed him gently, told him I loved him. He turned his head, tried to speak. I kissed his apologies away. We could talk tomorrow.

"I love you," I whispered, nuzzling his neck, the warm blade of his shoulder, the scent of his skin vinegar sharp with fear, sweet with adrenaline.

He pulled me to him, kissing me deeply; his tongue tasted of salt and of him, a taste as familiar to me as strawberries in May. He was back, the Gabe I knew. His rhythm and his words, the sweet words he whispered over me in the dark —"*Querida, mi vida, mi corazon. Tu me completas. Te amo, te amo, te amo . . .*"

His hands cupped my face, making me forget for a few breathless moments the physical throbbing of my bruised chest.

After we made love, he fell into a deep sleep, his breaths even, peaceful.

I lay awake, my chest aching, my heart filled with sadness, gratitude, fear, despair. I turned my head to watch my sleeping husband, this damaged man I loved, who seemed poised on a dangerous precipice, just out of my reach.

Lord, please come, I prayed, not knowing what else to ask. Come and see.

Chapter 5

Sleep eluded me until four a.m. The scent of coffee woke me up at six forty-five. Gabe's side of the bed was empty and cool, telling me he'd been awake for a while. My head felt like it was full of dandelion fluff. I couldn't imagine how Gabe must be feeling.

He was already dressed for work and stirring a saucepan of oatmeal when I walked into the kitchen. From the outside, I couldn't tell if what happened last night affected him at all.

"I'm meeting Isaac at the folk art museum today," I said, sitting down at the kitchen table and picking up a glass of orange juice.

"About his book?" he said, not turning around.

"Yes, and I still need your interview." We didn't discuss what had happened last night. I learned early in our marriage how defensive Gabe was about his nightmares, how much they embarrassed him. His strategy? Pretend they never happen. If I brought it up, he'd change the subject or just walk away.

He poured oatmeal into two ceramic bowls. "What's the subject again?"

"Home. What it means to you. Where you feel

at home. Just whatever you want to say about home."

He set the coffeepot on a wooden hot pad between us. "Do I have to write it down?" His expression was pained, like a schoolboy being told he had a report due on a book he didn't want to read.

I sipped my orange juice. "No, I'll ask the questions and write it down. It will be easy. Then Isaac wants to take your photo. He's trying to get a variety of San Celina citizens."

"We'll see," Gabe said, sitting across from me.

I kept sneaking glances when he bent his head to read the newspaper, wishing I could offer comfort, some words to make him feel better. Finally, I couldn't stand it. "Are you okay?"

He looked up from the paper, gazing at me from over his gold wire-rimmed reading glasses. "I'm fine. Why?"

Was he serious? I twirled my spoon in my oatmeal, my appetite gone.

"Who's Carlos?"

His expression froze. The clink of my spoon against the side of my bowl seemed magnified in the quiet kitchen. I had broken our unspoken rule—never ask about Vietnam.

"Guy in 'Nam," he said.

"A friend . . . ?"

"He was killed."

"Do you . . ."

"I apologize for last night." He folded the paper and set it next to his plate. "It won't happen again."

"It's okay," I said, instinctively touching the tender spot on my chest. He couldn't guarantee that, but saying so would be pointless. "Do you want to go out to dinner tonight, or do you want me to cook?"

He looked down at the newspaper. The headline proclaimed "Sniper Attacks Police Cruiser!"

"A little dramatic," I said, pointing to the paper. Right now, even talking about the sniper seemed less of a minefield than his bad dreams.

Gabe shrugged. "I'm not sure what my schedule is today. Everything is blown to heck with this sniper out there."

"How about I call you at work later? I don't know how much running around I'll be doing with Isaac, so I might not have time to cook."

"That's fine." He stood up, slipped on his suit jacket.

I went to him, straightened the already perfect Windsor knot of his black and gray diamond necktie. Did he realize that he telegraphed his emotions in his tie choice? No color today, as if any hint of color or brightness might reveal his uneven emotions. "You are unarguably the most handsome man in San Celina."

"Tiny pond," he said, not cracking a smile.

"You'd be the handsomest man even if we lived in New York City."

He brushed a kiss across my lips. *"Te amo."* He held my gaze, his pupils like smooth black stones in an icy ocean. "Thank you." He seemed to swallow the word. The shame in his eyes shredded my heart.

I touched his cool cheek. *"De nada,* Chief."

After taking Scout for a walk, I headed for work. Isaac's red Subaru Outback station wagon was already in the museum parking lot. I found him in the co-op charming the artists who'd come in early to finish pieces they would sell at the festival this weekend.

"Hey, Pops," I said, stretching up to give him a hug. He stood six foot four without his hiking boots and smelled clean and fresh, like just-cut alfalfa. His long cotton-ball-colored braid rivaled Dove's in length, reaching past his waist. "Did you take your photos of the folk art museum?" His plan had been to come early to photograph the museum's buildings at sunrise.

"I did. I also photographed Mr. Boudreaux. I think they'll be good ones."

"Can't wait to see them. I've done my interview with D-Daddy, just haven't transcribed it yet. Where're we off to today?"

"How much time can you spare? What with the festival . . ." His alert raisin brown eyes studied me.

99

"I've set aside the whole day for you. You and I planned this a long time ago. If anyone needs anything concerning the museum or the Memory Festival, they can call me on my cell."

"Wonderful. We have an appointment with a fellow in Pismo Beach. Then I would like to photograph the Oceano Dunes, the old depot and the Cowgirl Café, where I proposed to your gramma. What do you think of that as an anniversary present?"

"I think she'd love it. Sounds like a full day."

"If that's too much . . ."

"Not at all. I've been looking forward to this day for weeks." I linked his arm in mine. "We can keep going until you don't like the light anymore. Do any of these places include interviews?"

"Just the Pismo one. I thought we could really make some progress today. I'm anxious to get this book put together."

"No problem. I assume we're taking your Subaru. Want me to drive?"

"If you don't mind." His face, tanned brown as the pebbled leather cover of Dove's old Bible, looked tired. But his alert dark eyes missed nothing. "Benni, are you feeling all right?"

The question caught me by surprise. I thought I'd hidden my troubled emotions well with my cheery conversation. "Just a little tired. The rain kept waking me up last night." The lie skipped off my tongue as easy as spitting.

His expression told me he wasn't buying my explanation, but he didn't press me. Though Isaac might be the perfect person for me to discuss my anxieties about Gabe, I wasn't ready to relive last night.

Inside the car, I adjusted the seat for my short legs. "Ready to roll, boss man. So, what's the story behind our Pismo Beach guy?"

"His grandmother was a nurse who gave free health care to the Dunites back in the thirties. He lived with her for a little while and used to travel with her on her rounds."

The Dunites had been a controversial community of people who'd started living in the Pismo Dunes back in the thirties, flourishing there until the last community member died in the early seventies. They'd been often called California's first hippies.

"She probably told him some really cool stories," I said.

"Hope so. His definition of home should be interesting. His answer to the ad I put in the newspaper was very intriguing."

On the drive south on Interstate 101 to Pismo Beach we talked about the book. He was tossing around titles, still looking for the exact right one, though so far we hadn't been able to think of anything better than "San Celina at Home."

"I've completed sixteen interviews," I said. "I have your list and will be doing more of them next week once the Memory Festival is over. I might be able to conduct a few of them during the festival." I turned my head to smile at him. "Multitasking rocks."

"It does, indeed." He leaned his head back against the leather headrest, closed his eyes and gave a big sigh.

"Hard night?" I asked.

"Just thankful for a moment of quiet. With all the moving, building, switching things around these last six months at the ranch, it's hard to find a peaceful spot to take a nap."

Last summer my great-aunt Garnet, Dove's only sibling, told us that her husband, my uncle WW, had been diagnosed with Parkinson's disease. Everyone agreed that they should sell their house in Sugartree, Arkansas, and move to California. Their only son, Jake, had accepted a new job in Maine, but he didn't know how long it would last.

When Aunt Garnet and Uncle WW moved out here, we also unanimously agreed that the ranch house needed an addition. The sisters supervised the construction. To everyone's surprise, they worked in perfect harmony, having perfected the good cop, bad cop shtick. The contractors finished two weeks *ahead* of schedule, anxious to hightail it out of there. I couldn't *imagine* why.

The addition to the four-bedroom ranch house I grew up in included a wheelchair-accessible bedroom, a roomy bathroom with a walk-in shower, a sitting room and even an apartment-size kitchen. The plan was that they'd live a completely independent life with the comfort of knowing that Dove, Daddy and Isaac were only a hallway and a closed door away.

I glanced over at Isaac. This project seemed to have affected him emotionally; he'd been less jovial and teasing lately. Maybe it was the subject —home, family, memories. I wondered about what memories he carried of his upbringing. We agreed from the onset that we'd both be subjects of this book—that he'd interview and photograph me and vice versa. So far, neither had happened. We'd been too busy with our other subjects.

Was he having as much difficulty figuring out how to photograph me as I was trying to decide how to interview him? Though our relationship was comfortable now, even loving, it had begun because of a sad incident in his life. He'd come to San Celina a few years ago to look into the murder of his granddaughter, Shelby, a budding photographer attending Cal Poly. Her grandma had been his fourth wife, and though he and Shelby hadn't been related by blood, he'd known her since she was born and they'd had a special connection. Her murder had affected him deeply, I know, though he rarely spoke of it . . . or her.

During our "investigation" of Shelby's murder

he met Dove, fell in love and they married. Though initially I'd been suspicious of him, I'd grown to love him like a grandfather. Still, I wondered if it bothered him that, except for a few distant cousins, he had not one person in this world physically related to him. I glanced over at his face, golden brown from the sun, his silver and turquoise cross earring as familiar to me as his bear-size hands. I never knew his age until last year when Dove threw him an eighty-fourth birthday party. He would be eighty-five soon, though he didn't look it. He claimed it was Dove who kept him a young buck.

A freeway sign announced Pismo Beach at the next exit. I glanced over at Isaac, wishing I didn't have to disturb his nap. But we'd be there in a few minutes, and I had no idea where to find this person we were meeting.

He opened his eyes as I slowed down to take the turnoff to Pismo.

"Destination?" I asked.

"Harry's Bar," he replied, blinking his eyes.

That was a surprise. "Hmmm . . ."

He turned to look at me, one thick white eyebrow lifted. "What's that mean?"

"Bit of a rough-and-tumble place." I gave him a half smile. "Or so I've been told."

He chuckled and tugged at his ear. "Actually, we're meeting in front of the bar. He was going to be downtown anyway and said it would be easier if we followed him to his house. He said we'd know him by his unique vehicle."

"What's that mean?"

He shifted in the seat, pulled at his seat belt cross strap. "His name is Pete Kaplan. That's I all know."

Mr. Kaplan's vehicle was indeed easy to spot. When we pulled right in front of Harry's, the street quiet on this cold and foggy Tuesday morning, the old '60s Volkswagen bus looked like something right out of a history book. It was a faded blue, green or gray—hard to distinguish —and was covered with hand-painted Day-Glo orange and yellow daisies and crooked peace symbols.

The man who opened the driver's door when we pulled up also looked like someone from another era. He pulled off a navy knit cap show-ing a full head of curly, shoulder-length gray hair. With his silver-streaked beard, faded blue jeans and red and black tie-dyed T-shirt, Pete Kaplan could have played the part of the draft card-burning hippie in a Vietnam-era movie.

"Mr. Lyons?" he called, walking over to our car. His voice was as rich and smooth as the thrum of an oboe.

"Yes," Isaac said, unfolding himself from the Subaru's passenger seat. "It's nice to meet you, Mr. Kaplan."

The man smiled, revealing perfect white teeth

that were either a lucky genetic break or totally fake. I briefly wondered if this guy, who appeared to be in his late fifties or early sixties, was one of those rich kids who lived off Mom or Dad's money while living the free and "independent" life of a vagabond. Remembering what Gabe had gone through last night, I also wondered if this man had spent the Vietnam War in Canada or in a fancy college, saved from the draft by his parents' connections.

"The pleasure is mine," the man said. "Please call me Pete."

"I'm Isaac, and this is my granddaughter, Benni. She is also my assistant."

"Hello," the man said, giving me an easy smile.

We all shook hands, and then I leaned against the Subaru, waiting for further instructions from Isaac. I'd assisted him often on his shoots and learned my job was to stand quietly to the side, fetching equipment when he requested it. When he took photographs of people, he never just jumped into the session. He always talked to them first, looking for—he told me once—their core, the essence that made them unique.

"Some hide it better than others," he'd told me once. "That doesn't make them more interesting, just more difficult to find. People often mistake brooding or silence for depth. The truth is we are all deep. All humans have sorrows and joys, beauty and ugliness, gut-wrenching memories that both enrich and shame them. My job is to show their humanity honestly, without artifice. Sometimes that means showing not only who the person is, but who they aren't."

That was why I loved going out in the field with Isaac. I always learned something about photography and about life.

After a few moments of conversation with Pete Kaplan, Isaac came back over to me.

"We're going to follow him to his house. He said you could do his interview next week. I explained to him about your schedule this week."

"Thanks," I said. "This week is definitely a killer."

When we arrived at Mr. Kaplan's house, I realized that I had not been far off. He obviously wasn't hurting for money. It was a beautifully restored California Mission–style bungalow perched on a cliff overlooking the ocean. Even I could tell it was worth a lot of money. His living room boasted a huge picture window, its view of the sea like a constantly changing painting. His overstuffed leather sofa and chairs felt expensive and buttery soft. He served us cappuccinos from a fancy brass and silver Espresso machine in the kitchen. The freshly ground coffee beans scented the airy room with a sweet, nutty smell. The plain white walls of his living room were bare except for a large oil painting over the natural stone fireplace of a rustic cabin nestled among sand dunes.

After sitting down across from us, he started to tell us his story.

"The summer before my senior year in high school . . ."

I interrupted. "Excuse me, but is it okay if I take some notes?" I pulled a steno pad out of my backpack. "That way you won't have to repeat yourself next week."

"Absolutely," he replied. "That summer I was seventeen I lived with my grandmother. My parents were having troubles that summer, and they didn't know what to do with me. Grandma Jack was my dad's mother. Her name was Jacqueline Martha Kaplan. She'd been a combat nurse in World War II and was as tough as they come. That's where she acquired the nickname Jack. She and my mother never got along. Grandma Jack's bohemian lifestyle rankled Mother. The one thing they had in common was they both loved me. Those three months living here in Pismo and going out on rounds with Grandma Jack changed my life. Grandma Jack treated me like an adult, listened to my opinions. She taught me that I had a right, a duty, actually, to follow my heart, to live the life I wanted to live, not the one planned for me by my mother and father."

He stood up and went to the picture window,

stared out at the ocean. Next to me, Isaac quietly picked up his camera and snapped a couple of photos. Pete Kaplan didn't even turn around. His rich voice seemed to fill the corners of the airy room.

"I went to Harvard, like my father. I became a doctor like my father. Both decisions made my parents happy. But against their wishes, I chose psychiatry rather than Father's specialty, heart surgery. And I made a life outside of the hospital walls, outside of the privileged society I grew up in."

I glanced over at Isaac, surprised. Pete Kaplan was a psychiatrist? He certainly didn't look like one, though I'm not sure what I thought a psychiatrist looked like, since I didn't remember ever meeting one. Isaac's gaze didn't move from Dr. Kaplan.

Dr. Kaplan turned to look at us, the lines around his eyes softening in memory. "I was drafted in 1968, and despite my mother's demands that my dad 'fix it,' I chose to serve my country, even though I personally didn't agree with the war. I felt like I had something to offer the other young men who'd either been sent there without choice or went in voluntarily, not understanding what was truly going to happen to them. I arrived in-country two days before the Tet Offensive. Grandma Jack died of a stroke while I was patching up emotionally broken soldiers so they could be sent out to be broken again." He shook his head, his lips a straight line.

"Grandma Jack's best friend found her in her bed here in this house, just like she'd gone to sleep. Father died shortly after she did, ironically, of a heart attack. Mother moved back East to live with her sister in Boston." He rubbed his hands up and down his thighs, as if drying them. "She's still there, healthy and cranky as ever at eighty-nine." He gave a small chuckle. "Still tells me every time we talk that I've thrown away a perfectly good Harvard education."

He glanced over at the stone fireplace. A dark brown earthenware jar painted with daffodils sat in the center of the pale wooden mantel. "Father's buried in San Celina in the Catholic cemetery, and Grandma Jack is partly here." He pointed at the jar. "And partly out in the dunes she loved so much. That's why I retired here. After 'Nam, I practiced medicine in San Francisco, volunteering at the VA one weekend a month. When my wife died—we didn't have any children—I came here. Grandma Jack left this house to me in her will. I came because this is the first place I ever thought of as home."

I listened to his story, fascinated and feeling embarrassed that I'd misjudged him so completely.

Isaac took three rolls of thirty-six shots, some

of them outside in Dr. Kaplan's driveway, next to his hippie van, some with the ocean in the background. Then he switched to his new digital camera, and I watched his method change. He would take a shot, look at the screen, and then take another shot.

When Dr. Kaplan opened his garage door at Isaac's request, it revealed another vehicle, a more practical gray four-door Honda. Even I could see the juxtaposition of the image.

He patted the hood of the car. "I still volunteer at the VA hospital in San Francisco. I love my van, but it's getting too old to make the trip. My Honda is as dependable as the sunrise."

While Isaac photographed Dr. Kaplan, I faded into the background and let him work. I walked across the street to a small neighborhood park with an incredible view of the ocean. The concrete bench was cold enough to chill the back of my thighs through my jeans. The sun started inching out from behind the cloud cover, causing diamond-bright sparks on the ocean. The water seemed to turn from gray to blue before my eyes. I knew that Isaac preferred taking photos in the diffuse light of a cloudy day, so he was probably rushing, trying to find the image he sought before the sun burst out from behind a cloud.

I thought about what the doctor said about this being the first place he felt was home. It made me think of what I considered home—the Ramsey Ranch, of course. The Harper Ranch, where I was a newlywed . . . yes, that too. Otherwise, it wouldn't have bothered me so much to see a stranger wandering through the old ranch house. I thought about the house where Gabe and I had lived. We'd bought it less than five years ago. The first few months we were married we'd lived in the tiny Spanish house I'd rented in one of San Celina's older neighborhoods. I loved our present house with its built-in bookcases and Mission-style banister and fireplace. But did it really feel like home? I'd never say it out loud, but no. It was where Gabe and I lived. It was our house. But it wasn't my home. Not yet.

"Ready to go?" Isaac said behind me.

I looked up at him. Any fatigue he'd felt on the drive over had been banished the minute he picked up a camera. Something about taking photographs energized him, seemed to make him more vibrant, like a three-way lightbulb turned on high.

I'd mentioned that once to him, after we'd spent a day driving around the county while he took photographs of old adobes and cemeteries. Nothing excited Isaac more than a bunch of cracked, lichen-covered headstones.

He'd laughed and said, "There are many cultures who believe that when you take a photo of someone you steal a part of their soul. I do believe something special passes between the photographer and their subject. It's why during the time I spend with a person when I'm photographing them, it sometimes feels as if we have a relationship. And we do for that short amount of time. A good photographer can make you feel like you are the most interesting, important person in the world."

"And then you leave."

He'd nodded. "Yes, that can sometimes make a person feel abandoned. I've felt it myself."

I took down Dr. Kaplan's phone number and said I'd call him next week to set up an appointment to finish our interview. Then we loaded the equipment into the car.

"Where to now?" I asked Isaac.

"To the dunes. I want to test this digital camera on landscapes."

"Sounds good to me, Pops."

We spent the rest of the afternoon traipsing around the Oceano Dunes and the shoreline. While he took photos of birds and the few crazy people driving their dune buggies on this chilly Tuesday afternoon, I played around with the little Nikon he'd loaned me and took surreptitious photos of him. I'd packed us a lunch of Swiss cheese, Granny Smith apples, a loaf of San Celina's famous sourdough bread and Isaac's favorite drink, a combination of cranberry juice and sparkling lemonade. Though we did need to work on the book, this day had also been about Isaac taking a break from the intense Ramsey Ranch household. Though he'd been married five times before, he'd actually never lived with any of his wives. He had traveled the world, living out of suitcases and hotel rooms.

"The Ramsey Ranch is the only home I've known since I was a child," he said to me while photographing the shifting sands of the dunes, capturing subtle shadows and forms that I would be surprised to see in his final photographs. He told me something once that I've never forgotten because it occurred to me that it could apply to anything on earth—photographs, people, places, experiences, stories.

"What's not in the photograph," he'd said, "what you *don't* see, is often just as important as what you do see."

We ended up back in Pismo Beach, where he took photos of the Cowgirl Café for his anniversary gift to Dove. Right after dusk, we headed back to the Subaru. An icy wind had started to blow off the ocean, freezing our fingers and noses.

On the drive back to San Celina, with the car's heater turned to high, we were lulled into a comfortable silence. It was after six thirty and dark by the time we arrived at the folk art museum. The parking lot was empty except for my little purple truck and D-Daddy's green Ford F150 pickup.

"You go on home," I told Isaac. "I'll check with D-Daddy and see if anything needs my attention. I know you're itching to develop that film."

"Guilty as charged," he said, rubbing his hands together, looking about ten years old. "I think it's the sisters' book group tonight, so I'll steal myself a chicken salad sandwich or two and hide out in the washhouse."

Isaac had taken over the old washhouse where Dove's washer and dryer had resided before the addition of a laundry room to the main house. With plumbing already installed, he and Daddy converted it without much trouble into a perfect little darkroom. Isaac worked almost exclusively in black and white photography and rarely let anyone else develop his photographs. He believed that the artistry of a photograph lay not only in composition but also in the developing.

I gave him a fierce hug. "It was a perfect day, Pops. Thanks for letting me tag along."

"Thank you for being such a wonderful companion."

I unlocked the museum's front door and disabled the alarm. It was dark in the lobby except for the yellow moon-shaped night-light. After checking to make sure everything was in its place, I relocked and armed the alarm and headed around the building to the studios. My hand reached for the door when it flew open and D-Daddy's scowling face startled me.

"*Ange,*" he said. "You hear?"

"Hear what?" In that split second, a dozen scenarios flashed through my mind, none of them good.

"Sniper. This time he get one."

Chapter 6

After a moment of stunned silence, I said, "Where? Who?" Like a splayed deck of cards, my mind scanned the faces of the officers I knew.

"They didn't say," D-Daddy said. "But the reporters, they talkin' from the General Hospital parking lot."

"I'm going over there."

"Be careful."

"I will."

Before pulling out of the parking lot, I dialed Maggie's number at the police station. I didn't want to bother Gabe, but I needed to know the details. I wouldn't even let myself consider for a second that it might be him. Surely, someone would have called me on my cell phone.

She answered on the first ring. "Chief Ortiz's office."

"Maggie, it's Benni. Who got shot? How bad is it?"

"I can only talk for a second. The phone has been ringing off the hook. It was a patrol officer. Bret Mitchell. It happened over at Laguna Lake. He was answering an anonymous report that some boys were attacking ducks. When he stepped out of his patrol car, he was shot. The shooter got him in the thigh. Detectives are still over there, but so far they've not found anything."

"Officer Mitchell? The name doesn't sound familiar."

"Not sure if you've met him. Bret's fairly new. He has dark brown hair, about thirty years old. Came to us from Riverside PD last year. He's a pitcher on the baseball team."

"The one who pitched the shutout last summer?"

"Yeah, that's him."

"I remember him now." After the team's first choice for pitcher sprained his arm the first five minutes of the game, Officer Mitchell pitched a no-hitter in a charity baseball game against the San Celina Fire Department. No one had any idea he was a good ballplayer. The fire chief still ribbed Gabe about it, claiming Officer Mitchell had been a ringer.

"Is he okay?"

"He'll likely be off the job for a while, but the wound was clean. Everyone's spooked big time. Word among the officers is whoever is doing this is toying with us. Bret could have been killed. The sniper *chose* to shoot him in the leg."

"Gabe is at the hospital?"

"Yes, along with half the city, I think."

"Okay, thanks."

I sat in my truck a moment trying to decide what to do. There was no doubt that my presence at the hospital would only add to the frenzy, which Gabe definitely didn't need. Should I call him? Should I go home and wait? Waiting was not my long suit, but I decided it was the wisest course. So I drove home, fed and walked Scout, then sat out on the porch swing wrapped in a wool sweater, waiting for Gabe. The phone rang at ten after seven. It was Dove.

"How's Gabriel?" she asked.

"I haven't spoken to him yet, but I talked to Maggie. He's at the hospital. I didn't want to get in the way, so I came home. What's scary is the sniper could have killed Officer Mitchell and didn't. There's speculation the sniper is just toying with the police."

"Oh, honey bun, I'm so sorry. Do you need me to come to town? Garnet and I can be there in a half hour."

"Thanks, but I'd feel better if you'd all stay out at the ranch. These days, it's apparently safer."

"Call me when Gabe comes home. I won't be able to sleep otherwise."

"Yes, ma'am."

I went back out on the porch, Scout at my heels, and continued my vigil despite the cold breeze that swayed the tops of the trees.

119

Gabe finally arrived home around eight thirty. When he stepped out of his car, he walked toward the house as if he carried a two-hundred-pound weight on his back.

I waited for him on the top step. "How is Officer Mitchell?"

"He'll be fine," Gabe said, dropping his jacket and briefcase on the swing and pulling me into a hug. "This is bad, *querida*. We don't have any leads. My officers might as well have a bull's-eye painted on their chests."

I hugged him hard, my fingers pressing into his damp shirt. "Let's go inside. Have you eaten?"

He shook his head no.

I picked up his jacket and briefcase and opened the front door. "Let me heat up some soup."

While he changed, I called Dove, let her know he was home, then made us a quick dinner of tomato soup sprinkled with shaved Parmesan cheese, and fresh sourdough bread.

"Your detectives really don't have any leads?" I asked, pushing the plate of bread toward him.

He took a slice and buttered it. "The first one we just chalked up to a random nut trying to harass the police. Troubling, but not planned." He stopped, stared down at the piece of bread in his hand, a puzzled look on his face. "This second attack leaves little doubt this person is gunning for cops. And we don't have a clue why."

I reached across the table and touched the top of his hand, wishing I could say something that would help. But all I could think was—*I wish you weren't a cop. I wish you did anything else for a living. Anything.*

"What is your plan of action?" I asked. If there was one thing I knew about my husband, it was that he battled his fears by being organized, methodical and unemotional. A marine through and through. Semper fi.

His bottom lip tightened under his mustache. I could almost hear his breathing slow down. "Every available detective is assigned to the case. Detective Arnaud is heading the task force since she has a strong background in gang-related crimes. Besides, she headed a similar task force back in Louisiana."

"You think it might be gangs?" The thought chilled me. We'd had a run-in with a white supremacist group last summer during the Mid-State Fair, but would they have waited six months to retaliate?

"We don't know who or what it is, so we're checking out all possibilities. Fortunately, this is a slow time for us in terms of major crimes, so I'm authorizing overtime so that way officers can travel in pairs until we catch this person. I've set up a task force. The sheriff's department and highway patrol are on tactical alert. To make the mayor and the city council happy, I called the FBI. They're arriving tomorrow. Everyone's being cooperative . . ."

"As well they should be. So far it's been San Celina officers, but who knows what is going on in this crazy person's head?"

He took a small bite of bread. "Maybe the FBI will help with a profile, though I'm not thrilled about them being involved. They tend to take over."

I arched my eyebrows. Good luck with anyone trying to take over Gabe's department. He was usually cooperative about help, but he'd never step aside for any other agency.

"I'll take Scout for his walk," I said after dinner. "Why don't you shower and go to bed. Watch something shallow on TV. *America's Funniest Home Videos*."

"That's a stupid program."

"The dog videos make you laugh."

He smiled. "Yes, they do." He yawned, stretched his arms out. "Maybe I'll just go to sleep."

"Even a better idea."

"Stay close to the house. Better yet, take Scout out in the backyard."

"Okay."

After Scout's final constitutional, I hurried back inside the house, my cheeks and nose tingling with cold.

Gabe was in bed reading a magazine. Scout

crawled into his dog bed in the corner and collapsed with a deep sigh.

"I hear you, buddy," Gabe said.

"Now that I have my two guys settled, I'm going to take a shower and hit the sack myself." I pulled my sweatshirt over my head and peeled off my silk undershirt.

"What's that?" Gabe's voice was sharp.

Dang it, I'd forgotten about the bruise. I turned my back to him, tossing my clothes into the basket next to Scout's bed. "What?"

"Benni, turn around."

I turned slowly to face him, keeping my hands at my sides. For some some crazy reason, I felt *guilty*. He threw back the down comforter and walked over to me. Though we'd been married five years and I should have been used to his body by now, I couldn't help admiring his muscled thighs and strong forearms. Though he normally slept commando-style, tonight he wore the jockey shorts that I'd bought him as a joke for Valentine's Day. They had snarling Marine Corps bulldogs printed on them. The bulldogs looked exactly like the tattoo on his upper back.

"What happened?" He carefully slipped the strap of my bra off my shoulder and brushed his fingertips over the baseball-size bruise above my heart. Just the softest pressure caused me to wince.

I couldn't meet his eyes. If he wasn't standing

so close, if I couldn't feel his warm breath on my head, smell his familiar masculine scent—a tantalizing concoction of freshly washed cotton fabric and lemon—if I couldn't hear the raspy clearing of his throat, I might have been able to make up a story about falling off a ladder at the folk art museum or concoct some fictional accident with a stubborn calf. Heaven knows, my transparent redhead's skin usually always sprouted a bruise somewhere on my body.

"It's nothing," I whispered.

He cupped my chin and raised my head to look at him. The pupils of his eyes were tiny drops of ink. His touch was gentle, but his face seemed angry. He cleared his throat; still the words came out raspy. "Did I do this?"

"You didn't mean it . . . it was an accident . . . you were half asleep . . . dreaming . . ." I pulled away from his hand and hugged him; pressing my chest against his ribs, willing some of his pain to flow into me so he wouldn't have to bear it alone. "You didn't mean to . . ."

"Stop it!" He took me by the shoulders, holding me away from him. When I flinched again, he threw his hands up as if they'd encountered a hot branding iron. "Tell me exactly what happened."

Feeling suddenly chilled, I hugged myself, digging my nails into my upper arms. "Remember Sunday night when you had that bad dream? I tried to wake you . . . it was probably just stress from . . ."

He moaned and turned away from me, bending over slightly, pressing his balled fists against his temples. "I can't believe I did that to you . . . Why didn't you tell me . . . why didn't you show me?"

"You didn't mean it, Gabe. You didn't know it was me. I'm fine." I touched the small of his back.

He straightened up. In the golden light from our bedroom lamps, I could see his spine flex, the muscles move under his shoulders. His snarling Marine Corps bulldog tattoo leered at me. I wanted to cover its mouth with my hand, my lips. I wanted it to be erased forever.

He turned slowly back to face me, his expression as still and unemotional as I'd imagined he'd been while walking point in-country. He liked walking point, he once told me during a rare moment when he talked about Vietnam. He liked being the first one, he'd said, the one who knew what was happening before anyone else, what was going on in front of him. He wasn't afraid because at the time he felt like he couldn't die.

"I was eighteen," he'd said. "Stupid as a chicken. Besides, I felt like I had nothing to live for anyway."

His statement, spoken so blithely, had left me mute with sorrow.

"I'll sleep in the guest room tonight," he said.

"No, you will not."

"No argument. It's the only way to guarantee I won't hurt you again."

"Gabe, please . . ."

"Stop!" His voice was harsh and angry. Not at me, I knew. At himself.

At his loss of control. At his weakness . . . or what he perceived as weakness.

I felt hot tears well up, threatening to roll down my cheeks.

"*Querida.*" He ran his finger down my jawline. "Please, I don't want to hurt you . . ."

"You won't . . ."

He held up his hand. "And I can't have you to worry about along with everything else."

"I know." The words caught in my throat, hurting as they tumbled over the lump of salt.

"Once we catch this sniper, I'll take care of this."

How? I wanted to ask, but didn't.

He stared directly at my bruise. "Right now, you are safer in another room."

He picked up his reading glasses, unplugged his alarm clock and started downstairs to the guest room.

"No," I said. "Not the downstairs one. Up here." We had another room down the hall that I just recently furnished with a bed, nightstand and desk.

He turned to look at me, his expression questioning.

"Look," I said, pushing my bra strap back up. "When you have one of those dreams, you can't always come out of it quickly. I have to wake you. I can't hear you downstairs."

His expression was impatient and stubborn. "I don't want you near me when I'm . . . like that. That's the whole point of me staying in another room."

I could be just as stubborn. "If you sleep in the downstairs I can't *hear* you. If you go downstairs, I will too. I'll sleep on the sofa. I'll sleep on the floor outside your door."

"You are being ridiculous."

"Try to stop me."

He threw up hands. "Fine, I'll sleep up here. But if I have a dream, you stay out of the room. Yell at me from the doorway. Throw something at me."

"Okay," I lied.

He eyed me suspiciously, guessing that I would disobey his order.

"The sheets are new," I said. "Just bought them from L.L. Bean. You'll be sleeping on flannel pinecones."

One side of his mouth came up in a smile. "Sounds painful."

I slipped my arms around his waist and laid my face on his chest. The hair was soft under my cheek. I inhaled, holding his scent, like the deep breath a smoker would take from a long-anticipated cigarette. "I'll miss you."

He nuzzled the top of my head. "Me too. We'll figure this out."

"I know," I murmured.

While he set his alarm and placed his cell phone on the nightstand, I fussed with the blankets and pillows as if he were an invalid child.

"Go to bed," he said. "We both need some sleep."

After he crawled under the covers, I stood next to the bed, not wanting to leave.

"Come here," he said with a sigh.

I sat on the bed and leaned toward him. We kissed deeply, and the taste of him was still as intoxicating as a shot of whiskey; it made the hallway separating us feel like a vast canyon.

"Trust me," he said, cradling my face in his hands. His thumbs stroked my cheeks.

"I do, Friday."

On my way out, followed by a confused Scout, Gabe called out, "Close the door."

I turned to look at him, hesitating.

"Do as I say, Benni." His voice was firm, uncompromising.

I shut the door softly and went back to our king-size bed. It felt like a giant's bed without Gabe's presence. Scout stood next to me, bewildered by the unexpected change of routine. Gabe and I had slept apart before when we'd argued. Those times had upset Scout, who possessed a true diplomat's heart. He seemed to understand that it was a squabble, and he'd move between us, nudging our thighs with his nose, trying to communicate in doggie language —can't we all just get along?

But this situation confused him. There was tension but not anger. And his pack was sleeping apart. He whined, licked my hand, then went over and stood in the bedroom doorway, looking over his shoulder at me.

"I agree, it doesn't feel right, Scooby-Doo. But we have to let him handle this in his own way."

I read until past midnight, unable to sleep. Scout lay with his head on his front paws, his chocolate eyes wide and worried.

"All right," I whispered, crawling out of bed and tiptoeing down the hallway. I placed my ear against the guest room's cold door. I could hear Gabe's snoring, a soft rumbling that wasn't unpleasant, had never kept me awake. I carefully turned the knob and opened the door. Normally the sound would have instantly awakened him, but he must have been exhausted and in a deep sleep, because he didn't stir.

Scout watched me from the middle of the hallway. I left the guest room door open and walked back to our bedroom. "Is that better?

You can get to him now. And so can I."

Like so many other times when I swore he knew exactly what I was saying, he sighed and went over to his bed, curling up in a tight ball, his nose pointed toward the bedroom where Gabe slept. In a few minutes, he was asleep and so was I.

Chapter 7

"You look austere," I said the next morning while spreading blackberry jam on my English muffin. Gabe was dressed in a dark gray suit wearing another small-patterned tie, gray and burgundy this time. "And sexy," I added, hoping to make him smile.

Deep lines formed between his slightly bloodshot eyes. "I'll probably be talking to the press today."

"Well, you look very in control."

"Wish I felt that way."

"You'll rally, Chief. So, do you think the city will cancel the Thursday night farmers' market?"

Gabe shook his head, his jaw tense. "The town can't come to a sliding stop because of this idiot."

We finished the rest of our meal in silence.

Once he was gone, I called Dove. Though we'd always kept in close touch, once Aunt Garnet and Uncle WW moved to the ranch, I tried to call more often to see if there was anything she needed.

I was surprised when Daddy answered on the second ring.

"I'm leaving now," he said, his voice grumpy. "They . . ."

"Daddy? Is Dove there?"

"No one's here. They all left for town. Just me here. Me, the cows and the chickens." He gave a forced laugh.

"Is everything okay?"

"Just fine and dandy," he snapped. "Except for your gramma and her crazy sister trying to marry me off like some geisha girl up for sale."

The simile was not even close to accurate, since geisha girls were entertainers, not prostitutes, but I wasn't about to correct him and get my own head bit off. "Well, enjoy your time alone. I'll track Dove down."

"Whatever. I've got things to do." He hung up without saying good-bye.

"You have a nice day, too," I said to the dial tone. A cranky day for all the men in my life. Even Scout gave me a baleful look when I fed him dry kibble with his normal spoonful of canned dog food. Fortunately, his problem was easier to solve than Gabe's or Daddy's. I added a couple strips of cooked boneless chicken. His wagging tail was the nicest comment I'd received this morning.

This dating thing was really starting to upset my dad. It was past being funny now. I might have to take a chance on getting my nose bit off and speak to Dove and Aunt Garnet about poking into his love life. Though their intentions were honorable, maybe they needed to accept the fact that some people might be happier being single. Daddy certainly didn't seem dissatisfied with his life. But I'd talk to my gramma and aunt later. Right now, I had enough to worry about with the Memory Festival.

I dressed in comfortable old jeans, sneakers and a sweatshirt because I would be at the folk art museum today getting things ready for the museum's booth at the farmers' market. It would promote both the Memory Festival and the new museum exhibits. Would the fair be safe tonight? So far, there'd been no pattern to the ambushes—one in midday, the other after dark. Would there be a third attack?

I called Elvia at home to tell her what I knew about the latest attack. Her answering machine came on after the fourth ring. When I tried Blind Harry's, the clerk said that Elvia and Sophie were at the doctor's office.

"No message. I'll call her later. How's the Memory Fair flyer situation?"

"We're low," the bookstore clerk said. "People seem real interested."

"I'm heading downtown, so I'll bring more."

After dropping off the flyers, I decided to visit my cousin Emory. His office was located a couple of blocks from the bookstore on the second floor above the Ross department store.

Boone's Good Eatin' Chicken's West Coast offices were decorated with burnished natural oak furniture. Framed photos of 1950s advertising pages depicting chickens and eggs lined the sage green reception-area walls. *Oxford American* and *Reader's Digest* magazines flared out on the antique oak coffee table and an old wooden bowl filled with butterscotch and peppermint hard candies perched on the edge of the receptionist's desk, which was neat and empty this morning. The offices had the slightly distressed style of a Depression-era country lawyer. I think my cousin had grand illusions of looking like Gregory Peck playing Atticus Finch. The offices had not gotten any bigger now that my uncle Boone had moved out from Arkansas. Uncle Boone left the daily running of the company to Emory now, something that my cousin, who dearly cherished his leisure time, complained about constantly. "Welcome to adulthood," I always replied to his whining.

"Hey," I called out. My voice was a tinny echo in the empty reception room. Normally, one of two women ruled this area—a receptionist named Caitlyn or Emory's assistant, Birdie, whose office door, next to Emory's, was closed. No answer.

"Is anyone home?" I called.

"Only me and the chickens," my cousin

replied from his office, whose door was partially open. "Come on in, sweetcakes."

"Where is everyone?" I asked, glancing around his normally tidy office. Birdie was a fanatic about keeping it neat. Today there were files and papers everywhere, and the air smelled like burned almonds. "What have you been cooking?"

The smelly culprit turned out to be the coffee-maker on the credenza. I picked up the carafe and twirled the sluggish black liquid. "How long has this been sitting here?"

He ran both hands through his thick blond hair. "The ladies left for a computer seminar in Santa Barbara yesterday. I've been on my own. I made a pot yesterday and just turned on the coffeemaker to heat it up."

"Then forgot about it, right?"

He lifted one shoulder and grinned.

"Pathetic," I said, turning off the coffeemaker and unplugging it for good measure. "Why are they both gone at the same time? It's dangerous leaving you here by yourself."

He leaned back in his leather executive chair. "It's our new computer system. It'll hook us right up with the plant in Arkansas. The ladies need to take classes to learn how to use it and said it was better if they did it together. I was trying to catch up on some paperwork, but I'm thinkin' it might be smarter to close up shop until they return."

"I'm thinkin' you might be right," I said, flopping down in one of his visitor's chairs. "Is there anything so desperately important that you can't wait until they get back . . . when?"

"Friday. Not really."

I held up a palm. "Then you have time to talk to me. I need a sympathetic listening ear. Preferably male."

He grabbed the coffee brown Hugo Boss jacket slung haphazardly across his chair. "Trouble in paradise?"

"Something like that."

"Let's walk," Emory said, taking my hand and tucking it into the crook of his arm. "Tell Cousin Emory all about it."

Outside, a weak sun had made an appearance, drying patches of wet pavement. But, in the distance, dark clouds seemed to be gobbling up huge sections of the clean blue sky, warning us that another storm was on its way. Emory glanced up. "Looks like God is getting ready to spit on us real soon."

"I do hope you don't plan on explaining rain to Sophie with that particular metaphor."

He smiled. "Speaking of the most beautiful girl in the world next to my darlin' wife, we got the proofs back of the Easter photos." He let go of my arm and reached inside his coat, pulling out a thick envelope. "I paid extra to have them sent overnight."

On the way downstairs, I flipped through the photos, impressed by Van's ability to pick the exact right moment to snap the shutter. There were so many cute ones. "Wow, this Van guy really is good."

"Not bad for a guy who's more used to taking photos of hurricane damage, bombed-out cities and other natural and unnatural disasters."

"Really? Who did he work for?"

"Associated Press, I was told, and *National Geographic.* Then he went independent for a while, took some incredible photos in Beirut. And now he's a baby photographer. What a comedown."

"I'm sure that's not all he does." Out on the street, the sidewalks were busy with people trying to run their errands before the next storm hit. In California, when it rained, people stayed inside as if it were a blizzard.

"That's right, he also does college coeds . . . that is, he takes photos of them." He chuckled at his own joke.

"Why didn't he get a job at the *Tribune?* It seems to me they would snatch someone with his talent and experience right up."

"Ageism bites," Emory said as we passed by the studio where Van Baxter worked. Today there was a younger man sitting behind the desk, talking to three women holding babies. "I don't really know his story, but he is a bit long in the tooth . . ."

"That's crazy. He looks like he's around Gabe's age. Forty-eight is not old. Besides, isn't that against the law?"

"Call Gloria Allred and see if she'll take the case. These days a journalist in his late forties is considered over the hill and through the dale and way past great-gramma's house." He pulled out a photo of Sophie laughing at the camera, both her dark eyes wide open, sparkling like sunlight on water. "I like this one best. What do you think, three hundred cards?"

"Who in the heck are you sending three hundred Easter cards to?"

He looked chagrined. "Crazy, huh? I was thinking about sending them to all the employees at the plant back in Sugartree. With a Visa gift card for twenty-five bucks?"

"The gift card is thoughtful, but you should restrain yourself to sending her photo to those of us who love her. Her godmother would like five copies."

"Absolutely," he said, taking my elbow and leading me into the new coffeehouse I'd seen on the news the other day, Bitter Grounds. Two uniformed police officers sat at a table near the window. Emory lowered his voice. "So, how is Gabe handling this crazy-ass sniper business?"

"That's what I want to talk to you about. You know, this is the weirdest name for a coffeehouse." I chose a table in the corner, far from

138

the officers, hoping that no one could hear our conversation. "Seems to me people would steer clear of a coffeehouse that advertises bitter coffee."

"You know college kids. They adore absurdity. This is a happening place, I've been told." He put a finger over his lips. "We can't tell my lovely wife we were drinking at the competition, but I figure less chance of people we know over-hearing us here."

"Good idea." I took off my denim jacket and hung it across the ladder-back chair. The coffee-house was decorated in what might be described Tropical Hollywood Junkyard. The mismatched tables and chairs were painted bright reds, blues and yellows. Every cheesy Hawaiian and Tijuana trinket you could imagine hung on the walls—banged-up surfboards, red clay suns and moons that they sold at Cost Plus, *Beach Blanket Bingo* movie posters and way too many coconut shells with comical sand dollar ears and painted faces.

Emory bought me a Mexican hot chocolate and a large coffee for himself. They came in soup bowl–size mugs. "Here's a plethora of sugar and chocolate to sustain you. Now tell Uncle Emory all your problems."

I sighed and propped my elbows on the red table. Around us the bluesy music was low and inviting, and people's conversations were far enough away to be a comforting murmur.

139

"Gabe's not reacting well to this sniper attack."

"Completely understandable. I can't imagine what he's going through trying to figure out where this nutcase might hit next."

"It's more than that. He's having trouble sleeping."

Emory loosened his tie. "Insomnia?"

I shook my head no, wondering if I should have just kept my mouth shut. Emory had been my best friend since we were kids playing in Aunt Garnet's attic back in Sugartree, but it was awkward telling even him about something so personal. If Gabe found out I mentioned this to anyone, he would be humiliated and ashamed. I wrapped my hands around the wide, yellow mug. The heat burned my palms just enough to feel comforting.

Emory leaned across the table and covered my hands with his. His palms were dry and cool, their touch familiar. "This is Emory, your best friend in this whole wide wicked world. You can tell me anything."

I looked up and inhaled deeply. "I'm sorry, it's not really that dramatic. He's having nightmares again. The other night he accidentally . . . he sort of . . . hit me." I mumbled the last two words, my heart vibrating like a dentist's drill.

Emory bolted upright, his nostrils flaring in anger. "He what?"

"Please, don't overreact," I said, tears stinging

my eyes. "He was half asleep . . . he didn't even realize where he was . . ."

His furious expression told me he was not appeased. "Where did he hit you?"

"On my chest." My hand hovered over the spot above my heart. "Really, it's just a surface bruise. It's not that bad. I wasn't even going to tell him. But he saw it when I was getting undressed for bed last night." I picked up my mug with both hands and took a long drink.

"When did he hit you?"

"*Accidentally* hit me," I said, gesturing with my hand for him to lower his voice despite the fact that no one was even paying attention to us. "Monday night."

He gripped his own mug, his knuckles pale. "The first sniper attack was Monday afternoon."

"When he saw the bruise last night, he . . ." I swallowed, embarrassed to continue. I trusted my cousin, but it still felt like I was being disloyal to Gabe. "He was so upset. At himself, not me."

"Sounds like a post-traumatic stress reaction."

I nodded. "I'm sure the sniper attack brought it on. I've done some research about what triggers it."

"Has this ever happened before?"

"He's had nightmares before—maybe half a dozen times since we've been married. I've

141

always been able to wake him up. This time it was really hard. And this is the first time he's reacted . . . that way."

Emory stared down into his coffee cup. "Has he ever gotten professional help?"

"He's talked to Father Mark and to Pastor Mac, but I'm not sure how deeply. But he's never seen an actual therapist or a doctor. We talked about it once, but he never followed through. Being a cop, he's sensitive about the issue. And it could become public knowledge." I didn't have to say how disastrous that could be.

Emory raised his eyebrows. "The infamous permanent record."

"Yeah, except in his case, it's true. There are people here in the county who'd love to find some reason to pronounce he's not fit for the position of police chief." I looked down at the melting whipped cream, feeling too sick to drink any more. "Besides, you know how intensely private he is. If anyone found out, it would humiliate him. That's why I haven't told anyone, not even Dove."

Emory's voice was ragged. "Benni, what can I do for *you?*"

"What you're doing, listen."

"Keep in mind, any doctor Gabe talks to is bound by ethics to keep his confidence."

"Yes, but doctors have receptionists and office staff. He'd have to pass by other people in the

142

building. If we claim it on our insurance, there's a record."

"He could find a doctor out of town."

"I have argued those points with him, believe me. I know those are all the excuses he uses to avoid it. But I can't make him go if he doesn't want to." I pushed aside my half-finished drink. "I should let you get back to work. Thanks for listening to me vent."

Emory stood up, helped me with my jacket. "I feel like I didn't do anything except buy you something to drink."

"You listened. Sometimes that's the best thing a friend can do."

We walked outside where the sky had turned steel gray.

"Looks like another storm is brewing," I said, looking up. "I can't say I'm unhappy about it. We need the grass. The hills are already so green I almost have to wear sunglasses."

"Typical El Niño year," Emory said.

I couldn't help smiling. "Listen to you, sounding like a native Californian with your fancy-pants El Niño weather talk."

By the time we parted ways at the stairwell leading up to his office, the rain had turned into a steady downpour.

"You and Gabe still need to come over for some ribs," Emory said. "My barbecue's all put together now and working like a dream." We'd moved under the awning, but the wind was blowing the rain sideways. He flinched when a rain blast hit the side of his face.

I gave a small laugh. "Looks like we'll have to wait until the sun comes back out."

He kissed my cheek. "Sunny weather is just around the corner, I promise. Call me if you need anything."

In the ten minutes it took me to drive to the folk art museum, the rain turned into a deluge. At the museum, there were only four cars in the parking lot. One was Lin's gray Ford sedan, which, I noticed, still had a broken taillight, though she'd patched it with red tape. Though I don't know why, I felt compelled to write down her license plate number.

"You know, you're just looking for something to think about other than your own problems," I said aloud as I wrote the number on the only paper I could find in my purse, my checkbook register.

I checked the front door to make sure it was locked. The museum was closed on Wednesdays unless we had a special tour. It was also one of D-Daddy's days off, so the building felt especially deserted. His cheerful whistling of upbeat Cajun songs had become a dependable museum staple. Around back, the co-op building door was open. Conversation and laughter overflowed from both the woodworking room and the

144

alcove off the great room where we kept our two pottery wheels. The great room, where the quilters normally set up their quilting frames, was empty.

In the pottery alcove, both wheels were in use. Lin Snider worked the smaller one, wearing a snug gray T-shirt and stained blue jeans. She was even thinner than I'd first thought, since the two other times I'd met her she'd been wearing a jacket or a thick sweater. Bonnie, one of our regular potters, worked the larger wheel.

"Hey, ladies," I said, holding up my hand. "Nice day for pelicans."

"I love it," Bonnie said. "Takes me back to my childhood days in Portland. I'm part duck, you know."

Lin just smiled, not stopping her wheel, her hands expertly forming the smooth wall of a pot.

Back in my office, I puttered around, filing a few things, dusting my desk and bookcases. For once I was caught up on all my paperwork and really didn't have a lot to do except deal with the four messages concerning the Memory Festival. They all were easy and taken care of in twenty minutes. It felt strange being caught up with a free afternoon stretched out in front of me.

I called Elvia at the bookstore. "Hey, little mama. How was my goddaughter's checkup?"

"She's right on schedule," Elvia said.

"So, anything at the bookstore you need my

help with? I've got a completely free afternoon."

"No, it's very quiet here today. Everyone must have stayed home. You know cowardly Californians and rain. We duck and cover until the sun comes back out."

"Ain't that the truth. I can't believe I have a free afternoon with nothing to do. Maybe I'll go home and take a nap."

"That sounds heavenly. I may do that myself if it stays this slow."

"Okay, see you mañana."

The rain on the roof pounded harder, like a platoon of raccoons performing war maneuvers overhead. The weather outlook for this Saturday didn't look promising. How many exhibitors would cancel if it was raining this hard? How many people would decide to stay home and watch movies? Maybe having this festival in March wasn't the best idea in the world. The problem was, there weren't many free spots left on San Celina County's crowded events schedule.

A swoosh of wind rattled my office's small window.

"Yikes," I commented out loud.

"Indeed," Lin agreed from the doorway.

"Hey." I twirled my chair around to face her. "Is the wheel working okay? Any leaks in the ceiling?"

"Yes and no," she said, laughing. "Tell me, how often does San Celina have weather like this?"

146

"Not real often. This is real Pacific Northwest weather."

She chuckled. "Then I should feel right at home. I'm from Seattle."

"I apologize for any crazy drivers. Californians do not know how to drive in the rain."

"Nor do many from Seattle." She smiled and wiped her palms down the sides of her jeans. "My two hours are up. I have a question. Do you fire pots here?"

I opened my side drawer and took out the price sheet. "We have a small kiln out back. They fire once a week unless there's a bigger demand, like around holidays. The dates they fire are on the sheet."

"Got it." She folded the sheet into fourths and stuck it in her back pocket.

There was a moment of silence. The rain on the roof slowed to a steady thrum.

She glanced up at the ceiling, then back at me. "I know the weather's kind of bad, but you'd said you could possibly show me around San Celina. Are you free any time soon?"

"Actually, I'm free right now." The minute the words were out of my mouth, I regretted them.

"Great!" She looked down at her clay-stained clothing. "I brought a change of clothes. I can be ready in a few minutes."

"No hurry." I watched her walk out, wanting to slap myself in annoyance. Why was I giving up a rare free afternoon to give a stranger a tour of our county? Maybe because I was still feeling a little guilty about my inhospitable moment with her in Liddie's.

Too late now. I would have to make the best of it.

"What are you interested in seeing?" I said once we settled in my truck. "San Celina County is pretty diverse. North county is hilly ranch land, there's the coastal towns, wine country, even a kind of deserty plains out in east county. What type of situation are you looking to live in?"

She fiddled with the dark blue cashmere scarf she had wrapped around her neck in an intricate, fashionable knot that Elvia could probably name. "Oh, I don't know. I just keep thinking I'll know the place if I see it. How long have you lived here in San Celina? Are you a native?"

"Sort of."

She gave a low, pleasant laugh. "That's vague."

I pulled onto Interstate 101 heading north. "Let's work from the top of the county down. I'll show you Paso Robles, which has become a popular place for people to retire and then swing over on Highway 46 to the coast. You might like Cambria. It's a pretty little town that has a real artistic feel."

"I'm in your hands," she said, pulling a small notebook out of her leather purse. "I'll take notes."

"Have you been to the Chamber of Commerce?"

"I did that right away. A woman named Cyndi was a big help. I always send away for literature before I visit a place, then check the computer to see if the county has a website. So I do have a general idea about the places you're talking about."

"Cyndi Silva is amazing. No one knows this county better than she does. She and I went to Cal Poly together." I laughed. "Then again, I could say that about half the people in San Celina County."

Her expression was thoughtful. "That must be comforting."

I didn't answer, not certain what to say. I'd actually never thought about it in that particular way.

"Have you checked out a lot of other places?"

She turned to look out the window. "About seven or eight. Finding a home, the right home, is . . . well, it isn't as easy as it might seem."

Her choice of words startled me silent. I'd never doubted where home was, where I would spend my entire life. Even when Gabe and I married, we didn't discuss where we'd live. It went without saying that it would be in San Celina. His job was here and, well, it was my *home.*

But, a little voice inside me asked, what if he lost his job? Did that ever occur to you? What if he wanted to leave San Celina? Could you? Would you?

"Were you born in Seattle?" I asked.

There was a second of hesitation before she answered. "No, I was born in Illinois, where my mother was from. But I think I told you, my dad was in the army and we moved often. I haven't had any family in Illinois for years. My father died when I was in college. My mother died when I was five years old. Both my parents were only children and so was I." Her words didn't hold one ounce of self-pity that I could detect.

I stared at her a moment. "I'm so sorry. I understand, I mean, about your mother. Mine died when I was six and I'm an only child too."

"So you know what it's like to be alone."

I didn't answer, hoping that it appeared I was in tacit agreement. Truthfully, I had so many cousins, extended family members and friends like Elvia with large families who'd always accepted me as one of their own that I'd never felt alone. The sadness of her situation floored me.

"You said you were and weren't a native to San Celina," she continued. "What did you mean?"

Safe emotional territory. I grabbed for it immediately. "I was actually born in Arkansas, but my parents came to San Celina when I was a toddler, so I don't really remember living anywhere else." I smiled at her and took the next exit. "I'm going to swing through Templeton. It's where we bring our cattle to auction. Many people probably don't know that there are still working ranches in California and that we're actually the biggest agricultural state in the union."

"I didn't realize that. What about your husband? He's San Celina's police chief, right? Does he like his job? Is he a native?"

"Yes, Gabe is San Celina's chief of police. He's not from here." I braked to let a group of school-kids cross the street. It looked like they were heading for the stock auction buildings. It reminded me of a field trip our third grade class took to the Templeton Stock Auction. I'd been disappointed because I went there once or twice a month with Daddy to eat at Hoover's Beef Palace Café in front of the pens and watch the cattle being auctioned off so it didn't feel like a real field trip to me. "I guess he likes his job most of the time. I think sometimes we Californians might drive him crazy. He's from Kansas."

"Really? What part?"

"Derby. It's a town about fifteen miles south of Wichita."

She nodded while we watched the children meander across the street, the little girls holding hands, the boys pushing and shoving each other. "I've been to that part of Kansas. It's lovely. Midwestern people are very kind, I've found. More, I don't know, dependable than . . ." Then she caught herself. "Oh, my, I didn't mean to imply that . . ."

I waved a hand at her. "I know what you mean. Yes, Gabe is definitely dependable and it *is* real pretty around Derby."

"How'd he end up here in San Celina?"

The last child—a raven-haired boy in a red-striped T-shirt—crossed the street. He turned to wave at us. I waved back. "Like how many people get places, by accident, fate, God's providence, whatever you want to call it. After high school, he joined the service and served in Vietnam. After his tour was up, he went to visit his uncle Tony in Southern California and stayed for a while. He applied at the Los Angeles Police Academy and worked for LAPD. About six years ago he took the job as San Celina's police chief."

It was a condensed version of Gabe's life. When Gabe was sixteen, his dad died and Gabe started going wild. His mother sent him to live with Uncle Tony, his dad's older brother. When he turned eighteen, Gabe joined the marines and went to Vietnam. Once he came home, he applied to the LAPD, eventually working under-cover narcotics in East LA. He married, had a son, got divorced. He was also single with lots of other female relationships for more years than I liked to think about. *Then* he came to San Celina.

"Vietnam," Lin said softly. "I had some good friends who served there. They were never the same after they came home. Is Gabe okay?"

"Yes," I said, a little taken aback by her personal question. "It was a long time ago."

"Time is relative with things like that."

"Suppose so." My voice sounded more curt than I intended, but I didn't want to discuss Gabe's Vietnam years with a virtual stranger, even if I did sympathize with her situation. Changing the subject, I quickly went into tour guide mode. "Templeton's still a quiet little country town, but it's getting kind of upscale now too. There's a new neighborhood of custom-built homes over by the freeway. It might be a smart place to buy a house right now."

"Looks lovely," she murmured, turning her head to look out the window.

We drove down Templeton's Main Street, past the grain tower and Templeton Feed and Grain. I pointed out the bakery that baked incredible chocolate chip scones, the steak house that had won culinary awards for their tri-tip, the little hardware store where the staff were retired ranchers whose collective expertise had impressed an *LA Times* reporter enough to write a feature about them. At the end of the street, the Templeton Stock Auction buildings appeared to our right. The auction yards were closed today, but Hoover's Beef Palace Café was open.

"That's where the locals eat," I said, glancing at my watch. "Are you hungry?"

"As my daddy used to say, I could eat," she said, smiling.

I laughed and pulled into the crowded parking lot. "Yeah, my daddy says that too. Where did you say your father was from?"

"I don't think I did say. Actually, he was born and raised in Mississippi."

"My dad's an Arkie. They're practically cousins. I hope you're not a vegetarian?" I said when we reached the porch of the small café in front of the auction buildings. "If so, we can eat somewhere else. Paso has some good restaurants."

"Bring on the beef."

I waved to Sandy, one of the regular servers, and she brought over two menus. We both ordered open-faced, rib-eye steak sandwiches with French fries. While waiting for our lunch, I pointed out the wall of photographs of local ranchers dressed in suits and white cowboy hats.

"Those are all Cattlemen of the Year," I told her. "My dad was 1987. It was the highlight of his life."

She smiled. "You're proud of him."

I nodded. "He taught me everything I know about cattle and ranching. He taught me to ride and how to train a green horse. He's quiet, but a rock, you know?"

Her face relaxed slightly. "He sounds a lot like my dad. There's days I miss him so much I ache.

He was a big hunter. Taught me to shoot when I was six."

She looked around at the counter with the blue stools, almost every one occupied by men in Wranglers and straw cowboy hats. One wall was decorated with wooden plaques the size of license plates with local families' cattle brands burned into the glossy wood. Another wall held photos of famous local bulls. Thick white coffee mugs advertised the café and local businesses. "This is very authentic."

"As Western as it gets," I said. "A small town within a small town. Every rancher in San Celina County comes here at least once or twice a month."

"I like it," she replied. "In a strange way, it reminds me of the clubs on a military base. Kind of safe, you know? Where people know who you are."

Once they brought our food, we were quiet for a moment while we settled into eating.

She cut a small piece of steak and looked up at me. "Are you still close to your father?"

I finished chewing, then said, "Yes, I see him and my gramma Dove two or three times a week. Dove is Daddy's mom."

She put her fork back down on her plate. "Losing a mother so young is hard, isn't it?"

"Yes, but Dove was a great substitute. I would be crazy to shake my fist at God. I've really been very blessed."

"That's a wonderful attitude. Are you and Gabe going to have children?"

I stared at her a moment, suddenly uncomfortable with her probing questions. Was she interrogating me? Though I didn't want to go there, the vague thought that she had an ulterior motive made me wary.

"How did you end up in Seattle?" I asked, deciding to turn the tables.

She picked up her fork again. "Oh, like you said about your husband, in a roundabout way. I followed a boy to San Francisco in the early '70s. Lived there for a while. Took some history classes at UC Berkeley. Married the boy. Divorced him and then went back to college. Changed my major from history to accounting because I wanted to actually find a job that paid me enough money to live."

I gave a half smile at her comment and my own paranoia. She wasn't interrogating me. She was just being friendly.

"What?" She touched her chest with her fingers. There were still traces of clay beneath one nail.

"I majored in history."

Her cheeks blushed a dull red. "I'm sorry . . ."

I cut into my steak. Juice pooled around the sourdough bread slice, turning it a brownish red. "No, you're exactly right. My degree didn't do squat to get me a job. I worked as a waitress in

156

a truck stop café after college when my first husband and I needed the money for his family ranch, but that's about the extent of my formal employment."

"But your job as a museum curator. It's perfect for a history major!"

I smiled. "Yes, but I only landed it because my gramma has so much influence in this town. After my first husband, Jack, died in an auto accident, I was floundering. Dove pulled some strings. I think it started out as busywork because the museum was just getting started. The co-op was added to give the museum some, I don't know, legitimate reason for being there? My suspicion is both the museum and co-op started out being a big tax write-off for Constance Sinclair."

"Your patron of arts, I've heard."

"Yes. The hacienda belonged to her family. She's a descendant of one of the original Spanish land grant families. Anyway, she and my gramma . . . well, they're not friends, but they have lots of philanthropic interests in common." I shook my head, remembering. "It was something Dove had arranged to jolt me out of my depression, but it ended up being a great job."

The café door opened, and we both turned to look at the large group of laughing people who walked in. I waved at two of the ladies who were members of the Cattlewomen's Association. I turned back to face Lin.

"It's always been a part-time job, at least pay-wise. There's no way I could support myself on what I make. I do receive a small income from my cattle herd that I keep at my dad and gramma's ranch, but before I married Gabe, I was barely scraping by. I'm afraid now I'm a bit of a kept woman."

"Lucky you," she said. "I do mean that sincerely. Though with his job as police chief I'm sure you have a lot to do as his wife."

"Being a police chief's wife was certainly more complicated than I realized it would be when we got married." I picked up a French fry, inspecting it before dipping it in ketchup. "Then again, we didn't know each other long before we got married, so we *both* had lots of surprises."

"How long did you date?"

"I'm almost embarrassed to say. We knew each other only four months before we got married."

She sipped her iced tea. "You courted after you were wed."

"That about sums it up."

"How long have you been married?"

"Five years. Hard to believe sometimes."

"Good for you. Sometimes short relationships can be very intense, can change us for life, but it's not often that they turn into something long-term."

I tilted my head and looked at her without answering. It seemed such an odd thing to say.

158

She pushed her plate back. "This is delicious, but I ate such a big breakfast." Her cheeks were pale; her voice strained. She hadn't eaten more than a bite or two.

"Are you okay?" I asked, taking my napkin from my lap, ready to help her to the bathroom.

She held up a trembling hand. "I'm just getting over a little bout of flu. Please, excuse me for a moment." She stood up, faltered a little, gripped the edge of the table. "Really, I'll be fine."

I watched her walk toward the restrooms in back. She didn't look fine to me. I'd give her five minutes, then check on her.

She was back in a few minutes, composed and breathing more evenly. "I'm so sorry, Benni. I think I'm just a little shaky."

I stood up, picking up my jacket and purse. "I can take you home right now."

"No, please. I think if we just drive and not get out anywhere, I'll be okay."

I hesitated, not certain if I should take her word for it.

She laid a hand on my forearm. "I know how precious your time is and this free afternoon is rare for you. I want to continue our tour."

"Okay," I said, uncertainly.

"Let me pay for our lunch since I ruined it," she said.

She overrode my protests, so I let her pay.

When we stepped out of the café, a loud

shoop-shoop-shoop filled the air. Lin's head jerked up.

"It's just helicopters," I said in a loud voice. "They're probably flying out of Vandenberg Air Force Base."

She gave a nervous laugh. "Sorry, it just caught me by surprise."

On the drive up to Paso Robles, we stuck to trivial subjects—the weather in the different parts of San Celina County, the best places to buy produce, where the good cafés were. We drove through the tree-lined streets of Paso Robles, admiring the old Victorians and the small bungalows that made up "old" Paso. She exclaimed over the quaint downtown with the vaguely mission-style Paso Robles Inn and the redbrick Carnegie Library. Like the almost identical Carnegie Library in San Celina, it belonged to the local historical society. The modern new library sat within eyeshot of the original. We drove around the newer neighborhoods, and I pointed out the million-dollar mini-McMansions that now surrounded the town.

"Interesting mix of new and old," she commented. Once she was settled into the truck, her color seemed to return, though I could tell that the day was starting to wear on her by the strained skin around her bright blue eyes.

"Yes, it is. Paso Robles is definitely torn between the old ranchers and townspeople versus the 'city folk' who have a lot of disposable income to support the businesses owned by the ranchers and longtime citizens. It's an uneasy marriage, but seems to be working, for now."

"How is Paso Robles different from San Celina?"

I rolled my eyes heavenward. "Let me count the ways. In a nutshell, San Celina's a tad more liberal, what with the college and all. Paso is still, even with the addition of the city folk moving in, more rural. Still quite a few working ranches up here, though the wine people are rapidly becoming a force to be reckoned with in the ag community. The weather is milder in San Celina. In Paso, when it's hot, it can be blistering. When it's cold, it'll turn your bones to chunks of ice."

"I've lived in a place with extremes. It can be daunting. But exhilarating too, in a masochistic sort of way."

We pulled back onto Interstate 101 and took curvy Highway 46 over the hills to the coast. When we hit the summit, I pulled over. From this vantage point, you could see the rolling emerald hills, dotted with dark green oaks and the deep blue line of the Pacific Ocean in the distance. I had always felt like heaven would look exactly like this spot.

"Oh, my," she said, stepping out of the truck. The rain had softened to a fine mist. "This is breathtaking."

"Yes, it is," I said, feeling pride though I had nothing to do with its beauty. "It's even impressive in the summer when the hills are brown and tan, but in the spring, well, what can I say?" I leaned against the side of my truck. The cold, wet metal permeated my jeans.

Highway 46 ended at Pacific Coast Highway. A right turn would take us into the artsy town of Cambria, and a left turn south to Cayucos and Morro Bay, and eventually back to San Celina. After a quick drive through downtown Cambria, we headed south on Pacific Coast Highway.

I glanced at my watch. "I wish we could take the time to go through Cayucos and Morro Bay, but it's already four o'clock, and I have to be somewhere at six."

I had a meeting with the Coffin Star Quilt Guild at Oak Terrace Retirement Home. Normally our meetings took place during the day, but this meeting was a special one before the Memory Festival this Saturday. The ladies had been working on a quilt for the festival. It would be a silent auction item with the money going to the upkeep of the World War II veterans memorial in San Celina City Park. We planned on finishing it tonight.

"Oh, Benni, I'm sorry to take up so much of your time." She appeared genuinely distressed.

"No problem. It was a lucky break that my afternoon was free."

"I hope I'm not keeping you from a date with your husband."

"No, that's not it." I told her about the Coffin Star Quilt Guild and our quilt. "Though I wish it were with Gabe; he's been working triple time, what with this sniper out there shooting at police officers. I'm sure you've heard about it."

She nodded. "Yes, it's all over the news. It's quite disconcerting."

I quickly defended our town. "Nothing like this has ever happened here in San Celina. Gabe and his team will catch the person."

"I'm sure they will. It must be very upsetting to your husband."

"Yes, but Gabe's handling it like he does everything, logically and carefully."

"Like a true marine," she said, smiling.

I smiled back. "Isn't that the truth?"

We drove back to the folk art museum, and I dropped her off at her car.

It was only after I was halfway to Oak Terrace, while singing along with an old Tanya Tucker CD—". . . some kind of trouble . . ." —that it occurred to me.

I'd never told her that Gabe had been a marine.

Chapter 8

About three seconds later, I questioned my own memory. What had I said, exactly, about his military service? I remembered telling her he joined the service when he was eighteen and went to Vietnam. *Had* I mentioned he was a marine? I didn't think so, but I couldn't swear to it in a court of law. Though I didn't want to think it, my brain instantly started assessing everything about Lin Snider—her age, her backstory, that last bit of personal information about Gabe. Was she someone from his past? Another ex-lover wanting to rekindle a relationship? Was I doomed to repeat this same scenario as long as Gabe and I were married?

While waiting at Stern's Bakery to purchase two dozen chocolate cherry chip brownies, a favorite of the Coffin Star ladies, my mind quickly replayed the day with Lin Snider, searching for other words that seemed suspect.

I hated this distrusting trait in myself and consciously tried to suppress it. But I'd acquired it out of defense. Being married to a man with a complicated past, one that had winnowed its way into our present life more than once, had changed how I viewed everything.

The line at Stern's was long, and everyone's order seemed to be inordinately complicated. I shifted from one foot to the other, wishing it would hurry, wishing I knew someone in line so I could talk about the weather; how, as always, the students were driving the locals crazy; how I thought the Memory Festival would fare this weekend.

Anything to keep my mind from shifting back to the past, to a memory triggered by Lin Snider's comment. About another woman named Del. Gabe's ex-partner. Gabe's ex-lover.

In the privacy of the old Carnegie Library garden where underneath an ancient pepper tree I'd received my first grown-up kiss from Jack, I confronted Gabe with what I'd learned about his dinner with Del.

"What's the big deal?" Gabe said, his voice rising in anger, telling me I was smart to find a private place for us to have this conversation. "Don't people in this pathetic little town have anything better to do than gossip about innocent dinners between old partners?"

"Innocent dinners take place where people can see them," I said.

"Benni, I'm telling you nothing happened."

"Yet."

He glared at me, his eyes a blazing blue against his brown skin. "Is that what you think of me?

That I'm a person with so little self-control?"

I stared up at him, silent for a moment, then said, "Just tell me one thing. Are you still in love with her?"

His face looked shocked for a moment, then grew still. Not a muscle moved. Around us, a mockingbird flew from the pepper tree to the edge of the museum's roof to an old Martha Washington rosebush that was taller than me. His song was filled with distress and territorial anger and, I knew, a little bit of fear.

Finally, Gabe said in a voice low, rough, agonized. "I don't know."

"Next!" the counter clerk at Stern's Bakery called out, bringing me back to the present. "What would you like, ma'am?"

After buying the cherry chocolate brownies, I headed for Oak Terrace, my mind still dissecting the day with Lin. Was she someone, like Del, from Gabe's past? Had she and Gabe been lovers? It was not something I liked to dwell on, how many women he'd been with before me. But, sometimes, his past reared up, like a mythical dragon lolling in a cave, attacking when you least expected it.

By the time I reached the retirement home parking lot fifteen minutes later, I concluded that my mind was lost somewhere along Interstate 101. Was I crazy? One slightly suspicious comment,

166

and I had created a romantic scenario between my husband and Lin Snider. And the truth was, Gabe had rejected Del's advances three years ago and had never given me any reason since to think anything except that he loved me and was happy in our marriage.

Still, a niggling little voice inside my head prodded: What if she was the person poking around the Harper Ranch and why did she ask you so many personal questions and how does she know he was a marine?

Why didn't I just *ask* if she'd been out at the Harper Ranch? She probably had a logical explanation. I was making a mystery out of a molehill.

Wait and see. That was an adage that Gabe usually took with a situation when he didn't have enough evidence to act. Before undercover narcotics, he'd worked homicide.

"Sometimes," he'd once said to me about a stalled homicide investigation that was frustrating his detectives, "you simply have to wait for something to happen. You put out feelers, you gather information, you poke all the participants . . . then you wait. If something doesn't happen . . . you start poking again. If you're lucky, eventually someone talks or reacts."

"Or you find out there was nothing there to begin with," I muttered, pulling into the Oak Terrace parking lot. *Wait and see.* Gabe's advice seemed like the wisest move for me right now considering Lin Snider.

Oak Terrace had been a part of my life for the last six years, even before Gabe and I met. Shortly after I started my job as museum curator, Maxine, the recreation coordinator at Oak Terrace, asked me to start a quilt guild for the residents. Maxine was a member of the Cattlewomen's Association and, I suspected, she was put up to it by my sneaky but well-meaning gramma, who was trying to fill my lonely nights.

I reluctantly attended the first meeting of fifteen women, expecting a few sweet old ladies who smelled of Jean Naté cologne and needed someone to thread their needles and make them chamomile tea. What I found was a group of women who, though physically past their prime, were as mentally sharp and interesting as any of my friends. I did, indeed, thread their needles and make their tea, often spiked behind my back with someone's hidden flask of Jack Daniel's whiskey. I only knew this because I took a big gulp from my mug and almost sprayed my mouthful of whiskey tea all over the half-finished Courthouse Steps quilt stretched out on the quilting frame. They laughed and smacked each other like a bunch of preteen boys who'd put a tack on their teacher's chair.

"I'm glad I'm wearing my Depends," Thelma

Rook said, laughing so hard tears ran from her eyes. To this day, I have no idea who spiked my tea. I just made sure to keep my tea mug close to me since I did have to drive home.

To say these lively women saved my life would be an exaggeration, but since every one of them was a widow, some more than once, they were certainly the best grief counselors a young widow could have. Over the years, we'd discussed everything from the sad state of 1930s birth control to how to make a delicious cake without sugar to the similarities between the Korean and Vietnam wars. There wasn't a problem I could tell them without at least one of these women having encountered or experienced something similar.

They delighted in my and Gabe's courtship and marriage, hanging on every emotional bump and pothole along our rocky road to marital bliss. To think I could hide anything from them was being naive. Maybe that's why I moved slowly toward this meeting tonight. I wasn't sure if I was up to delving into what was happening with Gabe. At least not yet. These ladies had helped me through many rough times, including when he didn't know if he was still in love with his former girlfriend, Del. They were ready to take up arms (and canes) and go after her, making me laugh at their spirited solutions. Which, of course, was the point. We'd started out with fifteen women, but with deaths and additions, were holding at a steady ten or so, depending on who was having physical ailments.

"Father Always-On-Time is mowing us down like alfalfa," Janet Bottroff said at the funeral of one of our original members. Janet had been a professional tailor her whole life and had worked in the costuming department of MGM back in the thirties and forties. She claimed to have once been kissed by Clark Gable. "I've thought about asking San Celina Floral to consider offering seniors a punch card—buy ten funeral bouquets, get one free."

"Maybe we need to lower our age requirements," said Martha Pickering, her roommate. When we'd initially formed the group, the women had decided a person had to be seventy-five to join Coffin Star Quilt Guild.

"One of the youngsters over in Building C was complaining of age discrimination," Thelma said. That "youngster" was seventy-two. "Maybe we do need some younger blood."

"I don't know," said Pat Tobin, another new member who had just moved here from Washington. Thin and elegant as a flamingo, she'd sailed around the world three times in her capacity as an activities director for Holland America cruise line. She often kept us in stitches with stories about the crazy things people requested on cruises. "Those under seventy-fivers are kind of flighty." The other women murmured in agreement.

Before entering the pale pink and mint green lobby decorated with ivy wallpaper and pink baskets of fake Boston ferns, I dialed Gabe. Until this sniper was caught, I assumed every night would be a late one. There were task force meetings, meetings with the mayor, city council, and eventually, the FBI. All I could do was stand by and let him know I was there.

He answered on the second ring, his voice all business. "Chief Ortiz."

"Hey, handsome, you doing okay?"

"*Querida.*" His voice lowered, caressing the word that almost felt like my name now. "It's crazy here. I won't be home for dinner."

"I didn't think so. I'm at Oak Terrace with the Coffin Star ladies."

His chuckle was a cheerful tune in my ear. He loved the ladies and their sense of humor, though I often wondered if he'd adore them quite as much if he knew how much they knew about him. "Give them my regards."

"I sure will. I'll be here a couple of hours, then I'll head home. Any progress?"

His sigh was audible. "The FBI has started their profiling thing, but between you and me, it could be anybody for any reason. So many people hold grudges against cops. We're sifting through every letter and threat recorded in the last five years.

171

We're also checking recruits who didn't make it through the academy. Those college students who rented the apartment the first shooter used have practically had proctology exams we've dug so deeply into their backgrounds."

"Did you find anything?"

"Nothing. As far as we can see, they are just typical college kids who handed out too many keys to their apartment."

"Don't forget to eat dinner," I felt compelled to say since there was nothing else I could do for him. "Do you want me to bring you something?"

"No, but thanks. Maggie is making sure everyone's being fed."

"Be careful. I don't want you to be the next target."

"I will. *Te amo.*"

"Love you too."

Oak Terrace's ivy theme, executed during the retirement home's last remodel, continued in the waist-high stenciled ivy motif that circled the recreation room. Even the curtains on the long windows had an ivy and oak leaf motif. Six women waited for me, their wheelchairs pulled around the large rectangular folding table. I was surprised to see a new, brightly colored quilt spread out on the table.

"Where's the coffin quilt?" I asked, setting the pink Stern's Bakery box down next to the new Bunn coffeemaker. The scent of coffee surrounded me as the machine gurgled to its finish. "I thought we were finishing that."

"Oh, we finished that last week," Dorothy Harrington said, waving a chubby hand at me. She was round-faced with pale green eyes and ginger-colored hair. Every piece of clothing she wore was polka-dotted because her father used to call her Dotty. "It's over yonder ready for you to take to the Memory Fair." She shifted in her wheelchair. "I hope that's cherry chip brownies in those pink boxes."

"It is. And we've already sold nine hundred and sixty-two dollars worth of tickets for the raffle quilt." I'd been worried that the somewhat macabre quilt might be a hard sell. Instead, it had been one of our easiest raffle quilts to promote. Morbid apparently was all the rage, especially among college students. The ladies were considering making a second one.

"So, what've you got here?" I asked, sitting down at the head of the table.

"Spider Web quilt," said Pat. "My own design. We had tons of scraps, so we decided to use 'em up." She ran her hand over the double-size quilt top. The multicolored spider web design reminded me of exploding pizzas.

"Use it up, wear it out, make it do, or do without." Janet started the famous Depression-era slogan. The other women joined in, reciting the words in a singsong chant. Then they cackled like a bunch of Dove's hens. Pat gave me a mischievous wink.

"It's cool," I said, gazing over the quilt. Each separate spider web background was made with tiny triangles of colorful fabric; the spider's web itself was made with black fabric. At each corner of the two-inch black border were log cabin squares made with the same multicolored fabric as the insides of the spider webs. "Very bright and cheerful."

"My five-year-old great-grandson said the webs looks like pizzas," said Vynelle Williams, one of the guild's original members. "He called it the Spider Man Pizza quilt."

"My thoughts exactly!" I said, laughing. "So, what're we doing with it?"

"Top's finished," Pat said. "We thought we'd start quilting today."

"Sounds good. You all have some refreshments, and I'll set up the quilting frame."

In twenty minutes the quilting started. As needles flew up and down through the multi-patterned fabric "webs," so did the conversation.

"I was thinking we'd raffle this one off too," Vynelle said. "Maybe donate the money to the Alzheimer's unit here at Oak Terrace. They need a new karaoke machine."

"They can't sing to it, of course," Janet explained to me. "But the nurses use it to serenade the residents, and the folks seem to enjoy it."

Her springy curls, dyed as blonde as a canary's wings, were always as perfect as her bright red painted lips. "Bless their hearts." She pursed her lips. "But for the grace of God . . ."

The other women nodded their agreement.

"How are things looking for the Memory Festival?" Thelma asked in a few minutes, holding out an empty needle to me. I took it and handed her a threaded one. Threading needles for these ladies constituted a good part of my job at these meetings.

"Well," I said, "except for the possibility of a downpour soaking everyone and police officers getting shot by an unknown sniper, everything's peachy."

"Lordy, we've been a-watchin' that on the TV," Martha said, shaking her head, her eyes not leaving the quilt top as her needle rocked in and out. "Who do you think it might be?"

"Some kook hopped up on reefer, no doubt," Janet said.

"Listen to you," Pat said, poking at Janet with her elbow. "Reefer. For heaven's sakes, you sound like a hippie. Remember back when reefers were refrigerators?"

"Now you're really dating us," Janet said. "Isn't it funny how words change meaning?"

"How's Gabe taking it, sweetie?" Vynelle asked me. "He must be very upset."

I concentrated on threading the short needle in

my hand, thinking that I needed to get my eyes checked. It seemed to be getting harder to see the eye with every visit. "Oh, he's . . . you know . . . he's hanging in there." I stabbed the thread at the eye of the needle, missing it. I stuck the thread in my mouth again, wetting it, then trying once more. My jaw tightened in frustration; my eyesight blurred. I should have threaded the needles at home.

"Benni." Vynelle's scratchy voice was gentle.

"Yes?" I said, concentrating on my needle.

"Sweetie, look at me."

I swallowed, resisting the urge to wipe my eyes before looking up at Vynelle. All six women stopped quilting and watched me.

"Is everything okay?" Martha asked.

I didn't want to talk about it, but lying was out of the question. Though I wouldn't go into detail, I decided to be honest. "He is having some difficulty sleeping. Nightmares about Vietnam. It's . . . it's been hard . . . on both of us." I stuck the newly threaded needle into the large apple pincushion. "I think the sniper attacks set him off. Well, set off the post-traumatic stress."

Eleanor nodded, her wrinkled face grave. She'd been a high school history teacher. American history was her specialty. "That's what they call it now. Back in my daddy's time, World War I, they called it combat fatigue. Then in World War II, they gave it a fancier name—gross stress reaction." She clucked under her breath. "The men just called it shell shock. You know what they called it in the Civil War? Soldier's heart."

"Soldier's heart?" I repeated. That name seemed especially poignant.

"No matter what they call it," Eleanor said, "it's hard on the soldier, hard on his family."

"Or hers," Thelma said, whose oldest granddaughter was an air force pilot.

"Don't I know it," shy Miss Winnie Dalton said, speaking up for the first time. Her thin white hair was pulled back with a red velvet ribbon. Delicate blue veins crisscrossed the thin skin of her temples. She and her late husband, Frank, had owned Dalton's Deli, a popular sandwich shop and ice cream parlor down by the college. While attending Cal Poly in the '70s, Elvia, Jack and I used to buy ice cream there every afternoon, no matter what the weather. Jack used to call their pastrami burgers "manna from God." Miss Winnie, which was what everyone called her because it was what Frank called her, always gave Jack an extra scoop of ice cream because he'd replace the heavy five-gallon ice cream containers for her when Frank or their son, Billy, was busy.

"Miss Winnie was a nurse in World War II," Thelma said. "She's seen lots of battle fatigue."

I looked over at her in surprise. "Miss Winnie, I had no idea you were a war nurse!"

She blushed, looking pleased. "Glad I can still surprise someone. It wasn't as romantic as it sounds. Those were hard times. Though I did not know him yet, Frank was serving over in Sicily. He repaired airplanes." She reached over and patted my hand. "We met at the VA hospital, realized we were from the same state, got married shortly afterward. Frank had a real hard time." She looked down at the quilt and started stitching again. "His job was to clean the airplanes when they came back from combat. One time he had to pull a young tail gunner from the back of an airplane that was all shot up. He had to crawl down this long tunnel opening to fetch the young man. When he grabbed under the boy's arms and pulled, only half of him came out. Frank realized then the boy had been shot clean in two. Said he backed out of there quick as a frightened rat. Once he hit the tarmac, he vomited his guts out."

"That's horrible," I said, my stomach queasy. "How did they get the man out?"

She looked up at me, blinked her pale eyes. "Why, after Frank was done throwing up, he had to go back in and get the rest of him so they could bury the boy. It was his job. Said it was the hardest thing he ever did in his life. He wrote a letter to the boy's mama but never told her the full story, just said her son was a true hero. When he returned from the war, he never allowed fireworks near our house. He hated

Fourth of July. Always went camping by himself on that day, as far away from the celebrations as he could."

The rest of the women made sympathetic sounds.

"What did you all do?" I asked, gazing around at them. "I mean, how did you cope?"

They glanced at each other, their mouths thin lines. Pat spoke first.

"Each of us had different experiences," she said. "But mostly we all coped the same way. You just push through it the best you can. Most men saw combat back then. It affected them in different ways. Mostly we just let them work it out on their own."

"When Billy got back from Vietnam," Miss Winnie said, "he was all torn up, couldn't sleep, was drinking too much. That set Frank to remembering what happened to him in the war. With two of them wandering the house in the middle of the night, drinking and carrying on, it felt like I was living in a loony bin."

"Never ends," Thelma said with a sigh.

I faced Miss Winnie. "What did you do?"

"I flat-out nagged them into getting help. Frank didn't want to talk to the psychologist fella, but I told him that it was up to him to set a good example for Billy, that he could not expect his son to pull himself together if his own father wasn't willing to do the same thing. They went to the same doctor, and it was the best thing that ever happened to all of us." She nodded her head, remembering. "And I got help too. Found a real sweet doctor who helped me cope. Just let me talk and talk and cry and cry. Dr. Jean Malcolm. She passed on a few years ago, God bless her." Miss Winnie shifted in her wheelchair. "You just put one foot in front of the other and keep walking. You'd be surprised at what a body can survive. Excuse me, ladies, but I must go powder my nose. Don't tell any good gossip until I get back." She slowly wheeled herself out of the room.

After she was gone, Janet said, "Listen to her. Miss Winnie knows what she's talking about."

I picked up another needle to thread. "I know it's good advice, but . . ."

"No, I mean she *really* knows what she's talking about. She wasn't just a nurse during the war. She was stationed in the Philippines when the Japanese bombed Pearl Harbor. She was in a prison camp for three years."

"I had no idea." How could I have known someone almost all my life as I had Miss Winnie and not known something so important?

"She doesn't talk about it much," Martha said. "She saw the worst that men can do as well as the best, but she didn't let the bad become more important than the good."

When Miss Winnie returned, I couldn't help

sneaking glances at her, trying to discern what it was that enabled a person to survive the atrocities she'd experienced. Someone walking through Oak Terrace would likely look at her and think, There's a nice old lady, somebody's sweet gramma who probably won ribbons at the county fair for her angel food cakes.

It would probably never occur to them that they were looking at a hero.

At eight thirty, we decided to call it a night. After assuring the ladies that I'd be fine cleaning things up, I set the quilt frame on its side at the back of the room and tidied up the coffee area, putting the leftover brownies in the refrigerator after marking the box "Property of Coffin Star Quilt Guild—Eat At Your Own Risk." Beneath the words, I sketched a smiling skull and cross-bones. With the Coffin Star quilt wrapped up in an old pillowcase, I headed for my car.

In the pink and green flowered lobby, I ran into Van Baxter.

"Hey, what're you doing here?" he asked. Camera bags hung from both his shoulders, and he carried a long black bag that held the same portable portrait lighting that I'd lugged around countless times for Isaac.

"I teach a quilting class to some ladies who live here." I set down my own bag on the green commercial carpet. "Well, I don't actually teach them anything. I'm more a fetcher of coffee, threader of needles, and partaker of their wisdom. What's your excuse?"

"Taking some photos of Mr. Nakamura. He's turning one hundred in two weeks, and his family wanted a portrait."

"Wow, one hundred. Hard to imagine."

"He looks great. Says a glass of sake a day is his secret." He grinned at me. "I took a couple photographs of him taking a shot of his favorite beverage. Not sure his family's going to like those, but it sure made him smile."

I laughed. "Guess centenarians are a nice break from coeds and babies."

"You said it."

After a few seconds of silence, I said, "I'd better get going. Gabe'll be home soon. At least I hope so."

"I know what you mean." He struggled to move ahead of me to open the door, but his load made it an awkward dance.

"Please, let me be liberated," I said, holding the door open for him. "You can get it next time."

"Thanks. I'm all for women being liberated." He walked ahead of me through the door. The cold burst of damp air made me shiver. Outside, the sky had cleared, and the stars were silver sparks in the sky. "Like I said, I know what you mean about late nights. I've been chief cook and bottle washer quite a few nights with Lillian. I think she's growing more than a little tired of

Campbell's Tomato Soup and grilled cheese sandwiches. That's the extent of my cooking expertise."

"Lillian?"

"My mother-in-law. She had a stroke. That's why we moved here from Louisiana. A helper comes in when we both have to be gone, but it's expensive. Yvette and I try to handle the nights. But Yvette's had lots of late nights since she got this job, what with this or that case, trying to make her mark. Now there's this sniper business." His gray eyebrows moved together in irritation. Then he flushed, obviously remembering in that split second who Yvette's boss was. "Hey, I didn't mean . . ."

"I totally understand," I interrupted, shifting the quilt from one arm to the other. "That was whining from one law enforcement spouse to another." I mimed zipping my lips. "Doesn't go any further."

His expression softened in relief. "Thanks. I don't mean to sound ungrateful. When we had to move here to help her mom, we were just thankful that one of us landed a decent job. With insurance."

I smiled sympathetically. "So important at our age."

He grimaced. "Don't remind me."

"Why didn't you take Lillian back with you to Louisiana?" I flinched inwardly when I said it, embarrassed by my bold question. Spending time with the ladies did that to me, made me often forget that not everyone wanted to be as candid as we were. "Never mind. I apologize for asking such a presumptuous question. Please, forget I asked."

His Honda was parked next to my truck. He set his lights down and pushed the button on his key, releasing the trunk lid. "Don't worry about it. It's a legitimate question. Simply put, she's stubborn. She wouldn't move in with us or wouldn't let us hire anyone to stay with her or even consider an assisted living place."

"How long have you been taking care of her?"

"Almost a year. Yvette initially took a leave of absence, then realized that she'd . . . we'd . . . have to move here. That's when she applied at the department. Your husband was very kind to hire her."

"He is kind, but he wouldn't have hired her if she wasn't good," I said.

Van nodded.

"Does she have any other family to help?"

"A brother, but he's a mess emotionally and financially. Last time we heard, he was living in a trailer down in Baja California. All the responsibility is on Yvette's shoulders."

"And yours," I said, trying to be sympathetic.

He gave a curt nod, lifting the bags into the trunk.

"Maybe if you could get her down here to Oakview Terrace and meet some of the ladies in my quilt group she'd reconsider . . ."

"I wish," he said, slamming down the trunk lid.

"I'm sorry." I'd obviously hit a tender nerve.

He waited a second, then turned around to face me, his expression mild. "It's all right. I've traveled all over the world as a photographer and seen hundreds of people who have it worse than I ever could imagine. It's just not what I expected to be doing at this point in my life." He gave a wry half smile. "I suppose millions of baby boomers could say the same thing."

I nodded. "By the way, the photos you took of my goddaughter were incredible. You captured her perfectly." It seemed like changing the subject was the kindest thing I could do.

He stared at me a moment as if not comprehending my words. "Oh, yes, the bunny suit. Thanks. Not exactly Pulitzer work, but it helps pay the bills." He held up a hand. "See you round the campfire, as my dad used to say."

"Yes," I said, feeling totally stupid for bringing up Sophie's pictures. But I'd wanted to end with something positive. "Take care. You know, what you're doing, you're a hero too."

He rolled his eyes and saluted me with his keys.

It had to have been hard to uproot your whole life to go care for your wife's mother, I thought, starting my truck. I wasn't sure if I could do it. On the drive home I thought about that, whether I could leave San Celina and move to Wichita if Gabe's mother needed care and she refused to move. I loved Gabe, but that was beyond my capacity to imagine. How selfish was that?

Gabe finally came home at ten p.m., looking like he hadn't slept in a week. While he took a shower, I made him some warm almond milk, figuring he didn't need the extra stimulus from cocoa. I added a banana to his plate and some graham crackers spread with peanut butter. Kindergarten food, but comforting.

And that was what he needed right now— pure comfort. I waited for him in the kitchen, wondering briefly if Van did anything like this for his wife when she got home from a long day. He was a good guy, but after caring for his mother-in-law all evening, it seemed likely that both he and Yvette needed someone to pamper them.

"No leads?" I asked when Gabe sat down at the table. His black hair was dark and wet, the strands of gray at his temple just barely noticeable. He smelled of Zest soap and mint shampoo.

"No." He sipped the hot milk. "Do you mind if we talk about something else? Tell me about something that has absolutely nothing to do with my job."

"Sure." I sat down across from him, picked up

one of the graham crackers spread with peanut butter. "I spent most of the day driving around the county with Lin Snider." I glanced up at his face, waiting for a reaction.

"Who's that?" he asked, his expression guileless.

I told him how Lin and Amanda met at the health food store, how Lin was looking for a place to retire, had been at the folk art museum using one of the pottery wheels. During my explanation, I could tell his attention was wandering, probably thinking about the sniper.

A flood of relief washed through me. He wasn't acting. Lin Snider didn't set off any alarms.

"Then I went to Oak Terrace and helped finish another graveyard quilt with the ladies. Saw Van Baxter there."

Gabe cocked his head. "Who?"

"Detective Arnaud's husband."

"Right, I knew that. He's the photographer guy."

"Yes." I didn't mention what he and I had discussed. "How's she working out?"

"She fit right in without a wrinkle. Her experience with a similar situation to this sniper has been invaluable."

"Did they catch the sniper in . . . where was it?"

"New Iberia. Yes, they did. It was a disgruntled

oil rig worker, of all things, who was also a veteran."

"Wow, double cliché."

"No kidding."

I picked up his empty mug. "More?"

He shook his head no. "I need to get some sleep. Another long day tomorrow."

"I'll let Scout out in the back for a last trip outside, then I'll lock up."

After I'd locked the house and set the alarm, I went upstairs to our bedroom hoping to see Gabe in his usual spot. He'd turned both bedside lamps on and folded back the comforter, but he wasn't there. I walked down the hallway to the guest room.

"I think this is silly," I said, standing in the doorway. He was already under the covers, reading a magazine.

"Humor me," he said, not looking up. "At least until we catch this guy."

I crossed my arms and didn't reply.

He finally looked up. "Come here."

I walked across the room and climbed up on the bed, straddling him. I took his face in my hands and looked into his eyes. His jaw tightened briefly, then relaxed. I brought my face to his and brushed his lips with mine. "I miss you."

He kissed me back, hard enough to leave me breathless. "Give me a few more nights. I need to . . . figure this out."

Though I wanted to argue, I didn't. He didn't need more stress in his life right now. But when this sniper was caught, my husband and I were going to have a long talk about how to deal with his broken soldier's heart. About what I felt about it. Because it was about my choices too.

Until then, it appeared, we'd sleep apart. I kissed him again and repeated the words he said to me every night on the phone when we were dating, "Dream sweet."

Chapter 9

After Gabe left the next morning, I took Scout for a walk and ended up at Emory and Elvia's house. She had already left for work and Sophie was staying with her *abuelita* Aragon. Emory and I sat on the wide front porch in matching Shaker-style rocking chairs. It reminded me of his dad's house in Sugartree where he and I had spent long, hot Arkansas afternoons in the deep shadows of their Victorian front porch drinking sweet tea and eating banana pudding. This morning we drank tall mugs of Community Coffee, a regional brand he had shipped in from Louisiana.

"You and Hud," I said, sipping the strong, nutty-tasting coffee that I, like a coward—Hud always declared—blasphemed with cream and sugar. "You're determined to Southernize San Celina County."

"Detective Hudson has excellent taste," Emory said, toasting me with his red-striped mug. "At least in coffee. Community is the best caffeine delivery liquid on earth." He rocked slowly, waving at our elderly neighbors, twins Beebs and Millee Crosby, who were power walking in identical burgundy velour tracksuits and white visors.

"Signed up for cane fu," Beebs called out. "Dove and Garnet say it's the bomb. That's good, you know." She stopped, adjusted her visor, walking in place. "Doesn't mean something is going to actually blow up."

"Thanks for the clarification," I called back, winking at Emory.

"My cane is lavender," Millee sang out, matching her sister step for step. "With black lightning bolts."

"Very Harry Potter," I replied. Scout's tail thumped on the wooden porch. The Crosby twins were his favorite neighbors, as well as mine. Their treats—for both humans and canines—were always generous and homemade.

"Harry who?" Millee yelled, her arms pumping high as they continued their walk.

Emory chuckled and looked over at me. "So, how are things at home?"

I looked down into my tan coffee. "All right."

"Are you sure there isn't anything I can do to help you?"

"I'm sure."

"Seriously, Benni, this has been weighing on my mind since you told me. I want to help. If Gabe won't talk to a professional, maybe he'll talk to me."

"No," I said quickly. "Honestly, Emory, it's

better if you just leave it alone. I can handle this."

He started rocking faster, obviously agitated. I was beginning to regret telling him about Gabe. My cousin's innate instinct to protect me, probably heightened by his own new role as father, was reassuring, but I still needed to nip his desire to intervene in the bud.

"You know," I said, determined to distract him, "there is something you can do for me."

His rocking slowed to a more leisurely rhythm. "Name it."

"There's this woman I need checked out."

His chair came to a complete stop, his expression uneasy. "Why?"

I started rocking, trying to make my voice casual. "Just humor me, because this is going to sound nuts. But there's this woman who has sort of popped up in my life recently and I'm afraid . . . well, remember Del?"

"Say no more," Emory said, holding up a hand. "I still feel horrible that I wasn't there for you when that she-devil tried to break up your marriage."

I snickered. "She-devil? Shades of bad Tennessee Williams dialogue. You've been watching too many Southern B movies."

"Colic will do that to a person. You would not believe the movies they show at three a.m."

I reached over and patted his hand. "You were

in the midst of getting married when Del swooped down into my life . . ."

"Like a rabies-infested vampire bat," Emory said.

"Good analogy, but I made it through that, and it was much worse than what I'm going through now."

"So, what woman is trying to snatch your man this time?"

I leaned my head back against the smooth wood. "That's just it. I'm not certain she has anything to do with Gabe. It's just a couple of suspicious moments that, because I'm obviously emotionally raw and totally paranoid, I've worked into someone who is stalking us from his past."

"Details, my little kumquat," he said.

I quickly told him about spotting the person at the Harper Ranch, how Lin Snider just happened to meet up with Amanda and finagled meeting me, her probing questions yesterday, the fact that she drove a car similar to the one I saw at the ranch and the thing that bugged me the most, how she knew Gabe was a marine when I was absolutely sure now I'd never mentioned it.

"You know," I said, draining my mug, "actually stating my suspicions out loud makes me realize how lame my case is."

"It's understandable for you to be wary," Emory said.

"Except that situation with Del happened three years ago."

Emory nodded. "Yes, but something like that stays with a person a long time."

I set my mug down on the porch next to my chair. "Am I being totally crazy?"

He smiled at me, poking my calf with his leather house slipper. "Yes, but your suspicious nature is one of the things that makes you so intriguing. I can have her checked out, if you like. I know a discreet investigator I met when I worked at the *Tribune*." When Emory first moved here to woo Elvia, he worked for a short time at the *San Celina Tribune*. They still missed him, a friend of mine who works as the city editor, said. He always made sure there were doughnuts and bagels every day in the break room. "Give me her name and some details."

"Lin Snider. Short for Linda. I'd guess she's in her early to mid-fifties. Silver hair. Blue eyes. About five nine or five ten. Very thin."

"Where's she from . . . or rather, where does she *say* she's from?"

"Seattle area. Her dad was career military, died when she was in college. Her mom died when she was five. No siblings. On the co-op application, she put her 'in case of emergency' person as Amanda. But she barely knows her."

"That *is* odd. Like maybe she's hiding something?"

I stopped my rocker with one foot and scooted forward. "Exactly. I do have her license plate number. It is from Washington, so she wasn't lying there. It's in my purse. I'll call you when I get home."

He nodded. "I'll sic my investigator on her. Never hurts to do a little background check."

"Thanks, Emory. If nothing else, it'll just relieve my mind." I stood up to leave.

He stood up too and pulled me into a hug. "By the way, your clever little diversionary tactic didn't work. I'm still watching what's going on with you and Gabe. I'll step in if I have to."

I hugged him back and didn't answer.

"I'll call you as soon as I hear anything," he said, walking Scout and me down the steps.

Back at home, I dug out my checkbook and called the license plate number over to Emory. Then I contemplated my day. Everything was so organized with the Memory Festival that I didn't have much to do. Once I went to the folk art museum and gathered up what we'd need for the booth at the farmers' market tonight, my day was free. On the drive over to the museum, I wondered what precautions the police department was taking for the farmers' market. I couldn't be the only person worrying the sniper would strike again.

San Celina's Thursday night farmers' market had become one of the most famous farmers' markets in the state. It was actually a combination of street fair/farmers' market and became an eagerly anticipated event for tourists, locals and Cal-Poly students. Besides providing a seasonal variety of local fruits and vegetables, the weekly event offered grilled tri-tip, giant turkey legs, smoked chicken, ribs, barbecued Portuguese luinguiça sausage as well as homemade pizza, spicy carne asada tacos or Hatch green chile–cheese tamales. Then there was the deadly rich, home-style ice cream made by Cal Poly's Food Service department. Besides the food, there were craft booths, political booths, henna tattoos and face painting. And there was always some band playing—blues, zydeco, country, oldies rock, Cajun, or mariachi. Every Thursday night downtown San Celina was off limits to cars so people could wander the market on foot.

It was busy at the folk art museum with three school tours and dozens of artists working on last-minute projects to sell at the Memory Festival. I spent the next hour packing up the flyers, posters and raffle tickets for the booth tonight. We would be displaying the Coffin Star Quilt Guild's Coffin quilt and making another big push to sell raffle tickets. When I was finished, I called the ranch to see how things were going. Uncle WW answered.

"Hey, Uncle Dubya, Dubya," I said. "What's cookin'?"

"Not too much," he said, his gravelly Arkansas drawl reminding me of what Emory was likely to sound like when he was older. "The sisters are drivin' your daddy plumb crazy." Uncle WW gave a tiny chuckle. "He says he's got a plan."

That did not sound good. "What does that mean?"

I could picture Uncle WW's grinning face, the deep wrinkles pulled slightly up, one thumb hooked in the pocket of his denim overalls. "Not my place to tell you."

"I was just calling to check on everyone."

"We're all fine, now that the construction is over. The sisters are off gallivanting somewhere, and Isaac left early this morning, said something about the Bennett brothers?"

"They're the five-generation fishing family in Morro Bay. He's taking their photos for his book. I'm scheduled to interview them next week."

"Guess I'll be seeing you at the farmers' market tonight. I'm resting up. This dang ole Parker's Son disease just throws me somethin' awful, sometimes. Someone oughta smack that Parker fella and his ornery son."

I smiled at his nickname for the disease that was slowly taking away his freedom. That was Uncle WW, though. He could make a joke about anything, even his own disability.

"Are you going to be okay tonight?" The farmers' market could be a stressful place, but especially this week.

"That's why I'm home restin' up. The girls and me will be at the historical society booth tryin' to convince folks to come to the Memory Festival."

After we talked, I sat back in my chair, contemplating the second free day ahead of me. Setup for the farmers' market didn't start until five p.m., and I was caught up on all my paperwork. Though I certainly could clean house or do laundry, I wasn't in the mood for chores. Since Isaac was working on our book, I decided I should too. That seemed a better use of my time than mopping a kitchen floor that would just get dirty again.

I pulled out the green canvas L.L. Bean briefcase I bought specifically for this project and pulled out my list of interviewees. Isaac and I didn't start out with a particular agenda regarding whom we'd interview or photograph. We'd agreed that keeping it open this early in the process would allow the book to form itself. We'd let it unfold as we worked, getting inspiration from one person to seek out another. I glanced over my list. Who could I call on the spur of the moment? People were so busy, most interviews took some finagling to arrange.

I leaned back in my chair, staring at the pen-and-ink drawing of Scout romping through a field of sunflowers that Stewart Allison, one of the co-op's longtime artists, gave me last week for an early fortieth birthday present. Stewart caught the wisdom in Scout's eyes perfectly. After the Memory Festival was over, Scout definitely deserved a day out at the ranch, chasing squirrels and running through mud puddles.

Wisdom made me think of the Coffin Star ladies, specifically Miss Winnie. After finding out she had been a nurse in World War II and a prisoner of war, I thought again about how people were so often judged by their outside appearances.

Miss Winnie. Of course! Why didn't I think of it last night? She'd be a perfect person to interview for the book. Home had to really mean something special to someone who'd gone through an experience where they weren't sure if they'd ever see home again. But would she agree to it?

I flipped through my old school Rolodex and found her number. It was eleven thirty, so maybe she was already at lunch, but I took a chance and dialed her number. Miss Winnie answered on the second ring.

"Hey, Miss Winnie, it's Benni Ortiz."

"Hello, dear! You just caught me on my way to lunch. It's fried chicken day, and I want to get there while it's still crispy."

"I don't blame you. I won't keep you but a second. I have a huge favor to ask."

"Certainly. What do you need?"

I bit at a rough spot on my thumb. "I'd love to interview you for this book Isaac Lyons and I are doing. Then he'll take your photo. I . . . I want to ask about your experiences in the war and your feelings about what home means."

She didn't even hesitate. "Absolutely. When?"

"I know this is short notice, but I have this afternoon free."

"How about one thirty? We can meet in my room, and then we'll go out to the garden. It's been so rainy, and I want to take advantage of the brief sunshine."

"Thanks, Miss Winnie. I'll be there."

I hung up and gathered up my tape recorder, notebook and a couple of pens. A kernel of excitement tickled my stomach. It was the way I always felt when I was able to do what I loved the most, historical research. I loved my job as museum curator and I loved being a cattle rancher. I didn't even mind being a police chief's wife. But my passion was history, specifically oral history. It was the one thing that I felt was truly mine. I had a good feeling about this interview with Winnie Dalton. Depending on the photograph, I could imagine her being the cover of the book, though that was ultimately Isaac's decision, not mine.

Outside, the sky was a brilliant shade of blue that could only be called California blue, a blue so clear and clean with the palest shade of aquamarine hovering around the edges. Scattered across that sky were clouds so perfect they could be applying for a job modeling for a Hollywood talent agency—fluffy on top, flat on the bottom. They seemed to hang by thin piano strings moving just enough to imagine an unseen hand somewhere making them sway.

I was staring up at the performing clouds when my cell phone rang.

"Hello?"

"Have some info for my nosy cousin," Emory said.

I opened my truck's door and tossed my briefcase on the seat. "That was unbelievably fast."

"It's the computer age, my little backwoods cousin. It took my investigator about fifteen minutes. It's a short report, purely stuff she acquired from Internet sources. She could follow up, check it out in more detail by talking to folks, but I wanted to run what we have by you first. Unfortunately, I don't think you're going to like what I have to say."

I felt my stomach roil and the clouds that had looked so innocent moments ago now had tinges of gray in them. Dark gray. Like the sedan parked in front of the Harper ranch house. "What is it?"

"It is exactly nothing. She is who she says she is. Linda Snider. Born in Chicago, Illinois, in 1946. That would make her fifty-two. Divorced with no children. Both parents have passed away. No siblings. Started school in Berkeley, finished at Washington State. Major was accounting. Worked in the accounts payable department for twenty-three years for Humboldt Manufacturing. They make replacement parts for big assembly lines. You know, for companies like Nabisco and Coca-Cola. She took early retirement and still owns a condo up in Seattle. She is who she appears to be. A nice middle-aged accountant looking for a place to put down roots. Looks like your mystery balloon just lost all its helium."

I knew I should be happy that she wasn't some ex-girlfriend of Gabe's or someone else with a nefarious motive. It should have relieved my mind knowing that she was just who she said she was. So why was my gut still thick with something that felt like a huge knot?

"Thanks for humoring me," I said, not wanting to sound ungrateful. "I guess I was barking up the wrong tree."

"You sound disappointed. Seriously, you can trust this investigator. But if you want, we can dig deeper, maybe contact an investigator up in Seattle."

"No, no, that would be overkill. I guess my instincts were just off this time. It doesn't explain why she was checking out the Harper ranch . . ."

"*If* it was her."

"Touché. Maybe I'm searching for fleas when

202

it's just that the dog has an innocent itch."

"You sound more and more like Dove every day," Emory said with a laugh. "Let me know if there's anything else I can do. I have a copy of her driver's license if you want to pick it up here at the office. Betsy sent it as an attachment. I'll print it off for you."

"A private investigator named Betsy. Somehow that doesn't sound right."

"She has a master's degree in criminal justice and was a Detroit homicide detective for ten years. She didn't feel like she needed a macho name."

"Touché *numero dos*, cuz. See you tonight?"

"I'll be the one munching on a disgustingly delicious giant turkey leg."

On the fifteen-minute drive to Oak Terrace, I told myself to let this suspicion about Lin Snider go. If I'd had a therapist, I suspected what she or he would likely point out was that I was attempting to avoid the real problem in my life, a husband who was teetering on an emotional breakdown. What I really needed to concentrate on was figuring out a way to convince him he needed . . . we needed . . . professional help. The thought of sleeping in separate rooms for the rest of our lives was simply unacceptable. But being hit by my husband, even accidentally, was unacceptable too.

I found Miss Winnie in her room sitting in a

green and yellow calico easy chair. She cradled a bulky green leather photo album in her lap. The walls of her south-facing room were covered with a soft yellow wallpaper dotted with tiny white daisies. Photos of her family hung on all four walls—her late husband, Frank; her son, Billy; and her three granddaughters. The youngest granddaughter reigned as last year's Miss San Celina County at Mid-State Fair. Frank, who I remembered as a practical joker with a penchant for silly humor items like hand buzzers and whoopee cushions, died of a heart attack a few months after Jack's death.

"Hi," I said, setting my briefcase on the floor. "What have you got there?"

"I kept a few photographs and some articles about the nurses who served with me. A while back, some nice lady from back East visited me. She was writing a book about the nurses captured by the Japanese in the Philippines. We exchanged copies of pictures, so I have more now. Some of them were taken by Japanese photographers while we were in the camp, some after we were released." She patted the top of the album. "I don't think about it much anymore. Some days it seems so hazy, like it happened to someone else. But the proof is all here."

I reached for the album. "May I?"

"Certainly."

I took the album, lumpy with photographs and

articles, and sat down on the straight chair next to Miss Winnie, turning each bulky page slowly, trying to absorb the enormity of her history. She had divided her Philippines album in three sections—before, during and after her capture. Before photographs showed glamorous, classy-looking whitewashed buildings surrounded by palm trees. Inside they appeared airy and resplendent with tiled floors, sweeping staircases and tropical wicker furniture. The nurses wore spotless white uniforms and starched hats, smiling like movie stars. But in the smaller second section the photographs abruptly changed and showed blurred images of shanty-like buildings and tents, rows of people lying on the ground under a tangle of jungle trees, the nurses staring at the camera, their eyes sad and distant, their lips stoic. My expression must have given away my feelings.

"That's before we were captured, right after the war began," Miss Winnie said softly. "We had a full hospital out in the jungle to take care of our injured boys. It was hard and frightening, but at that point we were still free."

I looked up at her calm face. "I don't even know what to ask you. Isaac's book has to do with home, specifically San Celina as home." I looked down at a black and white photograph of a list of handwritten names. "What's this?"

She folded her hands in her lap. "When we

were captured in Bataan we wanted to leave a record of who we were. You know, in case they never found us. So we all signed this piece of bedsheet. See, there's my name." She pointed to her scrawled signature—Winifred Eliza Norman. "The photo was sent to me by one of the nurses I stayed in touch with. She lived in Washington, D.C., until she passed away three years ago. A historian she knew found the photo in some museum there, and he made a copy for her. I'm not sure if the original sheet survived the war."

I stared at the lists of names, trying to imagine what it must have felt like, how terrified the women must have been. "How long were you there?"

"Almost three years." Her brown eyes looked past me.

"Where was Frank?"

"He was over in Sicily, but we didn't even meet until after the war." She brushed at the crocheted afghan spread over her legs. "We became acquainted at the Los Angeles VA hospital in 1949. He was having a hernia repaired." Her laugh was a young-sounding tinkle. "I was his nurse."

"Tell me about him when he was young." I didn't want to jump right into her time in the prison camp. Talking about Frank would be a good warm-up. While she talked, I flipped through the third section of the album, photos of a triumphant return to the States and newspaper articles about their capture and time in the camps. What an invaluable piece of history. Though I was a little afraid it might sound insensitive, I wanted to make sure this scrapbook wasn't lost. After all, Miss Winnie was in her late eighties.

"I hope you're leaving this album to someone in your family who realizes its importance." I carefully closed the album, resting my hand on its cover.

"I am. The Coffin Star girls have been after me for ages to make sure that it was properly taken care of in case I unexpectedly kick the bucket." She gave another girlish laugh. "Not that it would exactly be unexpected at eighty-eight and a half. Actually, I've been meaning to talk to you about this. I want to donate it to the historical society with the assurances that it will be properly cared for."

"Miss Winnie, that's so generous of you! You know the historical society would love to add it to their collection. I'll catalog it myself. Are you sure it's okay with your family?"

She sat forward in her chair, pushing back the afghan. "Billy's fine with it. You can give him a call to set your mind at ease that you're not swindling an old lady. I think he was relieved not to have to deal with it. And my grand-daughters—they're sweet girls, but right now all they think is important is boys, shoes and those funny little things they carry their music on."

I smiled at her. "That'll change."

"One can certainly hope."

"I'll propose to the historical society that we have these pages scanned. That way I can have a copy made for your family. They have funds for this sort of thing." I would also look into having her copy bound into a book. I knew there were places that did that because Emory and Elvia had recently had Sophie's first six months of photos made into a bound book. I'd ask Emory where he got Sophie's done. No matter what the cost, I would pay for it myself.

"Take it with you," she said, waving her hand as if she were casually giving me the last two cookies in a Christmas tin.

"Not now," I said. "Don't you want to keep it so you can look at it?"

She tapped her temple. "I have it all up here, Benni. Nobody can take that from me."

I set the book on her chenille bedspread. "Now I want to ask you the questions for our book. Isaac will be in touch with you soon about taking your photo."

"Will you come with him?"

"Depends. Sometimes I do, sometimes I don't. Whatever makes you more comfortable."

She gave me a flirtatious smile. "Oh, I don't mind being alone with Mr. Lyons. He's quite the handsome gentleman."

I laughed. "Yes, he is. Did you know he was a photographer during the war? You and he could probably exchange war stories for days."

We decided to finish the interview out in the garden so she could get some sun and observe what was blooming.

"Flowers really became important to me when we were in the jungle hospital, before we were put in the camp," she said, while I pushed her wheelchair down the carpeted hallway toward the garden. "The flowers in the Philippines were gorgeous—bright red hibiscus and gardenias so fragrant you'd think you were living in a perfume factory. After a twenty-four-hour shift in the operating rooms, I'd sometimes lie on my cot and just stare at the flowers. Somehow, they gave me strength. Like God was telling me that there was hope."

We sat in the center of the garden where a stone bench dedicated to nature lovers had been placed by the local rose society. A western meadowlark landed on a stone birdbath and dipped her copy head to take a drink. Its marigold-colored belly exactly matched the knitted shawl around Winnie's shoulders.

"Are you warm enough?" I asked, glancing up at the sky, where large patches of blue argued with rapidly expanding battleship clouds. "Looks like we might get more rain soon."

"I'm fine," she said, stroking her covered arm.

"This cashmere shawl my granddaughters bought me for my birthday is surprisingly warm." She reached over and touched the bud of a tangerine rose. "You have some questions?"

I pulled out my tape recorder and turned it on. "Just a few. Once I write your story, I'll let you look at it to verify that I recorded the details correctly. Since the subject for this book is home, where were you born?" I scooted to the edge of the stone bench, resting my elbow on the armrest and holding the recorder a few feet from her.

She folded her hands in her lap. The thin diamond wedding band on her left finger twinkled in the wan sunlight. "I was born in 1909 in a little two-room house way up in north county. It's gone now. Termites ate it clean up. It was down the street from Mission San Miguel. Daddy was the foreman of a ranch up there about ten miles east. Mama came to town to stay with a friend when I was close to being due. She didn't want to be out in the middle of nowhere when I was born. She wanted another woman there. A midwife came up from San Luis Obispo to help deliver me, but I was fast. I got there a half hour before she did." She gave a delighted laugh. "I was always fast. That's why the surgeons liked me in the camp. The other nurses too, because I'd finish my work, then help them with theirs. They nicknamed me Speedy."

"How did you end up being in the Philippines?" This was off the subject of the book, but my historian's heart couldn't help delving into her incredible history.

"I was looking for adventure, so once I finished nursing school, I signed up for the army. Nothing scared me, not the meanest bull or the biggest rattlesnake." She smiled, her teeth the pale yellow of churned butter. "I killed many a snake in my younger days. When we were in the camp, I was the snake killer. Some of the other girls weren't raised out in the country, and snakes just scared them silly. Killer was another name they called me, but they weren't being mean. They appreciated my talent with the sharp edge of a shovel." Her round face, dotted with age spots, softened in memory. "The city girls had it so much harder than us country girls. We were used to doing things by kerosene light, used to critters like rats and spiders." She sighed. "I wanted adventure, and I sure got it."

"It must have been hard for your mother," I said.

"Oh, Lordy, it was. I was her only girl, you know. I had five brothers; all of them but one joined up. One in each service—army, navy, air corps and marines. The youngest, William—that's who my Billy is named for—had a bad heart, so he couldn't serve. He died a week after VJ day. But he was with Mama the entire war, helping her and Daddy on the ranch as best he could." Her eyes filled with tears. "He was a real comfort to her, especially when I was captured."

I reached over and took her hand. The skin felt like warm tissue paper. "I'm so sorry, Miss Winnie."

She pursed her lips; her head gave a small jerk. "But we made it. That's what is important. You know, I told some of my stories to that lady who was writing the book, but I didn't tell her everything. That would have taken much too long."

"Maybe what I can do is write up a bunch of questions to get you started, and you could work on it when you felt like it. I could read them, then ask you for more details where I think it's relevant. Only a little of it will be in Isaac's book, but I think it would be great to get your whole story down for people to read. People need to hear your story."

"I can do that," she said. "But, you know, the others have their wartime stories too. Did you know that Thelma Rook wrote me every day without fail the whole time I was in the prison camp? She didn't mail the letters because they probably would have never gotten to me. But she saved them and handed me the whole lot of them when I got back because she said she knew I'd be back. Took me a month to read them all. I still have them."

"Wow," I said. For oral history research, they

would be invaluable. So many of the people of her generation had passed on already, and who knows what happened to their letters, pictures and memories?

"Billy's got 'em. Bet he'd give those to you too if you asked."

"That is incredibly generous. Thank you." I clicked off the tape recorder. "You know, I love all this, but I need to focus now. What I'm here for today is something for Isaac's book, so we need to concentrate on home as a specific concept."

She shifted in her wheelchair. "Ask away."

I clicked the recorder back on. "What specifically did you miss about the Central Coast, about your home here, when you were in the prison camp?"

She pressed her lips together, thinking. "Besides the obvious things like my mama's voice and her sourdough biscuits, I guess I'd have to say that I missed the tule fog."

"Tule fog?"

"Just any kind of cool fog, actually. It was so hot there, so tropical. Now, at first, it didn't bother me. The first two months I lived there, before Pearl Harbor was bombed, it was like living in a paradise. We had a houseboy for the nurses' quarters, and he used to deliver us fresh-squeezed papaya juice every day. You could go to the movies, polo matches, bowling." She touched her cheek with her hand and, for a split second, the daring young woman with the dark lipstick returned. "Monkeys swung from vines and parrots darted through the trees with feathers as bright and pretty as circus balloons. I thought someone had dropped me off in heaven. It was so different from our ranch."

"You didn't think about home much when you first got there?"

"I thought about it, but like I said, it was the people I missed. Mama and I were very close. I'd only been away from her for the time it took me to attend school in San Francisco. When I went to the Philippines, I was unmarried and on my first big adventure. I thought I'd only be there a little while. I felt like home, my home here, was a place that would always be here."

"Once you were captured, what were your feelings then?"

"The jungle lost its appeal real quick once we had to live in it. And the poor boys who were trying to fight the Japanese . . ." She shook her head, sighing deeply. "They tried so hard. They were so *valiant*. But they didn't have a chance. We'd been caught by surprise, and no one was ready."

"How did you keep going? Specifically, how did thoughts or memories of your home keep you encouraged?"

"You know, some of the other girls and I used

to play a game called 'What do you miss most about home.' We'd play it when we were too tired or scared to sleep. Someone would start, and we could continue for hours. The memories would start out normal and expected, like I said, my mama's voice and the taste of her sweet milk biscuits. All the girls had similar memories. But we played it enough times that people began to get creative. We would try to one-up the other, see who could come up with the most original or unusual memory. We came from all over the United States, so we were learning about backgrounds other than our own. One girl from Chicago, an Italian girl with the most gorgeous black hair—Teresa Daniello, her name was—said she missed the meaty juicy Italian roast beef sandwiches her grandma made. Another girl, Bridget—oh, I don't recall her last name—she was from a Wisconsin dairy farm. She said she missed the feel of a cow's udder. Oh, we teased her about that one."

"What were some of your memories specific to the Central Coast?" That was exactly what I was looking for. Her answer might help Isaac decide how to photograph her.

She cocked her head, resting her cheek in her hand. "The smell of eucalyptus. Mama's Coty powder. Daddy's Saturday night boots."

"His boots?"

She laughed softly. "I missed the sound of the

215

shoe brush as he shined his good cowboy boots." She moved her hand back and forth over her feet. "*Shush, shush, shush.* It meant we were going to town. Mama, the boys and I went to the picture show at the Fremont Theater in San Celina, and Daddy met his friends for a beer at the Bull Corral. Then we'd all eat pancakes and sausage afterwards at the Golden Horseshoe. It was where Liddie's Café is today."

"The Bull Corral? The bar across from the Chamber of Commerce?" It was a bit of a dive bar now, where tourists poked their heads inside to see if they could catch a glimpse of a real cowboy.

"The very one. It has been there forever. Anyway, those were my original memories. Eucalyptus and Daddy shining his black leather cowboy boots. Those were the things that made me think of home." Her body seemed to sag slightly, and I realized we'd been talking for almost an hour. It was easy to forget that Miss Winnie was in her late eighties.

I stood up and brushed off the back of my jeans. "I have enough for now. Besides, I can come back another time. "Would you like me to take you back to your room?"

"That would be nice," she said, her eyes blinking rapidly. "All this remembering is making me crave a good long nap."

Back in her room, I helped her into bed and

arranged a white afghan over her legs. "I appreciate you talking to me, Miss Winnie. And I really appreciate what you did for our country. I know I'm not the first to say this, but you are a hero."

"Oh, pshaw," she said. "A lot of people sacrificed back then. It was hard, but you know, the main thing we knew is we were in it together. We had something to fight for. It sometimes felt harder when everyone got back home, truth be told. Women didn't always know what to do with themselves. The fifties were hard to figure out. So many boys were injured, and I don't just mean physically. Like my Frank, they were all jumbled up inside their heads from all the horrible things they saw and did." She sighed, closing her eyes. "But we made it through, most of us, anyway, by just tending to our homes and families, putting one foot in front of the other. When I talked to the man upstairs, it seemed like the answer always was to get back to work. There's comfort in good hard work. And remember that better times are coming. You mind that now, Benni. You and your nice husband. You'll get through all right because you're a hard worker and you don't give up. Your mama would have been so proud of you." Her eyes fluttered, and soon she was snoring softly.

"Thank you, Miss Winnie," I said softly,

touching her hand. Then I picked up the album and shut the door quietly behind me.

I was certain that Isaac would approve of putting Winnie Dalton and her story in the book. He'd have many picture possibilities with her. Maybe we could even go up to San Miguel, find the ranch where she grew up, if there was anything left of it, and take her photo there. I'd check it out first; see if it was possible to take her out there and if she wanted to go.

I drove back to the museum and locked the album in my file cabinet. Since the museum and co-op buildings had a security system, I figured it would be as safe there as at my home. First thing Monday I would see about scanning the photos and articles about the Angels of Bataan, as they were called in the articles. There was a historical society meeting next week. I had an idea that I hoped the members would like, a dual exhibit at the folk art museum and the historical museum honoring nurses throughout our county's history. Winnie Dalton and her story could be a huge part of the exhibit. More people needed to know about these remarkable women.

Excited about this new idea, my mind was already starting to write the ad I'd place in the *Tribune* asking nurses to come forward and tell their stories. It would be wonderful if we could have interviews from nurses serving in all the wars—World War II, Korea, Vietnam, the Gulf

War. I wondered if there were any nurses still alive from World War I. That seemed unlikely, but one never knew. Maybe I could convince a reporter to write an article about military nurses and as a sidebar ask any of them to contact the museum or the historical society.

I passed the historical society building, the old brick Carnegie Library, where I'd gotten my first library card when I was five years old, and noticed Dove's little red Ford pickup parked in front. I swung into the side parking lot. I was excited to run my idea by someone, and Dove was the perfect person. She and Aunt Garnet were no doubt there getting the historical society table ready for the farmers' market tonight. Wayne Burrows, my high school American history teacher, who'd retired last year, was staffing the front desk. He wore a brown and pink argyle vest and brown wide-wale corduroy pants.

"Hey, Mr. Burrows," I said. "Is Dove here?"

He straightened some brochures and nodded toward the stairs. "Down in the basement. She and her sister are boxing up the materials we're taking to the farmers' market tonight."

"Have many people asked about the Memory Festival?" The historical society had been one of the festival's biggest sponsors, memories being their forte, so to speak.

"A fair amount of inquiries." He rubbed a finger along the side of his ski slope nose. "The first time for anything is always a crapshoot. I have a feeling it'll do real well, though, which will make next year's more popular."

I grimaced. "I don't even want to think about next year. I just want to get through Saturday. Then we'll talk."

"Best laid plans of mice and women," he said, chuckling.

"Robert Burns," I called over my shoulder. "With some poetic license."

"Good girl," he called back.

Downstairs I found Dove and Aunt Garnet folding down the lids of two almost identical pasteboard boxes.

"*Hola, hermanas* Honeycutt," I said. "Do you need me to carry those anywhere for you?"

Dove looked up and smiled. "No, thanks, honey bun. One of the men is just going to walk them over with a dolly." Lopez Street, where the farmers' market took place, was only two blocks away.

"We're sharing a booth with the Paso Robles Historical Society," Garnet said. "They're setting up; we're in charge of taking it down."

"Sounds good. How are things looking for Saturday?"

"We've got our own booth for the Memory Festival," Dove said. "But don't you worry about it. We've got everything under control."

"Glad to hear that." I sat down on an office

220

chair in the corner and spun myself around a few times, then stopped myself with my toe. "Say, did you two ever hear anything about the Angels of Bataan and Corregidor?"

"Oh, my, yes," Aunt Garnet said, taping the top of her box closed. "They were famous. Back during the war, all the newspapers across the country wrote about them. We all thought they were incredibly brave and glamorous."

"Bet they didn't feel all that glamorous after eating weevil-infested rice and canned sardines for three years," Dove remarked, not bothering to tape her box. "That's if they were lucky, from what I hear."

"I didn't mean it in a bad way, Sister," Aunt Garnet said irritably. "I just meant we admired them. They were very brave."

"Yes, they were," Dove agreed. "But it couldn't have been easy coming back. After what they went through, which was more horrible than any of us could imagine, they paraded those women around like prize ponies. I bet a lot of them would have just liked to have gone straight home and take up their lives again without everyone asking them left and right what it was like, secretly itching to know all kinds of personal details they probably wanted to keep to themselves."

Aunt Garnet's face turned thoughtful. "I imagine you're right. Guess I didn't think about that. It was just such a special thing back then to see women being praised for their bravery. I think we all sort of wished a little bit that we'd been the ones celebrated." She rested her long fingers on the top of the box. "They represented what we all hoped we could be: brave and resourceful in the face of evil." She smiled at me. "I bet toy nurse's kits were probably the most popular Christmas request for little girls the year the Angels were going around the country talking about their time as POWs."

I stood up, picking up my purse. "Do you know Winnie Dalton was an Angel of Bataan?"

"I do," Dove said. "That's where I found out about how they were treated when they got home. She was proud to serve her country and tell her story, but she also told me that being asked to talk about it so much sometimes made it harder. Everyone expected her to always put on a brave face when all she wanted to do was go home, have about ten glasses of cold milk and take a long bubble bath." Dove looked down at her hands resting on the pasteboard box. "But she did her duty again, speaking wherever she was asked to speak until people's attention went to something else. Then the nurses were pretty much forgotten."

"She gave me her photo album," I said. "I mean, not me personally, but the historical museum. I was thinking we could do a special exhibit on nurses. All nurses in the history of San Celina County, but maybe military nurses could be the center of the exhibit."

"Sounds good to me," Dove said. "Once this festival is over, let's talk about it."

"Okay, I have to get going." I started out of the room, stopping when I reached the doorway. "Say, now that I have you two together and there's no one around, what's the deal with fixing up Daddy? Why, all of a sudden, are you interested in finding him a woman?"

Dove and Aunt Garnet exchanged a look that was similar to one of our ranch dogs when they were caught chasing calves.

"What are you two cooking up?"

"We only want your daddy to be happy," Dove said, crossing her arms across her blue chambray work shirt.

"He seems pretty dang happy to me," I said. "At least he was until you two started putting him up on the auction block."

"Now, we're not that bad," Aunt Garnet said primly, straightening a stack of flyers. "We merely introduced him to a select number of appropriate women . . ."

"And we've had to work darn hard at it," Dove interjected. "He's getting old. There's not that many women around his age who aren't married, dead or—forgive my French—loony tunes."

"Or have questionable families," Aunt Garnet added.

Tempting though it was, I didn't comment on the *questionable family* reference, since there were those—okay, *me*—who thought that comment could very well apply to our family.

"He's not old," I said. "He's only in his sixties."

"Too young to be alone," Dove said.

"Wait, I thought you said he was too old to find anyone . . ."

Dove waved her hands at me impatiently. "Don't you have somewhere to be? Don't you have important things to do before Saturday?"

"That's a subtle way of telling me to get lost."

"See you downtown, honey bun." She fluttered her fingers good-bye.

"Whatever," I muttered to myself, ascending the wooden stairs. Actually, she was right. I did have somewhere to be. Home. It was almost five p.m. I needed to feed Scout and hustle over to the Memory Festival booth. Some of the other committee members had agreed to set it up, but it would open at six p.m. when the farmers' market started with the blast of a loud air horn from in front of the Chamber of Commerce.

I brought in the mail, fed Scout and played ball with him for a few minutes, with promises for a longer session tomorrow. While grabbing a quick glass of orange juice, I glanced over the pile of mail I'd tossed on the kitchen table. Just the usual bills, junk mail, a couple of magazines and a white envelope with my name scrawled across it. I recognized Emory's handwriting.

The envelope contained a single sheet of paper. A fuzzy photocopy of a Washington State driver's license showed an unsmiling Linda Snider. I peered closely at her photo. It looked like her and it didn't, like many people's driver's license photos. Her hair seemed darker in the photo, though it was hard to tell from the copy. Everything seemed to match—height five ten, weight 148. She certainly weighed less now, but who ever weighed what they said on their license?

Eyes—blue, hair—gray. Her birthday was April 14, one day before Emory's. She was born in 1946. That made her twelve years older than me. She was born the first year of the baby boom. Closer to Gabe's age than mine. She'd see life more like he did, remember the Vietnam War in a completely different way than I did. To me, the war in Vietnam had been a fleeting picture on the six o'clock news. I was seventeen when the last marines left Vietnam in 1975. Boys my age, including Jack, hadn't worried about the military draft; it had ended two years earlier in 1973.

For some reason I thought of Winnie Dalton and the Angels. In a way, I understood what Aunt Garnet was trying to say in the historical museum, about being a little envious. Their courage had been tested, and they'd passed the test. Like men who'd never gone to war and would always wonder if they would have been a hero or a coward or something in between, I wondered how I would have fared had I been a POW like Miss Winnie and her fellow nurses.

Somehow, thinking about what Miss Winnie went through, what she survived, gave me hope that I could weather whatever life blew across my path.

Don't give up, she had said. Put one foot in front of the other. Tend your home. Remember that better times are coming. Get back to work. These were things I could do.

Chapter 10

"You sure couldn't tell that a crazy man with a gun was running wild in the city by this crowd," Emory said later that evening. The farmers' market had been open for an hour and a half. My cousin stood in front of the folk art museum booth gnawing on a giant barbecued turkey leg. He was right. The streets seemed more crowded than usual, and judging by the crowd's carnival mood, no one seemed especially concerned that a sniper might lurk in the shadows.

"That thing looks positively radioactive," I said, eyeing his juicy turkey leg. "No, that's not exactly the right word."

"Correct. It is not glowing." Emory took another bite and groaned with pleasure. Only my cousin, dressed in loose khakis, a dark brown cashmere sweater and a blue chambray shirt, could look classy as a Saks Fifth Avenue ad while eating such earthy street food.

"Okay, it's dinosaurian," I said, straightening a pile of Memory Festival brochures. We had already gone through four bags of Hershey's Kisses. They worked as a great draw to our booth. I just hoped the number of people who were willing to eat our free candy would translate into people attending the festival.

"Much more accurate description. You *is* a college-educated woman."

"I'm starting to get hungry myself." The clock above Marshalls Jewelry Store read seven thirty. Still an hour and a half to go before the farmers' market closed. I turned to Jan Nixon, a fiber artist from the co-op whose hand-loomed Navajo-style blankets depicting traditional quilt patterns sold for thousands of dollars to collectors. "Mind if I take a break?"

"Sure, I can handle things," she said. "I'm going to start rationing this candy, though. Some of the college boys have been here three or four times."

"I trust in your ability to fend them off," I said. She'd raised five boys on a cattle ranch in Southern Arizona before she and her husband retired to the Central Coast. If anyone could handle smart-mouthed college boys, it was Jan.

"Walk with me to the bookstore," Emory said. "I told my sweet wife I'd take Miss Sophie Lou to have her photo with Mr. Easter Bunny. I was waiting for the line to become shorter, but that doesn't look like it's going to happen."

"Seriously, Emory, more pictures?" I asked, walking with him toward the store. The three long blocks, closed off by sawhorse barricades, were as crowded as opening day at the Mid-State Fair.

Emory just grinned and licked barbecue sauce off his upper lip.

"I hope you two have another kid soon," I said. "Otherwise Sophie's going to develop cataracts from too many flashbulbs in the face."

A flash of worry furrowed his brow.

"Kidding." I elbowed his rib cage. "I'm sure that's not possible." Never, I reminded myself, underestimate the irrational worries of first-time parents.

We parted ways in front of Blind Harry's, and I kept walking, always interested in seeing what new products were for sale. At the end of Lopez Street, while standing in line for a grilled hot dog, I noticed Van Baxter's small booth. I remembered him mentioning he'd have a booth here when we spoke at Sophie's appointment the other day. Despite my growling stomach, I abandoned my spot in line and weaved my way across the crowded street. I was curious about his work, especially his career with the Associated Press and *National Geographic*. It must feel like such a letdown to take photos of college girls and babies after that kind of illustrious career.

As I made my way through the crowd, it occurred to me that he might like to join the co-op. Maybe the camaraderie of other artists would help him adjust to his new life here on the Central Coast. Tempting him with meeting Isaac Lyons might do it. Again, I sympathized with Van, thinking how hard it must be to uproot and change your life because of your spouse's family responsibilities.

The white canvas booth sat at the very end of the farmers' market, where people with less influence with the Downtown Association Committee were assigned. A hand-painted sign hung over the entrance—Van Baxter Photography. On one side of his booth was a woman selling gold and silver body jewelry. On the other side sat a booth with an astrologist who gave readings for ten dollars and sold homemade soaps. The jewelry booth and the soap-astrology booth both had more customers than Van Baxter Photography.

Van's back was to me when I walked up. He stood in front of a twelve-by-sixteen photograph of an exploding oil derrick, talking to a man in a red Hawaiian shirt. They appeared to be haggling price. I paused in front of a photograph of some young children playing hopscotch on a cracked sidewalk. Behind them loomed a tank bearing an American flag. Next to the tank stood an American soldier in a wrinkled uniform, his rifle slung casually across his chest. The caption stated simply—"Beirut." Another photo showed a lone cross-country skier standing in the middle of a snowy field pointing a rifle at some unseen target. The caption read—"Winner."

A woman who appeared to be around my age

walked up to me. She was taller than me by a head and had sorrel-colored hair pulled back in a low ponytail. She wore snug jeans and a white, tailored shirt with the cuffs rolled to her elbows. A filigree butterfly necklace was her concession to femininity. Her skin was an ivory color, finer than my freckled complexion. She, no doubt, spent less unprotected time in the sun than I did. Her features were sharp, her eyes slightly too close together but a beautiful shade of pewter.

"A good photograph actually needs no caption," she commented. Her voice was the exact opposite of her features—smooth as warm milk. Only because of my own background did I catch the slight slur at the end of her sentence, suggesting a Southern background. "My husband's words, not mine."

I stuck my hands in my back pockets. "That one of the tank and the kids. It feels like we're getting ready to take the next turn in the game. And the skier, it's . . . well . . . mysterious and . . . stunning."

She laughed deep in her throat. "The skier is me. In another, younger life I competed in biathlons." She held out her hand. "I'm Van's wife, Yvette."

"Oh," I said, taking her hand. *Of course.* Her handshake was confident. "I should have realized. I'm . . ."

"Benni Ortiz." She smiled at me, an open,

woman-to-woman smile now, no need to impress or seduce. "I've seen your photograph in the chief's office."

I grimaced. "The one on the horse. That photo totally embarrasses me, but for some reason, Gabe adores it."

Isaac had taken it at last year's roundup. I was riding a neighbor's green-broke horse. We were in a corral about a quarter mile from the herd. Isaac caught me when the brown-and-white paint horse was rearing. With my white Stetson and old leather chaps, I looked like something out of an iconic thirties Western, one of the original Pendleton cowgirls. The horse looked great, in my opinion, but I cringed at my serious and determined face. All I could think of when I saw the photo was I wasn't in control of my horse.

"A real Annie Oakley moment," she said.

Though her face appeared guileless, I wasn't sure if she was being sarcastic. Since being married to Gabe, I'd met quite a few female police officers, and I'd learned to be wary. Most female officers were great, just as down-to-earth as any of my civilian female friends. However, like some of their male colleagues, a few women became police officers for questionable reasons. They often started out with a chip on their shoulder, determined to prove they were as tough as any man was and certainly tougher than any other woman. And some resented my position as the police chief's wife. No doubt my face held a leery expression.

"I meant that as a compliment," she said quickly. "Seriously, I'm terrified of horses, so that photo really impressed me."

I felt my spine relax and made a dismissive gesture with my hand. "My dad threw me up on a horse when I was six months old. Riding is second nature to me." I cocked my head, thinking of the photograph and that she'd been a SWAT team sharpshooter. "Probably similar to the way you feel about your weapon."

She laughed, subconsciously touching her side, reaching for the spot where she usually kept her weapon. "You're right. My dad taught me to fire a twenty-two when I was seven years old. When I hear someone say they've never fired a gun, I'm amazed. I can't even imagine that."

"Was your dad in law enforcement?"

She shook her head no. "Just an avid hunter. He died when I was ten. That's when we moved from Louisiana to Santa Maria to be near my mother's people."

"I heard you were a Central Coast girl."

She crossed her arms loosely over her chest. "Half Californian, half Louisiana swamp rat. After I graduated high school and left for college in New Orleans, Mom moved to Arroyo Grande. I came back once a year to visit, eat a little Santa Maria barbecue. I do have a special feeling for the Central Coast." She didn't mention her mother's illness.

Van finished with his customer and walked over to us, his disappointed expression revealing he'd failed to make a sale. "Hey, Benni. I see you've met the better half of the Baxter-Arnaud household."

Yvette's cheeks flushed with rosy circles of color. The shine in her clear eyes as she looked at her husband told the world she was in love with this man.

"How's it going, Van?" I asked.

"Sales are slow to nonexistent, but then there's always the Memory Festival on Saturday."

"Don't worry," I said. "People tend to be a little looser with their money at the festivals rather than at the farmers' market."

"We'll have a better spot, for sure," Van said. "Luckily, the spaces were chosen by lottery, rather than seniority like tonight. I lucked out. I'll be over by the Santa Celine Mission, next to the fountain."

"That is a good place. A lot of tourists visit the mission." I was glad the committee had agreed to a lottery system in terms of deciding which vendor got which space. That way, no one could complain that certain vendors were getting special treatment.

Before we could continue, a group of women came into the booth and started asking about his photographs of Eola Bay and Port San Patricio, a few miles south of San Celina.

"I'll let you get back to work," I said, holding up a hand. "Good luck."

"Thanks," Yvette said. "We sure need it."

For a quick moment, Van's expression darkened, then turned neutral. Had Yvette realized how her comment sounded? I sympathized with Van, but I also understood her position. There had been many times I had said things that Gabe took the wrong way simply because I didn't think before the words tumbled out of my mouth. I sighed, feeling bad for them. Relationships were as precarious as minefields; there was no getting around that. And they seemed to get harder the longer you were together, not easier.

I lingered in the booth a few minutes, looking at Van's photographs. His style was emotional, intense and eclectic. He photographed everything from an exploding oil derrick to a group of protestors at the nuclear power plant to a series of shelter dogs up for adoption. The dog photographs were incredibly moving. He managed to capture their sad history with his close-ups of their liquid eyes and scraggly coats. Those might sell well as would his scenic shots. It must be hard to try to figure out where you wanted your career to go when you were used to being more controversial and important. I briefly wondered if he would be interested in coming out to our roundup next week. It might be something different for him to photograph, maybe the start of a new direction in his career.

As I stood at the front of the booth and studied one of Van's recent photographs of two elephant seals squaring off, their barrel-shaped bodies glistening, their necks arrogant and threatening, out of the corner of my eye I caught a familiar face.

In the astrology-soap booth next to us, Lin Snider studied the pastel-colored soaps. I knew I should go right over and say hello, but something in me decided to observe her without her knowledge. I edged closer to the neighboring booth, letting the thin canvas block me from Lin's view.

"That's pomegranate and lime," I heard a woman tell Lin. "My newest line."

"Smells heavenly," Lin said. "I've always loved homemade soaps, especially now that I'm older. They seem to react less harshly on my skin."

"I know what you mean," the woman replied. "Would you like some samples? I'm here every Thursday night. Are you local or just visiting?"

"A little of both. I'm searching for a place to retire."

At least she was sticking to the same story.

"San Celina's a wonderful place to live," the woman said. "Where are you from?"

"Seattle. From what I hear, the weather's

practically perfect here, despite the last few stormy days."

"Yes, it is. Say, would you like a reading? I could tell you what your astrological chart says about what's coming up in your life, maybe give you a hint about where you should settle down. What's your sign?"

Lin gave a small chuckle. "I'm not much of a believer in astrology."

The woman laughed with her. "A skeptic. Are you by any chance a Scorpio? Persistent, passionate, secretive and a bit suspicious?"

"Yes, I am! And I am embarrassed to admit that is a good assessment of me. I have nothing against astrology, it's just that . . ."

"No worries," the woman said. "Just take my card. It has my info on it—the soaps and the stars. I'm a pet psychic too, in case your puppy or kitty cat is having any issues. Diversification is the key to survival in these tough economic times."

"So I've heard," Lin said, her voice growing fainter.

I moved back, stepping deeper into Van's booth, and began flipping through a bin of five-by-seven matted photographs, my back to the street, hoping Lin wouldn't notice me.

Yvette came up beside me. "Can I help you find something specific?"

"Looking for something for my uncle," I

mumbled, hoping my voice didn't carry. "For his birthday." I grabbed a shadowy photo of the San Miguel Mission and handed it to her. "He's fascinated by the California missions. He's from Arkansas, but he lives here now." I dug into my jeans pocket and pulled out two twenties.

"Van likes them too," Yvette said, taking both the photograph and the money. "The architecture is so different from the Catholic churches in Louisiana. Van's gone to buy me a corn dog, or I'd have him sign this to your uncle personally."

"No problem," I mumbled and didn't speak again while she wrapped the photograph, not certain why I was so worried about Lin spotting me. I mean, it was logical that I'd be at the farmers' market and that we might run into each other. And she'd been perfectly normal with the astrology-soap lady, actually verifying the story she'd told me. So, why was I still suspicious?

"Are you okay?" Yvette handed me the photograph and my change. "You look a little stressed." She lowered her voice. "If it's about the sniper, please don't worry. There's a huge police presence here tonight."

"No, it's not that," I said, probably too quickly. "Actually, I just realized I've been gone from the museum's booth too long. Got to give Jan a break."

"Okay," Yvette said, tilting her head, her expression curious. "See you around, I guess."

"Definitely."

By the time I exited Van's booth, Lin had disappeared into the crowd. Ridiculously, I felt relieved, as if I'd dodged a stray bullet.

I started back toward the center of the farmers' market and the museum's booth. The crowd was dense tonight, despite the cold, misty weather. A rainstorm was definitely hovering. All we needed was for it to hold off another hour or two, then the farmers' market would be over. The last thing I felt like doing was scrambling to pack up our booth during a downpour.

After Yvette mentioned it, I did notice there seemed to be more police than normal tonight— San Celina police, county sheriff and many officers not in uniform, but whom I recognized from interagency social events. Like a dysfunctional but loving family, law enforcement officers might bicker among themselves, but they immediately united when one of their own was threatened.

Still, it didn't make a lot of sense to me to have so many officers patrolling downtown. If I was the sniper, this would be the last place I'd hit tonight. If he . . . or she were really trying to freak out the police, it would be more nerve-racking if they attacked someplace in the boonies, completely unpredictable, while all the police presence was concentrated here in San Celina.

"Hey, Benni!"

I turned around and saw Miguel, one of Elvia's younger brothers, a few steps behind me. He wasn't in uniform tonight, either working plain-clothes or just out to enjoy the farmers' market. He wore a bright turquoise and red Hawaiian shirt and blue jeans.

"Hey, Miguel. What's new? Did anyone tell you that it's, uh, winter?"

"You know me," he said, grinning. "Hot-blooded."

I shivered inside my gray sweatshirt. "You make me cold just looking at you. Everything copacetic on the streets?"

"So far, so good," he said, falling in beside me. He was about five ten and had a forty-four-inch chest, all muscle and macho bravado. He patted the side of his baggy shirt. "Great for hiding my weapon. If you knew how many people were packing tonight, you'd freak."

"Please, I don't want to know. Are you wearing your Kevlar vest?"

He put his finger over his lips. "Ruins my profile." He puffed his chest out a little. "Makes me look like I have a gut, like the old guys."

I nudged him with my elbow. "Miguel, that's so vain."

The crowds were thicker now, and a drum band had started a calypso tune that inspired a large group of folks to start an impromptu dance in the middle of the street. I stopped for a second, trying to figure out the best way through the bouncing, swaying crowd.

"Hey, are you going to see my sister anytime soon?" Miguel asked.

"We see each other every day, usually. Why?"

"I need to pick up a rosary we ordered for our mom's birthday at the mission gift shop and give it to Elvia so she can wrap it."

"So?"

"I'm leaving with some guys tomorrow to go down to LA to this concert and . . ."

"And you've messed around and haven't picked it up yet."

He grinned at me, looking for a few seconds like the five-year-old boy I used to babysit. "Want to walk with me over to the mission so I can pick it up?"

"Sure, then I'll take it to your big sis."

"Thanks," he said. "I have a late shift tonight. Eleven to seven. Then we're leaving."

"No sleep?" I commented, trying to remember when I was young enough to work all night, then leave on a trip.

He waved a dismissive hand. "I'll sleep in the car."

We tried to weave our way around the dancers, but they took up the whole street.

"Let's cut across the bridge and go around back," Miguel said. The mission was one block over on Monterey Street. Monterey ran parallel to Lopez Street. San Celina Creek meandered through the center of town and lay behind the buildings facing Lopez and in front of the mission. Over the years, the city had developed the land along both sides of the creek, turning the odd spaces into a series of miniature parks, brick-lined walkways and green spaces where people could picnic, lie in the sun, or play with their dogs or children. Bridges on the north and south ends of the creek made it easy to cut across the creek to go to the mission or the shops on Monterey Street.

It was quieter once we started walking across the long metal bridge, the sounds of the farmers' market muffled by the overgrown trees and the loud swoosh of creek water, the current stronger than normal because of the abundant rain this year.

"So," I said, when we reached the middle of the bridge, dimly lit from a streetlamp, "are you seeing anyone special? There's this new girl at the co-op and she's real cute . . ."

He turned his head to answer me, and then I heard a muffled *thump*. For a split second, his face looked surprised, his mouth a silent *oh*. He crumpled to the floor of the bridge, the metal and wood vibrating beneath my feet when his head hit metal. I dropped to my knees, screaming, "Help! Someone get help! Officer down!"

Miguel's eyes watched me, his mouth convulsing silently. Around us, I heard people shouting, water running, footsteps on the bridge. I threw my body over Miguel's to protect him.

"What's going on?" a young man shouted somewhere behind me. The bridge vibrated beneath us.

"Don't worry, don't worry," I said to Miguel, locking my eyes onto his. "You'll be okay, you'll be okay. Oh, God, please."

"Hey, do you need help?" The young man again.

I turned around and saw two teenagers—a boy in a red sweatshirt and a girl with a pixie haircut—their faces shocked, their bodies poised to flee.

"Call 911!" I screamed. "Tell them where we are. We need paramedics. Call 911. Now!"

"Okay!" the girl answered. "Wait there." She started running, the young man following her.

I pulled my sweatshirt off and laid it across his chest where blood had already seeped from somewhere in his chest.

I took his hand and said, "Help is coming. Hang in there, Miggy." His childhood nickname fell from my lips. He'd threatened Elvia and me with death if we ever used it around his law enforcement buddies. "You'll be okay."

Please, not Miguel, Lord. Please, let him live. Please, please, please.

It felt like forever, but eventually, around me,

I felt people moving, heard people yelling, shouting orders. Everything sounded muffled, like a television turned low. A white, hot buzzing in my ears. Miguel's dark-lashed eyes stared into mine, reminding me in that split second of how, as a little boy, he was always so quiet, so watchful. He would beg me to read *Charlotte's Web* to him over and over. He finally told me that he was waiting for the part where Charlotte doesn't die. To make him happy, I created an ending where she came back to life, saved by a caterpillar that was a doctor, got married, had children and grandchildren and great-grandchildren. In Miguel's version, Charlotte lived happily ever after.

Miguel could not die on a bridge out in the cold March night. Not before he even had a life. No, I thought. Not Miguel. *No.*

I bent closer, my lips at his ear. "Hold on. Don't move." His shallow breaths turned my heart to stone.

I lifted my head at the sound of a voice, someone saying something, calling my name. "Mrs. Ortiz." Dark blue filled my vision. "Don't worry, Mrs. Ortiz," the blue blob said. "Paramedics are on their way."

His hand touched my shoulder, slipped down to my upper arm, urging me up and away from Miguel.

"No," I said, jerking away. I couldn't leave. His

mother would never forgive me if I left his side. I would never forgive myself.

"Paramedics," a calm voice said behind me.

My brain clicked into rational thought. I released Miguel's warm hand and stood up. Two men in dark blue uniforms pushed past me, setting huge bags on the ground, stooping down, tearing open his shirt.

"GSW," one said, opening his bag.

"Hey, buddy," the other said to Miguel. "Don't worry. We'll take care of you." Their voices were too calm. Couldn't they see this was Miguel? Didn't they realize how important he was?

I coughed, choking on the thick liquid at the back of my throat. "He's a police officer."

"Yes, ma'am," one of them said without turning around. "We'll take good care of him anyway." Both the paramedics chuckled, their humor incongruous with their busy hands and efficient movements. But I couldn't be mad. It was their way, this gallows humor. I'd seen that same laughter in the face of death in my husband and his colleagues. I'd seen it in Miguel.

I felt a hand tug at my arm. It was a San Celina police officer. His baby face looked too young to be carrying a gun. He was young enough to be my son if I'd had a baby when I was seventeen or eighteen. Not an impossible thing.

"He's a police officer," I told the young man.

"Yes, Mrs. Ortiz, I know Miguel. We need to

move back and give the paramedics room to work."

"My husband. Someone needs to call Gabe. He's at home. He was going to watch a game, baseball, I think. No, basketball. Maybe. I don't know. I don't remember. Someone needs to call him."

"Come with me, Mrs. Ortiz," the officer said. "We need to take your statement while it's still clear in your mind. Someone's already called the chief. He's going to meet us at the hospital."

"It came from below us, I think," I said. "From the creek." My brain felt full of buzzing wasps. "Has Gabe been told? Someone needs to tell Gabe. I have to call Elvia. She's his big sister. She has to hear it from me. His mama! Señor and Señora Aragon, somebody needs to tell them. Is Miguel going to be okay? I have to get to the hospital."

The officer, whose name tag read G. Russo, said, "Don't worry, Mrs. Ortiz. Someone will take care of all that. I have orders to take you away from the scene."

"Whose orders? Where's Gabe?"

The young officer took a deep breath. Hysterical witnesses were obviously new to him, as were fellow police officers being shot in the street. What a baptism into the force. I wanted to burst into tears, pound somebody's chest, but this young man looked like he was ready to throw up himself. I swallowed hard, willed myself to stop trembling. I was the older person here. *Get a grip.*

"I'm okay, Officer," I said. "I'll do whatever you need. You're right, I need to give my statement before I forget anything. Someone can take me to the hospital afterward."

He nodded gratefully, leading me to where a half-dozen police cars seemed to have materialized out of nowhere. I was suddenly aware of chaos surrounding me—a perimeter had already been set up with black and yellow crime scene tape and dozens of officers were keeping back the onlookers. My mind flashed on Elvia, her mother, the rest of the Aragons.

Officer Russo opened the back of one of the squad cars. "You can sit here, Mrs. Ortiz. One of the detectives will be with you in a moment."

"Can I make a phone call?" Then I realized I'd left my cell phone back at the folk art museum booth with my purse. "Miguel's family . . ."

"Don't worry, Benni. They're being notified." The answer came from behind me. I turned to see Captain Jim Cleary, Gabe's second-in-command.

"Jim!" I flung myself into his arms and immediately burst into tears. I'd known him almost as long as I'd known Gabe. I didn't have to act mature and together with Jim, who'd seen situations of this magnitude many times in his thirty-year law enforcement career.

I sobbed out my terror and relief as he gently patted me on the back while holding me in a fatherly embrace. With five kids of his own, two of them daughters, he was an experienced comforter.

Once I calmed down, I leaned back against the squad car, wiping my nose and eyes with the sleeve of my flannel shirt. "I'm sorry for being so emotional."

"I wish I had a handkerchief to give you," Jim said.

"Here," another familiar voice said. "I always have one."

Hud moved through the crowd of officers and handed me a cotton handkerchief. "It's not the first time, is it, ranch girl?"

"Thanks, Hud," I said, taking it and holding it to my face, letting it absorb the salty tears.

"Here, drink this," Jim said, handing me a bottle of water. "Are you up to giving us a statement?"

I nodded, taking a long drink of water. I knew the sooner a witness was interviewed after a crime the more they were likely to remember. I wanted to do whatever I could to help catch this criminal. It was personal now.

"I know it's hard with all this chaos," Jim said, "but try to tell me exactly where you walked, what you saw and heard up to the moment when Miguel was shot."

Yvette Arnaud walked up, still dressed in the jeans and tailored shirt I'd seen her in earlier when I bought the photograph for my uncle. Where was that package now? I had no memory of dropping it.

Jim nodded at her. "This is Detective Arnaud's case. Why don't you tell her what happened?"

"Hey," she said softly, touching my shoulder. "Are you okay? Do you want another bottle of water?" She glanced around for someone to fetch one.

"No, I'm fine," I said, squeezing my almost empty bottle. "If I drink any more I'll just have to pee."

She gave a half smile. "I hear you. Why don't you just take a deep breath and tell me what you remember. I saw you run into Officer Aragon right after you left Van's booth. Take me through the last hour step-by-step. Take your time."

I closed my eyes, clutched the bottle of water and tried to quiet my mind, filter out the voices and confusion around us. I tried to recall the last half hour or so I spent with Miguel before he was shot. A sudden thought that it might be the last time I saw him caused a violent shudder to shoot through me, and I doubled over, wanting to throw up.

Yvette put her arm around me and carefully helped me sit back down on the squad car's seat, giving my shoulder a comforting squeeze. I closed my eyes and sat there for a moment, willing my stomach to calm down.

When I opened my eyes, her calm face was watching me. Hud stooped down, his hand lightly touching my knee. "Miguel's going to be fine. I heard the paramedics say the bullet missed his heart. There's some bleeding and a little damage. He might have a collapsed lung. That's serious but fixable."

I inhaled deeply, only slightly relieved to hear Miguel's prognosis. We wouldn't know for sure what was going on until a doctor examined him.

"Benni," Yvette said. "Can you tell us what happened?"

"We decided to take the bridge and cut over to Monterey Street," I said, glancing at Hud, then Yvette. "Miguel had to pick up a rosary for his mother. At the mission gift shop."

Slowly, I described our route, trying to recall every detail. I knew that often the seemingly most innocuous thing might be a clue for the detectives.

Once I'd gone through the whole scenario, she asked me to repeat it. Then she asked me to tell it a third time. My water bottle was empty now, and I was gripping it with both hands, the crinkling sound from the plastic somehow a comfort.

After my third telling, Jim Cleary stepped in. "I think we've picked her brain clean. Let's have an officer drive her over to the hospital."

I gave him a grateful look and stood up. For a moment, my legs felt numb, and I started to sway. Hud darted up and caught me before Jim could move.

"Take it easy," he said, his arm around my shoulders.

Jim called over the young officer who'd been the first to come at my cries for help. "Officer Russo, drive her over to General Hospital. Make sure she gets inside."

"Yes, sir."

"Are you going to be okay?" Jim asked.

I nodded yes, though I wasn't sure. "Do you know where Gabe is?"

"At the hospital. He called to check on you while you were talking to Detective Arnaud. He said he'd see you there."

Despite the crowds, Officer Russo maneuvered his squad car out and onto a side street. As we pulled away, I glanced up briefly and saw the hundreds of curious people. It occurred to me that the sniper was still out there. The person who shot Miguel might be standing in that crowd staring at the spectacle he or she had caused, as satisfied and sated as an arsonist who watches a forest go up in orange flames.

I hunched down in the passenger seat, turning my head, trying to ignore the gawkers. For a moment, I understood what it must feel like to be hunted by paparazzi. I felt vulnerable, scared and angry. On the drive to the hospital, using the officer's borrowed cell phone, I called Dove. If she hadn't heard about it yet, she would soon. The San Celina grapevine was as fast as a Japanese bullet train.

"Gramma?" I said.

"What's wrong?" My tone put Dove immediately on red alert. "Are you okay? Who's hurt? Where are you?"

Before I could answer, I heard her yell, "Ben, start the truck!"

"Wait," I broke in, my words tumbling over each other. "I'm fine, I'm fine. I'm on the way to the hospital, but it's not me. And it's not Gabe."

I heard her take a deep breath. In the background, I could hear my dad's gruff, worried voice. "Dove, what's going on? What's wrong?"

"Benni's fine," she told him. "So's Gabe." She came back on the line. "Why are you going to the hospital?"

"Miguel was shot. I was with him . . ."

"I'll be there . . ."

"No, wait. It would be better if you didn't. The hospital is probably a madhouse, and you'd have a hard time getting past the guards. I just wanted to let you know I'm okay. It's probably on the news right now. I gave my statement already, and an officer is taking me to the hospital . . ."

"Gabe?"

"He's at the hospital. I'll call you when we hear something."

"Honey bun." Dove's voice, as familiar and comforting to me as the wind, calmed my racing heart. "Our poor little Miguel."

"The paramedics said he'd be okay." It was a little lie, but she didn't know that. Maybe he would be. He *had* to be.

"I'll call the prayer chain," she said softly. "We'll start lifting him up. You tell Señora Aragon we're praying for her boy."

"I will."

At the hospital, we passed through two checkpoints set up by the San Celina police. A security perimeter that would rival a presidential visit had also been set up around the hospital. I glanced at my watch and realized only an hour and a half had passed. It felt like both days and seconds since Miguel was shot.

Officer Russo pulled in front of a side door off the doctor's parking lot where two police officers stood guard. After a few words with them, Officer Russo ushered me through the door. It led into someone's private office. I followed him through the office into one of the hospital's quiet, low-lit back corridors. We walked through places in the hospital I'd never known existed. In five minutes, we were in the Intensive Care waiting room. Elvia, her mom and dad, various brothers and sisters-in-law and my cousin Emory were in the room watching a news report of the shooting. A quick glance told me my husband wasn't in the room.

"Benni!" Elvia rushed over to me, Emory behind her. "Are you okay?" She pulled me into a tight hug. Emory put his arms around both of us.

"I'm fine. I would have been here sooner, but a detective had to take my statement while it was fresh. How's Miguel?" My first thought when I walked in was he had to be okay or people would have been crying.

"He's in surgery," Emory said, stepping back but keeping a hand on both my and Elvia's shoulders. "Apparently he had a collapsed lung, but the doctors seem to think the bullet passed through without any unfixable damage. They're worried about infection, of course, but he was darn lucky. A half inch to the side and . . ."

Elvia started crying, and I hugged her tighter. "Oh, sweetie, he's going to be okay. Miguel has always been a tough little nut. Remember when he fell out of the peach tree and got a concussion? He'll pull through this."

"I know," she said, her words muffled into my shoulder. "I hate whoever did this!"

"I know," I said, this time glancing up at my cousin's worried face. "How long will he be in surgery?"

"They don't know," Emory said.

At that moment, Sophie Lou, held by Señora

Aragon, let out a strangled cry. Elvia instantly released her hold on me.

"She's hungry," she said, taking Sophie from her mother. "Maybe they have an empty room I can use."

"I'll come," her mother said, glancing worriedly over at the door to the surgical unit.

"We'll come get you if we hear anything," Emory assured them.

After Elvia and her mother left, everyone found a place to sit. Ramon, Miguel's younger brother, changed the channel since the news report was over and a rerun of the television show *M*A*S*H* started playing. It showed the doctors in a bloody operating room cracking jokes, not something that any of us wanted to watch right now.

"Let's sit down," Emory said, pointing to a quiet corner away from the television set, which was now showing a basketball game. "Are you really okay? It had to be pretty scary for you." We sat down next to each other on the olive green tweed sofa.

"You know me, I'll collapse two weeks from now when I'm shopping for eggs or ice cream or something." It was how I reacted to things—days or weeks later when it made no logical sense.

"Maybe you should get checked out by a doctor," he said, taking my hand. "Your hands are as cold as a chunk of ice."

"Cliché," I said, giving him a weak smile.

"Who can be William Faulkner during a time like this?"

"I don't need to see a doctor. Who I need to see is my husband. Has he been here?"

"He dropped in for a moment right when they took Miguel in for surgery. Said he would be back before Miguel came out. I'm assuming he has someone monitoring it and keeping him informed." Emory squeezed my hand.

"He said he was worried about you, but that he'd made sure you were in good hands."

I nodded. I knew that. Once he heard I was physically okay, I didn't expect Gabe to come running to find me when he had this critical situation to deal with. Every minute counted right after a shooting. I had learned long ago that this was part of being a chief's wife. Our own personal fears and relationship would have to take a backseat until this was resolved.

I held Emory's gaze. "Did he seem all right?"

Emory's lips pressed together, a strand of blond hair falling over one eye. "He was completely calm and in charge. Same old Gabe."

I inhaled decply. "Yes, same old Gabe."

"Hey, guys," Ramon said, walking over to us. "I'm making a trip to the cafeteria. Need coffee or a soda or something?"

"Sounds good." Emory stood up and reached for his wallet.

"Got it covered, *hermano*," Ramon said, waving him back. "What do you want?"

"Black coffee," Emory said.

"Hot chocolate, I guess," I said.

After taking everyone's order, Ramon and one of his teenage nephews left for the cafeteria. Minutes later the waiting room door opened and a doctor still in green scrubs walked in.

"Mr. or Mrs. Aragon?" he said. His face was long with heavy jowls like a human equivalent of a basset hound.

"*Sí,*" Miguel's father said, standing up. "I am Miguel's father." His sons and their wives stood behind him in a semicircle. Emory and I stood behind them. Señor Aragon's gruff voice held a slight tremble. "How is my son?"

"I'm Dr. Chambers," he said. "Officer Aragon's going to be fine, eventually. It was a close call, but the bullet just nicked his lung. We have to worry about infection, of course, but he's a young, healthy man and with some time and rest should be almost good as new. I wouldn't recommend any strenuous exercise for a few months, but there's no permanent damage." He paused a moment. "He was very lucky. Another inch or two could have been a lot more serious."

No one spoke, contemplating his words for a moment.

"He can still work as an officer?" Señor Aragon asked. "He will ask me that first."

Miguel's family nodded in agreement. Miguel loved his job and would want to come back to work as soon as he could.

"No reason he can't do everything he did before," Dr. Chambers said, smiling. He glanced up at the television set. "Any news about the sniper?"

"No," said Rafael, the oldest of the six Aragon brothers. "Not that we've heard."

I turned to Emory. "I need to tell Elvia and Señora Aragon the good news. If Gabe comes by . . ."

"I'll keep him here until you get back," Emory said.

"And call Dove," I said. "I told her I'd let her know how Miguel was."

"Will do."

The hospital hallway was quiet, since visiting hours had ended an hour ago. Police officers guarded either end of the hall, and I wondered where else they were stationed in the building. Though I would never actually second-guess my husband and his work decisions, I could not help thinking—Miguel is the last one in danger right now. The sniper *already* shot him. Then again, I didn't know the whole situation, and Gabe was very good at his job.

I walked to the center nurses' station and asked where Elvia and her mom went to feed Sophie.

"Room sixteen," said a nurse wearing green

scrubs. "They . . . oh, there they are now." She pointed behind me.

I turned and saw them walking down the hallway toward me. Señora Aragon carried Sophie, so Elvia ran toward me.

"What . . . ?"

"He's out of surgery," I told her. "He's going to be fine."

Elvia crossed herself, then burst into tears. I put my arms around my friend and held her as she sobbed. Señora Aragon kissed the top of Sophie's head over and over, murmuring "*Gracias*, El Señor, *gracias, gracias . . .*"

"Can we see him?" Elvia asked.

"I didn't ask. The minute I heard, I came to find you. Your dad and brothers probably have more information."

Back in the waiting room, Gabe stood next to Señor Aragon, explaining something to him in Spanish. Seeing me, he said to Elvia's father, "*Un momento.*" He crossed the small room in two strides, pulling me into his arms.

"*Querida, querida,*" he whispered into the top of my head. "Are you all right?"

"You heard about Miguel? He's going to be okay."

"Yes, I had someone here keeping me informed. I'm sorry I wasn't there when you were questioned . . ."

I pressed my cheek into his chest, trying to

259

absorb his warmth. "I was in good hands. Jim was there. You had a job to do."

He hugged me again. "I have to go on camera in a few minutes. For the eleven p.m. newscast."

I looked over at the large black and white clock next to the muted television. It was a quarter to eleven. "I can't believe it's this late."

"What are you going to do?" he asked, glancing over at Elvia and her mother.

"I'll offer to spend the night, but I know they'll refuse. They'll probably take shifts, and the ones staying will keep everyone else informed. You know Señora Aragon won't leave."

Sure enough, a few minutes later Elvia called her family together and they started drafting a chart, deciding who was staying, who would go home and sleep, who would come back tomorrow and relieve the night watch. Neither Miguel nor his parents would ever be alone.

"I'll meet you by the rose garden in twenty minutes," Gabe said, kissing my forehead. "The interview shouldn't take long. There's not much I can do except tell them we, the sheriff's department and every agency who can spare someone are working on it. And that there's now a $75,000 reward for information leading to the capture of the sniper."

"Maybe that'll convince someone to step up and give information."

Gabe's face was shadowed, his cheekbones

stark, like they had been laser cut from a hunk of granite. "We can only hope. Right now, we don't have enough information to do much."

For some unrealistic reason, I felt guilty. "I'm sorry I couldn't be more help."

He stroked my cheek with the back of his knuckles. "Yvette said you were great. That you remembered an extraordinary amount of detail."

"It happened so fast. I hope something I told her will help.

"You never know what will be the link. Chances are this person knew this area well enough to use the woods by where you and Miguel were walking, then run down the creek bed so that it would be difficult to find any trace of him. Whoever is doing this is smart."

"What can your detectives do then?"

"There's a group of homeless people who tend to camp down by that section of the creek, so we're interviewing them. Every spare officer I have is on this. The FBI is working up a profile. The bullet they cut out of Miguel is on its way down to the forensic lab in Santa Barbara with a rush on it."

I took his hand and squeezed it, wishing there was something else I could do to help. "Good luck with your interview."

"Thanks, I'm going to need it."

Chapter 11

"Is there anything you need?" I asked Elvia a few minutes later. She sat next to her mother on the waiting room's scratchy sofa. While I was gone, the crowd of Aragon family and friends milling around in the Intensive Care waiting room had thinned considerably. "Where's Sophie?"

"Emory took her home," Elvia said. "Maria went with him." Maria was her brother Jorge's wife. "I have breast milk in the refrigerator. My nieces and nephews think it's great they get to camp out at our house." Elvia gave a tremulous smile.

I sat down on the other side of Señora Aragon, whose face was hollow-eyed from exhaustion. I touched the top of her cold hand. "Señora, you know that God and the San Celina PD are watching over Miguel. He's safe here."

"*Gracias, mija*," Señora Aragon said, her voice thick. It was probably the fiftieth time she had thanked me for being there when Miguel was shot. "I know my Miguel safe. I know *doctor* say he is fine. God is good." She clutched her ruby-colored rosary to her chest. I put my arm around her fragile shoulders.

"He's a tough boy," I whispered to her. She smelled of talcum powder and the sweet cucumber soap she liked. "A strong man. He's going to be up and teasing you again in no time."

I could feel her tremble in my embrace.

Elvia walked me to the waiting room doorway. Gabe was at the end of the hall talking to some officers. I gestured to him that I'd join him in a minute.

"Will you be okay?" I asked Elvia. Her eyes were red-rimmed, but after the initial shock, in her typical type-A fashion, she'd taken charge of Miguel's welfare.

"I'm fine. I'm worried about you, though. Are you sure you're okay?"

I gave her a crooked smile. "I'll fall apart when I can fit it into my schedule."

She touched my cheek with her fingers. "You take care of yourself, *hermana*. Try to convince Gabe there is no way he could have prevented this. It hurts my heart to see him blaming himself." Though I knew that Emory had kept his promise to me and not told her the details of Gabe's emotional struggles, this woman knew me. And she understood Latino men, having been surrounded by them her whole life.

"I'll do my best, but you know how he is."

"I'll call you tomorrow."

Our drive home was silent. I rested my hand on Gabe's thigh, wanting to say something com-

263

forting but not able to think of one single thing.

Scout sat inside the front door, his anxious expression like a mother too fretful to sleep while her teenage kids were out on a Saturday night. He accepted my neck rub and words of apology with his usual patient forbearance. His eyes seemed to say—why must you worry me like this?

"Do you want to shower first?" Gabe asked, his voice tired and hoarse.

"You go ahead. I'll close up downstairs."

He turned and went up the stairs; his back had been ramrod straight throughout our time in the waiting room, befitting his police chief role. Now I could see the slight slump in his shoulders, the defeat he felt. However, I knew my husband. By morning, his resolve would return, and no one except for me would ever know that he felt any doubt.

After my shower, I went into the guest room to kiss Gabe good night, Scout at my heels. He lay on his back and stared at the ceiling.

"Are you sure you want to sleep alone tonight?" I asked.

He didn't move. "I can't talk about that right now."

I waited a moment to see if he'd say more. "Well, good night, Friday."

I sat down on the edge of the bed and kissed his lips.

His hand slipped behind my neck and pulled me closer. I thought for a moment that I felt it tremble.

"Good night, *querida*," he whispered.

When I walked down the hallway toward our bedroom, poor Scout stood halfway between the rooms, torn between where to sleep. Finally, with a sigh, he followed me and flopped down next to my side of the bed.

"You can go sleep with him," I told him, reaching down to stroke his velvety head. "I won't be insulted."

But Scout stayed next to me. No doubt, he knew that even if he went to sleep with Gabe, he would be sent back with the admonition to "protect Benni."

I picked up my cell phone and dialed Gabe.

"Chief Ortiz." His voice was strong, in control.

"Don't you look at the screen before you answer?"

"My eyes are closed."

"I just wanted to say good night. And that I love you."

"Me too. You know, you could have just yelled down the hallway."

"That's a little too Waltons, don't you think? This is the modern version of good night, John-boy."

"Dream sweet, *querida*."

"You too, Friday."

Though I thought I'd have a hard time falling asleep, I didn't. If Gabe had bad dreams during the night, I didn't hear them. I couldn't help feeling guilty when he came into the room early the next morning and opened the closet door.

"What time is it?" I mumbled from beneath the down comforter. Rain beat on our roof in a regular, heavy rhythm most likely messing up any evidence that the police might have found in the woods by the creek. Had the sniper been smart enough to do this on a night right before rain was expected? The cold-blooded calculation of that possibility made me shiver even in my warm cocoon.

"Five thirty," Gabe said. "Sorry to wake you up, but I need to get to the office by seven. I'm going by the hospital first, to see if Elvia or her mother need anything. The nurse on duty said Miguel had a quiet night, thank God."

"That's good," I said, sitting up. "Where's Scout?"

"Downstairs. He's already gone outside and is waiting for breakfast."

"I'll get up . . ."

"Go back to sleep. I'll feed him before I leave."

The warm bed tempted me for a few seconds, but my better self won the battle, and I threw back the covers. "No, I have a million things to do to prepare for the Memory Festival tomorrow." I swung my legs out and searched for my house slippers. A gust of wind and rain rattled the bedroom windows. "That is, if the festival is still on."

His back was to me while he flipped through his shirts. "Will you cancel if it rains?"

"Depends on how hard it is raining. But I was wondering if it would be canceled because of the sniper."

He turned around, a white shirt and his darkest gray suit in his hands. "No, same reason we didn't cancel the farmers' market. We have no idea when or where or even if this guy will strike again. You can't cancel life."

"Or she," I said, wrapping my robe around me.

"Doubt it's a woman."

I shrugged, feeling cranky. "I'm just saying."

"Nevertheless," he said, opening his sock drawer. "As far as the police department is concerned, your festival is good to go."

"Then all I have to worry about is rain."

By six thirty we were both walking out to our respective vehicles. The rain had turned into a fine mist, and the normal neighborhood sounds were muted, as if a thick blanket covered the whole world.

"Don't forget to eat breakfast," I said, standing on tiptoe to kiss him good-bye. His lips were damp and salty, his mustache warm. "Two cups of coffee is not the breakfast of champions."

"There'll be food at the station," Gabe said.

"Maggie's making sure we are all eating healthy. She's amazing."

"Yes, she is. And so are you. You're going to catch this person soon."

"Let's hope so."

I contemplated going by Liddie's for breakfast, but I needed time alone to go over my schedule and the half-dozen separate lists concerning the festival. At Liddie's I was sure to see people I knew. We would start talking about the sniper, what happened last night, Miguel's condition, and then two or three hours would be gone. I did not have the time to spare today. I would probably be answering those questions ad nauseam tomorrow. A less public place for breakfast was needed.

So I decided to drive twelve miles north to Morro Bay. Though I knew a few people in town, I wasn't as well known as I was in San Celina. My chances were better for a breakfast unencumbered by curious questions.

Fifteen minutes later I was driving down Main Street in Morro Bay. Since it was a Friday morning in March—not a premier time for tourists—I had no problem finding a place to park on the Embarcadero. I walked a block enjoying the cool, damp air, watching the fishermen work on their boats. There were still a few families who made their living by fishing, though, like cattle ranching, it was becoming a part of the bucolic past in this town that was built on commercial fishing. I decided to have breakfast in a new coffeehouse called Bertie's Bad Beans. It reminded me of the coffeehouse Emory and I went to a few days ago. Was advertising bad coffee a popular trend in coffeehouse marketing these days? I went inside the pink clapboard building and was pleasantly surprised to find an extensive bakery selection. I ordered a large coffee and chose an almond croissant and a cherry turnover. Unlike Gabe, who reacts to stress by losing his appetite, I react by craving food, specifically sugar and carbs.

There were only two other people in the coffeehouse besides the young man who worked the counter. Neither of them knew me. I looked at my watch. It was almost seven thirty. I took a chance and, hoping they weren't asleep, called Elvia and Emory's house.

"Did I wake you?" I asked when Emory answered.

"We have a baby, sweetcakes," he said with a sigh. "Remember? Miguel had a quiet night."

"Yes, I know. Gabe called the hospital first thing this morning."

"Elvia came home at six a.m. after she took her mama home. Papa Aragon took over the day watch along with Gilberto and Jose. Ramon is still there. He's the only one who won't throw out his back sleeping on the waiting room sofa."

Ramon was the youngest of the six Aragon sons. "Looks like Miguel is going to be fine."

Hearing those words again, I felt my tight stomach start to relax. "Tell Elvia I'll drop by the hospital sometime today. I imagine it's quite an ordeal to get in to see him."

"Security is tight, but you shouldn't have any problems. They'll clear you at the front desk."

"Is Elvia available?"

"She's taking a shower. Want her to call you?"

"No, tell her to get some sleep. I'll call her later."

"Stay safe."

"It's not me they're after."

Once I heard Miguel was doing well, I ate my croissant and went through tomorrow's schedule, making a list of who I needed to contact today to verify details. The cherry turnover saw me through writing out tomorrow's hour-by-hour schedule. I deliberately put any thoughts of the sniper out of my head, at least for the time being. Surely, he wouldn't dare try again tomorrow?

After I finished both my work and my breakfast, I decided to drop my notebook off at my truck and take a walk through Morro Bay. The sun was just starting to peek out from behind the clouds, giving me hope that tomorrow might be rain-free. First chance I got, I'd check the forecast.

I walked down the almost deserted

Embarcadero. The sound of the ocean, the gulls, the casual shouts of the fishermen were a soothing backdrop to my thoughts. Though my mind had been occupied for the last twelve hours by the attack on Miguel, it now wandered back to Lin Snider. I felt rather foolish about eavesdropping on her last night at the farmers' market. She was beginning to be an obsession, probably an unwarranted one. Even if she did have a past with Gabe, right now, in the light of this sniper situation, it was small potatoes. By the time I reached the end of the Embarcadero and started up Bay Street toward downtown, I'd decided that once this festival was over, I was going to be mature and invite her into my office. I would flat-out ask her if she had ever known my husband. If there were something nefarious about her hanging around San Celina, I would bring it out in the open, and like mold exposed to bleach, it would fade away.

When I got to Main Street, I lingered in front of a new quilt shop that had replaced the one that closed when the owners, Tom and Tina Davis, moved to Washington State to be near their kids. The new shop—Cotton Ball Quilts—was owned by a mother and son quilting team—Judi and Rob Appell—who had taken the quilting world by storm. They'd been big supporters of the Memory Festival, donating a special quilt designed by Rob called Ocean Memories, featuring extinct and almost extinct ocean creatures. I admired the memory quilt display, glad to see the poster advertising the festival prominently placed. The quilt shop had a booth right in front of San Celina Creamery—our town's favorite ice cream parlor.

I started back down the hill to the Embarcadero and my truck, when I happened to glance in the window of Kitty's Café, a local breakfast haunt that always made the top ten lists of favorite San Celina County restaurants. There were the normal array of colorful ball caps and stained cowboy hats, ranchers and retirees being the only ones usually up and out this early for breakfast. Weather this soupy was a good excuse to go to town to chew the fat with other ag folk, an acceptable alternative to actual work.

What I saw caused me to stop in the street, my mouth open in shock.

My dad. Sitting at a window seat. His head thrown back in laughter. Empty breakfast dishes in front of him. In front of *them.* Because he wasn't alone. And the person he was having breakfast with was a woman. Who was also laughing. A woman I'd never, ever seen before in my whole life. She had bright red hair pulled back in a high ponytail. She had big gold hoop earrings. She wore a leopard print headband. Her bright green Western shirt was a paisley print, and she wore a chunky man's watch.

That was as much as I comprehended before I turned tail and headed back the way I'd come, praying they hadn't seen me. When I got to the corner, I crossed the street and went down one block. Once I was out of sight, I slowed down, feeling silly for panicking. So what if my father was having breakfast with a woman I'd never seen before? He was free to do that, right? Except my dad didn't ever have breakfast with people he didn't know. He didn't have breakfast with *women* he didn't know. Especially ones who wore leopard print headbands. What's more, he never ate breakfast in Morro Bay. Like me, Liddie's was his territory. He came to town twice a week and always ate there. The only reason he occasionally went to Morro Bay was to buy something at Cy's Feed and Seed. He did that mainly to support Cy Johnson, our neighbor. Daddy just preferred to go to San Celina.

If he was eating in Morro Bay, it was because, like me, he was trying to avoid running into people he knew.

Maybe it was because I was feeling edgy anyway, but the thought of my dad dating, something that seemed so funny when Dove and Aunt Garnet talked about it, didn't seem very humorous when I was presented with reality.

Oh, quit it, I thought. You remember what it was like when Dove dated Isaac. This isn't any different.

Except Dove didn't sneak around. She dated Isaac right out in the open for the whole world to see.

Okay, I reasoned, that was probably why Daddy decided to see this woman on the sly. We were, by no means, the type of family who stayed out of each other's business, and he didn't want everyone's two bits worth of advice.

I walked around the corner and thought about how I could avoid Bay Street and sneak back down to the Embarcadero to my truck. If Daddy wanted to keep his tête-à-tête to himself for the time being, who was I to question that? I'd drive the back road out of Morro Bay, past the golf course, and try to pretend I hadn't seen him with the redheaded woman.

Still, it had appeared that they were finished with their meal. What if they saw me? Morro Bay was such a small town and my purple truck was a beacon. I thought about this as I walked past Cy's Feed and Seed, so I decided to duck in and kill some time there, give my dad and his companion time to leave. Cyrus Johnson's parents owned one of the ranches that bordered the Ramsey Ranch. They were our closest neighbor. Cyrus, the Johnsons' only child, was a bit older than I was, so we knew each other growing up but didn't hang out in the same crowd. His wife, Love, was helping at the historical society's Vietnam War booth tomorrow. Like Gabe, Cy had served in Vietnam.

I opened the door of the red shiplap building. The familiar feed store scents of leather, hay, chicken feed and sawdust reminded me of the sweetgrass smell of summer.

Cy was alone behind the counter. He had a thick auburn beard and shaggy hair that covered his ears. Love was always after him to trim it. His red and black checked wool shirt and denim overalls gave the impression of an Irish Paul Bunyan. It wasn't an inaccurate comparison. He had huge shoulders and the stamina of a teenage boy. I'd seen him buck hay bales long after men ten years younger than him had given out.

"Well, hey," he bellowed out in the empty store. "If it isn't the heroine of the moment gracing my fine establishment."

I waved my hand in protest. "Please, I just happened to be there. All I did was yell for someone to get the police."

"You'll always be a hero to me," he said, giving a wide smile.

"Mr. Johnson, you are an outrageous flirt."

He came around the counter and gestured to the coffee area over next to the saddles for sale. "Care for a cup?"

I really didn't need more coffee, but it would give Daddy and his breakfast date time to leave, eliminating any chance of us running into each other and experiencing a very awkward moment. I guessed that he probably wouldn't be stopping by Cy's store today.

"Sure," I said, taking the coffee he poured. It was strong and thick as used motor oil. I softened it with a liberal dose of cream and sugar. "How's business?" I sat down on one of the wooden armchairs arranged in a semicircle around a potbelly stove. A rotating group of retired and active farmers and ranchers normally occupied them. "Where is everyone?"

"You missed the early crowd," he said, sitting down across from me. "They're here when I open at five a.m., waiting for their first cup and to squabble over my newspaper. Kitty's Café doesn't open until six a.m." He glanced at his large black Timex watch. "Second group should be here about ten a.m. They hang out until lunch."

I laughed, sipped my coffee. Even with cream and sugar, it was so strong that my eyes widened a little. The buzz from it would certainly keep me going today. "Sounds like you ought to charge a membership fee."

He rested his massive hands on his knees. "Probably should, but most of 'em are like me, broken-down old ranch or farm boys who just need a place to let off a little steam about how tough ag folks have it. They just sit around and tell old war stories and such. Figure it's better they commiserate here than tying one on at the local bar, maybe driving away drunk and hurting someone." A drunk driver had killed Cy and Love's only son, Tommy, so I knew this was something Cy felt strongly about.

"Telling war stories, huh? I should send Gabe down here."

Cy cocked his head, picking up my ironic tone. "Does he need to talk about being in-country? You know, we do get into talking about 'Nam sometimes. Seems to help some of the guys to talk about it."

I looked down into my coffee, my reflection small and odd-shaped from the overhead lights. "I was just kidding. Gabe keeps to himself about Vietnam."

Cy shook his head. "Mom always says that bad feelings are like an overflowing pot of oatmeal; the goop has to go somewhere."

I looked up at him. His dark brown eyes were sympathetic, and I almost blurted out everything that was going on between Gabe and me. Instead, I asked, "How are Polly and August doing?" His parents still lived on the Johnson ranch, about five miles inland. Cy and Love moved to a bungalow here in Morro Bay, and they helped at the ranch when his parents needed it.

He ran a hand over his broad face. "They're doing fine. Dad is kicking up a fuss about being at the World War II booth tomorrow, but Mom is making him do it. She even had his uniform cleaned and pressed."

"That's great. I'm hoping we see lots of uniforms tomorrow."

"Gabe going to wear his?"

I inhaled, set down my half-finished coffee. "I doubt that he'll even be there. I mean, what with Miguel being shot and the sniper still out there . . ."

"That's bad news. I'm praying it's not a veteran. We have enough bad press as it is with post-traumatic stress problems." He stared down at the dark concrete floor.

Before I could stop myself, I heard the words tumble from my lips. "Did you ever have it? Or bad dreams or . . . whatever." The minute the words came out of my mouth, I was horrified. "Oh, Cy, I'm sorry . . . that is so personal . . . what was I thinking . . . I'm so sorry . . ."

He held up a hand for me to stop. "Now, you just said what was on your mind, and you know that's how I prefer it. What you asked is a perfectly legitimate question from a friend who is married to someone who served in 'Nam." He scratched the side of his head with his knuckles. "To be honest, I didn't come back with some of the bad trauma that some guys did. I saw a little action, but not like some men." His lips narrowed, hidden by his thick beard. "But even with what I experienced, it flashes back to me at odd times. It can make me break out in a cold sweat or, as Love can tell you, talk in my sleep."

"Do you ever . . ." I stopped, not certain how to put it without giving away what happened with Gabe and me. "Do you have nightmares?"

"Occasionally. But Love can always shake me out of them. Is Gabe having some problems?"

I looked away, embarrassed and angry with myself for betraying my husband so easily. Tears burned my eyes. Desperately I tried to think of a way to extricate myself from the conversation.

"It's all right," Cy said softly. "Just remember this. He's not alone. You need to know that, and he needs to know that. I understand he's in an awkward position being a police chief, but there are ways he can get help. One of our guys goes to a great doctor recommended by the VA. He specializes in post-traumatic stress . . ."

I jumped up, sloshing coffee on the floor. "Oh, geeze Louise, I'm such a slob." I set the cup down, grabbed a handful of napkins and stooped down, trying to mop up the brown liquid. The napkins became sopping wet in seconds. There was still coffee puddled on the floor.

"It's okay, Benni," Cy said, his voice never changing timbre. "It's just a concrete floor."

I stood up, holding the wet napkins in front of me. "I need to throw this out."

He nodded at the counter. "Trash can is over there."

I threw out the wet napkins, wiping my damp palms down the sides of my jeans. What I had meant to be just a quick dodge to avoid my father and his mystery breakfast date had turned out to be an encounter with the reality of my and Gabe's situation.

"Look," Cy said, coming over to me. He laid a hand on my shoulder. "The name of Bill's doctor is Pete Kaplan. He lives over in Pismo . . ."

"I met him! Isaac is taking his photo for this book we're doing about what home means. His gramma used to be a nurse to the Dunnites way back when."

He squeezed my shoulder. "So, keep him in mind."

I nodded. "I will, though I doubt Gabe would ever agree to talking to him. He thinks that once this sniper is caught, he . . . things . . . will get back to normal."

"He could be right, but what about the next time? That's what is so insidious about PTSD. It can hide for years, and one unexpected gunshot, one car backfiring, a scent of something can bring it back."

"So, what could a doctor do?"

Cy shrugged. "I never asked Bill, but I do know that it sure made him feel better to talk to Dr. Pete. I imagine doctors have things they do, maybe even pills. That's something you'd have to talk to the doc about." He patted my shoulder, then walked back behind the counter. "You let me know if there's anything I can do, you hear?"

"I will. Right now, the most important thing is finding that sniper. I know Gabe won't do a thing for himself until that's solved."

"Then let's pray that it's solved quickly."

I smiled, knowing that he would do just that. I glanced down at his counter, thinking I should buy something while I was here when I saw the flyer.

"Are you with the right horse? Get an astrological reading of you and the horse you are contemplating buying and see if you are compatible. Free bar of homemade soap with every equine reading."

"Hey, I saw her at the farmers' market," I said, laughing. "An astrological reading to see if you and your horse are compatible?"

He laughed, his cheeks turning slightly pink with chagrin. "Yeah, I put about as much stock in astrology as I do the man in the moon, but she's a sweet lady. Buys all her feed from me and always donates money to buy food for shelter animals and to the fund we have for kids who can't afford Girl Scout and Boy Scout uniforms and dues. I figured I could spare the counter space."

"Have you had any takers?"

He chuckled. "No, but I've gotten a lot of ribbing from the fellas around the campfire." He nodded at the circle of chairs. "They say I'm a pushover."

"What do you say back to them?"

He gave a mischievous grin. "That it's a common trait in an Aries."

"Is it?"

"I have no idea. I was born in April so I used the only sign I know—mine. It was a good comeback."

I laughed, suddenly glad that I'd confided in Cy. I knew he could be trusted to keep my confidence and that he'd be there if I needed to talk to someone who might be able to tell me what Gabe was going through. "So, you and Emory are compadres. He was born on April thirteenth."

"Good month in which to be born. They say we are often very creative." He mock-polished his nails on his chest and gave a deep belly laugh. "Which might be another way of saying we are darn good liars."

It was only after I'd walked the three blocks to my truck, not even paying attention to whether my dad spotted me or not, that it occurred to me that Lin Snider also shared the astrological sign Aries with Cy and Emory because her birthday, according to her Washington State driver's license, was April fourteenth, the day after my cousin's.

So, why had she told the woman at the astrology-soap booth yesterday that she was a Scorpio?

Chapter 12

Lin Snider's error suggested one thing. She was not an experienced liar.

Gabe and I had occasionally discussed the art of lying. Years before we met, he'd worked in undercover narcotics. Gabe's life and the lives of his fellow officers had depended on him being a convincing liar. Learning to lie, Gabe said, taught a person how to spot deception in others. He maintained that people usually slipped up on the small details rather than the big ones.

"In undercover work," he'd said, "often an officer works so hard at the big picture of who their character is that sometimes he or she gives themselves away with the smallest detail. And, believe me, the bad guys are looking for that. We're lucky that most criminals are stupid, narcissistic or both. Still, one rookie I trained almost blew his cover simply by ordering the wrong kind of beer."

So, if a trained undercover agent could mess up a detail, an inexperienced civilian like Lin Snider . . . or whoever she was . . . might be able to lie about her birthday if she was *thinking* about it. But when someone mentioned your astrological sign in a casual conversation, it would be natural to answer without thinking. Especially if you weren't adept at living with an alias and you assumed no one was listening.

I drove into the folk art museum parking lot with two questions I was determined to answer. Who was Lin Snider, and why had she come to San Celina? Then there was that even more worrisome question: Should I tell Gabe? He really didn't need another problem right now, especially if it might not even be real but simply my paranoid delusion. It certainly wouldn't hurt to think about it for a few more hours before running to him. In the meantime, I would drop by the folk art museum and see how things were going.

The gift shop was busier than I expected, and there was a good-size crowd in the main gallery. We'd run an ad in the *Tribune* about the Memory Festival and our new exhibits at the museum. It had obviously worked.

"You have three messages on your answering machine about the festival," said Sally Parker, a docent who had just completed training. She was a retired art teacher who'd recently moved here from Idalia, Colorado. "I heard two of them because I was walking by your office. They sounded frantic."

"Day before the festival jitters," I said with a grimace.

"I have some spare Valium if you need it," she said, grinning. Then she brought one hand up to her cheek. "Oops, forgot who you were for a minute."

I laughed. "Don't worry, even police chiefs' wives occasionally need pharmaceutical intervention. Shoot, maybe we need it more than the average person does. I'll keep your offer in mind."

Back in my office, I listened to the messages. Thank goodness all three problems were easy enough to solve, and I did so within fifteen minutes. I leaned back in my chair, feeling smug. That feeling wouldn't last. By this time tomorrow, I'd likely be tearing out fistfuls of hair, hunting down Sally and begging for that Valium.

"Hey, Benni," a voice came from my doorway. It was Robbie, one of our Cal Poly art student interns. "There's no more room on the shelves in the big room for all the pots waiting to be fired. What should we do?"

"Let me see what I can do," I said, standing up and stretching.

Storage had recently become a problem at the co-op. There was no way for us to expand the buildings, because one of the stipulations that Constance Sinclair gave concerning the museum and co-op buildings was that they had to retain their original exterior. She felt it properly honored her ancestors, and who were we to argue? She owned the whole kit and caboodle. When the co-op first started over five years ago, there had been only ten or eleven artists, so the studios felt positively spacious. Sixty-three artists belonged to the co-op now, and though they kept most of their work at home, by necessity, works in progress often remained at the studios. That meant storage space was prime real estate.

I went into the great room where the wood-workers had built shelving along the south wall to accommodate the green ware waiting to be fired in the kiln. Each pot was supposed to have a tag inside to identify its owner.

"Let me check the shelves in the kiln room," I said.

"There's one free row," Robbie said. "Sandy just came by and picked up five of hers." Her brow furrowed in apology. "I didn't feel like I had the right to choose which pots to move."

"No problem. That's my job. I'll move a few that are waiting to be fired over to the kiln room. And I'll leave a note telling the potters to check back there if they can't find their work."

"Thanks," she said, relieved.

I grabbed a chubby gallon pot with elaborate etchings on the side. Inside, the identification tag said Lin Snider.

"Wouldn't you know," I murmured, hugging the pot to my chest.

"What?" Robbie asked. "Do you need some help carrying them?"

"No, let me do it. That way if anything is broken, it's on me."

Another relieved look. "Thanks."

I walked to the back of the building to the room that held our kiln. Many of the potters took their work to a studio in Santa Maria where there were three kilns, all bigger than ours. However, if your pot was small enough and you were not in a hurry, our price was right . . . free.

I set Lin Snider's unfired pot down on the table and inspected it closely. She'd etched miniature spider webs in one continuous strand around the belly of the pot. Around the rim, tiny spiders danced across the clay.

A quicksilver of cold ran down my spine. My suspicions gave her choice of images a whole other meaning than if she would have carved sunflowers or ladybugs. I slipped the pot on the shelf, tucking the identification tag back inside.

While rearranging the other pots, I lectured myself. So what if the woman liked spiders? That didn't mean anything. Besides, spiders always got a bad rap. They were good, not bad. At least most of the time. Dove had been telling me that since the first time I saw a spider as a girl and screamed bloody murder.

"Gardens need spiders," she had said to me. "God made them for a good reason, and even though there's some that might hurt you, as a whole, they are a heap more helpful than a cockroach or a weevil. Now weevils, there's an insect that should make a body scream. I don't think it's a coincidence that evil is part of their name."

So I diligently tried to rationalize away any underhanded motivation behind the spider motif. Maybe she was a gardener. Maybe she thought, like in quilting lore, that spiders brought good luck. For Pete's sake, maybe she just *liked* spiders. By the time I arrived home, I still hadn't come to any conclusion that gave me peace. I sat in our driveway still unsure about whether I should tell Gabe about this woman.

Because the truth remained, what exactly could I tell him? What had Lin Snider really done? I added up the charges against her in my head. She'd snooped around the old Harper Ranch. I was almost certain that had been her. She'd "accidentally" met Amanda Landry and finagled an introduction to me. By asking to rent the pottery wheel, she'd maneuvered her way into being in physical proximity to the folk art museum and, again, me. She'd quizzed me a little too much about my life and revealed she knew that Gabe was in the marines despite the fact that I had never told her what branch of service he served in. (Though it had occurred to me that his service was public knowledge, but even so, that meant she went out of her way to find out his branch of service.) What tripped her up was forgetting that she and the real Lin Snider had different birthdays. Of course, I was assuming that she'd stolen someone's identity. Her driver's license photo was indistinct and her weight way off, but the same could be said for many people's license. Were these facts enough to alert Gabe? Especially when he had a situation much more important to worry about?

My brain's defense and prosecution still debated the dilemma while I brought in the mail, flipped through it, fed Scout, washed the kitchen counter, and turned on the heater so our chilled house would feel welcoming when Gabe finally arrived home tonight. The more I argued my reasons to investigate her, the more flimsy they sounded. Like the calculated plot of a television crime show, it felt like I was trying to force the clues to fit the scenario. Still, it niggled at me enough that I decided to walk down to Emory and Elvia's house and run it by one of them.

I knocked on the door of their Victorian. When no one answered, I opened it and stuck my head inside. "Hey, any Aragon-Littletons in the house?" I knew there were or the door would be locked.

"Kitchen," Emory yelled back.

He was standing in front of the stove stirring something that smelled buttery and delicious in a large cast-iron frying pan.

"What're you cooking?" I asked, peering over his shoulder at the now almost translucent onions, celery and chopped fresh garlic.

"My famous Cajun Kitchen Sink Soup for Miguel. This is just the base. There's the good stuff." He nodded over at the counter to a pile of shrimp, scallops, diced smoked ham, cooked chicken, okra and tomatoes.

"Looks delicious." My cousin's Cajun soup, learned from Miss DeLora True, the woman who raised him back in Arkansas after his mama died, could convince even a vegetable phobic like me to eat healthier.

"There'll be enough to share. Just mosey on back here in a couple of hours with your empty pickle jar."

We smiled at each other. That was exactly how Miss DeLora used to store her soup.

"I might do that. Gabe will be late again tonight, no doubt."

He turned to look at me while the vegetables continued sautéing. "Hear anything about the sniper?"

I shook my head no and leaned against the black and white speckled granite countertop. "How's Miguel? Gabe called this morning and was told he'd come through the night well, but I haven't heard since." I assumed he was doing okay or someone would have called my cell phone or tracked me down.

"He's doing great considering he had a collapsed lung. Elvia said he was already complaining about the hospital food. That's why I'm

290

making the soup. He's not on any special diet."

I grabbed a piece of smoked ham and popped it in my mouth. "Then he must be okay. How's Mr. and Mrs. Aragon doing?"

"Both are hanging in there. Mama Aragon's already made him and half the nursing staff her magic flan."

"Yum. I'd agree to minor surgery for her flan."

He turned the heat down low on his Viking stove and wiped his hands on the white tea towel tucked into the waistband of his jeans. With two long steps, he was across the kitchen and opening their Sub-Zero refrigerator. Their house might be Victorian, but their kitchen was pure Williams-Sonoma. "You and the chief are in all kinds of luck, sweetcakes. She left a big bowl of flan for y'all. Said the chief was probably missing his mami's flan."

"Wonderful, though I'm not sure Kathryn made flan." Gabe's mother was Anglo of the Pennsylvania Dutch persuasion; his father was Mexican. Until she retired, Kathryn had been a teacher, a working mother who didn't happen to be the homemaking type. "But I do know his *tía* in Santa Ana did."

Emory handed me a clear Pyrex bowl covered with plastic wrap. The top of the flan was the color of ripe wheat, the bottom rich amber. The caramel on the bottom would become a silky, delicious topping when I flipped the bowl over. I don't know what Señora Aragon put in it, but it was so addictive it had made more than one adult unabashedly lick their bowl as if they were five years old.

"This will be just what Gabe needs tonight," I said.

"Mama Aragon's exact words," Emory replied, turning back to his pan. He scraped the softened onions, garlic and celery into a five-quart stockpot.

"I want to run something by you."

Emory disappeared into the walk-in pantry. "Keep talking," he called, his voice muffled. "I'm listening."

But I waited until he came back out holding three boxes of Trader Joe's organic chicken stock. "I'm not sure what to do."

"About what?"

I set the bowl of flan on the kitchen table. Inside this warm kitchen filled with the comforting smells of butter and chicken stock, my worries about Lin Snider seemed silly and self-involved. A sniper was targeting San Celina police officers, a dear friend of mine had been one of his victims and I was concocting a mystery about a woman who was simply looking for a place to call home.

Still. Her small lies and evasions bothered me. I inhaled deeply, feeling completely paranoid, and then told Emory my latest suspicions about Lin Snider.

He listened patiently while I reeled off the list of reasons I thought this woman was up to no good. When I finished, he waited a beat or two before answering.

"Frankly, I don't think you have enough information at this point," he said, stirring the soup. "Certainly not enough to bother Gabe. That's my two cents minus inflation, which makes it worth about a quarter of a cent."

"You're right," I said miserably. "But it also seems wrong to do nothing. I mean, what if . . . what if . . ." My mind searched for a scenario that would justify my reasoning. "What if Lin Snider is the sniper!"

The statement caused Emory to turn and look at me in surprise. The idea was so preposterous that it could be true.

He shook his head and laughed. "Maybe if this was an episode of *Murder, She Wrote*." He peered down into his soup pot. "Or *Saturday Night Live*."

"It's not that crazy. Gabe's best SWAT sharpshooter is a woman."

"How old did you say this woman is? And what kind of shape is she in?"

He had a point. About the age, anyway. "She's fifty-two according to her driver's license. If it is *her* driver's license." I laid my hands flat on the table, studying my fingers. "She does look around that age. I guess she's in okay shape. A little on the thin side. She kind of looks . . . delicate?"

"In shape enough to go running through a creek bed lugging a rifle?"

"I heard Gabe say Miguel was shot with a .22. They aren't that heavy. I know she can shoot. Her dad was a hunter, and he taught her."

He arched one eyebrow. "You have to admit, it's reaching. A female sniper? There can't be too many of those."

"But it's *possible*. Don't be a chauvinist."

He turned his back to stir his soup, giving an annoyed grunt. "I'm cooking dinner for my working wife and will probably get up twice during the night to feed my baby girl and change her diaper. Your accusation is just flat-out mean."

"Boo-hoo," I said, laughing. "But, you're right. I'm making . . ."

"Roux with store-bought margarine."

"When isn't margarine store-bought?"

"Forget my lame analogy. I'm trying to support you in this, but unless you come up with something more substantial, all's I'm sayin' is, I think you shouldn't oughta bother your stressed-out husband with it."

"And I'm tellin' you that you are right, dear cousin. But I'm still going to keep my eyes open."

"As well you should. As well we all should."

When I got home a few minutes later, the blinking answering machine informed me that in the hour I'd been gone, two people had left messages.

"Honey bun," Dove's voice demanded. "I need a list of all the single women at the co-op who are over the age of fifty. Garnet and I are running out of possibilities, and that computer dating business is nothing but a scam. We are not getting the cream of the crop, in my opinion. Call me as soon as you hear this." She'd called me at six forty-five p.m.

The second message was from Daddy.

"Benni, girl, get me a rope," was all he said. The time was about a half hour after Dove's. Men's voices murmured in the background. Was he at the Farm Supply? A bar somewhere? The bus station? Maybe he was going on the run. Then shouldn't he be asking for a suitcase, not a rope?

I put the flan in the refrigerator and considered the myriad things Daddy could have meant by his comment. Did he want a rope to hang himself, Dove, Garnet, the ladies they were forcing on him? The possibilities were endless.

Like Dove's message, I decided ignoring it was the better part of valor. I had enough emotion on my own plate to contend with tonight. I puttered around the house, folding clean clothes and playing ball with Scout, waiting for Gabe.

At eight thirty, I became hungry and contemplated walking back to Emory's for some of his soup but decided to make a grilled cheese and tomato sandwich instead. After my lonesome dinner, I settled down on the sofa to watch TV. What felt like minutes later, Scout's happy bark woke me. The front door opened, and Gabe walked in. I glanced at the television. The eleven p.m. news had just started.

"Hey," I said. "Anything new?"

"No," he said, tossing his jacket on the chair. "I'm beat."

"Are you hungry?"

"No, I'm fine."

"How about some hot cocoa?"

"That sounds good."

"Señora Aragon made you flan."

That brought a tiny, half smile to his face. "I'll have some tomorrow."

While he took a shower, I changed my mind and made him warm almond milk. More soothing and conducive to a peaceful night's sleep.

It was waiting for him when he came down wearing sweatpants and a white T-shirt, his black hair glossy from his shower.

"Almond milk," I said, pointing to the mug next to his brown distressed leather recliner. "I'm going to take a shower."

"Thank you, sweetheart. I'll be down here watching Leno. 'Jaywalking' is on right now."

"Your favorite," I said, hoping the comedy routine would relax him, make him forget things, if only for a few minutes.

By the time I came back downstairs, he was

296

stretched out in the recliner, asleep. Scout lay on his side next to Gabe's chair, snoring in tandem. I quietly turned off the television and covered Gabe with a quilt. Then I went around the house clicking off lights and locking up. After I finished, I found my travel alarm, set it for five a.m., then lay down on the sofa and pulled a wool blanket over me. Though it wasn't our bedroom, at least tonight we'd be sleeping in the same room. That was good enough for me.

His moan woke me like a gunshot. I bolted up, trying to focus my eyes in the dim light. Scout stood next to the recliner, alert but silent.

"It's okay," I whispered to Scout, then went to Gabe. He thrashed in his sleep, his fists clenched tight.

"Gabe," I said, keeping my voice a normal tone. He continued twisting and moaning, caught in that nightmare place. Angry Spanish words tumbled from his lips.

"Friday, wake up!" My voice raised an octave. Though it went against every instinct I possessed, I stayed out of his physical reach.

"No!" Gabe yelled suddenly. "Stop! No! There, there . . . no, no, no . . ."

Before I could stop him, Scout barked, then moved closer to Gabe.

"Scout, no." I grabbed his collar and pulled him back. He strained against my hand, sixty pounds of dog ready to defend me if he thought I needed it.

"Gabe!" I yelled his name as loud as I could.

Gabe bolted up, his eyes wide and unseeing. In the dim morning light, he looked gaunt and old.

Scout's bark turned to a low growl.

"No, Scout," I kept my voice firm, calm. "It's okay." I placed my free hand on his neck and massaged it. I glanced around, looking for something soft to throw at Gabe, to jolt him from his dream.

"Gabe!" Scout tensed under my hand.

"I'm awake." His voice was sharp, angry. He pulled the recliner upright, staring at me with bleary eyes, finally seeing me. He turned on the lamp. In the soft glow of the light I could see sweat glisten on his upper lip, drip down the side of his neck.

"Gabe, you were . . ."

"I know." He stood up and left the room without another word. His footsteps on the stairs were slow, heavy. I heard him walk into the master bathroom and slam the door. Minutes later, the shower came on.

The mantel clock said four-thirty. Underneath my hand, Scout whined softly.

"Sorry, boy," I said, letting loose of his collar. "I bet you have to go outside, don't you?" I let him out into the backyard and started a pot of coffee. I'd planned to get up at five a.m. anyway.

There was a festival committee meeting at six a.m. inside the historical museum, our designated command post. I needed to run by Stern's Bakery and pick up the muffins I'd ordered. The muffins, coffee, energy drinks, sodas, fruit platters and energy bars I'd stock in the historical museum's break room would hopefully sustain the committee through this long day.

After sticking some canned biscuits into the oven, I went upstairs and dressed for the day, glancing out our bedroom window. The sun was now a hint of pink on a cloudless horizon. *Thank you, Lord.* I dressed in dark blue Wranglers, an old long-sleeve T-shirt and an off-white fisherman's knit sweater Aunt Garnet knit for me. Though it didn't look like rain, according to the weather report last night, it would be a chilly day. The shower had stopped, and no sound came from the bathroom. I considered knocking but decided to give my husband the space he needed.

While reaching for my watch on my bedside table, I saw the envelope containing Lin Snider's driver's license. I pulled it out again and looked at the photocopied picture. I studied it closely, thinking again how it both looked like her and didn't.

Before I left, I made a quick call to the Intensive Care waiting room phone to check on Miguel. Ramon answered with a groggy "Yeah?"

"Hi, Ramon, it's Benni. Sorry if I woke you. Just want to know how Miguel is doing."

"No worries," Ramon said, giving a loud yawn. "Doc says he's doing good. Mama's crazy to get him home so she can nurse him back to health."

"Anyone else there?"

"Nah, I told everyone to take off. They're all old and looking kinda wretched."

I chuckled. Ramon was still in his early twenties while some of his older siblings were in their mid- to late-thirties. "You are such a rock star."

"Nah, just tougher than the rest of them. Oh, Sam came by last night. Said he'd be back today."

Sam, Gabe's son, had been down in Southern California helping his mom get settled in her new condo in Newport Beach. She and her second husband had recently divorced. Sam lived and worked at the Ramsey Ranch when he wasn't attending Cal Poly where he was, at least for the moment, studying culinary arts.

"Dove said she called him about Miguel." I guessed she'd also told him about the sniper attacks. Gabe and his son had come to a better place in their relationship where Gabe didn't try to control him as much and easygoing Sam cut his by-the-book dad some slack. Personally, I thought Gabe should have called his son and told him what was going on, but that was Gabe. It never occurred to him to clue Sam in, which probably was part of their relationship problems.

"Say hey to Miguel. Tell him I'll drop by as soon as this Memory Festival is over."

"You're up way early."

"The festival starts at nine a.m., but I have a meeting with my committee in . . ." I glanced at the bedside alarm clock. It was five thirty-five. "Yikes, twenty-five minutes. Are you in a booth today?"

"I'll be helping record oral histories in the Everyone Has a Story booth at one p.m. I'm getting extra credit for it for my history class." Ramon was a senior at Cal Poly . . . still. He'd changed his major four times in three years, much to his parents' consternation. He was, according to Elvia, enjoying the social aspects of college way too much.

"Okay, see you at the festival."

The bathroom door opened and Gabe came out, toweling his hair. Two places on his face were bleeding from his shave, unusual for him.

"Hey," I said. "There are biscuits in the oven. They should be ready by now. Want me to make some gravy?"

He shook his head. "Biscuits are quick. I need to get back to the office."

I wanted to suggest he try to get more sleep. The blue-gray circles under his eyes looked like old bruises. But right now, sleep was the enemy. "There's a meeting at six a.m. at the historical museum. After that, I'll be cruising the festival all day. I'll have my cell phone on."

He blinked twice, draping the blue towel around his neck. He looked at me a long moment, then said, "I'm sorr—"

Before he could finish, I was in front of him, my hand over his mouth. "No, don't. There's nothing to apologize for. I think . . ." It was on the tip of my tongue—*I think you should see someone.* As if he knew what I was about to say, his expression grew cold, halting my words.

"I'll call you during the day," I said, laying my head against his bare chest. It was warm and damp and his heartbeat steady. "Is there anything we should do? I mean, what should I tell my workers to do if the sniper tries again?"

His sigh was deep, filling his chest. "If you hear shots, find cover. Call 911. That's about all I can say. We'll have a lot of police there, not that it seems to matter to this person."

I kissed his damp chest, then looked up at him. "Called the hospital and Ramon answered. Miguel's doing good. Oh, and Sam's back in town. He went by the hospital. Gotta run. I'm already late."

"Maybe I should have called Sam. But I didn't want him to worry."

"He's a big boy now." I patted Gabe's chest. "Be careful, Chief. I love you. Don't forget the biscuits."

"I won't. *Te amo, querida.*"

I swung by Stern's, picked up the muffins and was only five minutes late to the meeting in the basement of the historical museum. All fifteen committee members were there as well as Dove and Aunt Garnet.

"I'm so glad you two are here," I said, hugging Dove, then Aunt Garnet. "If I make it through this day without having a stroke, it'll be a miracle."

"You'll be fine," Aunt Garnet said, handing me a mug of coffee.

"We'll be patrolling the festival with our canes," Dove said.

"Us too," called out the Crosby twins, holding up their colorful canes. "That sniper better not get near the festival today, or he'll have us to contend with."

"Our whole class will be out there," Dove said. "Thirty-six of us."

"Thanks, I think." Thirty-six seniors with cane fu skills they were dying to use were too much for me to contemplate this early.

I quickly went over my lists, reminding everyone where they were supposed to be and what they were supposed to be doing.

"I'll be traveling between the booths all day. You all have my cell phone number, so call me if you need anything. The Cal Poly history depart-ment and many of the history students are also there to help you. They are all wearing purple

T-shirts with Memory Festival Volunteer in big white letters on the back. Their job is to help with moving things, unpacking, getting water or food, whatever you need. Each of you has booths assigned for you to supervise, so tell your people about the volunteers. Utilize them. They are all getting extra credit for participating in this event."

I checked my clipboard. "Okay, that's it for now. Have fun, and to quote one of my favorite cop shows, 'Let's be careful out there.' "

As the rest of the committee started leaving to check on the booths under their jurisdiction, I perused the muffins, settling on a cherry-almond. I would give myself ten minutes to eat it and drink another cup of coffee before heading into the fray. The antique clock hanging over the snack table said seven fifteen. The festival started at nine a.m. I inhaled deeply, letting it out slowly, trying to calm my jittery stomach. Everything would be fine.

I felt a familiar hand rubbing a circle on my back.

"Honey bun," Dove said. "How are you doing?"

I took a bite from my muffin before answering. "Fine."

"Don't talk with your mouth full," she said automatically, though her tone was light. "Are you sleeping all right?" Her sharp blue eyes searched mine.

"Sure," I mumbled around a mouthful of muffin.

"You look right tired."

I swallowed, then took another bite. "Big day. Got up early."

"Don't talk with your mouth full."

I wrinkled my nose at her and, like when I was a kid, opened my mouth to display my half-chewed breakfast.

"You're a bad girl," she said, pinching my cheek gently. Then her warm hand moved to my chin, caressing it even while holding it steady so I couldn't look away. "Whatever you're going through, you know you can always come to me, don't you?"

I nodded, swallowing. The cakey wad stuck for a moment in my thick throat. "I know, Gramma. Everything's okay. I promise." Though I longed to tell her what was happening, I also didn't want Gabe diminished in her eyes. A fierce part of me wanted to protect him, even from someone who loved him as much as Dove did.

I could smell the flowery scent of her Coty face powder, a smell as familiar to me as my own. "Liar. But you'll tell me when you're ready." She gave my chin a tiny shake. "See you round the flagpole, Sadie." It was how she used to say good night to me when I was a little girl.

"Yes, ma'am."

By eight thirty, I'd toured all the booths, taken

305

care of numerous last-minute problems and now stood on the top step of our outside amphitheater near the mission, where the children's storytelling marathon would take place. Blind Harry's Bookstore, the San Celina County Library and the Central Coast Storytelling Guild sponsored the all-day event with storytellers performing every half hour. Though it was still a half hour before the festival officially began, I could already tell the storytelling area would be a popular stop. Parents and kids were already filling the amphitheater seats. I bought a cup of hot chocolate from a vendor's first batch and watched the final preparations for the storytelling marathon.

In the grassy area next to the amphitheater, Memory Mountain, a local scrapbooking store, presented a free "make it and take it" scrapbooking class for kids where they could have their picture taken with their favorite storyteller and make a scrapbook page. Storytellers mingled with the crowd. They were dressed as pirates, fairy godmothers, railroad engineers, Native Americans, cowgirls and cowboys, farmers and zookeepers. There was even a man dressed as a dinosaur.

"Looks like fun," someone said behind me. "And that hot chocolate looks delicious."

I turned and faced Lin Snider. She was dressed in dark jeans, a maroon sweater and a navy wool jacket. My mind flashed back to the person who had walked through the ranch house a few days ago. He or she had been wearing a dark blue jacket.

"Are you a fan of Elvis Presley?" I blurted out.

Her blue eyes widened a moment before she regained composure and smiled. "He was never my cup of tea. I'm more of a Beatles fan. Why?"

My heart fluttered in my chest. What was I thinking asking her that? I sipped my cocoa and asked, "Which storyteller do you think the kids will like best?"

She contemplated the eclectic group of story-tellers. "I'd guess the pirate for the boys and the fairy godmother for girls. But that's just what my . . ." Her words stopped abruptly, and she coughed daintily into her palm. "What my choice would have been at that age."

A group of kids ran in front of us, accidentally bumping me. Hot chocolate sprayed down the front of my sweater.

"Dang it!" I jumped back, holding the paper cup of cocoa in front of me. "Slow down!" I called after them.

She dug through her big leather purse and produced a packet of tissues. "I hope your sweater will be okay."

"Thanks," I said, taking the tissues and dabbing at the fist-size stain on the corner of my sweater. "I should remember how crazy kids get at these things."

She cocked her head, studying my face. "So, this must be a nightmare for you. All these kids, I mean. Not like the peaceful life you and your husband are accustomed to. Does it make you glad you never had any?"

I stared at her a moment, thinking, What an odd remark. "It's not a nightmare at all. I'm glad a lot of kids are here. That's sort of the point."

She stuck both her hands into the pockets of her jacket. "I'm sorry, that was rather insensitive. I should know better. People always assume that those who don't have children are irritated by them. I . . ." Her voice trailed off.

"Not having children of your own doesn't make a person a children-hating ogre," I said stiffly. As another childless person, she should have understood that. The older I became, the more I was annoyed when people assumed things about me before knowing whether their opinions had any basis.

I shrugged, still a little irritated. "It's okay." I glanced down at my watch. "Wow, it's almost nine a.m. The festival is good to go. You enjoy yourself, okay?" Right at that moment, I needed to get away from her and the worry she'd brought into my life. I turned and started walking toward the mission.

"Benni, I have a question," she called after me.

I turned back around, hoping I didn't look as impatient as I felt.

"You're really busy today, so I understand if you can't answer right away, but I'd love another couple of hours on the pottery wheel. Do you know if it's free tomorrow?" Her face looked almost desperate.

I do not know what came over me, except that in the last few years, with my unexpected and totally innocent forays into crime solving, I had developed a bit of a criminal mind.

"What a coincidence!" I said, faking enthusiasm. "Actually, it is free at noon. I just had someone cancel last night. How long would you like?" I actually had no idea if a wheel was open, though there was a good chance that the Sunday right after an event like this the co-op studios would be empty. But even if the wheel was booked, I was ready to beg, bribe or mug someone to make sure Lin would be using that wheel. Because during that time, I was going to finally discover if she was someone for me to worry about. I would find a way into her motel room in Morro Bay.

"Two hours?" she asked.

"No problem. I won't be there, but someone else will."

"I sure appreciate it. My good fortune."

I smiled at her, feeling a bit like a grifter. "Yes, it is."

While I watched her walk away, I heard someone come up behind me. It was Evangeline

Boudreux, D-Daddy's daughter and a longtime member of our co-op. "Oh, your friend found you," she said.

I looked up at Evangeline. "What?"

She pointed at Lin. "The lady in the peacoat was asking after you."

"She was?"

"Well, asking about you. I was helping Princess Perfecto set up her scepter-making supplies, and your friend kind of just started talking to us. She said she'd seen me around the co-op. I guess she's a new member?"

"Not actually. She's renting the pottery wheel. She's a friend of Amanda's."

Evangeline mimed wiping sweat from her brow. "Glad to hear that. She was asking some odd questions, and I wasn't quite sure what her motives were."

I felt my breathing slow down. "What was she asking?"

"Oh, just whether you ever participated in the children's art activities and if you seemed to enjoy it."

"That is odd."

"Yeah, I thought so too. I almost asked her if she was investigating you to be a foster parent or something." She flipped a strand of dark curly hair from over her left eye and laughed. "Are you?"

I gave a forced laugh, hoping Evangeline

wouldn't notice. "It would be news to me. Did she ask anything else?"

Evangeline shook her head no. "I told her that *you* were the one who not only designed all our children's programs, but that you harassed people for donations and you finger painted along with the kids. That seemed to make her happy. Why do you think she was asking?"

"I don't know, but thanks for the good report."

After Evangeline walked away, before I forgot, I called the folk art museum and asked one of the docents to check tomorrow's schedule for the pottery wheel.

"I need to know if it's free from noon to two p.m." Waiting, I fidgeted from one foot to the other. Finally, the docent picked up the phone in my office.

"It's free all afternoon."

"Thank you. Would you please write in Lin Snider?"

"Sure."

After I arranged Lin's session, I shoved my mounting worries about who she was and what she wanted to the back of my mind. Would I really break into her motel room tomorrow? Right now, I was ready to do so, especially after hearing how she'd questioned Evangeline about me. But would I be so gung ho tomorrow? Well, like Scarlett, I'd think about it then.

I stopped off at the historical museum and

managed to wash away the worst part of the chocolate stain. I considered taking it off, but walking around in this cold weather wearing only a long-sleeve cotton T-shirt wasn't appealing. The rest of the day ran so smoothly I kept looking for the Oz-like tornado on the horizon. But Mother Nature was kind and benevolent, presenting us with a breezy, if cold, day. A few storm clouds lingered far enough away that I wasn't worried . . . much.

"Please, not until six p.m.," I murmured more than once while glancing at the distant pewter-colored clouds.

If attendance was the only thing that counted, the Memory Festival appeared to be a success. People's spirits were high, and there was an equal amount of laughter and emotional tears. Though their presence wasn't obvious, I recognized quite a few San Celina police officers. Many of them were working plainclothes detail. It relieved me, despite knowing that if this sniper decided to attack again, the officers might not be able to stop it from happening.

I took photos at every booth to record the fair's technical aspects so next year's chairperson, which I was determined would not be me, would have an idea what to expect and how to plan.

At the historical society's oral history booth people were asked to fill out a "Where were you and what were you doing?" questionnaire about their memories on various common incidents in our country's history like the bombing of Pearl Harbor, John F. Kennedy's assassination, the murder of Martin Luther King Jr., the *Challenger* explosion and the death of Elvis Presley.

Down on Lopez Street, the VFW's booths, which emphasized military memories, took up almost a block. There were so many men in eclectic uniforms milling about that you would have thought someone was filming a movie. The background music of Tommy and Jimmy Dorsey and the Andrews Sisters caused more than one older couple to break out in spontaneous dancing, much to everyone's delight. A wiry man in a World War II leather bomber jacket and a chevron cap pulled me into a quick jitterbug, maneuvering me with expertise. He had no doubt been quite the ladies' man in his time. Or maybe still was.

The Vietnam and Korean war veterans seemed a more casual group, more sober than those of World War II, maybe because their memories were less softened by time. Some men dressed in immaculate uniforms, others with long, shaggy hair wore tattered camouflage military jackets with purple hearts pinned to their chests. The music from their CD players was more familiar to me, though I'd been in elementary school during most of the time they were fighting in Vietnam—Iron Butterfly, the Beatles, Led

Zeppelin's "Stairway to Heaven," even the song "Last Train to Clarksville" by the Monkees.

At the Vietnam War booth, a woman with short auburn hair wore dark green fatigues and shiny black combat boots. Two pairs of scissors were tucked into her shirt's front top pocket and pens filled a pocket on the upper part of her left sleeve. She wore a stethoscope around her neck and was talking to three teenage girls dressed in almost identical tight narrow-legged blue jeans, black Nikes and midriff-baring sweaters in bright sixties prints showing peace symbols and doves.

"You were only twenty-one when you went to Vietnam?" one girl exclaimed. "That's, like, so young! I'm nineteen! That's, like, only . . ." She turned to her friends, her glossy mouth open. One ear was rimmed with tiny gold and silver earrings.

"Two years older than you," the woman said. She appeared to be in her early fifties with sun-roughened skin. Her shirt had the last name, Bennett, written over her breast. She gave a high, quick laugh that didn't reach her dark eyes. "I graduated nursing school only two months earlier. I wanted to get away from home. I wanted to be on my own. I wanted adventure." Her laugh was more cynical this time. "Boy, did I get adventure."

"Was it, like, scary?" one of the girls asked,

sipping from her sixty-four ounce Taco Bell drinking cup.

The woman nodded. "Very scary."

"Like how? Did you, like, get shot at? Did you see gross stuff?" The girls exchanged looks, poked each other and giggled.

"Our hospital came under fire many times. Yes, there was lots of gross stuff." She rubbed the side of her nose and glanced over at me.

"Did you kill anyone?" the tallest girl asked. She wore her blonde hair long and straight and parted in the middle. She thrust one hip out in an arrogant stance. "My dad protested against the war. He, like, told me that people who went to Vietnam were not all that smart. That they totally wasted their lives."

Her words made me gasp.

"Britney!" one of her friends exclaimed. "You're such a mean girl." Then she giggled and shoved Britney as if they were kindergartners.

The woman looked calmly at the girls, her expression neutral. "It was gross beyond your imagination," she said, her voice as unemotional as if she were reading from an instruction manual. "There were maggots and rats and snakes and lice. There were times when I couldn't see the floor because it was covered in sticky blood. Did you know blood was sticky? It reminds me a little of maple syrup."

One of the girls gagged. Blonde-haired Britney just stared, openmouthed.

The woman continued as if she were talking about a day the beach. "I saw hundreds of boys die, screaming, full of maggots, their guts spilling out of them like spaghetti from a jar. There were piles of bodies and trash cans filled with amputated legs. That's what we did with the legs, you know, throw them out. What else were we going to do with them? Boys burned by napalm stank and screamed and cried for their mothers and they died in the few minutes it took me to type their blood. Then we just moved on to the next one. Because there always was a next one. Vietnam was hot and sticky and dry as dust and dirty as shit and it was the most beautiful land I've ever seen. When I got home, people thanked me by spitting on my shoes and calling me a baby killer. I didn't kill babies. On my days off, I went to orphanages and took care of babies. I immunized them and cleaned their sores and I rocked them to sleep. There are men walking around today who are here because I helped save them. The boys who went to 'Nam did so because they were told it was the right thing to do for our country. It was a war started by men who were forty years older than the boys carrying the guns. Like most wars, it was just a pissing contest between old men with naive young men and women paying the ultimate price. Oh, and just for the record, your dad is an ass."

Behind the shocked, sputtering girls, I started slowly clapping. In seconds two men in marine uniforms and a woman dressed in a World War II WAC uniform joined me. Then the rest of the small gathered crowd joined in. While we applauded Nurse Bennett, the young girls walked away, cursing under their breath.

"Good on you, as my grandma used to say," one of the silver-haired marines said to the nurse.

I stepped closer to the nurse. "More people should hear those things."

The expression on her face was rueful now. She fingered the stethoscope around her neck. "I'm kind of sorry I got so graphic. They're just girls. I should know better than to go off like that."

She peered at the badge around my neck that read Memory Festival Chairman. A hand came up to her mouth. "Shoot, are you the one in charge of this festival? I am so sorry. I guess that wasn't exactly the kind of memories you were expecting . . ."

"Stop," I said, holding up my hand. "It's exactly the kind of memories this festival is about. This isn't just the *good* memories festival. All memories are legitimate. Those girls were spoiled brats who needed to hear your story. And I totally agree that girl's dad *was* an ass."

She gave a sad smile. "You love someone

who served in 'Nam." It was a statement, not a question.

I nodded. "My husband was a marine. He was there in '68 and '69."

"Where?" one of the marines asked.

"I don't know all the places, but he's mentioned Khe Sanh. He was there at the end of the siege. April of '68, I think. He was only eighteen."

"That was some bad shit," the marine said.

"Is he okay?" the nurse asked.

"Mostly." There seemed to be knowledge in her liquid brown eyes, as if she had seen through our closed window shades and witnessed his agony.

She took my hand and squeezed it. "Good luck. He's fortunate to have you on his side."

I stared into the face of someone who got it, who really understood. "He was injured there and because of a nurse, because of many nurses, he eventually came home. Thank you."

"Semper fi," she replied. "I'd do it again. All my guys, well, they were special." She smiled. "I mean it. I'd go again, if only for them."

During my rounds, I stopped to sign my name to the Memory Quilt, sponsored by the San Celina Quilt Guild and the Alzheimer's Association. It was a huge Log Cabin design that had places for eight hundred people to sign their names, more if they used the plain muslin back. The Alzheimer's Association booth was surprisingly upbeat with purple balloons and free grape Tootsie Roll pops. They sold greeting cards created by the memory impaired. I bought a set made from a painting by a man named Lefty. It showed a purple and red cowboy boot filled with brown flowers. The juxtaposition of the colors made me smile.

Next to their booth was the official Memory Painting, sponsored by the Central Coast Plein-Air Society. Using acrylic paints, people were encouraged to paint a two-inch section on the large six-foot-by-six-foot canvas. The finished painting would be displayed in the Arne Nybak wing of the San Celina Art Center. Arne Nybak had been one of our most famous regional artists. His daughter, Christine, owned Tea and Sympathy, where I'd given Elvia her bridal shower.

In one booth, sponsored by Deck Connors and promoting his newest business, Backdrops, people were photographed with their favorite object. They were given a free five-by-seven of the photograph and a discount coupon for a photo session at Backdrops. I expected to see Van Baxter there, but Tiffany Connors was helping in the booth, obviously pressed into service by her father.

The booths for each decade—1900 through 1990—were especially fascinating. They featured clothes, books, gadgets and advertising from each decade. A group of Cal Poly history students, those not working security, sponsored each booth.

The memory garden booth presented by our local nurseries and the Farm Supply made me want to start a memory garden filled with pansies, sunflowers and roses to remember my mother. There were booths promoting memory stones, flag cases and condolence lamps. One of my favorite booths was Kitchen Memories, which sold kitchen gadgets from every era. The Day of the Dead booth demonstrated how to make an altar in honor of your loved one. It even sold little sugar skulls and cookies in the shape of tombstones.

Though the Parkwell Mortuary's tombstone booth should have been a little depressing, it was actually interesting with its clever display of funny tombstone sayings. Mel Blanc's "That's All, Folks!" and "Here Lies Ezekial Aikle. Age 102. The Good Die Young." My favorite was "I Would Rather Be Here Than Texas" which I photographed so I could tease Hud with it. The explanation of the tombstone was the deceased's ex-husband was buried in Texas.

It was no surprise that the booths celebrating the passing of pets were popular. They sold pet reliquaries and hand-blown glass urns gorgeous enough to sit on anyone's mantel. In one booth, ashes, fur or a small photo could be sealed in silver and gold lockets. You could even have your dog or cat's paw print made into a pendant or charm.

Along with our usual food vendors selling tri-tip steak sandwiches, hot dogs, turkey legs and pizza slices, we chose vendors that sold food the committee felt represented old-fashioned memories—a root beer float booth, cotton candy, a penny candy store filled with Walnettos, jelly mints, Fizzies, chicken bones, Necco Wafers, Bit-O-Honey, Mary Janes, wax bottles and sassafras drops. There was a popcorn ball vendor, a saltwater taffy booth and a booth selling hot chocolate and marshmallows.

The hot chocolate booth was also selling doughnuts made by the home economics department of San Celina High School. That was where I found Dove and Aunt Garnet.

"Put that back," Aunt Garnet was saying to Dove, who was reaching for her favorite, a chocolate doughnut with sprinkles. Though they'd been getting along wonderfully up until now, the fact that Uncle WW was pretty much doing okay and Daddy was avoiding them and their matchmaking meant all they had left to do now that the festival was rolling along was pick at each other.

"Mind your own beeswax," Dove said, taking a big bite. Aunt Garnet had been getting on Dove to lose a little weight. Dove, at five feet nothing, wasn't fat but was definitely on the chubbier side of the equation. Aunt Garnet, despite being from the exact same gene pool, had four inches on Dove and weighed about twenty-five pounds less. The thing was, I had no doubt that Dove was in better shape. She'd worked on a farm or ranch since she'd been married to my grandpa, and once Aunt Garnet got married at eighteen, she had become pure city mouse. Truth be told, Dove could probably outrun, outride, outwork and certainly outlast Aunt Garnet.

"Do you realize how much fat and sugar is in one single doughnut?" Aunt Garnet said, pulling a banana out of her pocketbook.

"Do you realize that I don't give a hootenanny?" Dove answered. No one stood between Dove and her doughnuts. "Wrap me up that orange one to go." She contemplated the selection a moment, then added, "And two maple bars."

"Dove!" Aunt Garnet exclaimed. "That's just pure bingeing. I read about it in *Reader's Digest*." She gave the teenage girl selling the doughnuts a stern look. "Don't you dare sell her one more doughnut."

"Ignore the old biddy," Dove told the girl. "Add that jelly one."

Aunt Garnet's face was horror-stricken, as if Dove had said, "Barbecue me that cute little bunny rabbit while you're at it."

"Sister," Aunt Garnet said, "all I have to say is what would Jesus do?"

Without missing a beat Dove said, "Oh, please, God understands overeating. I'm betting Jesus binged once or twice in his life. We have no idea *how* much he ate at the Last Supper. Our Lord *was* under a lot of stress."

With Aunt Garnet sputtering a shocked and incoherent reply, I decided it was time for me to move along. I walked the length of Lopez Street, found everything going smoothly, so I headed over to the Mission Plaza.

I stopped by Van Baxter's booth to see if sales were going better than they had been the other night.

"How's business today?" I asked.

"Much better," he said. "I think the sun coming out might have loosened people's hold on their wallets." He grinned at me, then held up a finger that he'd be right back when a female customer asked him a question about a photograph showing the silhouette of a young woman on skis at the foot of a mountain. A rifle on her back mimicked the line of the skeleton trees.

"That's my wife," I heard him tell the customer. "She was training for a biathlon." The woman decided to buy the photograph for her sister.

"How far did your wife get in her training?" I asked him after he finished the transaction.

He wiped one hand down the side of his brown cargo pants. "She was good. Probably could have gone to the Olympics."

"What happened?"

"You know, her mom got sick, my job got hinky, money . . ." He shrugged.

"Life intervened," I said. "I totally . . ."

Before I could finish, a loud rat-tat-tat made me jump. The screaming was like a horrible flashback from a few days ago. I froze in place, my head telling me to move but my body feeling thick and slow.

"Get down!" Van yelled, shoving me to the ground.

I hit the ground with a jarring thump, my hip sparking with pain. But the pain revived me, and I fumbled for my cell phone, punching 911. Two uniformed officers ran past Van's booth. My mind went into overdrive—where were Dove and Aunt Garnet? Were the shots near the amphitheater? Was another officer shot? Would they catch the sniper this time?

"Nine-one-one, what's your emergency?" the dispatcher said.

"Shots fired at the festival downtown."

"Already reported, thanks," she said, hanging up.

I started to stand. "I have to go see what's—"

"No!" Van said, pulling me back down. "It's safer here."

In that moment I spotted a young girl, not more than four or five, running across the grass, screaming. I pulled away from Van and headed toward her. When I heard another pop-pop-pop, I slid across the wet grass, caught the girl's heel and pulled her to the ground. I instinctively curled my body around hers.

"Ashley!" I heard a woman scream.

I lifted my head slightly, keeping the girl's head pressed into my chest. People were running for cover into the mission gift shop, the chapel, behind walls and trees, though no one had any idea where the shots came from or if anyone had been hit.

Beneath me, the little girl trembled and whimpered. "Mommy. I want my mommy."

"Lie still, sweetie," I said, keeping my voice calm and steady, though I felt like crying myself. "We'll find your mommy."

Seconds later I heard D-Daddy's voice over a handheld PA system. "It's okay, folks. Just some kids and firecrackers. It's okay."

I slowly sat up, still holding the little girl, who was crying hysterically now. Her mother, a young woman who seemed barely out of her teens, dashed up to us. "Ashley, are you okay?

"Thank you, thank you," the mother said while I helped her brush grass and dirt off Ashley's pink corduroy. "We were at the cotton candy booth and I turned my back and then the shots started and she lost sight of me and ran and . . ." The mother herself was two seconds away from complete hysteria.

"It's okay," I said, putting my arm around her gangly shoulders. "She's okay and so are you. It was just firecrackers. Look."

I pointed to the activity about twenty feet away. Four plainclothes and two uniformed officers had surrounded three very scared-looking teenage boys. We watched while they handcuffed them and walked them toward a cruiser parked in front of the historical museum.

"Jerks," the young woman said.

"Are you sure you're okay?" I asked her.

The woman nodded, clutching her little girl to her. "Yes, we're fine."

"Okay, don't let this ruin your day. Don't forget to go paint a square on the Memory Painting."

"We won't," the woman said. "Thank you again."

I caught up with D-Daddy. "Walk through the festival with the PA system and reassure people for as long as you think necessary. I want to find Dove and Aunt Garnet, make sure they're okay."

"Saw them over at the historical museum," D-Daddy said.

Trailing behind the officers and the boys, I circled wide around them and ran across the museum's grass. Dove and Aunt Garnet stood on the top step rubbernecking.

"What in heaven's name is going on?" Aunt Garnet said. She looked at the front of my sweater. "And what happened to your sweater?"

I looked down at the beautiful sweater she'd made me and felt sick. My slide to catch the fleeing girl had added mud and grass stains to the hot cocoa stain. "Some idiot teenagers decided to shake everyone up by setting off firecrackers, and I had a mishap with a cup of cocoa and a scared little girl."

"Hooligans," Aunt Garnet said, patting her hair. "I hope they send them right up the river. Give me the sweater. I'll take it home and get the stains out."

"Typical teenage boys," Dove said, rolling her eyes as I pulled off my sweater. "They just don't *think*. Or rather they think for about two seconds and not always with their brains." Dove, having raised three teenage boys, was a little more tolerant of their craziness than Aunt Garnet, whose only son had been a mild-mannered boy whose favorite pastime was reading Isaac Asimov and playing chess.

"Still, they need to be severely reprimanded," Aunt Garnet said.

"Oh, Sister, they will be, I'm sure, once their mamas hear about it."

We watched as the boys, who looked around fourteen or fifteen, were helped into the backseat of the police car.

"I hope it doesn't cause people to leave the festival," I said with a sigh. "D-Daddy's going around with his portable PA and reassuring everyone. Maybe I should go by all the booths and do the same."

"I'll come with you," Dove said. She turned to her sister. "I'll meet you back here in about an hour. Do you want me to bring anything from any of the food booths? A doughnut, perhaps?" She grinned wickedly.

"You are a disgrace," Aunt Garnet said but smiled back. "Don't worry about your sweater, Benni. I am the queen of stain removal."

"She is, indeed," Dove said.

While my gramma and I walked toward the plaza, I asked, "Are you and Aunt Garnet doing okay?"

She waved her hand. "Pshaw. We're just frustrated and taking it out on each other. It's your daddy we're really annoyed at. He is just flat-out avoiding us."

"Gee, for the life of me, I can't imagine why."

"Do I hear sarcasm?" She pinched my upper arm.

"Maybe Daddy doesn't *want* a woman in his life." I thought about the red-haired woman with the leopard headband in Kitty's Café. *Maybe he already has one.*

"Okay, I'll lay off Ben for a moment and concentrate on you. What's going on between you and Gabe?"

I kept walking and didn't look at her. It appeared that the little firecracker incident hadn't scared the crowds away. Everything looked like it did an hour ago. "We're fine."

"Huh."

"No, really."

She grabbed my upper arm and pulled me toward a bench next to the creek. "You look about as happy behind that phony smile of yours as a duck in a desert. Now sit yourself right down and tell me what's going on, or I'm going to go directly to the chief himself and ask."

I sat down hard on the stone bench. "Please, don't call him. Gabe is under enough stress. He's just having nightmares, and we're both having a hard time sleeping. I think this sniper thing has rattled him. We're handling it." I stared down at the tips of my dirt-smudged boots. I'd scraped one toe when I hit the ground in Van's booth.

"Is there anything I can do to help?" she said, placing her hand in the middle of my back.

I swallowed hard, wanting to lay my head on her chest like I did when I was a child. But I wasn't a child anymore and this wasn't her problem to solve. "I can handle it. We'll be fine." I said the words, but I couldn't look at her. If I did, I knew I would burst into tears, and I couldn't afford to do that right now. I had to be strong.

"Okay," she said softly, reaching her arm around me in a hug. "But, remember, don't become weary in doing this good thing. In the right time, if you don't give up, God promises you will reap a harvest."

"Yes, ma'am," I said.

"And, honey bun. Trust your heart. It'll tell you what to do."

I rested the side of my head on her shoulder for just the tiniest moment, swallowing my tears. "I'll sure try."

Chapter 13

The Memory Festival concluded at five p.m. without any further excitement. At four thirty, Tiffany Connors took a break from her father's booth and interviewed me for the evening news. When I dressed that morning, it never occurred to me that I would be on television or that my beautiful fisherman's knit sweater would be out of commission. I bemoaned those facts later that evening while we watched the eleven p.m. news and Gabe massaged my aching feet.

"Look at my hair!" I said. "My French braid looks like I slept in it for three days. Look at what I'm wearing!" Front and center on the television screen was a T-shirt that I'd never have chosen to be interviewed in. It had been a gift from Emory last Christmas. Across my chest in bold, black letters it whined—"I Feel Like a Banjo 'Cause Everyone's Pickin' on Me."

"You look cute," Gabe said, his fingers kneading the ball of my right foot.

"Yes, cute is exactly the professional image I was going for. Oh, right there. Yes, yes!" I gave a loud, dramatic groan. "That feels better than sex."

"Thanks a lot." He tickled my instep.

"Stop, stop, stop!" I struggled to pull my foot away. He laughed, held tight and then started massaging my left foot.

When he hit a particularly sore spot, I groaned again. "I just meant right at this moment it feels better than sex. Don't get your Jockey shorts all in a wad."

"Tell me, Mrs. Ortiz," Tiffany said on the television. "Do you think we'll be having a second Memory Festival next year?"

"I have no idea," the TV me replied, looking wild-eyed. "Any volunteers to head the committee can contact me at the Josiah Sinclair Folk Art Museum." I grinned at her, looking a little maniacal. "Are you busy, Ms. Connors?"

She gave a practiced chuckle. "I'll leave the memory making up to you. This is Tiffany Connors for KSCC signing off."

"Sky King, over and out," I said, leaning my head back and closing my eyes.

"I loved that show."

"Me too, though I actually saw the reruns, whereas you are so old you probably saw the original episodes."

He good-naturedly slapped the bottom of my foot. "The last original episode ran in 1954. I was four years old. *I* saw the reruns too."

"Well, excuse me, Mr. Trivial Pursuit," I said, laughing. "I pined to be Penny King and have

Daddy change his name to Sky. I used to bug Daddy about getting an airplane. I had visions of us flying over our cattle herds in a spiffy little Cessna."

When the news was over, I turned off the television, and we were quiet for a moment. Bedtime had definitely become awkward between us. I contemplated whether I should mention Dr. Kaplan, how he seemed like a nice man and, even more important, was recommended by Cy Johnson, whom Gabe respected. But something inside warned this wasn't the right time. Trust your heart, Dove had said. My heart was saying, *Keep your trap shut . . . for now.*

"What happened to the boys who set off the firecrackers?" I asked, trying to ease the discomfort between us.

"All three were fifteen years old, so we scared them a bit, then called their parents. They weren't bad kids. None had records. They were just being squirrely and used some very poor judgment, considering the situation right now."

"For a few seconds there, it really did scare people. This sniper has the county on edge."

"The reward is up to $100,000. Deck Connors put up $25,000 himself."

"Really? That's interesting. Wonder why?"

He patted the top of my feet before lifting them off his lap. "No doubt he plans on running for some political office."

While Gabe took a shower, I let Scout out for his final constitutional. Normally I'd walk him up and down the street, but with the sniper out there, I heeded Gabe's request and stuck to our own backyard.

I took my shower, wrapped my robe around my still-damp body and padded across the hallway to the guest room. Gabe was already under the covers, hands laced behind his head, staring at the ceiling.

"Quarter for your thoughts," I said, sitting down on the edge of the bed.

"Not worth that much. Just trying to relax. Tomorrow will be another stressful day."

I gave him a long kiss. "Want company?" I murmured against his lips. Both his hands were already tangled in my hair.

He pulled back slightly, his eyes dropping down to my chest, hidden by my robe. "Benni, I don't want . . ."

I touched his lips with one finger. "Shhh. Not all night. Just long enough to help you relax." I undid my robe and let one side, the side without the bruise, slip off my shoulder, revealing his favorite thing for me to wear to bed—nothing.

"That ought to do it," he said with a smile, reaching over and trailing a finger down the center of my damp breasts.

I reached over and turned out the bedside light, knowing that if he saw the bruise, it would break his heart again. I let my robe slip to the floor and I crawled under the covers, pressing myself against the hard length of his body, forgetting everything except this moment, this time and place where the world went dark and all I felt were his hands on my skin and his lips on my mouth.

Early the next day, when the light coming through our lacy curtains was still gray and dawn a rosy hint behind the hills, Gabe came into the master bedroom where, after we'd made love, I'd slept alone.

"I'm taking Scout for a run. Sleep in, *querida.*" He nuzzled my neck, his early morning beard as scratchy as a cat's tongue. "You earned it."

"I did . . ." I agreed, burrowing deeper into the quilts.

The next thing I heard was a dresser drawer open. I sat up, yawning, in time to see the bathroom door close.

"Gabe?"

"Sorry," he called. "Didn't mean to wake you, but I put off taking a shower as long as I could. I'm going down to the office for a few hours."

"What time is it?" I mumbled, stretching the kinks out of my legs. The bedside clock read ten forty-five. "Shoot, I need to get up. I have to be at the folk art museum by noon."

"What?" Gabe yelled over the shower flow.

"Nothing," I called back, swinging my legs out of bed.

I was dressed and downstairs in fifteen minutes, attempting to smooth the wrinkles out of a dark blue plaid flannel shirt while waiting for a piece of toast.

"Where're you off to in such a hurry?" he asked.

"Folk art museum. I promised someone they could use the pottery wheel today at noon." *Oh, I'm also going to do a little breaking and entering, but enough about my plans . . .*

"Don't you have people there who open up on Sunday?"

"This person is new to the co-op," I said quickly, concentrating on my toast. "I want to show her around."

"You'd better wear a jacket," he said, pulling on his hiking boots, not suspecting a thing. I must be getting better at lying. "Looks like rain."

I glanced out the kitchen window. Murderously dark clouds filled the sky. "If it rains, maybe the sniper will stay home."

Gabe gave a noncommittal grunt.

I spread peanut butter on my toast and folded it in half, so I could eat it on the run. "Now that I think about it, jogging this morning probably wasn't your smartest move. What if he was out there waiting for you?"

He was silent, which usually meant I'd struck a nerve and he agreed with me but wasn't going to admit it.

"I stayed close to home," he finally said.

I shot him a look because we both knew it was an illogical remark. No one could predict this sniper's agenda. "I'm just saying . . ."

"Your comment is duly noted." He came over, lifted up my hair and kissed the nape of my neck. "You were incredible last night. Have you been reading *Cosmopolitan* or something?"

"Oh, please," I said, pushing him back with my butt. "A *Cosmo* girl I'm not."

"Well, ma'am," he drawled, encircling me with his arms. "I thank you kindly for the scintillating and titillating evening."

"You are so full of baloney, but you're welcome." I took a bite of my sandwich. "How long will you be at the office?"

"I have no idea. I'll call you. Want to go to Morro Bay for dinner tonight? I'll buy." His smile was more relaxed than I'd seen it in days. It never ceased to amaze me how a roll in the hay could totally transform a man. Temporarily, anyway.

"Sounds good to me. It also sounds like a bribe."

"I prefer the word seduction."

"Shoot, I'd sleep with you for half a shredded-beef taco, but if you're offering a lobster tail and some clam chowder, I'll take it. Love you mucho muchly." I blew him a kiss and headed for the front door.

"*Te amo mucho, querida*," he replied.

I arrived at the museum by eleven forty-five. Lin pulled in as I was stepping out of my truck.

"Do you mind if I start early?" she asked, while we made our way to the co-op buildings.

"Go right ahead. No one is using it before or after you. Take all the time you need."

She walked down the hall, and I went into my office. I paced back and forth in the small room, realizing I finally had to get on the bus or watch it drive away. There was only a small window of time for me to drive to Morro Bay and attempt to break into her room. I looked down at my black plastic Daffy Duck watch. Gabe had given it to me a few years back with the comment that Daffy and I had similar smart mouths. I pictured the silly watch being listed under "prisoner's personal property" after I was arrested. That would give everyone at the station a big laugh. It would also be an amusing anecdote at my funeral, because after the Morro Beach police arrested me, I had no doubt that Gabe would kill me. But my determination to find out what Lin was doing in San Celina was stronger than my fear of Gabe's wrath.

Please, I thought, not calling it a prayer as that would be wrong on so many levels, let the hotel patrons be transient tourists and the maids be uninterested or deaf or blind or all of the above. *Let me be a ghost.*

And, I added, help me find a way into the room.

Because it now occurred to me that was the part of my plan that I'd not figured out. A possible scenario rattled around in my head. Maids usually cleaned rooms around noon while people were busy checking out. I could pretend Lin's room was my room and I forgot something in it and my key was in my car . . . yes, that was good. Except for one thing . . .

I didn't know her room number.

Dang. How would I find that out? What was a believable reason for me to ask her that information? Why hadn't I worked all of this out last night?

Okay, I knew the Spotted Pelican was probably new because I knew most of the hotels in Morro Bay and the name didn't sound familiar. Maybe I could ask Lin about the hotel, if she liked it, did her room have a view and, by the way, what room *was* she staying in?

Lin had already set up and was starting the wheel when I walked into the small back room.

"If you need anything, just ask one of the other co-op members," I told her. Though it was slow, there were a couple of other artists working. "Or ask the docent in charge."

"Thank you so much for arranging this," she said, rubbing her wide forehead with the back of one hand. Pale lavender stained the thin skin under her eyes. Though it had only been a few days since we'd spent the day together, something about her seemed different, an air of desperation or fatigue. "I'm stressed and need time with the clay."

"No problem," I replied, feeling like the biggest phony on earth.

I lingered for a moment, trying to figure out a way to ask about her hotel, when I saw her large leather handbag sitting on the floor.

"Would you like to keep your purse in my office?" I asked. "It might get dirty out here. I'm on my way to run some errands. I can stick it in there on my way out."

"I suppose," she said, staring at her lump of clay, already in that artistic fugue I'd become familiar with working with artists. "But it's already pretty dirty."

"No use making it worse," I said, keeping my voice light. I picked the bag up and slung it over my shoulder. "It'll be in the right bottom drawer. My office door will be closed, but feel free to go right in."

"Thanks," she murmured, starting the wheel.

Once I was in my office, I closed the door, almost crowing like a rooster at my cleverness. I dug through her purse, past her wallet, some prescription medicine bottles, a couple of energy bars, tissue and a brush. I finally found the paper key packet stuck in an inside pocket. A cartoon character of a pelican who appeared to have chicken pox was printed on the packet along with the address—55 Ocean Bluff Way. *Room 312.* And there were two plastic room keys. So even if she looked through her purse while I was gone, there was a good possibility she wouldn't immediately realize one of her keys was missing.

From the folk art museum, it was a twenty-minute drive to Morro Bay.

I figured that gave me an hour, tops, to search her motel room. That left forty minutes to drive back to the folk art museum and replace the key before Lin's time was up. Since there wasn't anyone else scheduled on the wheel, there was a good chance she'd work past her time so she could finish her project.

Sitting in my truck, I checked my Thomas map book. The Spotted Pelican hotel was on the corner of Main and Ocean Bluff Way, overlooking the Embarcadero and Morro Rock. I found it easily, tipped off by a five-foot metal sculpture of a pelican in front of the black and white fifties-era motel. The three-story building appeared to have recently been renovated. Neatly trimmed trees dotted the parking lots and bright red and yellow flowers in barrel-size terra-cotta pots bookended the office's double glass doors. Five or six cars parked in front had open doors and people rearranging possessions, obviously checking out.

I parked my truck around the corner, out of

sight of the office, and walked around the building looking for a door that would allow me entrance to the hotel's inside hallways without meandering through the lobby trying to pretend I belonged there. I was in luck. An outside staircase led up to the second and third floors. I walked up, opened the security door with my stolen key, keeping my head high, willing myself to look like I was just dashing back to my room for a forgotten item.

My acting job, for whatever it was worth, was unnecessary, because I didn't meet one person before I reached her room on the third floor. I passed by a couple of open doors, blocked by heavy metal room maintenance carts loaded with clean towels, tiny soaps and shampoos and packets of coffee. But the maids were busy cleaning the rooms and didn't even give me a second glance. I slipped the key into room 312, took a deep breath because at this very moment I knew I was breaking the law, and opened the door.

Her room had already been cleaned. That was a lucky break. I'd attempt to put everything back exactly where I found it, but if I didn't, it was believable that the maid might have moved something, so Lin wouldn't suspect her room had been searched. I surveyed the room. The walls were painted a pale aqua and the room was decorated with black-framed copies of Audubon's detailed bird illustrations. A white and navy striped comforter covered the king-size bed. One overstuffed chair and ottoman were upholstered in the same fabric. The curtains and carpet were solid navy. The maid had opened the drapes halfway, allowing natural light to filter through the white sheers.

I looked at my watch. Forty-five minutes left. Be methodical. There's no time to waste.

I started with the bathroom. Her few cosmetics and skin care products were placed neatly in the corner of the counter—toothbrush, toothpaste and dental floss; Neutrogena night cream; Aveeno day cream SPF 15; Burt's Bees lip gloss; that ubiquitous green and pink tube of black Maybelline mascara; Cover Girl liquid makeup and matching face powder; a travel-size jar of Vaseline; a travel-size container marked "hand lotion." I opened the container and brought it to my nose, inhaled the familiar cherry-almond scent of the original Jergens. The same lotion Dove and Aunt Garnet used. The same hand lotion many of the women in the Coffin Star Quilt Guild used. The scent always seemed to be part of anything I did with the older women I loved and admired. I'd always imagined that when I reached a "certain" age, the age of wisdom is how I thought of it, I'd stop using my favorite hand-cream-of-the-month and permanently graduate to Jergens.

On the floor sat her overnight bag, that old-fashioned square kind that reminded me of movie stars in the 1950s like Marilyn Monroe or Doris Day. The glossy leather case was gray with black stitching, worn at the corners from use. I poked through its spare contents. It didn't reveal much more than the products on the counter—an expensive, wood-handled boar's bristle hairbrush, three more packets of tissue like the one she'd given me after my cocoa spill, two pairs of thin wool socks and a manicure set in a green leather pouch. There was also generic aspirin, calcium tablets, fish oil capsules, Tylenol PM and a small, unmarked prescription bottle filled with red and white pills. I opened the bottle, shook one out. No markings that I could see. The shower revealed only a pink disposable razor and an unwrapped hotel soap bar.

I went back into the room and checked her nightstand. On the surface was a travel clock, a pair of eyeglasses in a maroon case, a small jade animal that looked like a bull with curvy horns, and a shiny blue dish that looked like a young child made it. A pair of silver hoop earrings and a handful of seashells filled the dish. I picked up the dish and looked at the bottom. A small thumbprint was pressed into the baked clay. I walked around the bed to the other nightstand that held only a hardback book: *Losing It—An Easy and Practical Guide to Facing Your Past and Moving Forward.*

The author, a psychologist from Portland, Oregon, had visited Blind Harry's Bookstore a few months ago as part of his book-signing tour. His book was recently featured in *USA Today*. He'd talked about moving forward from every type of loss a human could experience—divorce, death, health, family, income, job, friendship. His simple steps to deal with those losses seemed to hit a nerve with the seventy or so people who came to the signing. Elvia had sold out of his books.

I turned the book over. The price tag was from a store in Oklahoma City. Oklahoma City? That seemed odd since she claimed and her license plate verified that she was from Washington. A bookmark held her place on page 197, approximately halfway through the book. The chapter had to do with the pros and cons of seeking out people in your past to whom you never said good-bye and making peace with them.

I set the book back on the nightstand, my stomach churning. What had I expected? It was becoming clear that Lin Snider was someone from Gabe's past—*another someone.* Was I doomed to repeat this scenario until we died or until it finally broke us up?

I shook my head, forcing myself to ignore the self-pity welling up inside me. I had a job to do and not much more time to accomplish it. I opened the nightstand drawer. Nothing but a black Gideon Bible and a Morro Bay telephone book. Next, I checked the dresser drawers in the cabinet that held the television. It held a neatly folded flowered nightgown, a pair of soft pink socks and a black cashmere scarf. A plastic sack from a local grocery store held what appeared to be her dirty clothes. The second and third drawers contained only extra pillows and blankets.

That left only her suitcase. I stared down at the closed suitcase. It was made of bland black fabric and was just a little too big to be a carry-on. I unzipped it and opened the lid, carefully feeling through her clothes, trying not to disturb anything. A woodsy scent floated up from her clothes reminding me a little of the patchouli that was popular with teenagers when I was a little girl.

In the bottom of the suitcase, I found a plastic CD cover—Elvis Presley's Greatest Hits.

Ha, I thought. It *was* you out at the ranch.

Well, maybe. Only a gazillion people had Elvis CDs.

I looked through each inside pocket finding only cotton underwear, beige bras and another pair of black socks. Then, just as I was about to give up and conclude that my illegal search had been in vain, I hit the jackpot.

Chapter 14

Well, a penny jackpot. But, at least it appeared to be something personal. Something that connected her with someone.

It was a photograph. A three-by-five photograph of a Hispanic girl who could be anywhere from her late teens to late twenties. It was hard to tell because she had the almond-shaped eyes and smooth, almost ageless facial features of a person with Down syndrome.

The smiling young woman stood in front of a large bottlebrush bush covered with bright red flowers. She wore loose jeans rolled to her calves, a yellow blouse with ruffles down the front and pink high-top Converse tennis shoes. Dark glossy hair cut in a chin-length bob with thick, slightly uneven bangs framed her soft face. Her mischievous grin made me guess she might have trimmed them herself. She looked like at any minute she would burst out in laughter and run out of camera range.

In the distant background was a hospital, one I recognized from many years of watching the soap opera *General Hospital* with Dove. A lot of people didn't know that the hospital pictured in the opening credits that was supposed to be in fictional Port Charles, New York, was actually a photo of Los Angeles County–USC Medical Center.

I turned the photograph over. On the back was written—Tessa at place of birth—1997.

I stared more closely at the photograph. Who was this girl? Lin told me she didn't have any children. Was this a niece or a friend's daughter?

It hit me like the first jolt of an earthquake. I sat down hard on the bed, clutching the photograph.

The girl was Hispanic. There was no doubt about that. Who knows how many women Gabe had been intimate with before we married. It was something I didn't like to think about. But Gabe had lived in Los Angeles for many years.

My head started to feel light. I leaned forward, resting it on my knees.

Was that the reason Lin had been asking questions about me and how I felt about children? Was she trying to find out how I'd react if she presented Gabe with a daughter?

Lord, help me, I thought, my head still on my knees. This is big. I'm not sure I can do this.

I don't know how long I sat there, but a knock on the door jerked me out of my frozen state.

"Housekeeping," a female voice called.

I called through the door. "Yes?"

"The room, it is okay?"

I peered through the peephole. A middle-aged Hispanic woman held a clipboard. "Yes, it's fine. Thank you."

I watched her check off the room and walk away.

My watch told me I'd been sitting on the bed holding Tessa's photograph for longer than I thought. It was almost one thirty. I should have left a half hour ago. I dug through my purse, propped the photo on the nightstand next to the travel clock and took a quick photo of it.

I put Tessa's photograph back inside of the suitcase, surveyed the room one last time and left. Halfway down the hallway, I walked by one other person, an older woman wearing binoculars around her neck.

"A good day for ducks," she said cheerfully. Her wet sandals squished when she walked.

I smiled without answering. Outside, a light rain had begun. I started my truck and pulled onto Main Street, not realizing how nervous I was until I came to the first stop sign. I started trembling so violently that I had to pull over to a side street. As I listened to the rainstorm grow stronger, it struck me that this moment was one I'd always remember. I'd always remember that this was the day I'd first seen the photo of a girl who might possibly be Gabe's daughter. I stared out of my truck's blurry windshield feeling like my and Gabe's life together seemed perched over a precipice ready to fall into a deep, unfathomable canyon.

While the rain grew harder and throttled the roof of my truck, I wondered again if I was overreacting, jumping to some huge conclusion. I contemplated what I really knew about Lin Snider. That she was curious about me and my relationship with Gabe. That she was either Lin Snider or posing as Lin Snider. That she was from Washington. That she carried the photo of a young Hispanic woman with Down syndrome who may or may not be her daughter. It was all such a jumble of suppositions. Should I go to Gabe? If it turned out to be nothing, he'd be upset that I'd manufactured a mystery where there wasn't one. If there was something to it, did he really need to deal with it right now?

Except for one thing. I knew this man's integrity. I knew this man's heart. If this young woman, Tessa, was his daughter, he would take responsibility for her. He'd never turn his back on her. He would love her. Of that, I was certain.

Could I handle it, him having another child? Yes, I thought I could. Gabe loving another child didn't bother me. Gabe having feelings for another woman. That was different. If this was his child, what had he felt for her mother, Lin?

I rubbed my aching temples, wishing there was an easy solution to this situation, wishing I knew more. I wanted to go to Gabe, not with suspicions, but with real facts.

I started the truck and drove back to the folk art museum. Right now, I had to sneak this key back into Lin's purse before she realized it was gone.

The museum parking lot was almost empty when I drove in. I breezed through the museum and headed straight to the co-op buildings. Inside, a lone quilter, a woman named Sadie, was rolling up a half-quilted Log Cabin quilt.

"Hey, Benni," she said.

"Hey, Sadie. Where is everyone?"

She chuckled. "Rain scared 'em off. Honestly, you Californians." Sadie was from Oregon. "I told 'em I'd lock up when the potter is finished." She jerked a thumb toward the hallway.

"I was born in Arkansas," I said, laughing, without breaking stride toward my office. Down the hall, I could hear the chattering sound of a pottery wheel moving. I sent up a quick *thank you*.

I went into my office and locked the door. Then I shoved Lin's hotel key back inside the paper key packet. I placed her purse back in the drawer, took a deep breath and unlocked my office door, feeling safe for the first time in hours. It felt like I'd run the Boston marathon. Twice.

She was just removing a pot when I wandered into the room.

"Hi," she said, looking up and smiling. "Did the rain mess up any of your errands?"

I plastered a smile on my face and said, "Not at all. I got everything done that I'd planned."

"Glad to hear that," she said. "I'll be finished in a minute. I accomplished much more than I anticipated."

"Good. Well, see you later. Just let Sadie know when you're leaving so she can lock up. I've got a dinner date."

After saying good-bye to Sadie, I decided to go to the Target in Atascadero and have my roll of film developed at their one-hour photo. Normally I took my photos to Lopez Street Drugstore downtown, but they knew me too well there. They always flipped through my photos, and someone would want to know what the story was behind my photograph of a photograph.

An hour and a half later, I had my photo of Tessa. Not that I knew what to do with it.

The truck's clock said four o'clock. I called Gabe on his cell.

He answered after the first ring. "Ortiz at your service. Day or night. Night preferred."

I gave him the laugh he was angling for. "I'm assuming you looked at the screen and saw it was me. And I'm assuming you're alone?"

"Who is this?" he asked.

"Ha-ha. What time are we going to dinner?"

There was a long silence.

"How about hot chocolate with marshmallows in our own home?" I asked, saving him from making an excuse. Anything to do with the sniper had to come first. "Whenever you get there."

"I'm sorry. A new FBI guy just came into town and wants an update right away. I'm meeting him and Detective Arnaud at my office in a half hour. We'll probably grab dinner downtown."

"It's okay, Friday. Really." Actually, I was glad our plans had changed. I was afraid I'd be distracted tonight and that, somehow, he'd pry out of me why. I needed a few hours to regain my composure. "I'll be waiting."

"Thank you," he said softly.

"Run like a rabbit." It was one of his favorite lines from the Pink Panther movies.

I hung up and sat in the Target parking lot, thinking about who I could talk to about my latest suspicions. There was really only one person who knew as much about this situation as me.

I called Emory at home. He answered on the fourth ring, his voice groggy. "Umm . . . hello?"

"It's Benni. You sound terrible. Are you sick?"

"No. Sophie. Colic. No sleep. Napping."

"Oh, Emory, I'm sorry. I didn't mean to wake you. Is my goddaughter okay? How's Elvia holding up?"

"Sophie's fine. She finally went to sleep two

hours ago after sixteen hours of walking the floor. I mean us walking the floor holding her. Elvia's in the master bedroom dead to the world. I'm in Sophie's room sleeping on the floor. Mama Aragon is asleep in the guest room."

"Wow. Again, I'm sorry."

"Is there something you need?"

"No, just calling to say hi." I wasn't about to lay my latest problems on him right now. "I'll catch you tomorrow when you're back in the world of the living. Sweet dreams."

"Love you," he mumbled and hung up.

Okay, that left only one other person since my two best friends were out of commission. I found his number on my phone's address list and dialed.

"Hey, ranch girl," Hud said. "What's up?"

"Are you free for dinner?"

"Depends on what you're cookin'."

"I'm not cooking anything, but I'd be happy to buy you dinner. I have . . . a dilemma."

"Hmmm . . . sounds interesting. Where and when?"

"Liddie's in a half hour? I don't want this to look like a date, because it isn't. I just need some law enforcement advice."

"Your husband can't help you?"

I was silent for a moment, wishing now that I'd called someone else. But who else could I call? "He's kinda busy right now. In case you hadn't noticed, there's a crazy person with a loaded gun roaming the streets of San Celina."

"This is about that lady the other night." No grass grew under Detective Ford Hudson's fancy alligator boots.

"Yes. I . . ." I chewed on my bottom lip. It was dry as a desert. "I sort of investigated her hotel room when she wasn't . . . uh . . . there."

"Breaking and entering!" Hud's voice was positively gleeful. "A felony. Oh, *catin*, you are such a bad, bad girl."

"I know," I said, feeling miserable. "I really need to talk to you."

"I'll meet you in ten minutes. I'll be the excited-looking one holding a yellow rose between my teeth."

The thing about Hud was, silly as he often acted, especially around me, he understood about the need to not always do things exactly by the book. The only other people I would have trusted with this information were Emory and Elvia, but they had enough on their plate right now. I'd tell Hud the whole story and, if necessary, beg for his help.

Because the fact was, Ford Hudson was a real Texas oil millionaire. He had resources that I couldn't even begin to touch, and I wanted him to use every one of them to find out exactly what was Lin Snider's story.

He made it to Liddie's before I did and had

somehow, despite being a busy Sunday evening, begged or bribed Nadine into letting us have the much-in-demand back booth. It was as private as you could get at Liddie's.

"I've ordered you a grilled cheese sandwich, a green salad with ranch dressing and water. I'm getting the tri-tip Cobb salad."

"I always get a cheeseburger," I said, sliding across from him. "And French fries."

"Change is good. If you're giving up Cokes, you might as well start eating healthier."

"Who died and made you my food coach?" I grumbled.

He took off his dark brown Stetson and placed it, crown down, on the red bench seat next to him. "Quit whining. If you're good, I'll buy you a piece of pie. Butterscotch tonight."

That perked me up. Butterscotch was my favorite. "I don't know where to begin."

He sat back in the seat, one arm resting over the back. "You might start with who is this lady whose hotel room you broke into and why you felt the need to break into it. There's a good start."

I leaned forward. "Shhh! I don't need this to get around town. Right now, no one except you knows about my, uh, foray outside the law."

He grinned and grabbed one of my hands. "I feel so honored. And, strangely, a little excited."

I jerked away and slapped the top of his hand. "You are always excited. You're like a junk-yard dog that's never been fixed."

"Now I'm *really* excited."

"Shut up and listen." I swallowed. "Please."

The slight catch in my voice immediately sobered him. "Go ahead, ranch girl."

It took me most of our meal to tell everything because Nadine kept interrupting us to refill our water glasses, bring Hud more biscuits, offer me a Coke on the house.

"She knows something is going on," I whispered to Hud after her third offer of Coke. "She's dying to know what it is."

"We probably should have gone somewhere else," he said.

"No, because we'd likely have been seen and Gabe would have been told and it would have looked like we were doing something illicit. You know this town. The only place we can eat together without people talking is Liddie's. I can tell Gabe we just ran into each other."

"Lie to your hubby?" He picked up a chunk of tri-tip with his fork and waved it at me, unable to abstain for long from teasing me. "Shame, shame. You are really racking up the bad-girl points this week."

"Would you let me finish?"

After my story ended, he continued eating without commenting.

"Well?" I said after a minute. "What do you think?"

"Give me a minute," he said, contemplating a strip of yellow bell pepper before sticking it in his mouth. "I'm trying to process everything."

While he thought, I fretted about whether telling him everything had been a mistake. I concluded that I'd had no other choice. I needed help from someone with vast and generous resources, and I needed it fast.

By the time a very irritated and curious Nadine brought our dessert—butterscotch pie for both of us—Hud had decided to bestow his opinion on me.

"Here's what I think. I need to do a deeper investigation on her than you can. You said that your cousin Emory had an investigator on board?"

I nodded, picking at my pie. "Someone named Betsy?"

"Betsy Twain. I know her. She's good. I'll tell her I'm working on it too and we can compare notes. But I have resources even she doesn't . . ."

"That's what I was counting on."

"It'll take a day or so. Are you okay until then?"

"I guess I'll have to be. I just hope if what I think about why she's here is true, she doesn't show up at our front door with this girl's birth certificate. I'm not sure Gabe could handle the shock right now."

Hud watched my face closely, his own emotions unreadable. "Is there something else going on with you and the chief?"

I concentrated on my pie. "We're fine. He's just stressed about the sniper. Anyone in his position would be." My tone was defensive, and I didn't care.

"Okay, another question. This girl. If she is Gabe's daughter, how do you feel about that?"

I looked him directly in his dark brown eyes. In the years I'd gotten to know Hud he'd become almost like a family member. Though I was absolutely in love with Gabe, till-death-do-us-part love, I knew and Hud knew that under different circumstances, I could have fallen in love with him. That made our relationship tricky, but somehow we managed. All I knew was I trusted him and he trusted me because we had been through some hard times together.

"I knew he had a past when I married him, Hud. If this girl is his daughter, then I'll accept her and we'll deal with it. She's not my worry . . ."

"The woman."

I nodded. Had Gabe loved her? Would that love be rekindled once he realized they had a child together? All of that was too much for me to contemplate right now.

"Thank you for your help," I said, touching my fingertips to the top of his hand. "You're a dear friend and I love you. If you ever need me, I'll be there. I mean that."

"I know you do," he said, shoving the dinner bill across the table to me. "Now buy my dinner and skedaddle home. I've got work to do."

That night Gabe had another nightmare. I managed to wake him up by yelling across the room, though it took me ten minutes. When I heard Gabe's voice cry out, I'd locked Scout in our bedroom, not wanting to deal with him and Gabe. Scout's clawing at the door was so frantic, I knew we'd have to sand and repaint it.

Every time I tried to move close to Gabe, he cursed, swung his arms out in defense and I backed up. If he hit me again, I knew he'd never forgive himself. So I stood in the doorway and yelled and cried until something broke through the mental hell he was in and he bolted up, sweating, his complexion as pale as parchment paper.

We didn't discuss his nightmare the next morning. Even so, it lay between us like the invisible pulse of an electric fence. He looked as if he hadn't slept in a week. I worried about his heart. His father, Rogelio, had died of a heart attack when he was younger than Gabe. Something needed to be done about these nightmares. And soon.

"Now that the festival is over," he asked, setting his breakfast dishes in the sink, "what are your plans this week?"

"I'm meeting Isaac this morning. We're going out on the ranch and taking each other's photos for the book."

"Sounds fun. Wish I was coming."

"Lobster dinner tonight?" I asked.

"I promise, no matter what."

We both knew that wasn't true, that it did matter what happened. If the sniper struck again, all bets and dates were off. But I'd been a cop's wife long enough now to accept that. So I played along.

"Can't wait," I said, hugging him around the waist.

I called Isaac, and we agreed I'd be at the ranch by nine a.m. so we could ride up to Big Hill. He wanted to photograph me with my horse. I thought a photo of him with the hills of San Celina in the background might have the grandness that his portrait deserved.

"Dig out your old Hasselblad," I said. "I think I want that in my photo of you." I'd always loved that camera. It looked like a piece of modern art to me.

The ranch was quiet when I arrived. The day was cloudy with thick marine fog blowing in from the ocean. A perfect day for photos, I knew Isaac would say. He was alone in the kitchen sipping a cup of coffee.

"Where are the girls and Uncle WW?" I asked, plopping down on a stool next to him.

"Went to town. WW's got an early doctor's appointment."

"I'll saddle up Misty. Are you taking the Jeep?"

Isaac nodded. "It's all loaded. The girls packed us a lunch."

"Bless 'em."

Misty was my favorite mare, a stout little buckskin that stood just over fourteen hands. She was smart, quick and good in an emergency. But she also knew how to relax, seemed to understand when we were taking care of cow business and when we were just out for a pleasure ride. Not all cow ponies were good leisure horses.

"Perfect day for photos," Isaac said, while we walked out to the barn.

I gave a small laugh.

"What did I say?" he asked, his expression perplexed.

"Nothing. Where's Daddy?"

"He lit out of here early, before the girls were even out of their housecoats. Said he had some cows to check on."

"His truck is gone."

Isaac pretended to study the green hills behind me.

"You know where he is. Spill the beans, Pops."

He looked down at me, his weathered face miserable. "I'm sworn to secrecy."

"To save you any agony, I've seen Daddy with his girlfriend or whoever she is, so the gig is up.

362

They were laughing it up Friday morning at Kitty's Café in Morro Bay."

He wiped the back of his huge hand across his forehead in a gesture of feigned relief. "I'm glad I'm not the only one carrying the burden of Ben's secret love life now."

"Who is she?" I opened the barn door. The scent of sweet hay, earthy horse and the buttery odor of saddle soap greeted us. It was a smell as comforting and familiar to me as Dove's macaroni and cheese. "Where did they meet?"

"Her name is Dot Haggerty. Short for Dorothy. They've been seeing each other on the sly for about six months. They met at the Snaffle Bit Futurity in Reno last October."

"I went with Daddy to the Futurity! I never saw him with any woman."

Isaac leaned against the stall while I slipped a halter around Misty and led her to the hitching post. "How much did you and he hang out?"

"Good point." Daddy and I enjoyed our annual trip up to the Snaffle Bit in Reno. It was one of the few times during the year when we were alone for an extended period. On the long drive, we talked, ate salty snacks, drank RC Cola, laughed and complained about the new country music. We agreed that there would never, ever be another Patsy Cline or Merle Haggard and that MoonPies and original flavor CornNuts were the perfect road trip food. If Dove went to the

Futurity, she usually drove with a bunch of her girlfriends.

However, once Daddy and I actually arrived in Reno, we saw each other only to wave because we both had dozens of old friends that we wanted to visit—he from his years of ranching, me from my Cal Poly and 4-H days. We always stayed in the same hotel-casino in separate rooms, often on different floors. I knew so many people attending the Futurity, I never had trouble finding a ride to the arena. Daddy could have met someone, courted her and had a wedding with a three-piece jug band and I'd probably not hear a word about it until the ride home.

"Where's this Dot lady from?" I asked.

"She owns a little ranch with her brother outside of Reno. They run about a hundred head of red Angus. Brother never married. She's a widow, like Ben. Has one daughter who lives in Nashville who's a studio musician. Dot grew up in Oklahoma. Did a little trick riding back in her thirties. She designs jewelry now."

I tilted my head and gave him a wry smile. "You sure seem to know a lot about her."

"Ben and I talk."

I brushed the light dusting of soil and loose hay off Misty's back and settled the red and brown Navajo-patterned saddle pad on her back. "So, are you going to ever tell Dove about Daddy's paramour?"

"Not on your life," Isaac said, his eyebrows shooting up. "That's Ben's row to hoe." He lifted my saddle off the wooden rack and set it easily on Misty's back without even having to swing it up and over. For not the first time I thought about how much easier life would be if I were that tall.

"But don't you think it would make everything easier if you told Dove and Aunt Garnet that Daddy is, apparently, doing fine in the love department? They would leave him alone and move on to improving some other lucky person's life."

"That's just it, they *wouldn't* leave him alone. They'd want to meet her, invite her for dinner, for Sunday brunch, for the weekend. They would quiz her within an inch of her life. They would want to know about her *people* all the way back to her great-great-greats. Then their friends would hear about her and then Dot and Ben would become the toast of San Celina ag society because no one ever expected Ben to date again so everyone would want to meet the woman who caught him. Ben and Dot are wisely trying to figure out if they actually have something together before they give the rest of the world time to dissect it." It was the longest, most impassioned speech I had heard Isaac give since . . . well . . . ever.

I stared at him, hands on my hips, my mouth open. It didn't take a genius to recognize a little of his and Dove's courtship difficulties in that speech. Then again, my dad wasn't a famous photographer. His and Dot's relationship wouldn't cause quite as big a stir, though it would surprise a good many people.

I had to admit, when I thought about Daddy actually being in a romantic relationship, my stomach felt a little queasy (seriously, what kid wants to think of their parents doing anything resembling what Gabe and I did on a regular basis?). However, I liked to think I learned something from my spoiled brat behavior when Isaac courted Dove. If it killed me, unless Dot Haggerty was some kind of black widow man-killer out to hurt him (in which case, all bets were off), I was going to be open-minded and accepting of this woman who may or may not end up being my stepmother.

I'd let Dove and Aunt Garnet be the interrogators. They would be much more competent and thorough at it than me anyway.

I pulled the cinch around Misty's belly, checked it and stretched my legs, getting ready to mount. "What are you going to do?"

"Mind my own business. Let chips fall where they may. Take the high road. If all else fails, run for cover."

I laughed, lifted my leg and mounted Misty. "A virtual Cobb salad of clichés, all of which fit the situation to a T."

"Cliché number five," he said, licking a finger and making a mark in the air.

"And I agree with all of them. Let's go take some pictures and leave Daddy to the Honeycutt Sisters Matchmaking Service." I touched Misty's side with my heel. "I'm taking the long way there, so I'll meet you at Big Hill in about an hour. I need some time to relax and think." It would take him about twenty minutes to get there in the Jeep.

"Good, it'll give me time to set up, check things out."

It had been the first time I'd been out for a ride since seeing Lin Snider at the Harper Ranch last Monday, a week ago now. It felt good to be on horseback again, especially with Misty who could practically read my mind. I didn't have to pay as close attention as I did riding Trixie. With all that had happened this week, I needed some time to decompress.

The cattle path to Big Hill was an easy one, traveled by generations of cattle to one of our higher pastures where the springtime sun caused the grass to grow deep green and thick. During roundup this was one of the first places we came hunting for cattle. The misty air deadened the sound around me, the cool weather keeping the usually buzzing insects asleep and waiting for the sun to come out. But there was plenty of other activity by squirrels and birds. I even caught a glimpse of a red fox, unusual for this time of year. A western bluebird followed Misty and me for a little ways, scolding us for riding too close to her nest.

Isaac was puttering with his equipment when I rode up. We discussed our photos and took them quicker than I thought possible. He used both his new digital and his old Nikon, using the digital as a sort of fancy Polaroid test shot. I had to admit it was fun seeing the pictures just as we took them, though the screen was small so details were hard to make out.

He took a bunch of me with Misty—both holding her reins and sitting on her back.

"I know one of these is it," he said. "But I won't know for sure until they are printed."

Using his new digital camera, I took some of him sitting in the Jeep, standing with the hills in the background, his Nikon hung around his neck. Then I got a little artsy and told him to hide part of his face behind his Hasselblad. In the background there was just a hint of hills. The minute I snapped the shot, I had a feeling it was the one.

His mouth turned down at the corners, impressed, when he looked at my photo of him on the digital screen. "You have a good eye," he said.

"I have a good teacher," I retorted.

Once our shoot was over, we ate the lunch that

Dove and Aunt Garnet had packed for us—egg salad sandwiches, pickles, carrot sticks, ranch dressing and two huge oatmeal cookies. The frozen bottles of water I'd stuck in the Jeep had melted enough for us to drink. I spread all our lunch out on an old wool army blanket next to a blue oak tree.

"How're things going with Gabe and this sniper investigation?" Isaac asked, leaning his back against the oak tree.

I lay back on the blanket and looked up through the oak's leafy branches.

"Oh, you know. It's stressful. It's . . ." I couldn't go on. I didn't want to lie to Isaac, but I also didn't want to talk about Gabe's nightmares or anything about him. What I wanted to do this afternoon was *not* think about Gabe and his past.

He scooted down, took his beat-up Panama hat, the one he liked to wear when he was working, and moved it low over his eyes. "Did I ever tell you I was in Vietnam during the war?"

I sat up and crossed my legs. "No, but I'm not surprised. You've been everywhere."

He chuckled under his hat. "Not everywhere, but a darn lot of places. Anyway, Gabe and I were talking a few months back and realized that we'd been in Vietnam about the same time."

"Wow, that's weird."

"Yes, quite a coincidence. We might have crossed paths, though chances are we didn't. I was there for *National Geographic*, so the military treated me well. I ate and drank with the officers. Gabe, being a marine grunt, didn't get my perks, though he and his buddies certainly deserved them more than I."

"I hate that about the military, all that hierarchy stuff. I would be a horrible military wife. If someone tells me I can't go somewhere, that's exactly where I want to go."

"I think God placed you exactly where you should be."

"So, what did you photograph in Vietnam? I don't know much about it because I was so young when the war was going on. When you and Gabe were over there, I was ten years old, learning my times tables and how to groom a steer for show at the county fair."

He inhaled deeply, crossing his arms over his chest. Above us I could hear birds rustling, the sound of a woodpecker. Misty snorted, pawed the ground, then settled back down. "Vietnam's a beautiful country with wonderful people. What we did to it . . . well, don't get me started on my soapbox. I may be a bit more left-wing than most about the devastation heaped on that little country."

"Were your photos political at all?"

"No more so than any war photography. I concentrated on the beauty of the country, the warmth and resourcefulness of the people, the incredible landscape. I was trying to show what Vietnam was like before the war as well as during the war."

"Did you photograph any soldiers?"

"I did for another assignment, one for AP. Anyway, to answer your original question, what I loved most in Vietnam were the people and their animals. Specifically how they interacted and worked together as a team. I was thinking about compiling some of those photographs using that theme. Kind of like the photograph I just took of you and Misty. It would fit in quite well."

He'd snapped a shot of me blowing into Misty's nostrils and Misty fluttering her lips in response. It was our special way of greeting each other.

"Did you take photos of Vietnamese kids and their dogs?"

"It was their relationships with water buffalos I found so fascinating. Water bos, our guys called them. They're the symbol of Vietnam, you know, and most farmers owned one. They were extremely important to their livelihood. I loved watching the kids ride them like circus elephants, making them obey as if they were pet dogs. Those long, curved horns always reminded me of handle-bar mustaches. Even the bravest soldiers and marines were very cautious around the water bos. The kids were fearless and used to laugh at how scared our troops were of the water buffaloes."

It was later, when I was pulling into my driveway, that Isaac's words struck something in me.

Those long, curved horns always reminded me of handlebar mustaches.

I dug through my purse and found the photos I just had developed at Target. I flipped through the photos of the Memory Festival until I found the photo I took of Tessa's photo. Next to it, only partially visible since it wasn't the focus of my photo, was the tiny jade animal with the big, curvy horns.

A water buffalo.

Chapter 15

Had Lin been in Vietnam? Or perhaps Gabe sent her that gift or gave it to her after he returned. I leaned my head against the steering wheel, suddenly so weary of this whole scenario that I wished I could take a pill that would make me sleep for a month. I looked at my watch. It was almost two p.m., and I didn't have a place I needed to be or a thing I absolutely needed to do.

So I called Elvia to see how Sophie was doing.

"She's fine," Elvia said. "The doctor said it's common and that we did everything we could. Apparently, babies just have to grow out of it."

"I'm glad to hear that. How's Miguel? I meant to call this morning, but I figured you'd call me if there was bad news."

"He's fine. Driving everyone nuts because you know how he hates to stay still for very long."

"Unless he's playing video games."

Elvia laughed. "Yes, that's true. Actually, he's bored with all his games."

"How about I get him a new one."

"He'd love that. He's dying for *James Bond 007*."

"I'll run by Norman's Toy Store."

Fortunately, the toy store had the game Miguel wanted. In the parking lot of General Hospital, I called Hud's cell phone. It went right to voice mail after one ring.

"Hey, Clouseau," I said. "Any information yet? Call me as soon as you get this message. I have something to run by you about . . . our subject."

The security around Miguel had relaxed a little, though there was still a police officer posted in the lobby and another one next to Miguel's door. The officer at his door dutifully checked my identification despite knowing perfectly well who I was. He probably didn't want me reporting to his boss about any lax in security.

Miguel sat up in his hospital bed wearing a small-print hospital nightgown and dark blue sweatpants. His room looked like a combination balloon store and funeral parlor. The sweet scent of the flowers fought with the lemon-pine scent of the hospital's room cleaner. A basketball game blared from the overhead television. Miguel was playing video hangman with Gabe's son, Sam.

"*Madrastra*!" Sam said. "Long time, no talk."

"I've been around."

"He's been down south surfing, lucky dog," Miguel said.

"Hey, I was helping my mom move too, bro," Sam retorted.

"How're you doing?" I went over and kissed

Miguel's cheek. "I'm so glad you're okay," I whispered in his ear.

"I'll live. So, how come you've only visited me twice in the last week? I've kept track, you know."

"I sent a basket of cookies, magazines, some balloons and, you're right, I visited twice, but both times, you were asleep. Beside, you were not the easiest person to see. For a few days, this place was worse than Fort Knox. Your lovely sister and your handsome boss have kept me up on your progress. I don't think you've been lonely one little bit."

"He hasn't," Sam said. "You should see the girls who want to visit him."

"Man, getting shot is totally better for getting girls than walking a puppy."

"Walking a puppy probably hurts a lot less," I commented.

"For sure," Miguel said. "They said I can maybe go back to work in eight weeks. I'm already bored."

"When are they saying you can go home?" I asked.

"Maybe next week." His full mouth turned down at the corners. "I wish I could work this case. Man, I'd like a crack at the guy who did this." His broad face tightened in anger.

"They'll get him," I said, patting his hand. "Is there anything I can do for you? I can't imagine what else you need." I handed him the video game. "Oh, Elvia said you wanted this."

"Wow, thanks! I was getting bored with the old stuff." He turned it over in his hands, his face resembling the five-year-old Miguel I remembered. Inside my chest, it felt like my heart shrank a little when I thought about how we could have lost him.

"I'll come by your parents' house in a few days," I said. "Do what the doctors tell you to do. Don't get all Latino male macho on me."

"Ah, what do you know about Latino males?" Sam said, grinning at me.

I shot him with a finger pistol. "You, young man, need to come visit your father."

Sam's face turned serious. Except for his brown eyes and the darker hue of his coppery skin, he could have been Gabe twenty years ago. Though Sam's gregarious personality could sometime grate on Gabe's nerves, his son was also one of the few people who could make Gabe laugh. "He needs you right now, Sam. He needs some laughs."

"I'll come by," he said. "You know, I came back when Dove called me about Miguel. No one from *my* immediate family called me."

I grimaced. "Guilty as charged. Someone should have. I apologize. What is it you young folk say—my bad?"

"Young folk?" Sam said, making a face at

Miguel. "What is this, *Little House on the Prairie*?" They both burst out laughing.

"Glad I could amuse you two. You know, someday you *young folk* are going to be old, and we'll see how funny you think it is."

"Never happen," Sam said. "Our generation's going to find a cure for that."

"For sure," Miguel said.

"Good luck with that. I'll catch you crazy boys later," I said, smiling at their naïveté.

"Love you, *mama dos*," Sam called after me.

"Me too," Miguel echoed.

It made me happy that Sam would stop by to see his father. Now that their relationship had evened out—mostly because Gabe had learned to accept his son for who he was and not expect him to be a carbon copy of Gabe—they were really good for each other. Sam might be lacking a little in the ambition department, but that might change. With his easygoing personality, I had no doubt he'd always find a job of some kind.

The main parking lot for the hospital had been full when I'd arrived, so I'd had to park over on the side lot near the emergency room. So when I reached the lobby, I turned left to go through the emergency room waiting area, a shortcut to my truck. In the hallway outside the emergency room, I ran into Yvette Arnaud.

"Hey, Detective Arnaud," I said. "Fancy meeting you here. Are you here to talk to Miguel again?"

"No, no," she said. "My mother. She fell . . ."

"Oh, I'm sorry," I said, instinctively reaching over to touch her arm despite the fact I barely knew her. "Is she hurt badly?"

"She hit her head. She's getting a CT scan right now." Her hand shook as she touched her mouth. "No one was there. I was working and Van was supposed . . . She was alone and then she fell. She lay there for hours. I . . ."

"When did she go in?" I asked.

"About ten minutes ago. They said she'd be there for about an hour."

"Then you have time to get a cup of coffee. Let me take you down to the cafeteria . . ."

"No, I couldn't . . . I mean . . . drink more caffeine." Her smile was tremulous when she held out her hand. It was visibly shaking. "Glad I'm not working SWAT. Couldn't shoot the broad side of an elephant today."

"How about some herbal tea, then? Or a strawberry malt? Believe it or not, they make great shakes and malts in the hospital cafeteria. They won second place in the *Tribune*'s Best of San Celina competition."

She hesitated, then said, "Okay."

On the elevator ride down to the basement where the cafeteria was located, she told me some of the details about her mother's dilemma.

"She has one of those neck things, you know, where you press the button and summon help?"

I nodded. I'd seen and made fun of the commercials for that product along with everyone else. Now that I had so many aging relatives, the product didn't seem quite so funny. "Is that how she got help?"

"No, I found her. She was knocked unconscious, so she couldn't press the button."

A fatal flaw in the system, I thought. How could technology fix that?

"She wouldn't have pressed it anyway," Yvette said, her voice bitter. "She thinks the lifeline is stupid and a waste of money. But she won't agree to assisted living and won't agree to someone staying there during the day. It's all on Van and me, and it's getting . . . hard. Thank God his parents are dead."

She glanced over at me, her face blanched. "Oh, that sounds horrible. I didn't mean . . ."

"It's okay. I understand what you were trying to say."

We reached the cafeteria and stood in line. I ordered a strawberry malt and some French fries; she chose skim milk and a toasted bagel.

"I'll try a malt another time," she said. "My stomach's a little upset."

"Absolutely understandable," I said, motioning at her to put away her wallet. "This is on me. What with this sniper business and now your mom, I'd have an ulcer or three by now if I were in your shoes."

She gave a half smile and picked up her tray. "You don't fool me, Benni. Things aren't all that rosy for you these days, I'm sure."

"You're right," I said, thinking, You have no idea. "But I was just trying to make you feel better. Misery loves company and all that jazz." I pointed my tray toward a table in the back of the busy cafeteria.

Once we sat down, we ate silently for a few minutes. I was beginning to think she'd regretted taking me up on my offer to talk, when she spoke.

"It's just so hard," she said, her head down, studying her bagel as if the answer were written there in sesame and poppy seeds. "I can't seem to make her happy. I can't make Van happy. He hates it here. My mother drives him nuts. I can't get a handle on this sniper . . ."

I ran my finger down the side of the icy silver shaker that contained part of my malt. "You have a lot on your plate right now. Anyone would be overwhelmed."

When she looked up, her expression was panicked, as if suddenly realizing who I was, who I went home to after this. "I can handle this task force. I did it in New Iberia. We caught the sniper. He was a disgruntled oil rig worker, angry because they'd cut off his disability check. The only disability he had was a fear of hard work."

Her face grew hard. "We'll catch this guy too."

"I know you will," I said, quickly realizing I'd hit a sore spot. "Gabe thinks very highly of you."

"I shouldn't be talking to you . . . I . . . this is . . ." She shoved the bagel aside. She'd only taken two small bites. "I'm not usually this unprofessional."

"Having feelings isn't unprofessional. Having feelings is human."

"But men . . . your husband . . . they don't respect an officer who breaks down. I can handle this." She started to stand up.

"Wait," I said, reaching out. "Anything you tell me stays with me. I promise. Do you have any friends here? I mean female friends?"

She slowly shook her head no, the hard lines of her face softening.

"Look, you need help to get through this. I . . ."

Before I could finish, her tough cop mask was back. She pushed aside her tray a little too forcefully, causing her half-empty glass to clink against the plate. She slid smoothly out of the booth. "Thanks for listening, but I can handle this. Please excuse me, I need to see about my mother."

I watched her walk away, her back straight and unyielding. I wanted to do something to help her, but what could I do? She didn't want my help. I looked down at my half-eaten French fries, my appetite gone. I cleaned up both Yvette's tray and my own and walked out to my truck. Once inside,

I tried calling Hud again. Again I got his voice mail on the first ring. I was getting the feeling he was avoiding me.

"Hud, call me. Right now. If you can't find anything about Lin, that's okay. I just need to know. Bye."

I stared at my cell phone for a moment, then dialed another number.

"San Celina Sheriff's Department. How may I direct your call?"

"Sheila? It's Benni Harper. Uh, Ortiz."

"Well, which one is it, girl? Believe me, if I was married to that hunk of a police chief, I'd never forget my last name." Sheila gave a loud, honking laugh, followed by a fit of coughing. "Sorry, my allergies have been driving me nuts. Doc says it's mold. I said, hey, I might be old, but I'm not moldy . . . yet." Another wet laugh.

"With how cranky Señor Ortiz has been the last few days, I'd sell him to you for one of your caramel cakes." Sheila Waterston, the receptionist at the sheriff's department for the last hundred years, also baked the best cakes in the county. She rarely made them for money but would bake one for charity, for a gift or for a friend.

"This sniper business has all the boys and girls here with their hands hovering over their weapons, jumpy as a cat in a yard full of pit bulls. I'm afraid to sneeze, to be honest with you. Someone might turn me into Swiss cheese."

"Something has to break soon. So many agencies are working on it."

"That may be the problem, sweetie pie. So, what can I do you for?"

"Is Detective Hudson in his office?"

"No, ma'am. He's gone with the wind until further notice."

"What?"

"Took some vacation time. As of yesterday. Easy for him to do that since he works the iceboxes." That was what Sheila called the cold cases. "Want to leave a message?"

"No, thanks. Wasn't urgent. Catch you later."

I dialed Hud's cell phone again. Voice mail. "Okay, Hud, quit playing games with me. I just called your office and they said you're on vacation. I'm assuming you are working on what I asked you about, but I don't know for sure because *you won't answer my calls!* Call me back immediately. I mean it."

I sat for a moment in my truck, not sure what to do. Yvette's dilemma kept coming back to me, and I wondered if I should do something, tell someone.

But who? Certainly not Gabe. I'd promised her I wouldn't reveal any confidence, but she and her husband were definitely in a tough spot and needed help.

I sighed and turned my ignition. There was nothing I could do except make myself available if she needed to talk. Her situation wasn't unusual. Another woman torn between her demanding job, her spouse and his needs and her aging parent's needs. It was a sad, familiar story. What I wished Yvette Arnaud understood was, it was a heck of a lot easier when you had girl-friends. Somehow I couldn't imagine her opening up in the same way to any of the male detectives working with her. Apparently, she hadn't made any female friends yet in San Celina.

Gabe actually did make it home early that night. We drove into Morro Bay, ate lobster tails and filet mignon, walked along the Embarcadero and talked about everything except the sniper. I told him about Dot Haggerty, Daddy's secret girlfriend, which gave him a good laugh. We speculated what the girls would do when they eventually found out about Dot. We watched the sun set behind Morro Rock and listened to a blues guitarist at the Bayou Blues Club.

While I watched the fishing boats bob gently in the waves, Gabe's arm around my shoulders, his breath soft and warm in my ear, in that moment, despite the sniper, despite Lin and Tessa and the changes they might bring into our life, at this very moment, I was happy; I was content. And I was old enough now to appreciate the rarity of that feeling, knowing enough to enjoy it and to wrap the memory carefully in tissue and save it for later, for the hard times that would, as cer-tain as the setting sun, descend upon us.

Chapter 16

When we got home from Morro Bay that night, we made love, the perfect ending to a perfect evening. Except it wasn't the real ending. The real ending was when he kissed me one last time and left our bed, making that long walk down the hallway to the guest room.

"Stay," I said.

"Wait," he replied.

Our marriage problem in haiku. Though Gabe had a good night, that is, one free of troubling dreams, I'd decided the next morning that was enough. We needed help. After Gabe went to work, I called Dr. Kaplan. I had the perfect excuse: my need to interview him for Isaac's book. While I was there, I'd casually ask him about post-traumatic stress in veterans. If he couldn't help me, maybe he could point me in the direction of someone who could. At least I wouldn't be sitting around doing nothing.

"Do you have any free time today?" I asked him on the phone. "I'm sorry for the short notice, but I happened to be off work today. I'm trying to do my part of this book in between my real life."

"Fortunately, you caught me on an off day. That is, I'm off from work. Not off as in crazy." Dr. Kaplan's laugh was deep and full; it seemed to fill up the phone. "Though there are some who know me who might beg to differ."

I couldn't help laughing with him. "Do psychiatrists actually use words like *crazy?*"

"Only when we're not using the word *nuts* or *cuckoo,*" he said. "How about two o'clock?"

"I'll be there."

That meant I had the morning to kill since it was only nine a.m. Though I knew it was probably useless, I tried Hud's cell phone. Voice mail again.

"You are in big, big trouble, Detective Hudson. *Mucho* big trouble. It was somewhat amusing yesterday, but I am pissed now. Call me back." I punched the off button with vehemence, though he'd never know it. It was something that was completely unsatisfying about cell phones. It was hard to make a dramatic point like slamming down a receiver. This younger generation had no idea what delightfully dramatic gestures they were missing.

I spent the rest of the morning getting our physical house back in order. This last week, Gabe and I had both neglected household chores while he was dealing with the sniper and I was supervising the Memory Festival. Last night I'd used the last clean bath towel. It was time for someone to do laundry. Normally we did chores together or split the work. Despite his macho Latino male tendencies in some areas, Gabe had always done his share of household chores. He liked order and was willing to pitch in to make sure our house was neat and clean.

So this would be my gift to him today—Mr. Neatnik Marine Corps. When he arrived home tonight, he would find a clean house, clean towels and, if I got back from Dr. Kaplan's in time, maybe dinner on the table . . . or warming in the oven, since his schedule was so unpredictable.

I did draw the line at wearing a frilly apron.

I turned all our radios and the downstairs stereo on to our local country-western station—KCOW —and let Brahma Bob and George Strait encourage me in my housework.

Before I knew it, it was one p.m. and the house sparkled. I took a quick shower, gave Scout a dog chew and headed for Pismo Beach. I pulled up in front of Dr. Kaplan's house with two minutes to spare.

He had his front door open before I closed my truck door.

"Right on time!" he called.

"What does that say about me?" I gave a nervous laugh and tucked my notebook under my arm.

"That you're punctual?" He gave a hearty laugh, setting me at ease. "Forget I'm a psychiatrist, okay? I'm just a guy you're interviewing for your book." He opened his front door, sweeping his arm out in front of him.

"I'll try," I said, feeling foolish.

"Now, don't feel silly," he said, causing me to give him a surprised look.

He laughed again. "No, I'm not psychic. I've just been a psychiatrist for a long time. I'll tell you a secret." He lowered his voice as if there were a crowd of people straining to hear his words. "Sometimes I tell people I'm a mailman. Then all they ask is if I've ever gone postal. I lift my eyebrows slowly and then they immediately change the subject."

"That's so bad," I said, laughing.

He grinned, looking as impish as a twelve-year-old boy. "Fun, though."

"I'll bet."

Inside, he asked me what I'd like to drink, giving me a list as long as a Starbucks menu.

"I know, I know," he said, holding up his hands. "I sound like I was a barista in a former life. It's how I relax, learning to make new drinks."

I chose a chai tea latte.

"Good choice," he said, making me feel oddly like I'd gotten an answer right on some imaginary test. "I'll have one too."

He talked the whole time he made our drinks, his deep voice booming from the kitchen. He'd taken his boat out this morning and had seen what he thought might be a blue whale. His grandma used to collect whale knickknacks. He once tasted whale blubber while on a trip to Japan.

"It *doesn't* taste at all like chicken," he said, carrying our drinks into the living room on a teakwood tray. Cardamom and honey scented the air, intermingling with the smoky scent from the oak wood fire.

When I didn't react, he said, "That's a joke. Admittedly, a lame one."

I gave another nervous laugh, took a sip from my drink, then set it on the ceramic coaster on the coffee table. "I have some more questions and also need to recheck some of the things you told Isaac and me when he took your photo."

"Have you seen the proofs?" he asked.

"No, things have been a little . . . busy in my life."

He nodded. "Isaac came by yesterday with the contact sheets. I have to tell you, I felt as excited as a teenage boy on the first day of football practice. It's a real honor to be photographed by your grandfather."

I almost corrected him. Not because I was ashamed of being mistaken for Isaac's grand-daughter. There wasn't anything that would be more wonderful than to be actually related to him by blood. I just didn't want it to look like I was trying to be someone I wasn't.

Dr. Kaplan took a sip of his drink. "Don't worry,

Benni, I know he's not your natural grandfather. But he obviously loves you like you were his own."

My mug of tea stopped halfway to my lips and I stared at him. "How *do* you do that?"

One eyebrow lifted just a fraction of an inch. "I've been observing people for a long time. Most of us wear our whole lives on our faces. Psychiatrists and dogs know that."

"Now, that's an interesting observation." I sipped my tea and set it back down. "You're right. I think our dog, Scout, knows what is happening between Gabe and me before *we* do. It's scary, sometimes."

"Not so much, when you really think about it. They spend their whole lives watching us, trying to decipher our moods, figure out our intentions. They depend on us for everything—food, shelter, affection—so it is definitely in their best interest to know us very well." He held his mug up to me. "So, let's cut to the chase, shall we? You didn't actually come here to interview me for the book. What's going on with you and Gabe? I'm assuming it has to do with this sniper. Has it set off his PTSD?"

I didn't immediately answer. My first thought was, *Thank you.* Tears suddenly stung my eyes. "He has nightmares. Bad ones."

He nodded and sat back in his chair, holding his mug in both hands. "Tell me about them."

For the first time in a week, I completely let down my guard about Gabe's nightmares. Though I'd talked to Emory and the Coffin Star Quilt Guild ladies, I'd tried to keep a positive spin, tried to hide my fear.

But with Dr. Kaplan, because of who he was, because I didn't feel the need to "keep Gabe's cover," I was absolutely candid. He let me talk and talk and talk, gently prompting me with questions, until hot tears were flowing like a mountain stream down my cheeks. He silently stood up, fetched me a box of tissues, and let me cry and talk, cry and talk. The only thing I could not bear to talk about was Lin Snider and Tessa.

An hour later, I sat hiccupping and emotionally drained, an embarrassingly large pile of tissues covering my lap.

I looked down at them in dismay. "Do you . . . where can I . . . ?"

"Trash is under the sink in the kitchen," he said. "Bathroom is down the hall to your left. I'll make us both another chai latte."

Once I'd used the bathroom and rinsed my swollen eyes, I went back out to the living room. Dr. Kaplan was standing in front of the picture window, his back to me. He turned around and smiled when he heard me enter the room.

"Feeling better?" he asked.

I nodded. "I'm so sorry, Dr. Kaplan. I did

mean to ask you about Gabe, but I didn't mean to totally fall apart."

"No worries," he said. "And call me Pete. Or Dr. Pete, if that makes you more comfortable. I asked and you responded. Healthiest thing you could have done. For you and, ultimately, we can hope, for Gabe." He gestured at me to have a seat. He sat down across from me on a matching love seat. "Tell me, do you think Gabe would talk to me?"

"I doubt it. He'd probably kill me for even mentioning the nightmares to you." My hand came up to my mouth. "Metaphorically speaking, of course. He has never been violent with me. I mean, not consciously." I'd told him about Gabe striking me in his sleep.

Dr. Pete waved his hand. "That wasn't you he was lashing out at. Though there's nothing simple about PTSD, it definitely sounds like that is what is going on with him, likely set off by this sniper situation."

"That's what I thought." I took another tissue, twisting it in my fingers. "What do you think I should do?"

He gave a wry smile. "Are you asking what can *I* do about it?"

I nodded mutely.

"Well, talk therapy can help. Maybe some anti-depressants or sleep medication as a temporary measure. He and I can do many things. However, the magic words are, of course, he and I. You can't do this for him."

I looked down at my hands, clenched around the wad of tissue. "Yes, I know."

"Is there any way you can convince him to talk to me?"

"I can try. But I can almost guarantee he won't while this sniper is still out there."

"Fair enough. Let me give you my card." He stood up, went over to a door next to the entry and opened it. From where I was sitting, I could see it was an office with a desk, two easy chairs, a credenza and a couple of bookshelves. He came back out and handed me a cream-colored card with simple raised black letters—Peter Kaplan, M.D. Psychiatry.

He turned it over and jotted something on the back. "That's my cell number and my e-mail. Let Gabe know he's free to use either one." He handed it to me. "You too, for that matter."

"Thank you," I said, sticking the card in my back pocket. "I'll talk to him about it as soon as . . . it's possible."

"You'll know the right time. I have a feeling that Gabe knows that this is more than he can handle this time. Sometimes a person in trouble just needs someone else to do the footwork for them. Please, don't give up hope."

"I won't. The fact that Cy Johnson thinks highly of you . . . that'll go a long way in your favor."

"Cy's a good man. He has helped many troubled veterans. He kind of sees it as a mission from God. I like him a lot."

"Me too."

I stood up and picked up my backpack. "I'm sorry for taking up so much of your time."

He held up a hand. "No apologies. I was glad to help."

"I feel like I should pay you something. This is what you do for a living, after all."

"Then make a donation to a veterans' charity. They always need money."

"I will. I promise."

It was four thirty when I started home. By the time I reached the turnoff for Port San Patricio, I realized that I was going to need another hour or so before seeing Gabe, to allow my swollen eyes to calm down. I drove the winding, two-lane road to the pier and parked in front of the Fat Cat Café, a local twenty-four-hour diner that was a favorite of late-night drinkers and fishermen. I called Gabe at the office, excuses for being late forming in my head. Maggie answered.

"He's in another meeting," she said. "The FBI is getting antsy, trying to take over. Chief is getting territorial, growling back, ready to bite some-body's balls. It's a jungle in there. The mayor has called three times. If something doesn't break soon, I'm going to find that sniper my own self and twist his or her little head off with my bare hands. I'm sick of this."

"In other words, I shouldn't bother making dinner?"

"My guess is he'll be in the boxing ring for another couple hours. I'd say don't bother cooking, but have a Prozac milk shake ready."

"I wish," I said, thinking about what Dr. Pete had said about drug therapy in tandem with talk therapy. Would Gabe ever agree to either?

"You take a sip too, sweetie. And save some for me."

"Hang in there, Maggie. Try to make sure he eats something."

"I'm doing my best."

Then I tried to call Hud again. This time he answered.

"Hey, Señora Ortiz, what's new?"

"Haven't you gotten any of my messages? Where have you been? Why did you say you'd help me and then just take off? I should have known better than to trust . . ."

"Hey, hey," he broke in. "Calm down, ranch girl. I've been working hard on our case. I was just getting ready to call you, as a matter of fact."

"Liar."

"That's not a very nice thing to say to someone who just might have solved your mystery woman dilemma."

I straightened up, my heart pounding. "What did you find out? Where are you?"

"I'm closer than you think. I'm at the airport walking out to my truck. Are you at home?"

"The San Celina airport?"

"No, Bangkok International. Of course the San Celina airport."

"Where did you go?"

"Seattle. And have I got some interesting things to tell you."

"What?"

"No, I want to see your face. Where are you?"

"I'm not at home. I'm at Port San Patricio."

"What are you doing there?"

I stared out my truck's front window at the peeling, dry-docked boat in front of me. Someone had named it *Wishful Thinking*. "Long story."

"Do you have dinner plans?"

"No, Gabe is working late."

"Then I'll meet you at Fat Cat's. I can be there in twenty."

Fortunately, Fat Cat's on a Tuesday evening was not crowded. The fishermen tended to eat here either early in the morning or late at night. And the college students, who loved the huge three-cheese omelets and home-fried potatoes as a way to counteract an overindulgence of beer, tended to patronize the café more on the weekends after two a.m. Tonight the café was quiet, with only a few booths filled with what appeared to be local residents. I chose a booth by the window so I could watch Hud drive into the parking lot. True to his word, he was there in just under twenty minutes.

He waved at me when he stepped out of his truck and was sliding across from me two minutes later.

"Did you order yet?" he asked.

"No, I'm not really hungry."

"Well, I'm starving. Let me order and then I'll tell you what I found out."

I waited patiently, drumming my fingers while he perused the menu, whistling softly under his breath. After ordering a cheeseburger, French fries, a chocolate shake and a dinner salad, he took a sip of his water, looked up at me and grinned like a maniac.

I slapped the table once. "Tell me what you found out."

He pulled a photograph out of the top pocket of his leather jacket and placed it carefully down on the table between us. He pushed it toward me with one finger. It was a photo of a woman wearing a black sweater and long, dangling silver earrings. It was Lin Snider. Except she had shoulder-length hair.

"So?" I said. "You have a photo of Lin Snider before she cut her hair."

"Look closer, *ma petite jolie blonde*."

I leaned closer and peered at the photo. It

wasn't Lin Snider, but looked enough like her to be her sister. The face was a tad narrower, the cheekbones more pronounced. And, if you looked closely, there was a Marilyn Monroe–type mole next to her lip.

"So, who is it? Her sister?"

He grinned again. "Benni Harper Ortiz, meet the *real* Linda Snider. Of Seattle, Washington. Linora Snider's coworker and friend."

Chapter 17

"What?" I grabbed the photo and looked more closely. "I don't get it. Linora Snider? Linda Snider? Who's the woman here in San Celina?"

"I know it's weird, but here's the story in a nutshell. The woman staying at the Spotted Pelican is Linora Snider *posing* as Linda Snider."

I sat back in the booth. The cold from the vinyl seeped through my cotton shirt, and I shivered. "I still don't get it."

He pulled off his leather jacket and handed it over the table to me. "I don't have the whole story because the *real* Linda Snider didn't have it. She and Linora are casual friends. They worked for the same company in Seattle and became acquainted when people kept getting mixed up."

"Okay . . ." It still wasn't clear.

"This is what Linda told me. She and Linora were called Lin One and Lin Two at the company where they worked. To keep things straight as I tell this confusing tale, keep in mind that Linda is the real Linda Snider, my Seattle contact, and Lin is Linora Snider. They were only six months apart in age and, as you can see by the photo, fairly similar in appearance. They had remarkably similar lives, down to being only children with both parents dead. They even retired within a month of each other. Linda said they lost touch for a few months while figuring out their new lives. Linda did some traveling, visited her nieces and nephews who live around the country. The real Linda Snider never had children." He paused for dramatic effect. "Lin has one daughter. Her name is Tessa."

The girl in the photograph. I felt myself start taking short, shallow breaths. Stop it, I told myself. You'll pass out. Breathe normally. "Okay. What else?"

"After they retired, they went almost a year without seeing each other, though they did send a few postcards and had a telephone conversation or two."

His food arrived, and Hud stopped talking while he messed around with it. "You can talk and play with your food at the same time, can't you?" I said impatiently.

He tilted his head and took a French fry, calmly putting it in his mouth. "The longer I know you, the less I envy Gabe."

"Trust me, Hud. You don't want to tease me right now."

He pushed the plate of French fries to the middle of the table. "Help me eat these. Okay, where was I? So eventually they had lunch together. Linda said that Lin seemed a little quiet and troubled. It was over lunch that Lin asked Linda for a favor."

I took a French fry, contemplated it, then put it back. "What?"

"Now, pay attention here. Linora asked Linda if she could borrow her identity."

Nervous, I picked up the French fry again and bit it. "Why?"

He lifted his shoulders. "Got me. Linda didn't know either. Lin wouldn't tell her but assured Linda that she wasn't going to do anything illegal. Lin implied that it was to throw someone off who she'd once known. Still, Linda felt funny about it. She was an accountant by trade and by nature. She liked things to be in their proper place. When she tried to find out more about why Lin needed her identity, her friend was too vague. So she turned her down."

"This is getting too weird and convoluted for me. How did Lin get Linda's identity?"

"She bought it, I'm guessing. Easy enough to do, especially since she'd worked in payroll and knew Linda's important numbers like her driver's license and Social Security number. Even her license plates are copies of Linda Snider's. Believe it or not, they have the same car. Phony documents are way too easy to buy."

"But why? I still don't get why."

"That part, unfortunately, Linda couldn't help

with. When I quizzed her more thoroughly about Lin's life, she was not that forthcoming. She was still a little suspicious of me and protective of her friend, despite her friend's mysterious request. Until, of course, I showed her my badge." He took a big bite from his cheeseburger, groaning with pleasure. After he swallowed, he said, "It's amazing how accommodating people can be when I flash that baby."

"Can you stop patting yourself on the back long enough to tell me the rest of the story?"

"Testy, testy. Linda told me what she knew about Lin, which, surprisingly, fits a lot of the story our Lin told you. Lin didn't borrow Linda's entire life. She didn't have to. Both were only children. Both of them have lost their parents. However, there was one little thing Lin left out of her history. I'm guessing it was probably the reason she borrowed Linda's identity, in case someone did do some checking. Someone like you . . . or Gabe."

I leaned closer, feeling my stomach churn. "What's that?"

"Before Lin was an accountant, she was a nurse."

I slowly closed my eyes. "She served in Vietnam."

"Well, shoot, you took away one of my surprises."

I opened my eyes and asked, "Her daughter, Tessa. How old is she?"

"Twenty-eight, according to her birth certificate. She was born . . ."

"In Los Angeles," I finished. "In 1970."

He took a long drag from his chocolate shake. "So, you know most of this already. Why did you need me?"

"I didn't know it. I guessed it."

"When was Gabe over there?"

My words came out in a whisper. "1968 and '69."

His lips tightened for a minute. "What're you going to do?"

I stared at my hands. "I don't know. It's . . . right now isn't the best time to spring something like this on him. But I might not have a choice. I want to tell him before Lin does."

"What can I do to help?" His face was open, nonjudgmental.

"Nothing, except what you've already done. Thank you. I'm sorry if I was snappy with you."

"Forget it. If you weren't snapping at me, I'd have to check your temperature, make sure you didn't have malaria or beriberi or something."

"Finish your dinner. I need some time to think."

Hud silently ate his cheeseburger while I played with a plastic straw, bending it around and around my finger. It started to get dark around us; the café started to fill up. It was a cold night, and this was probably the warmest spot for miles.

"I fell off this pier once," I told him, tossing aside my tortured drinking straw.

"You did? When you were a kid?"

I turned my head to look at my reflection in the window. "No, as an adult. Not that long ago. When Gabe and I were first dating. A murder suspect pushed me." On the edge of my reflection, I could see the lights from the fishing boats start to sparkle on the black ocean.

"Why doesn't that surprise me?"

I looked back at Hud's boy-next-door face. "It was around this time of year, and it was one of the scariest moments of my life. All that dark, freezing water. My clothes were so heavy. I thought I was going to die. I saw my mother's face. And Jack's. At least I thought I did. Then Gabe's face replaced both of theirs, and he told me to swim toward him. So I did. And I was saved."

Hud smirked at me over his coffee mug. "Okay, I'll admit your husband is a good-looking son of a gun, but he's not God."

I rested my chin in my hand. "I don't mean that way. I was literally saved. I was pulled out of the water."

"By Gabe?"

I gazed out through the window into the darkness. "No, by a guy named Clay O'Hara. An old boyfriend of mine. He lives in Colorado. He was in love with me. Or thought he was. Gabe proposed to me that night, and I accepted. We were married three days later."

"So some old boyfriend who has the hots for you saves you from drowning and you marry the chief? Doesn't sound fair."

"I guess life mostly isn't, is it?"

"I guess not."

I glanced over at the yellow and black Felix the Cat clock over the cook's pass-through. "It's almost six thirty. I need to go home. Scout's probably chewed off his front paw in hunger."

I slid out of the booth, pulled off Hud's jacket and laid it on the seat next to him.

He grabbed it and threw two twenties on the table.

"That's a big tip," I said.

"Someone may as well have a happy night."

At my truck, he gave me a hug and whispered, "Call me if you need anything. Even just to talk. Promise?"

"Thanks."

On the drive home, I worried the information about Lin Snider as if it was a piece of tough steak. A part of me wanted to confront Gabe right off, ask him if he'd had an affair with a nurse when he was in Vietnam. An affair that might have resulted in a child. But was that my place? What if I was wrong? What if Lin Snider had absolutely nothing to do with Gabe?

My gut and the facts told me that wasn't the

case. But my gut had been wrong before. Still, there were all these facts. What I needed to do before anything was talk to Lin herself. I needed to confront her with what I had discovered and ask her flat-out what she was doing in San Celina, what she wanted from Gabe, from us.

The trouble was I couldn't even imagine how I'd begin.

Chapter 18

It was past seven p.m. when I arrived home, and poor Scout was starving. In penance, I gave him an extra scoop of canned food along with a sprinkling of cheddar cheese, his favorite treat.

"I promise to never be this late again," I said, stroking his broad, shiny back. He ignored me and kept eating. He knew I would likely break my promise and he would forgive me. It's what dogs do best, forgive with grace, a lesson straight from God.

The minute Gabe walked through the door an hour later, I heard the thump of his briefcase when he dropped it on the entryway floor. Muttered Spanish curses followed seconds later. I didn't ask him if there'd been any progress. His defeated expression told me there hadn't been. I heated some chicken soup, made him garlic toast and left him to eat dinner in front of the television.

Upstairs, I puttered around the bedroom, folding clothes and straightening my dresser drawers. It was busywork, but I needed something to do while I mulled over what I should do about Lin Snider. By the time Gabe came up to shower, I'd made my decision. I was going to call her tomorrow, tell her I knew her real identity and that I wanted to talk face-to-face. Before Gabe found out, I needed to know what she wanted. I knew that he'd be annoyed when he found out that I'd not come to him right away. But one look at his face when he came in tonight told me that one more emotional problem would send him over the edge. A fierce part of me wanted to protect my husband. If this child were his, we would deal with that. But before I'd let this woman turn our lives upside down, I wanted to know all the facts. It was a lesson I'd learned from Dove from the time I could understand her words.

"Learn all the facts you can about a problem," she would tell me. "Then wait a day. If you apply that to everything you do in life, you'll end up being a lot better off."

When I was old enough to see the disparity in her advice and her own living, she'd cut me off with, "Do as I say, not as I do. I am a wise woman, but not wise enough to follow my own advice."

I never quite knew how to answer that.

"Going to bed early?" I asked Gabe, when he opened the dresser drawer.

"Thought I would. I'm beat."

"I'm going to walk down to Emory and Elvia's house. She has something I need to give Dove tomorrow." It was a totally manufactured errand.

What I was going to do was call Lin Snider and demand to see her tomorrow. That was *almost* waiting a day, right?

"Be careful," he said.

"I'll take Scout. He can use the exercise."

Fortunately, I'd not cleaned out my leather backpack in the last week. Lin Snider's cell phone number, carelessly written on a crumpled Post-it, was at the bottom under a half-eaten package of M&M'S. With Scout on his leash, I walked toward Emory and Elvia's house, turning at the block right before their house, and headed downtown. I found a quiet spot on a low brick wall in front of a closed nail parlor and dialed Lin Snider.

"Hello?" Her voice was tentative.

"Lin? This is Benni Ortiz."

"Benni!" Her tone grew warmer. "How are you?"

"Fine. Look, I won't waste your time. I know who you are and I know about Tessa. We need to talk."

"Oh." The word was part sigh, part exclamation.

For a moment, I felt like a jerk. Then I remembered that she was the one who came into town under false pretenses, she was the one determined to mess up my life. "Whatever you have to say, I want to hear it before Gabe does. He's under tremendous pressure right now, and he doesn't need any added stress. His health is my primary concern."

"I agree. This might be hard for you to believe, but I don't want him hurt either. I care about him deeply."

Her words were an arrow through my heart. "When can we meet?"

"How about tomorrow?"

"Morning?"

She hesitated. "How about early afternoon? One p.m.? I've not been sleeping well. Mornings are sometimes hard."

"One p.m. is fine. Shall we meet at your hotel?"

"Yes. I'm staying at the Spotted Pelican in Morro Bay. Do you need directions?"

"I know where it is. See you then." I hung up and sat on the brick wall for a while watching Cal Poly students wander up and down the street, laughing and goofing off, clueless to the complex adult world that lay ahead of them.

After a few minutes, I started back toward home. Halfway there, I realized that Gabe might notice that I didn't bring anything back from Elvia's, my excuse for leaving. I'd wing it, come up with some reason I returned empty-handed. It ended up not being an issue because he'd already gone to bed.

"I'm home," I said, sticking my head through the guest room doorway. He lay on his back, staring at the ceiling. "Everything's locked up tight, Chief."

"Good night," he said without turning his head.

"Are you okay? Dumb question, I know . . ."

He patted the mattress next to him. "I have something I've been thinking about lately, and I want to talk to you about it."

I sat down beside him.

"I'm considering turning in my resignation."

I stared into his eyes, the pupils black dots against a blue-gray as unfathomable as the ocean. "How long have you been thinking about this?"

"A little while now. You know I love the work. I love my officers, but the politics"—his jaw turned to steel—"I hate the politics."

He was considering something that I'd often silently wished for, that he leave the police force, become a civilian. But, to be honest, now that it was an actual possibility, I struggled to imagine what would come next.

"What would you do? I mean, for a living. What . . ."

"Good question." He bent his head, rubbing his temples with his thumbs. "I don't have any idea." He looked up, his face intent, as if dissecting my reaction. "I need to know one thing. Would you stay with me? Would you go with me? I mean, if we have to leave San Celina?"

"Of course," I said, though I could not imagine leaving my home. But, still, I said it.

The lines of his forehead smoothed out. "It's not something we have to decide tonight. It's

411

just that my life has gotten so complicated. More than I ever dreamed possible."

"No, we don't have to decide anything tonight." I moved toward him, kissing his lips, thinking, Complicated? Oh, Friday, you have no idea how much more complicated your life might be getting.

Chapter 19

The next day was cold and gray, matching the somber atmosphere around our house. Even Scout, normally a cheerful dog, seemed morose. Right after his breakfast, he slunk over to his bed in the corner of the living room and buried his nose under his fuzzy blanket.

"Scooby-Doo, that's exactly what I feel like," I told him, stroking his smooth back.

Gabe left for work at his normal time, but I could tell he was dreading whatever the day had to bring.

"Something is bound to break soon," I said, hugging him. His crisp white dress shirt felt cool and familiar against my cheek. "Something good," I felt compelled to add.

"I'll call you when I can," he said, kissing the top of my head.

Once he was gone, I dressed in jeans and a sweatshirt, then decided to do the human equivalent of Scout's canine escape of burying his head under blankets—watching daytime talk shows with my front window blinds closed.

When the doorbell rang a half hour later, I considered ignoring it. But Scout bounded off his bed with his tail wagging, which meant it was someone we knew. I turned off the television and answered the front door.

"I could use a cup of coffee," Aunt Garnet said, standing on my front porch, leaning on her new cane. "I have maple bars." She held up a white bag with a tiny grease stain on the front. "Dove said they are your favorite."

"You are my favorite aunt of all time," I said, gesturing for her to enter. "I'll put the coffee on."

"WW is getting a haircut," she said, following me into the kitchen. "He loves his time at the barbershop. He's made some friends there and I want to encourage it, so I'm looking to kill some time. Dove's over at the historical museum. We're all going to Emory's chicken place for lunch. It's Free Wing Day."

I scooped coffee into the coffeemaker's basket, poured water in the top and flipped it on. "Free Wing Day?"

Aunt Garnet opened a cupboard and pulled out a dinner plate. "Anyone who buys a sandwich or a meal gets an order of free hot wings with their meal." She placed two maple bars and two jelly doughnuts on the plate.

"Yum, jelly's my second favorite."

"Yes, I know. I don't really like wings, but we figure we'll help fill some seats, make Emory's place look busy. Shills, I think they're called in Vegas."

That made me smile. "You're getting downright hip, Aunt Garnet."

A small frown darkened her face as she scratched at a place on the plate. "Just trying to help out family." She looked up. "You might need to change your automatic dishwashing soap."

"Yes, ma'am." Emory's chicken restaurant was doing just fine, but I thought it was sweet of her and Uncle WW to care. "Maybe I'll join you for some wings. My schedule is wide open until one p.m." And I knew I'd only mope around the house and brood if I was alone. Right now, thinking too much about what to say to Lin Snider might not be a good idea. The more I tried to plan my words, the more awkward they sounded in my head. A distraction from my thoughts would be good.

"What's going on at one p.m.?" Aunt Garnet asked, placing a pitcher of milk between us. Behind her, the coffeemaker chugged and sputtered.

I sat down at the table and took a maple bar. "Just meeting with a new co-op member." I concentrated on tearing my doughnut in half, then fourths. Aunt Garnet didn't know me as well as Dove, but I wasn't famous for my poker face, and I didn't want to provoke any curious questions.

"Uh-huh," Aunt Garnet said. The tone of her voice informed me she wasn't buying what I was selling. Still, she gave me a pass. "Did you hear who won the Coffin Star Quilt Guild's graveyard quilt raffle?"

"No, who?" The fireworks incident at the festival had thrown me off, then I'd concentrated on getting everything closed up and secure.

Aunt Garnet carefully cut her maple bar into six neat pieces. "Parkwell Mortuary."

I almost choked on my doughnut. "No way! What are the chances of that happening?"

"It is amusing, isn't it? The *Tribune* is going to do a story on it. Thelma Rook called me from Oak Terrace and said they were over there interviewing the quilt ladies yesterday. Joel Parkwell bought three hundred tickets, so he must have really wanted it. The quilt raffle raised almost three thousand dollars."

"That's wonderful news. I'll have to take the Coffin Star ladies some cupcakes to celebrate. That's the most money one of their quilts has ever earned."

"They're already planning their next one. It's another graveyard quilt, but they're going with a Day of the Dead theme." Aunt Garnet winked at me over her coffee mug. "Apparently, death sells."

"Apparently. And their label on the back is an added extra." I'd designed a special Coffin Star Quilt Guild label for the back of the graveyard quilt. It had the names of all guild members beneath a smiling skull wearing a garden hat decorated with roses and daisies.

While we were finishing our doughnuts, the phone rang.

"Honey bun," Dove said. "Have you seen my sister?"

I smiled over at Aunt Garnet, who was rinsing off our dishes and putting them in the dishwasher. "She's right here, Dove. Uncle WW is catching up on world events at the barbershop, and Aunt Garnet brought me doughnuts."

"Hypocrite."

"What?"

"Garnet, not you. Tell her to quit stuffing her face with junk food and get over to the historical museum. Things are a mess here."

I glanced at the kitchen clock. It was only ten a.m. "I'm not doing anything until this afternoon. Want some extra help?"

"When can you get here?"

"If Aunt Garnet feels like it, I think we'll walk over . . ." I glanced over at Aunt Garnet. She nodded her assent. "We'll see you in a half hour."

On the walk downtown to the historical museum, I maneuvered the conversation to Daddy and his love life, hoping I could convince Aunt Garnet that she and Dove should leave him alone without revealing that he had solved his love problems all on his own.

"What's new on the 'Getting Ben Hitched' front?" I asked.

Aunt Garnet sighed and tucked her arm through mine. "Dove and I are about ready to surrender. Poor boy just seems to want to be alone."

I patted her hand. "Sometimes it's better to let nature take its course. Maybe you inspired him enough to start looking on his own."

"One can hope," Aunt Garnet murmured.

When we reached the museum, we went around to the back door. The museum was closed today, so the parking lot was empty.

"Where's Dove's truck?" I asked.

"Ben dropped us all off downtown. He's over to the Farm Supply. He's meeting us at Emory's place at noon."

Aunt Garnet rang the service bell, and a few minutes later, Dove opened the door.

"You two get in here," she said. "We've got a bunch of stuff to put away."

We walked down the long hallway and came out at the ground level of the old Carnegie Library, where most of the historical museum's displays were located. The room was cool and quiet, smelling as it always did of citrus oil, old wood and dust. Everything appeared to be neatly in its place waiting for the next open day.

"Where's the mess?" I asked.

"Downstairs," Dove replied. "People just up and dumped everything from the festival yesterday right in the middle of our meeting room. We have to move it out of the way. There's a historical society meeting tomorrow morning."

"Where's everyone else?" I asked. There were at least twenty other people involved with the historical society's fair booth presentations.

Dove rolled her eyes. "Everyone's exhausted or thrown out their back or has grandkids that need tending."

"In other words, it's up to the Honeycutt sisters," I said, following her down the wide, wooden stairs.

"What else is new?" Dove grumbled.

Once downstairs, I saw the mess wasn't as horrible as she made it out to be. Mostly it was just a matter of moving boxes into a spare room. I found a small dolly in a back closet and started stacking boxes.

"We'll get this done in no time," I said. "What's the saying, 'Many hands make light work'?"

"I love those old sayings," Aunt Garnet said, folding the top of a loose box closed. "Why aren't there any new ones, I wonder? Seems like they stopped back in World War II."

"Oh, there's still sayings being invented," Dove said. "They're just crazy. Like, 'Make love, not war.' "

"If people did that instead of shooting at each other," Aunt Garnet said, "maybe the world would be a better place."

"Certainly a more populated one," I added. "Is anyone thirsty?"

"I could use some water," Dove said. "There's some in the refrigerator in the break room."

"I'll come with you," Aunt Garnet said. "I need to use the ladies room."

We climbed the stairs to the main floor and were walking down the hallway toward the back of the building when we heard a quick—*pop, pop . . . pop, pop.*

"Now who's playing with fireworks?" Aunt Garnet said, reaching for the bathroom door.

"Probably a car backfiring," I said uneasily, not wanting to alarm her. I recognized gunshots when I heard them. Whatever was happening outside, we were most likely safest right where we were.

While she was in the bathroom, I went to the front of the building and peeked out a window. Since Dove hadn't come barreling up the stairs, I guessed she'd not heard the shots. In front of the museum, people were dashing for cover; a young woman abandoned her flat-tire bike and ducked inside the public bathrooms; a mother and her two kids ran in after the girl. Was it the sniper? In the middle of the day? Or was it indeed a car backfiring and people were just jumpy? Maybe I could hear more out in the garden.

I went back to the hallway where the closed door told me Aunt Garnet was still in the bathroom. I turned left down the hallway and through the door that led to the outside garden. The garden, surrounded by a six-foot brick wall, had always been a special place for me. When this Carnegie-built building was still a public library, I spent many happy hours in this garden reading my first books—*Curious George*, *The Runaway Bunny* and eventually, *Old Yeller*, *Five Children and It* and *Beautiful Joe*.

The garden was empty, and I couldn't hear anything more than some shouting and distant screams, so I turned to go back inside. My hand was on the door when behind me I heard a rustling, then a loud grunt. I swung around in time to see Van Baxter jump down from the brick wall, his face red and sweating.

"Van?" I stuttered, shocked.

"Well, crap," he said and pulled a pistol from his waistband.

Chapter 20

"Don't say a word," he said, pointing it at me.

I stood absolutely still, my hands at my sides. My mind frantically tried to assess what just happened. Van Baxter jumped over the museum wall and was holding a gun on me? *What,* a hysterical voice in my brain screamed. *What?*

"Get inside," he said, motioning me with the pistol to open the door to the museum.

Inside? I froze, my body instinctively refusing to obey. Dove and Aunt Garnet. Van had a gun. He had me hostage. Dove and Aunt Garnet were inside the museum. I needed to protect them. Think. *Think.*

"What is going on, Van?" I said, forcing my voice to sound calm. I moved in front of the solid oak door and tried to send a mental message to Dove and my aunt—Leave, run *now*. If ever I wanted to believe that mental telepathy worked, please, God, it was this moment.

"Get away from the door," he said.

I stood my ground, hoping to give Dove and Garnet time to figure out that something was wrong.

"You're the sniper," I stated.

"The prize goes to the police chief's wife."

I stared at his flushed face. "Why?" I finally said, trying to buy myself time.

He scowled at me. "Seems to me you would understand."

The taste of sugary maple rose up in the back of my throat and I resisted gagging. "But I don't."

His eyes locked with mine. "Maybe you don't. Maybe you don't know what it's like to give up your life for someone who doesn't appreciate it."

I stared at him without answering.

He shrugged. "The first time? I just wanted to see if I could get away with it. Then . . . then it became kind of fun. I like the adrenaline. Reminded me of when I was taking war photographs."

I didn't respond, but just watched his face while I frantically tried to think of what to do.

"C'mon," he said. "You've got a reputation for getting involved with murders. I bet you love the thrill of it."

Anger heated the back of my neck. "I don't try to kill cops."

A flicker of some emotion flashed across his face. Regret? Fear? Then he scowled again. "I wasn't trying to kill anyone."

Before I could answer, Aunt Garnet called my name.

"Benni?" Her voice sounded muffled through

423

the heavy old door. She pushed at it, sending me stumbling toward Van.

"Stop!" he yelled, backing up.

Aunt Garnet's head poked through the doorway. "Oh, my Lord in heaven," she said, opening the door wider. "What is going on out here?"

Van's face tightened in anger. "Who else is here?"

"Uh . . ." I said, again trying to buy time.

"Young man, put that thing away." Aunt Garnet stepped into the garden and pointed a knobby finger at him. "That's just plain dangerous."

"Back inside, old woman." The cords of his neck bulged. His eyes glittered, a crazy light from somewhere inside him.

"Why, there's no need to get nasty—" Aunt Garnet started.

"Do what he says," I hissed, taking her elbow and maneuvering her back inside the museum.

"But—" she said.

"No talking," he commanded.

I felt the gun barrel stab the center of my spine.

"Is there anyone else here?" he asked again.

Hide, Gramma, I thought. *Hide.*

He pointed toward the stairs. "This place have a basement?"

"Yes," I said.

He shoved the gun deeper into my back. "Get going."

Aunt Garnet walked ahead of me. "Dovey," she

called as we clumped down the wooden stairs. "It's just us. Don't be scared. Don't try to get up."

I stared at the back of her gray curls, completely mystified. What kind of warning was that?

"How many more people are here?" Van asked.

"Just my sister," Aunt Garnet said in an unnaturally loud voice. "But don't you worry about her. She can't even walk. She's *crippled,* poor thing. Got the polio when she was six years old. Spent a lot of her life in an iron lung. Weak as a sparrow."

My tongue stuck to the top of my dry mouth. What in the world was Aunt Garnet babbling about?

Downstairs in the large meeting room, Dove sat on an old Queen Anne chair in the corner, her arms resting casually on the carved arms.

"What's going on?" she asked, her face perplexed.

"We seem to have a problem, Sister," Aunt Garnet said. "Actually, I think this young man here might be our sniper."

Dove nodded her head, bringing one hand to rest on her Hawaiian-print cane. "That would be a problem."

"You two shut up," he said, shoving me into Aunt Garnet, almost toppling us over. "I have to think. Sit over there." He pointed at two folding chairs across from Dove.

He looked around the room, his movements

frantic and jerky. "I need time. I am not going to hurt you unless you don't cooperate. But I need time."

He spotted a box of extension cords we'd used in the booths. "I'm going to tie you up and tape your mouths shut. When does this place open next?"

"Tomorrow," I said. "At ten a.m."

"Then someone will find you then. I'll be long gone." He took a length of cord and handed it to me. "Tie her up." He pointed at Aunt Garnet.

He watched me pull Aunt Garnet's arms behind her and tie her wrists. She winced at the discomfort.

"I'm sorry," I whispered.

"Don't worry about it, sweetie pie."

He handed me another set of cords. "Now tie her to the chair." After I'd helped her sit down and tied her feet, he looked over at Dove. "Now, her."

"Oh, for heaven's sakes, young man, she can't even walk," Aunt Garnet said.

I couldn't believe they were still trying to pull one over on Van. Would he fall for it? Had he ever seen Dove around town? This whole handicapped charade depended on Van never having seen her.

He studied Dove a long moment. She gave him her best impression of a sad, scared old lady. "Then just tie her arms."

"The polio has made her circulation bad," Aunt Garnet said. "Please, don't tie her up until right before you leave. It could cause permanent damage."

He could not be that stupid, I thought, looking from Van's face to my gramma's phony expression. Then again, Dove usually won the family poker tournaments simply because we never knew for sure what was going on with her. And it appeared that Aunt Garnet was just as conniving as her sister.

I did not say a word, hoping that my face would not give away their completely insane charade.

"Fine," he snapped, sticking the gun in the waistband of his jeans. "I'll tie up Benni and then the old lady. But you're all getting your mouths taped."

He turned his back to Dove and started wrapping the extension cords around my wrists. He pulled them so tight, I grunted with pain.

The next thing I saw was a whirl of color.

Dove's cane struck the side of Van Baxter's head. With one tiny whimper, he slumped to the ground.

"I decided to go with the metal insert," my gramma said, looking down at him.

"Good call," her sister replied.

After Dove untied us, I called 911.

"Nine-one-one. What's your emergency?" the dispatcher asked.

"It's Benni Ortiz. We're over here at the San Celina Historical Museum by the mission, and I believe my gramma . . ."

"And your aunt," Dove called.

"And my aunt Garnet have captured the San Celina sniper."

"Say what?" the dispatcher asked.

"Yeah, you'd better send in the troops. Oh, and you might include the paramedics and an ambulance. I think the sniper just might have a concussion."

After I hung up, I called Gabe's cell.

"First, I want to assure you that Dove, Aunt Garnet and I are okay." Then I told him what happened, including who the sniper was so, if possible, he could tell Yvette before anyone else did.

"Did he say why?" Gabe asked.

"Yes, I'll tell you the whole story when you get here. Please hurry."

"I'll be there as quickly as I can," Gabe replied.

Within a half hour, every branch of law enforcement you could imagine swarmed the museum. Dove and Aunt Garnet greeted them at the front door of the historical museum, inviting them in and pointing to the staircase to the basement.

"Cool as a couple of Victorian ladies inviting us in for tea and cucumber sandwiches," Janice, one of Gabe's field sergeants, told me later. She had been first on the scene because she was working a case nearby.

I wasn't up there, having been the one elected to stay with a groggy Van Baxter, whose hands we'd duct-taped together. Not that he was in any shape to attack anyone. Like I told the dispatcher, there's a good chance Dove's whack from her cane had given him a concussion.

Gabe arrived only minutes later. The paramedics were still checking Van's vital signs and getting him ready to go to the hospital.

"Are you all right?" Gabe asked, touching my face with his hand.

"I'm okay. It was crazy. It was . . ." I looked up into his face, feeling a hysterical laugh start to bubble up out of me. I swallowed hard, knowing that if I started laughing, I wouldn't be able to stop. What kind of picture would that present to the reporters waiting outside the museum? "Dove and Aunt Garnet were incredible. You aren't going to believe what they pulled off."

I told him the detailed story, while paramedics checked out Dove and Garnet. By the time I finished, Gabe's mouth had turned up into a wry smile.

"I should be embarrassed," he said. "No doubt I'll be ridiculed for the rest of my career about our big sniper case being cracked by sheer accident and my wife being rescued from a hostage situation by two crafty old ladies and a trick cane. But, truthfully, all I can say is, thank you, God."

"Sometimes," I agreed, resting my forehead against his chest, "that's the only thing appropriate to say." I pulled back. "You called Yvette?"

"She was at home. She took the day off because her husband had some business to take care of."

"Oh, no. That will be funny someday, I guess."

"Or not," he replied, his face sober now. "She'll be here as soon as she can. She had to find someone to stay with her mom."

"I wonder if she had any idea that Van was . . ."

"No," Gabe said, his voice firm. "She couldn't possibly have . . ."

He didn't finish his sentence. We locked eyes. His begged me not to say anything more on it. Were we thinking the same thing? She might have suspected, but couldn't face the truth. Sometimes a person wanted something so much that they ignored what was obvious, what was right there in front of them.

Outside, crime scene tape completely circled the museum property, keeping the curious public and the media at a distance. The paramedics were wheeling Van's gurney across the museum's wooden floor when Yvette arrived. Without looking or speaking to anyone, she went to her husband, took his hand and looked down into his face. Everyone froze for a moment, waiting.

"Van," she said in a harsh, agonized voice. "Why?"

He turned his head away and didn't answer. She watched them wheel him away, her back as straight as an iron post. She turned and walked over to Gabe.

"Detective Arnaud," he said, his voice kind. "You are relieved of your duties on this case."

She nodded, swallowing a few times before she spoke. "I don't know what got into him. Really, I don't know why . . ." Her voice faltered and her eyes brimmed with tears. "I should have known."

"He'll need an attorney," Gabe said. "Why don't you take some time off?"

"Excuse me, Chief," one of the uniformed officers broke in. "The media wants a statement for the evening news."

"I'll be right there," Gabe said. He placed his hand on Yvette's shoulder. "Will you be okay, Detective?"

"Yes, sir," she said, raising her chin slightly. "I'll be fine."

We watched Gabe walk toward the front doors where the media waited.

"Are you really okay?" I asked Yvette. "Would you like some water?" I held out a bottle of water that someone had given me. "I didn't drink out of it."

"No, thanks. I'm fine."

A group of detectives came up the stairs, chattering about Van's capture. When they reached the top and saw Yvette, they instantly stopped talking. They glanced at each other, then looked away, embarrassed and unsure about how to react around her.

"C'mon," I said, grabbing her arm and pulling her into a side office where we kept brochures, extra supplies and where docents stored their personal items while working at the museum reception desk. I closed the door behind us. "You'll have some privacy here."

"Like I'll ever have privacy again," she said bitterly. She looked past me, her face rigid with anger. "I had no idea. How stupid is that? I had *no* idea. I feel like such a fool. Why would he be so stupid? I don't understand why."

"I don't know. Maybe he'll tell someone when . . . I don't know . . . maybe he'll tell you why." My babbling embarrassed me into silence.

She dropped her head, covering her face with her hands. In seconds, I could see her shoulders start to shake. I wasn't sure what I should do. Though it felt awkward, I stepped closer to her and touched my hand on her shoulder. Her head jerked up. Her eyes were flooded with tears.

"You know what's crazy?" she said. "I still love him. Isn't that nuts? That I could still love a man who tried to kill cops, who tried to kill my friends?"

"We can't help who we love." I held out the water bottle. This time she took it. "What will you do?"

She gripped the water bottle in her hand. "I don't know. I'm all he has. His parents are dead. He has no siblings and no friends. How can I walk away?" Then she looked up, her eyes full again. "But how can I stay?"

I had no answer.

We stood inside the room for another ten minutes without speaking. Through the door we could hear a muted symphony of men's voices, like the murmuring conversations in a troubling dream. Finally, there was a knock at the door and it opened.

Gabe stuck his head in. "Benni? Someone said Detective Arnaud . . ."

"I'm right here, Chief," Yvette said.

"You need to come to the station."

"Yes, sir." She turned and handed me the half-empty bottle. "Thank you, Benni."

We watched her walk out the door.

"How are Dove and Aunt Garnet doing?" I asked.

Gabe rested a hand against the back of my neck, unconsciously kneading it. "They've been troopers, but they're looking tired. They've given their statements and were interviewed by the *Tribune*. I was going to see if you could convince them to go home. Your dad and uncle are parked over by the mission. I'll have an officer escort them out."

"I'll try."

I found them sitting on a maroon velvet sofa in one of the Victorian exhibits. Gabe was right; they did look exhausted.

"Hey, you hooligans, lounging on the exhibits is against museum rules. I'm going to report you." I perched one hip on a carved sofa arm. The wood dug into my flesh. No wonder the Victorians were so cranky-looking in photographs.

"Gabe says we're all done," Dove said.

"For now. Your chariot awaits. Or at least Daddy in his truck awaits. He and Uncle WW are parked a block away. Gabe said an officer will walk you out."

"Are you sure they don't need us to give our statements again?" Aunt Garnet asked. She and Dove both seemed to be thoroughly enjoying their fifteen minutes of fame. But I also saw the fatigue and fragility in both their faces.

"You'll have the remainder of your lives to talk about this," I said. "Aunt Garnet, you are now officially my favorite hostage partner. You're a rock star."

"Why, thank you, Benni. I take that as a compliment."

Then I hugged my gramma, not wanting to let go. "You were simply magnificent. An Oscar-worthy performance. I'm proud to be related to the Honeycutt girls. Where would I have been without you?"

"Oh, pshaw," Dove said, patting me on the back. "You'd have thought of something if we hadn't. You know my favorite saying . . ."

"Old age and treachery always win out over youth and skill," I filled in, laughing.

"Amen, honey bun. You go on now and take care of your husband."

I leaned down and hugged her. "I'm going back to the station with Gabe. I think I'm gonna bird-dog him for the next few hours so he doesn't get too stressed out."

"Keep us in the loop," Dove said.

"You know I will."

It was after four p.m., and I was sitting in Maggie's office at the police station waiting for Gabe when I finally remembered my appointment with Lin Snider.

"Oh, no!" I said, jumping up.

"What is it?" Maggie asked, alarmed, turning from the tea she was steeping for both of us.

I looked at my watch in panic. "I had an appointment to see someone at one o'clock."

Maggie laughed and turned back to her china teapot. "Sister, that train has left the station. I'm sure if they watch the news they realized you were a little tied up." She giggled. "I mean, literally. It's been the lead story for every broadcast. I heard AP picked it up. They might be hearing about you in Wichita."

"I'd better remind Gabe to call his mom and sisters. And his uncle and aunt in Santa Ana. But this appointment was really, really important, and I'm not certain she would be watching television today."

Maggie nodded over at her phone. "So, call her. Surely she'll understand why you had to reschedule."

"Thanks." I called the cell phone number I had for Lin, but there was no answer. Then I tried her hotel. They put me through to her room, but, again, no answer.

Okay, I thought, I'll try again in an hour. Maybe she gave up waiting for me and went out to eat.

In the next few minutes, Gabe finished up with the last of his meetings with various agencies involved in the sniper investigation. He stood in the doorway to his office, his face pale with fatigue.

"You ready to go home?" he asked me.

"Past ready." I followed him into his office, waiting while he sat down behind his desk and turned off his computer. I went over to his window and looked out over the maintenance yards where two men in overalls were bent over the open hood of a black and white cruiser.

"Gabe, there's someone here to see you," I heard Maggie say.

I turned around in time to see Lin Snider walk into the room. She wore businesslike dark slacks, a white shirt and a tailored jacket. Her back was straight and her cheeks flushed. A surprised gasp lodged silent in my throat.

I glanced over at Gabe, who was still fiddling with his computer.

"Who is it?" he said.

She said simply one word. "Ortiz."

He looked up. There was a moment of absolute quiet, when all I heard was my own breathing and the ticking of Gabe's desk clock.

Then, to my surprise, he straightened up and his hand slowly came up in a salute.

"Lieutenant Spider," he said.

She laughed, then answered, "At ease, Marine."

Chapter 21

They grinned at each other. Then Gabe walked across his office and put his arms around Lin, pulling her into a fierce hug. I stood there watching my worst nightmare come true.

"I was going to wait until all of this sniper business was over before I came to see you," Lin said, finally pulling away. "But I was worried about you. Old habits die hard, I guess." She gave a sound that was half laugh, half sob.

"I can't believe it's you," Gabe said. "After all these years. How are you?"

"We can talk about that later," she said. "Right now, please, let's fill Benni in. I can imagine what she must be thinking."

Gabe turned to me, his face lit up like a young boy's at Christmas. "Benni, this is Lieutenant Linora Snider, R.N. She served three tours in Vietnam. Toughest soldier I've ever met, bar none. Tougher than most marines. And she wraps a mean bandage too."

Lin laughed, sounding young and carefree. "That hurts to say that, doesn't it?" She arched an eyebrow at me. "I'm army, so that's a real compliment from a marine. And he's only saying that because I used to sneak him extra desserts. What I never told him was I did that for hundreds of guys."

"What?" Gabe exclaimed, a huge grin still on his face. "And I thought I was special."

She touched the side of her neck like she was going to brush hair away. Her hand fluttered nervously to her side. "Actually, Benni and I met a week ago, except I didn't tell her I knew you."

Her candor flabbergasted me.

Perplexed, Gabe looked from Lin to me then back to her. "Will someone tell me what's going on?"

"Shall I start or would you like to?" Lin asked me.

"It's a long story," I replied. "Let me call my cousin and ask him to feed and walk our dog. I think we all need to go someplace quiet for dinner and talk."

"Great idea," she said.

We took Lin to our favorite Italian restaurant downtown, Daniello's. Gabe and I were regular customers, so they accommodated our last-minute request for the private dining room in back. We ordered wine, antipasto, garlic bread, salad and lasagna. Daniello's served their food family style.

While we filled our plates, I asked Gabe the first question. "I'm curious about something. When Lin walked into your office, am I crazy or did you call her Lieutenant Spider?"

Gabe grinned. "That was my nickname for her. When I was brought in with my injury from the Bouncing Betty, I also had a bad concussion and a high fever."

"Malaria," Lin said, sipping a glass of wine.

"I was in and out of it for a day or so," Gabe continued. "She introduced herself, but my brain was so fuzzy that I thought she said her name was Lieutenant Spider. I called her that for days before someone finally corrected me. By then, it had become a kind of joke, and everyone started calling her that."

"Yeah, thanks so much for that, Ortiz," she said.

Gabe just couldn't stop grinning. "Nicknames were big in 'Nam. It meant you were liked."

"Unless it was a bad nickname," Lin said.

Gabe nodded and winked at me.

"So, Lin was your nurse," I said, trying to keep my voice light. Is that all? The photograph of Tessa kept coming back to me. Would Lin mention the girl?

"He was a big help to me once he got better," Lin said. "Before they shipped him back." She reached over and touched Gabe's hand. "I missed you when you left."

Gabe took her hand; his expression softened. "Do you ever hear from any of the other guys? Little Joe? Packie? Arturo?" He looked across the table at me. "We were the four amigos. At least, that's what we called ourselves. We weren't in the same platoon, but we all were Lieutenant Spider's patients at the same time."

Lin pulled her hand away and picked up her wine. "You didn't keep up with them?"

Gabe looked down at his plate. "No, I got busy. You know."

"Packie committed suicide in 1992. Pills and booze. His wife found my name and address in a journal he kept. The address was an old one, but the landlord knew where I was living, so he forwarded the funeral program to me. I wrote his wife and she wrote back telling me about how he died."

A flicker of pain wrinkled Gabe's forehead. "Man, that sucks."

"Yeah," she said.

"What about Little Joe?" he asked. "And Arturo."

"Little Joe lives in Oklahoma now. He's been married and divorced four times. Works at a tire place. Drinks a lot, but he's doing okay. He's making it day by day."

"Wow," Gabe said, shaking his head.

"Yeah."

"Arturo?"

She hesitated, and an expression of pain flickered in her eyes. "He died in a car accident."

Gabe was silent for a moment. "When?"

"A long time ago. In 1978. On the Fourth of July. Crazy, huh?"

"I never knew. I didn't . . . keep up with many people. Just a friend from Kansas. Dewey." A friend who ended up betraying and almost killing him. "I didn't really want to talk about 'Nam when I got back to the States so I never looked for anyone."

"Most of us felt that way. It wasn't that kind of war. Not like our fathers' war." She turned to me, attempting to include me in the conversation. "We didn't come back in huge groups like our fathers did after World War II. It felt like once we were done with our tour in Vietnam, our country was ashamed of us. It felt like they were trying to sneak us back into society one by one through the back door. It almost felt like they didn't want us to find each other. And what's really awful is many of us accommodated them."

Gabe nodded in agreement. "For almost ten years I didn't tell anyone I was a Vietnam veteran."

In the dim light of the restaurant, her half smile was sad. "That's sort of what I want to talk to you about." She reached down and pulled something out of her purse. It was the photo of Tessa in front of the bottlebrush bush in Los Angeles.

"Who's this?" Gabe asked, picking up the photo.

"Tessa, my daughter."

He studied the photo closely, then smiled. "She's lovely. What a beautiful smile." His words were sincere; his expression was not condescending or full of pity. He meant what he said. Which was one of the reasons why I loved him.

Looking at her face when he said it, seeing the expression of pride and shy joy at his compliments, I knew in that moment that whatever happened from this encounter, it could only be good.

"I need your help, Gabe," she said, taking another sip of her wine. "Yours too, Benni. I don't have anyone else and . . . Arturo . . . he always told me if I ever needed help, that I should come to you or Packie or Little Joe. That you were men who could be depended on . . . that you'd help me."

Gabe set the photograph down. "What do you need?"

She looked down at the photo. "She's Arturo's daughter. She was conceived in Vietnam. The war will follow her always. He adored her."

After hearing her first sentence, relief washed over me like a flooded river. My feelings shamed me, but selfishly, I was glad that Tessa wasn't Gabe's child.

"How can we help you, Lin?" Gabe asked.

"I want you to take my daughter."

"What?" Gabe's eyebrows moved together, perplexed.

"Please," she said. "I'm dying."

Chapter 22

"The cancer is inoperable," she said. "It's in my pancreas, my liver and now they've found spots in my brain. The doctors say it could be a month, six months, a year. No one knows. But I'm definitely dying."

"I'm so sorry," I said. "Oh, Lin, I'm sorry."

She looked from Gabe to me, clutching the photo of Tessa. "This is crazy, I know. But I have no family. Neither did Arturo. Tessa lives in an assisted living home with other Down syndrome adults. She'll have my pension and my Social Security. I have it set up in a trust with an attorney. Financially, she'll be fine, but . . ." Her voice faltered. "The people who run the home are great, but . . ."

"She needs a family," I said.

"Yes, yes!" she said, tears flowing freely down her cheeks. "It's crazy, but for the last month I've searched out six people who I knew back in 'Nam, people that Arturo knew and trusted. But none of them fit. None of them seemed right. I mean, it can't just be them, but their family has to be okay with it and . . ."

Her blue eyes pleaded with me. "I'm sorry it

444

appeared I was stalking you. I just had to know. I had to make sure that if I asked this of Gabe that his wife and family would be okay with it. I don't want Tessa to live somewhere she isn't wanted."

"Why did you go through the ranch house where my first husband and I lived?" I asked.

She blushed, looking chagrined. "It's silly, but I wanted to know all about you, who you were, what your life in this community was like before Gabe, how you and Gabe came to be together. There was something I liked right off about San Celina and about your family." She smiled at me. "I envied you your life once I looked into it. You have a wonderful family."

"I do," I said. "Why the phony identity?"

"What phony identity?" Gabe asked.

Lin and I looked at each other and smiled.

"I'll explain later," I told Gabe.

"Honestly, I didn't need to do it, but I had this crazy idea that I'd be recognized, so I wanted a cover of some kind. I realized, of course, that all I had to do was avoid Gabe. No one else knew me here. Avoiding him was easy enough to do since he was so completely absorbed in the sniper investigation he was rarely in the same place as you."

She pushed her barely eaten pasta around on her plate. "I have a few other people on my list, but I don't want to continue. I don't need to continue. I want you to be Tessa's legal guardians.

I know it's asking the moon and stars and . . ."

I squeezed Gabe's hand. He squeezed back in silent agreement.

"Of course we will," I said.

"It would be an honor," Gabe added.

She looked directly at me. "You know the moment I knew you'd be the right one to ask?"

I shook my head.

"When you covered that little girl's body with your own when we thought the sniper had attacked again."

"What?" Gabe said, turning to me. "What is she talking about?"

"The Memory Festival," I said. "It was firecrackers. But everyone thought it was the sniper. A little girl got away from her mother, and I went after her. What's ironic was I was standing right next to the real sniper when that happened."

"Life is strange," Lin said.

"That," Gabe replied, "is the truth."

Epilogue

Eleven days later
Roundup

"Pastor Mac's getting ready to bless the herd and the workers before we start," Dove said, looking up at me. "You and Bonnie will have to vaccinate. My fingers are hurtin' too much this morning. Darn arthur-itis."

I sat astride Trixie next to the sun-faded RV we'd used for the last twenty years during roundup as a combination office, women's bathroom, prep kitchen and gossip central. Most of our herd was in the corrals waiting to be sorted, vaccinated, castrated, branded and tagged. The calves were big this year and a little wild. It would make for an interesting day.

"No problem," I said.

Pressing the vaccination needle's sticky plunger hundreds of times was tiring even for young fingers. No doubt I would be munching an extra-strength aspirin and Tylenol sandwich myself tonight. "But only if you save me a piece of red velvet cake." Though she always made three of them, if you didn't nab a piece right away, you were out of luck.

"Already set you a piece aside. But there's plenty this year. We have five cakes now that Garnet's helping. And her red velvet is much better than mine."

I rested one hand on my saddle horn and resisted a smart-aleck comment. This detente between Dove and her sister still occasionally caught me by surprise, but I was not about to do anything to quell it.

"You know I'm partial to yours, Dove." My gramma didn't raise no dummy. The wise comment earned me a satisfied smile from her and probably a second piece of cake. "Tell Daddy I'll be there in a little bit. That speckle-faced cow that he likes so much is still hiding. He wants me to find her."

Trixie tip-tapped nervously beneath me. She and I had just ridden down from hills thick with rosy pink wild hollyhocks and dusty yellow clusters of footsteps of spring, a wildflower so appropriately named you had to smile when you heard it. Pollen coated everything with a fine, buttery dust, making the air thick, like breathing through a yellow fog. Aunt Garnet was handing out decongestant and antihistamine tablets like a Saturday night drug dealer trying to hook new customers.

For about twenty of us, the day had started

before sunrise, driving cattle out of the valleys and hilltops where they'd been hanging out with their new calves. One of the riders this year was Daddy's new lady friend, Dot, whom he officially introduced to the family last night at dinner.

"She'll be riding with us tomorrow," he'd said last night. He took off his white straw cowboy hat, holding it in front of him while he made his announcement. "We're . . . courting." He said the words with as much dignity as he could muster.

His ears had flushed a deep merlot when Sam let out a loud, enthusiastic, "Whoo-hoo, Ben! You hound dog." We all laughed when Daddy smacked Sam with his hat.

"I'm looking forward to riding with you," I said to Dot after dinner when she offered to go out to the barn with me to fetch more blackberries from our extra freezer.

"I care about your daddy." Her words were clipped, no-nonsense, her small pointed chin level and firm. "I'm not after anything that belongs to you. And I'm not . . ." She left the sentence open, but we both knew what she meant. She wouldn't try to take my mama's place.

I smiled at her and handed her a frozen package of blackberries. "Daddy has been alone for way too long. I'm happy for him and for you."

It was the truth. She seemed like the exact right person for my dad. Not flashy, an earthy, somewhat bawdy sense of humor and she loved cattle ranching. In fact, Dot reminded me more than a little of Dove.

Later, when I was alone in the kitchen with Dove and Aunt Garnet, I said, "See, everything worked out with Daddy. You didn't need to do all that manipulating. He already had a girlfriend."

"Yes, dear, we know," Aunt Garnet replied primly, sprinkling roasted almonds over the individual dishes of pound cake, blackberries and homemade vanilla bean ice cream.

There was something about the way she said the words that made me suspicious. "What do you mean?"

Dove and Aunt Garnet exchanged a look, then burst into laughter, sounding like two teenage girls rather than two women way past the age of qualifying for Medicare.

"We *knew*," Dove said. "All along."

"You knew? About Daddy and Dot?"

Dove waved an impatient hand at me. "Oh, for cryin' in a bucket. We knew two minutes after they started dating. When your daddy got back from Reno last October he went over to Penney's, bought himself four new shirts and changed his brand of cologne. He might just as well have taken out a billboard on Interstate 101. My boy was in love."

"I never noticed any new shirts," I said. "He

doesn't use Old Spice anymore?" For some reason, that made me a little sad.

"We do his laundry," Aunt Garnet said. "He can't hide from us."

"Polo by Ralph Lauren," Dove said. "But only when he's going to see Dot. Old Spice is still for everyday."

"All those other women you introduced him to . . ." I began.

"Just a way to out him," Dove said. "He would have snuck around forever if we hadn't stepped in. He needed some encouragement. Dot's a sweet lady, and we figured she wasn't going to push him."

"Whereas we had no compunction about shoving him right over the love cliff," Aunt Garnet said, sounding more and more like Dove the longer she lived here. Or maybe they just started sounding more like each other.

"So we pushed!" Dove said, her voice gleeful. "I'm thinking a summer wedding would be right nice."

"We could get Sam to build a gazebo over by the oak tree in the front pasture," Aunt Garnet said.

"Good idea, Sis!" They gave each other satisfied smiles.

You didn't stand a chance, Daddy, I thought. None of us does. Heaven help anyone who ever went up against these sisters. Team tagging, they could rule the world.

"Honey bun," Dove said, bringing me back to the present. "Turn around and look up." She pointed to a small rise behind us. About a quarter mile away, there stood Daddy's speckle-faced cow calmly gazing down on us, her white-faced calf glued to her side.

"Well, she's one sly mama. We've been looking for her for over three hours."

"Smart," Dove said. "And probably stubborn."

I laughed. "Must be a Ramsey."

Dove chuckled and squeezed my shin. "I'll tell Ben you'll fetch her down. Be careful now."

I turned Trixie around and headed up the small hill to persuade Miss Speckled Face and her baby to join the party. Mac's voice grew softer, though I could still make out his words. Like many of us, Pastor Mac was raised back in the day in churches that couldn't afford fancy PA systems. He had developed a Broadway-worthy speaking voice that came in especially handy during roundup. "Bless and keep everyone to your loving care, Father. Grant mercy and safety upon all your living creatures . . ."

Bless the beasts and the children, I couldn't help adding.

When I reached the wayward cow, I waited a moment, allowing her to enjoy a last moment of freedom, though by evening she'd be back out here grazing this thick, lush grass. A rainy winter had turned the grassy hills so green and plentiful that everyone would have to buy less hay this year. A blessing for all ranchers.

I turned Trixie back to face the corrals. From my perch, the sound of people, cattle, dogs and horses was a faint, pleasant buzz. We were working three hundred head this year. About fifty family members, friends and neighbors had come to the roundup to help, visit, take photos and enjoy the barbecue at the end of the day. Dozens of horse trailers, cars and one-ton pickup trucks were parked haphazardly in front of the corrals where we'd driven the last of the cattle minutes earlier. Kids ran and screamed with the sheer joy of freedom from constant parental supervision and the delicious feel of the cool, sunny day. It seemed only yesterday that I was one of them, darting under the fences, looking for snakes and grabbing a cold soda from the never-ending supply in the ice-filled aluminum tubs.

Men joked and slapped each other with their work-stained caps and straw cowboy hats. Women organized and rearranged and counted—plates, cups, cookies, brownies, sandwiches, soda cans, bowls of potato and macaroni salad, bags of chips, racks of ribs, dozens of tri-tip steaks and ears of corn. Dogs barked and calves bawled, panicked by their first temporary separation from their mamas. It was a cacophony of sound and activity as familiar to me as the Mother Goose nursery rhymes I'd learned in school.

Next to me, the speckle-faced rebel cow chewed contentedly, her curly-faced calf rubbing its nose against her side like a child nuzzling a favorite blanket. Even at this distance, I could pick out people I loved—Gabe, Maggie and her sister, Katsy, on horseback, already sorting cattle; Emory and Daddy checking out the chutes with Sam and Hud; Señor Aragon and Ramon working on their portable grill, getting ready to make their famous tacos; Garnet's and Dove's heads bent over the long table filled with covered dishes, cake plates, Tupperware containers and huge metal coolers filled with iced tea, lemonade and water. Dot moving back and forth from the RV, setting condiments on the table, fitting in as if she'd been there for years. And, sitting under the shade of a huge oak tree, two new visitors who were experiencing their very first roundup, Lin Snider and her daughter, Tessa.

Lin had left to go back to Washington the day after our dinner at Daniello's when she asked Gabe and me to be Tessa's legal guardians. Gabe and I discussed her and Tessa long into that night. We sat at the kitchen table facing each other.

"Are you sure you want to do this?" he said.

"Yep," I said. "Are you?"

"I am."

It was probably the most solemn vows we'd made to each other since we'd gotten married.

"One more thing," I said to Gabe that night. "I think we need to convince Lin to move down here as soon as she can. Tessa will need time to adjust to her new home. It's going to be hard. And Lin will need people to help her, too, as her condition advances. We need to plan for those things."

He took both my hands in his and brought them up to his lips. His thick mustache tickled my cold knuckles. "I love you."

I smiled. "Back atcha, Friday."

It took me a few days, but I finally convinced Lin that we really, really wanted her to live in San Celina and that it would be no trouble at all moving her and Tessa down here.

"Tessa needs to get acquainted with all of us," I said. "I've got a big family and lots of friends."

She was hesitant, afraid to be a burden.

"We have good doctors here and lots of people to help you," I said, giving her my best pitch. "You don't need to go through this alone. Moving you and Tessa down here will be a cinch. There's me and Gabe and Emory and Elvia and her brothers and Hud and Dove and Aunt Garnet and Daddy . . ."

"Stop, stop," she said over the phone, laughing. "Has anyone ever told you that you are one determined woman when you want something?"

"It's genetic," I said. "The Ramsey women want to rule the world. But only because we'd do such a bang-up good job. In our humble opinion, of course."

She was silent a moment. "Benni . . . I don't know what to say. Thank you. You are . . . For Tessa . . . It's a . . ."

"Pshaw," I said. "Let's see how grateful you and Tessa are after you've lived around my crazy, interfering family for a month."

From my perch on Trixie, I watched as kids danced around metal tubs of ice-chilled bottles of root beer, cherry Coke, orange and grape soda. Tessa fit right in. She and Lin were accepted and welcomed by our family and our friends, just as I knew they would be. Tessa was dressed like a western princess in new pink cowgirl boots, pink Wranglers, a white Western shirt and a pink cowboy hat. All presents from Aunt Benni and Uncle Gabe courtesy of the fashion department of San Celina Farm Supply.

"I'm a cowgirl now," she said proudly, pointing to her hat when we dressed for the roundup this weekend. They were staying with Gabe and me, but we'd be moving them down from Washington soon. "I'm gorgeous."

I laughed, pushing the front rim of her hat down with a finger like my dad used to do to me. "Yes, you are incredibly gorgeous."

Dove and Aunt Garnet and all their friends had taken Lin and Tessa into their hearts and were busy fixing up a house we'd rented down the street from Gabe and me. The owner of the little Spanish bungalow was an old friend of our family and a veteran himself. He was thrilled to be able to help another veteran. Tessa would live with her mother while we looked into group homes here in San Celina. Elvia and Emory had both offered Tessa part-time jobs. It would be up to Tessa to decide where she wanted to work.

In the circle of webbed lawn chairs, Uncle WW, Beebs and Millee, Jim and Oneeta Cleary, some of the Coffin Star ladies and other older folks sat gabbing. They were likely telling stories of past brandings, reliving that wild ride when they almost wrecked or the year the cattle stampeded because a rattlesnake slithered into the corral. Miguel sat among them this year, still mending from his injuries. He'd be back on horseback next year, no worse for the wear, to hear him tell it. And though I didn't see him, I knew that Isaac lurked somewhere taking photos. I watched Elvia try to fit one more platter of food on the packed folding tables while Señora Aragon swayed in place, holding Sophie Lou, stopping occasionally to readjust her daisy-shapcd sun hat. Next to her, Tessa chattered like a little bird, touching Sophie's hat every so often, then adjusting her own. There would be a trunkload of pictures of Sophie at her first roundup and of Tessa too.

After eleven days, the sniper story barely made

the newspaper's third page. Van Baxter had been charged and arraigned with two counts of attempted murder. Amanda told me it would likely take a year before it went to trial.

Gabe assigned Yvette to desk duty until they could figure out what would be the right thing for her to do. She needed her job, but I couldn't even imagine the humiliation she felt going to work every day. If it were me, I'd never want to see my colleagues again.

I thought about Yvette a lot and wished I could reach out to her. But the few times I saw her in the office, though I tried to make conversation, she was polite, but distant. I understood a little. Maybe because I saw her at such a vulnerable moment, the last thing she wanted to do was be friends.

"Why do you think Van really did it?" I asked Gabe a few nights ago. "I just can't believe it was only for the thrill of it. Do you think he wanted attention? Was it because he was angry, jealous of her job, evil, what?"

He shrugged. "I quit wondering why years ago. Why do people shoot innocent employees of companies they have a beef with? Why do people kill their families and then commit suicide? Why do people torture animals for pleasure? I can't answer any of those questions, Benni. I'm not sure anyone can."

He was right, of course. Van wasn't talking to

anyone, probably on the advice of his attorney, about why he stalked and shot at police officers. I was sure a doctor like Pete Kaplan might have some ideas. Maybe I'd ask him if I ever got a chance.

The reward money went to Dove and Aunt Garnet, who donated part of it to the historical society, part to a local veterans' group and the rest they were using to redecorate Lin and Tessa's new home. The historical society agreed that their part would go, at my suggestion, toward a new exhibit honoring military nurses that I agreed to curate. I prayed and hoped that Lin would be around to see the exhibit when it opened in the fall.

Something about this situation with Lin and Van and Yvette changed Gabe. His shell had cracked. I saw my opening and told him about Dr. Pete. He agreed to see him once, if only to make me feel better. I thanked him and told him I loved him and I'd be there for him no matter what he decided. I trusted that Dr. Pete would be the perfect doctor for him. I was right.

Gabe started seeing Dr. Pete every Sunday afternoon. We paid for the sessions ourselves so no one would know. Since his nightmares hadn't affected his ability to do his job, Dr. Pete agreed with us that his therapy was something we could keep private. In fact, he told Gabe he had nothing but admiration for him for deciding to get help.

"You know," he told Gabe. "There are too many people in positions of power who need help and aren't getting it because they are fearful of what people would say or how it will affect their job. So they suffer and their employees suffer and their families suffer." Dr. Pete shook his head. "People still have a long way to go in their acceptance of mental health issues. I hope someday people see that *not* getting help is much more frightening and dangerous to themselves and to society."

I could tell the times they touched on deep issues; Gabe came home as exhausted and depleted as if he had run a marathon. But I could also tell after a few weeks that he was feeling better, happier. Dr. Pete had prescribed some medication that helped Gabe sleep, and his nightmares hadn't returned. That's not to say they never would, but at least he—we—had somewhere to go now for help.

The night after his first session with Dr. Pete, after my shower, I crawled into the guest bed with Gabe and refused to leave.

"You will have to physically carry me out," I said. "And even then I'll come back." Scout flopped down on the floor next to the bed. He laid his head on his front paws and stared up at us.

"See, Scout's staying too," I said, folding my arms across my chest.

Gabe studied me a moment, the only movement on his face the jaw muscle under his left ear. It twitched like a moth trapped under his skin.

Then he smiled. "You both are loco."

"As loons," I agreed. "Though I have no idea why loons are called crazy. I mean just because you sound crazy doesn't mean you are."

He was smart enough to know he wouldn't win this battle. We all moved back to the master bedroom.

"I don't trust myself," he said, settling down next to me that night. "I don't want to hurt you."

"How about I trust for both of us?"

Scout was relieved to have both of us back in the same room where he thought we belonged. His contented sigh as he settled into his dog bed made both Gabe and me laugh. The pack was reunited.

All of these moments swirled around in my mind as I sat on Trixie and watched the scene unfold below me. Isaac had emerged and was taking photos of the women now. Dove, Garnet, some of their friends and even Dot Haggerty locked arms, kicking their legs like chorus girls. I heard a collective whoop rise up into the air and the sound of clapping. I was struck about how lucky I was, how important it was to guard and cherish each happy moment, like my night with Gabe in Morro Bay, to save them up for the hard times that would come just as surely as the blue lupine in spring.

I hoped Yvette had some beautiful moments saved up to sustain her through this terrible time of her life. "Lord, help her," I whispered, picturing her solemn face. "Please, give her hope."

Would I still feel thankful one year from now? Five years? What if Gabe's nightmares returned? What if Dr. Pete couldn't help, what if Gabe unintentionally hurt me again? What if things got worse? A lot worse? What if Gabe had to quit his job? What about the stress of being Tessa's guardian? Of Lin's eventual death? What if the stress of all this broke up our marriage? What if . . .

Faith, said a voice in my head, a voice that was a combination of Dove and Aunt Garnet and Father Mark and Pastor Mac and all the women in the Coffin Star Quilt Guild—all the wise people in my life who had helped form the woman I had become. Have faith. Have hope. But what if faith wasn't enough? What if hope seemed in vain? What was left?

Of course, I knew the answer. It was as simple and complex as a blade of grass. Then you love. Whom we love, why we love, when we love—all so incomprehensible. But it was the answer.

"You know what's crazy?" Yvette had said. "I still love him."

"The heart has reasons that reason cannot

know." One of Gabe's favorite quotes by Blaise Pascal, a mathematician who understood about faith and hope. A mathematician and a philosopher who understood about love.

Beneath me, Trixie shifted impatiently, telling me we needed to move this stubborn cow down to the rest of the herd, telling me she was ready to get back to work.

"C'mon, sweet mama," I called to the rebel cow. "Everyone's waiting on us. I promise, it won't take that long. Before you know it, we'll all be back home."

Center Point Publishing

600 Brooks Road ● PO Box 1
Thorndike ME 04986-0001 USA

(207) 568-3717

US & Canada:
1 800 929-9108
www.centerpointlargeprint.com